This book is a work of historical fiction. Names, places, characters and events are the product of the author's imagination and used in a fictitious sense, excepting those from real history included to establish background and context for the setting.

Copyright © 2024 by B. Lawson Hull

Cover design and illustration copyright © 2024 by B. Lawson Hull

The distribution or copying of this book, in whole or in part, is strictly forbidden under copyright law without express permission from the author. No AI tools of any sort were used in the writing, plotting or outlining of this novel.

BLH Books

author@blawsonhull.com

ISBN: 979-8-9908048-0-7

This book uses British spelling for English words in keeping with the setting.

Printed in the United States of America

Emelyn Morley and the Waking Dark

Saunmoor Book 1

For Mom, Dad, Laurie and Susan

Chapter 1
The Woman in Black

Hastelbrook village, southern England by the sea, Thursday June 2nd 1735

The shadow steeped courtyard split with light as the kitchen door opened, and Marta Denlund peered outside. A wearied young woman in bonnet and apron over her skirts, Marta eyed the bleak rolling sky with suspicion, holding back a diminutive pair of tawny headed girls as they tussled to see around their mother. "Inside my girls! There's a dreadful chill about . . ."

A large man in working vest and rolled sleeves stood in the cluttered courtyard, searching about him by the meagre flame of a hooded lantern. "Ah, here be the sodding thing," he grumbled, moving an ill-mended cradle to take up a well-worn axe.

"Again tonight, the cats won't go out," Marta said, watching as he dug up a leather satchel.

The man grimaced, slinging the bag over his shoulder. "That'll be enough of your superstitions."

"There's a curse about, mark my words," Marta insisted, "witch lights up the hill by the big house, walkin' shadows in the cemetery; you ask those boys at the log yard if they haven't heard the same!"

"Nay woman, you're the only curse on this village," he snapped, stepping closer. "I'll be on my way now, and I'll have those biscuits."

"You've et them all, leaving none for the girls I might add."

"Then I'll be coming home to that stew hot, and the squealin' brats abed," he said, lifting her chin with his finger. "Not a bite gone missing, or you'll feel my boot again so help me."

Marta cleared her throat, barring the children behind her. "I s'pose we'll make do; wages tomorrow after all," and taking a heavy growler jug from its shelf she passed it with deliberate care into the grasping hands of her husband.

Hefting the axe the big man turned to lope away, his lantern clinking against the jug.

Marta watched the bobbing light as it faded around the fence. "Philip Denlund, you mind your drinking tonight!" she called, gathering her courage. "And no cards with the lads; tomorrow's for buying what's needful, not refillin' your spirits! I'll not have my girls sleeping for their suppers, do you hear me?"

Chasing the girls to their bed she kissed them both, and after a wary stare at the front door she unwrapped a stout carrot that had been kept out of the stew, breaking it for them to share. The little ones crunched quietly as a scrawny cat leapt upon the windowsill to hiss at the dark. Rising from the bed Marta removed her bonnet, and she took her seat in the old rocker, to creak by the fire as the wind rattled the panes.

With a crack of splitting wood the guttering lantern jostled on its hook, and the broad backed Mr. Denlund lay his axe against the wall of the woodshed. The sky tumbled starless overhead, the night being blessedly cool though the work was slow, and with a weary sound he set another log on the stump, pausing to rub well calloused hands.

The log yard had a good view of the estate road, and in the distance, beyond narrow lakes and garden parks, the vast chimney studded stronghold of Hastelbrook Hall, which rose from the hill in three uneven storeys of natural stone. The seat of power for Mr. Hiram Morley, squire of the parish and lord of the manor, it was a house Denlund knew for the grandest ballroom in Sussex, though he'd never been inside, nor had he seen the storied greenhouse behind it, domed in facets of glass, except from the road. Tonight the great manor twinkled from ground floor windows to dormers in the unfinished garret high above, though his eyes were drawn to the candle flicker of one room in particular, his favourite to watch: the upstairs apartment of the eldest Morley daughter, the beautiful Emelyn.

"Long day for our fire-haired princess?" he said with a smirk. "Dressing for bed now I'll wager . . ."

A sharp gust moved through the wood, murmuring about him, and looping the growler handle he tilted the jug for a long spicy draught, spluttering with a satisfied cough. Stacked high against the fence, the wood remaining to chop taunted him, and wiping his mouth he breathed a curse, snatching the axe from its rest.

"Extra guests for the season," he huffed, kicking the new split logs aside. "Oh please my lord, let me chop all night!" and he brought down the axe, splintering the waiting log into thirds. "Can't have the gentlefolk chilly in their downy beds now can we . . ."

A light rain began to tap the ground, and Mr. Denlund mopped his brow. "The cats won't go out," he repeated, wheezing with chuckles as he raised the axe, but a chill ran its fingers over his back, and he turned to find a solitary hooded figure, standing in the middle of the yard between himself and the gate. By her litheness of shape it was a woman, swathed in black, with untamed raven hair long and loose about her shoulders.

There was a stillness to her he did not like, but he stood the axe in the dirt, leaning on the handle. "Is that Miss Emelyn Morley, come to make my happiness?"

"Philip Denlund," the woman said. Her voice was soft and silken, and as she came into the light he found her suddenly alluring, though eerily so, as though he looked upon the cold porcelain features of a beautiful doll.

Denlund leered at her. "Not Miss Morley then, but common baggage," he said, determined to find nothing strange in the encounter. "Long way from home I'll wager . . . How d'you know my name?"

"I have never tasted the village," she said, watching him with an unblinking stare.

"Too right you haven't." Denlund chuckled with scorn, unstopping the growler for another swig. "Little wretch wants a keeper does she? But you're in the wrong place love, or shall we wake the constable?"

"You are rotten," the woman said, her eyes opaque as ink in the low light.

"All right keep it up!" he bristled, dropping the jug. "I'll take you for free if I likes."

"Rotten," she repeated, drifting closer.

"Bugger off!" he growled, hefting the axe, "lest I cleave those little bird bones!"

But in a blink she was upon him, and he lost his feet. Turned and pressed into the woodshed he dropped the axe, fangs like sharpened steel plunged into his side below the arm, and his cry died breathless, smothered against the icy crush of her hand.

Blood surged from his veins as the woman in black drank deep.

Darkness encroached, the pulse of life abandoned his body, and she pulled him close. "Thank you, Mr. Denlund."

Laughing voices punctuated the air, a group of young men approaching the gate with cheerful lanterns. The vampiress dropped her prey, turning with a hiss, and like a whip of shadow she was gone.

■■

Friday June 3rd

Emelyn Elizabeth Morley opened her eyes, finding herself still on the cushioned bench in the bay windows of Hastelbrook Hall's corner library, her well-worn journal open across her lap, a copy of the *London Gazette* folded in the centre, with a stack of books at her side. For several blinks the recurring dream lingered in her mind: haunting, sonorous voices on the wind, a ghostly woman shrouded in black, both enchanting and frightful, leading her always through a high iron gate on a mist creeping road toward some foreboding place she never reached before waking . . .

At twenty-three years of age, and the eldest daughter of three, Emelyn was by all accounts a great beauty, if unapologetically red of hair which, contrasting her green eyes was aflame in the early evening light, gathered up tightly with a few rebellious strands trailing to the neck of her day gown, smartly cinched with bell sleeves.

Today's *Gazette* was uncharacteristically dour, citing a sharp rise in cases of murder and grave robbery along the Thames. After reading this and a survey on the ravages of gin addiction among the poor, Emelyn felt a touch unwell, and sorrowing for the afflicted she gazed across the drive at the wet leafy walls of the garden labyrinth, and the angel topped fountains standing sentinel by its entrance, their waterworn bodies smooth and dark. Of sharply pruned hedges in towering concentric rings, Hastelbrook's verdant maze blocked her view of the vale and lower gardens, where the carriage drive would wend its way around, bordered by flowering paths until it broke free to find the tenant village over and beyond the lakes.

Putting the newspaper aside for a stretch, she caught sight of a pair of collared doves as they circled the old Greco-Roman gazebo; its domed limestone pavilion marking what once had been the centre of an even grander boxwood maze, until an eccentric ancestor had churned up the sloping southern half, to plant open groves between hill and water. A soft daydream settled in, and she imagined how the gardens would appear from so high above, poppling rows of bushy colour splashed on a canvas of green.

But at a noise in the hall she sat up, marking the conspicuous footfalls of her youngest sister, the elfin blonde Isabelle Marie. Fresh from her debut in society at newly sixteen Isabelle was still round-faced and childlike, and though she did not share Emelyn's renown or quite her celebrated beauty, in haste to vocalize her thoughts she was without peer.

Flush with frustration, as was often the case, Isabelle dashed to her elder sister's side. "Emie I will not bear it!"

Emelyn concealed a yawn with the back of her hand. "Hello Bell, but are you returned already? Have the shops taken a holiday?"

Isabelle blinked at her. "No, Mama refused us to go; did you not hear the bells this morning?"

"I came down late, was there a fire?"

"Not a fire, no; some terrible accident in the village last night."

"Accident?" Emelyn asked, bestowing her full attention. "What sort of accident?"

"Mama wouldn't say. But it doesn't matter; my spirit is tattered, and it shan't be repaired."

"Oh dear, and who has tattered your spirit?"

Isabelle took a great breath. "Sarah is a spiteful gnash-gab! She raves on about *ghosts* or somesuch, and I only told her to stop, and she tells *me* to shut my mouth about John Lawford! When she knows how I ache for him! She's a beastly sister and I shall never speak to her again."

Emelyn puzzled at her. "*Ghosts or somesuch?* My dearest Bell, I'm sure she only wants you should find a man worthy of your affection, as do we all."

"Well she's a hateful way of showing it; my Mr. Lawford has been much maligned."

"He injured a gentleman," Emelyn said, standing from the bench, "in a brawl of his own making."

"A lawyer, not a gentleman," Isabelle scoffed. "But he will exonerate himself, I know it!"

"Come now, it's been three months. You needn't long for your lawless lost Lawford any longer."

"You're making fun of me," Isabelle said, rubbing her eye.

Emelyn marvelled to see her so affected. "I don't mean to . . . here," she said, handing her a kerchief. "But you deserve better than the likes of

John Lawford, that's the truth."

"Do I?"

"Isabelle Marie Morley is not to be trifled with," Emelyn said. "Now, you must forgive Sarah as soon as you decently can, and I should like to write a bit more, before the clouds get any darker."

Isabelle shrugged with a sniff, dabbing her face. "Fine then I shall go; what have I to do but attend my broken heart."

"I will pray for your swift recovery," Emelyn said. "But before you go, I can't imagine Sarah raving; whatever do you mean *ghosts or somesuch?*"

Isabelle dropped the kerchief on the bench, wrinkling her nose. "She insists she saw one, or something scary out her window, north up the hill among the headstones."

"Did she? Well I'm sure it was only a nightmare."

"But are we not plagued by foul rumours enough without her inventions?" Isabelle flustered. "I've never seen a ghost, and I should very much like to . . . Oh and I've meant to ask, shall I have your room when you move away?"

"What? Heavens Bell I'm not engaged yet; I've not even a prospect. You shan't have my room while I'm making perfectly good use of it."

"Then I shall move to the rose room," Isabelle said with a shrug. "I don't want Sarah's next to mine," and she turned to swish away, back into the hall.

Emelyn stared after her, and as rain began to play upon the windows she resumed her place on the bench, taking up her journal to continue:

'Accident in the village last night. Sarah seeing ghosts? And Isabelle still on about John Lawford. But I could never do as she does, drop my heart at a man's feet, in hope that he bends his knee to return it. The sooner she forgets him, we're all the better for it.'

The little droplets washed higher on the panes, and she watched vacantly a few moments, before resuming:

'Yet for all that, Bell speaks true. Have I not promised before God and family to be married by summer's end? So I must be grateful for life and present liberties, at least until third week September.'

Emelyn tapped the pencil on her lip, and casting about for distraction she dwelt again on the dream of the woman in black, which by now had all but faded, leaving only a persistent sense that she'd met the woman before, somewhere.

The rain increased, shadows lengthened over the wind washed gardens, and clutching her leather-bound journal to her chest Emelyn determined that should her supernatural visitant appear again while she slept, every detail must be put to paper.

Saturday June 4th

Late spring at Hastelbrook was cool and pleasant, and after breakfast Emelyn took her customary stroll through the western gardens: a hedge bordered fantasia of blooming parterres beneath pink Morello cherry trees. Today the wind blew crisp as she walked, and she paused to enjoy the fragrant colours, purple iris in particular, and soft spears of delphinium that rose from their lily beds, with green plants of summer yet sleeping between them. Beyond the southern boundary of the hedge her path descended through flowered banks down the hill, past benches where oft she would read or think, and over a bridge at the narrow place between the lakes, which her great-grandfather had designed. After crossing the bridge her way rounded the reedy banks, to pass by a vast gnarled oak tree, that as far as she knew had been there since the world began.

Morning surrendered to afternoon, and for some while she sat thoughtfully in the little garden temple, listening to the spring frogs as she watched the sky in the water.

"Ghosts or somesuch," she murmured. "All right Sarah, let's have it."

Seeking her middle sister's side of the story Emelyn found her upstairs in the music room, adjacent to a railed gallery overlooking the ballroom. Sarah Anne sat at the harpsichord, playing a few sombre notes of Handel's *Sarabande* as she stared through the keys. At twenty she was three years younger than Emelyn, though taller, lithe and pretty, if boyish of figure, with curly auburn hair and freckles.

"I thought to leave you to it," Emelyn said, coming to join her on the bench, "but without my sisters laughing I find the house too quiet."

Sarah tilted her head as she played but did not respond.

"You needn't have lectured Bell over John Lawford," Emelyn continued. "I suspect we shall never hear from him again," and finding no response she joined in the music, tapping the keys at random.

Sarah stopped, resting her hands in her lap. "You never could be bothered to learn . . ."

"Perhaps if I might have practiced out of doors," Emelyn mused. "Anyway, there can be no danger of Isabelle's entanglement with Mr. Lawford now, so if you only meant to distract her with ghost stories . . ."

"She's been a ridiculous brat," Sarah said, "though after what I've seen I could not care."

"And what do you imagine you've seen?" Emelyn asked, giving her a nudge. "Not a ghost, surely."

"A monster then, watching the house from the cemetery."

"A monster?" Emelyn repeated. "Sarah, really . . ."

"Or it was the most horrible man I've ever seen, huge and hunched, with eyes that burned like lanterns. I screamed and hid from the window, and when I looked back he was gone."

"Well I hope you've kept it from the staff," Emelyn said, "or we shall have gossip all the way to the village," but at the look on Sarah's face her smile faded.

"I'm not the only one to see such things," Sarah protested. "What of the time you nearly fell in the cistern? Was there not a *great long shadow* that frightened you home?"

"Frightened me from the edge to safety more like," Emelyn said. "But I was a child Sarah, it might have been anything. I have disquieting dreams as well . . ."

Sarah stood sharply, upsetting the pages of music. "It wasn't a dream," she insisted. "I was awake; I know you shan't believe me . . . I am alone," and she began to shake, holding herself as though to ward off a chill.

The sight of her sister in such a state was not a little unnerving, and Emelyn stood from the bench to embrace her. "Hush now; there's nothing to fear."

"But I wish it *were* a dream," Sarah muttered.

"You're always welcome in my room," Emelyn said, patting her back. "But you must allow dreams can *seem* very real indeed; sometimes I see a strange woman in black, even imagine I've met her in the waking world."

Sarah released her. "By heavens who is she?"

"Well, but she is no one of course," Emelyn said. "That's the point; she is a dream character, just like your monster."

Her sister nodded with a frown, looking none the happier.

Emelyn sighed. "All right, if the monster returns you must come and fetch me; I won't tease you for it."

Sarah grunted, lowering the cover over the keys of the instrument. "Thank you, Emie . . . I might very well," she said, leaning to collect the scattered papers.

Emelyn leaned down to help, grabbing a few of the farther sheets. "I do not believe in ghosts, nor monsters," she said, her words sharper than her conviction. "What matters now is you must mend fences with Bell."

Sarah stood to accept the pages, replacing them on the music rest. "I tire of her endless wailing over that hopeless man, but you're right, perhaps I shouldn't have bullied her . . . tell-tale though she is. I'm sorry she bothered you."

"Oh I don't mind," Emelyn said, picking at her nail, "in truth we do not commiserate, not as we used to, and I rather miss it."

"You've grown up too quickly for us," Sarah said, arranging the pages against the board. "And now you are to be married in all haste . . . and save us all."

Emelyn swallowed. "I wish Mama would abandon this fantasy that I shall lift us from gentry to royalty."

"Well if the *Belle of Brighton* can't marry above her station, what hope for the rest of us," Sarah said, staring at the windows. "But then how should we ever get on . . . I shall miss you awfully."

"Isabelle wants my room, and you shall miss me awfully," Emelyn said, feeling a clench of nerves. "If you please, I'm still here."

A handsome wigged footman, Adam Comberland, appeared at the arch opening to the gallery. "Miss Morley, Miss Sarah," he said clearly. "Dinner is to be set."

"Thank you Comby," the ladies replied together.

Changed for dinner into a slender gown of candy green, Emelyn sat at the table gazing into nothing as laughter and conversation buzzed around her, her mind distracted by her sister's distressed recounting of the monster in the cemetery.

Today the service was spicy curried soup and savoury pies, to be followed by turkey and chickens Dutch dressed over rice, with sweet peach comfit for after. Dinner was taken in the large northeast dining room, to accommodate those the Morleys' only son, her elder brother Deacon, called the *happy vanguard*— those familial guests who made a point of arriving a day early for every engagement. Emelyn sat crowded between two of her mother's largest relations— her uncle Mr. Fallworth, whose wife was perpetually ill, and their son Tynan, a portly young fellow of seventeen. Altogether four couples had joined the table, the men in long open coats with folded cuffs, high white cravats at their necks, while the women wore flowing gowns with shawls and soft colours for the afternoon.

Emelyn's father, Mr. Hiram Morley, a narrow, wizened man in long periwig and spectacles, sat at the head of the table to Emelyn's left, while her mother perched with regal gravity on a high backed chair at the south end. An enchanting woman of fifty-two, Mrs. Antonia Morley's stern features and silvery red hair belied the cheerful cream of her gown. Deacon was predictably absent, confined to his room by a renewed complaint of health, while Isabelle and Sarah chattered at either side of their mother, their quarrel having run its course.

"Mother sent me with some advices for you, that is on the matter of attracting a suitable match," red cheeked cousin Tynan said, glancing at Emelyn.

"I was hoping she might," Emelyn said dryly. "Of course we languish without her company. How is she?"

"Mother is very well thank you," Tynan answered. "She is taking her physick in Bath," and he huffed with a sorrowful sound. "But what a hopeless, terrible business."

Emelyn looked at him. "Is it?"

"No no, I mean the man in the village, who died. Was it accident? Did you know him?"

"Oh, Philip Denlund," Emelyn said, feeling little remorse for the man's passing, "I knew him only by reputation; he was a hard man. But the investigation has only just begun . . ."

"Yes, good," Tynan said, finding his smile. "Well, on a gladder note the clouds are breaking, the air is brisk in the trees; tomorrow shall be very good for testing partridge."

"Will you shoot them nesting in the trees?" Emelyn asked.

"In flight my dear," her uncle interjected. A roundly robust gentleman, Mr. Fallworth was ever ruddy of face as though perpetually recovering from laughter. "There is a wondrous new firearm for birds," he went on, "a mixed shot of lead balls, which spreads when fired! Any fool can shoot a bird on the ground; far more sporting to give them a start don't you find?"

"Yes, very thoughtful," Emelyn said, sipping her wine.

Uncle Fallworth chuckled, and the gentlemen's conversation continued around her, moving on from hunting to shipping, addressing rumours of terrible storms over the western sea, while the ladies rounded back to gardens, Mrs. Morley insisting the pleasure boats for the lake were to be finished this year, though Emelyn knew her father could never afford them. Her soup had lost its heat making the long journey through servants' corridors from the kitchens, but the flavour was pleasant, and she gave a sigh as the footman whisked it away for tablecloths and dishes to be reset in preparation for the main course.

One of her mother's closest confidants, the sombrely costumed Lady Malvary, baroness in her own right, sat across the table by her Lilliputian husband Mr. Wipplehem. "My dear whatever do you use for your skin, you must tell me," the baroness inquired, staring as though Emelyn were made of wax.

"Lemon in the mornings," Emelyn said, "with sugar."

"But I confess our dear Hester does the same," Lady Malvary said, addressing Emelyn's mother, "yet her skin is never so buttery as that."

"Our Emelyn is a natural beauty my lady," Mrs. Morley pronounced from the end of the table.

Perusing a bowl of olives, Isabelle was selecting favourites with her fingers to jab on the end of her fork, for eating in the French style. "And not a day goes by but you'll find Emie in the bath," she observed.

There was a collective murmur, and Emelyn groaned, focusing on the plate set before her.

"Daily baths?" Lady Malvary decried. "But my dear Antonia think of your daughter's health!"

Emelyn's mother shook her head with closed eyes, as though to warn her off the topic.

"But are you mad my dear girl?" Lady Malvary persisted.

"Is Queen Caroline mad?" Emelyn asked, cutting deeply into her turkey. "She herself espouses the benefits of daily baths, with clear water to rinse. I find her regimen rejuvenating, and very good for the skin."

"Well I have never heard such a thing," Lady Malvary said, forking into the dwindling olives as her little husband spluttered in agreement.

Uncle Fallworth laughed again. "Let us consider the matter settled; I know better than to cross my niece! Now Hiram," he said, dabbing his mouth with a napkin as he addressed Emelyn's father. "I've an announcement!"

Mr. Hiram Morley sat with his usual air of agreeable fatigue, looking up as the footman ladled sauce over his dinner. "Fallworth my good fellow," he said, "I daresay your news has ripened long enough."

"By your leave sir," Fallworth said cheerfully, catching hold of Emelyn's knuckles with a wide, warm hand, "I've a most delightful information concerning your lovely eldest!"

"Deacon is the eldest, dear Uncle," Emelyn corrected, bracing for the news.

"Yes of course!" he chuckled, but as her uncle spoke again the words were far away, Emelyn's mind returning unbidden to her sister's horrifying sight in the cemetery. Forcing a smile she strove to listen: someone was coming to visit, though she had missed the name . . .

"Emelyn, my dearest can you not hear your uncle's voice?" Mrs. Morley asked loudly.

"Yes Mama," Emelyn said, sitting taller, "of whom are we speaking?"

"Why Miss Poppy Loganbrek!" Uncle Fallworth responded. "Are not the pair of you fast friends? She writes of course on behalf of her adoring brother, my good fellow Geoffrey George. Now tell me, have you written after her latest?"

"Oh!" Emelyn said, her heart sinking. "Alas, not yet." Overflattering and dependably tedious, the correspondence of her most persistent suitor, whom she had never met, appeared on the tray with alarming frequency. A celebrated magnate of shipping many years her senior, Geoffrey George Loganbrek was by his letters a literary man of eloquent and gushing praises, if transparently keen to win her for the prospect of attractive offspring. Every page was ostensibly written by his sister, to satisfy convention, though the hand might as well have been his. "But the Loganbreks are still in India," Emelyn said hopefully.

"Certainly not," Mr. Fallworth said, dabbing his mouth again. "He is returned to Scotland, and she with him. His sister resumes her post at his estate in Edinburgh, but Geoffrey himself shall be in attendance here tomorrow night!" And he leaned at her with a long wink.

"That is wonderful news, just in time for the party!" Mrs. Morley said brightly.

"He may not be handsomest of the lot," Uncle Fallworth went on, "but it's long odds finding a fellow flusher, or more admiring!"

Emelyn smiled, lamenting that her plan to keep the Loganbreks at a safe distance by exchange of letters, at least until the sea swallowed the land, would be cut short.

"Well my dear?" Mrs. Morley called. "Have you nothing to say? But how grateful we must be," she continued, addressing Emelyn's uncle, "that our dear Mr. Loganbrek should return home after travelling so long, and think only of her," and clasping her hands she hummed for joy as Fallworth raised a glass to Mr. Morley, who did the same, his face a veneer of enthusiasm.

"Her seventh season indeed," Fallworth crowed. "Splendid lucky number that; I believe she may keep her promise yet, what do you say?"

A mortified anger rose in Emelyn's breast. "Excuse me," she said, standing from the table.

Retreating to the expansive drawing room, Emelyn crossed the room to stand by the fire, where over the mantle loomed the stark portrait of her great-grandfather, the eccentric Samuel Bastian Morley, who after losing his young wife had spent feverish years expanding the manor into the byzantine monument it became. Thin as a wraith, with disdainful silver brows to match the falling curls of his wig, her grave ancestor was posed on a stone bridge, with the gnarled fanning shape of the eldest oak on the property behind him. Emelyn's eyes were drawn to the brilliant ruby topped cane he leaned upon, an object which by family folklore had disappeared upon his death, though likely it was buried with him, in the largest Morley plot behind the house.

"Emelyn Elizabeth you shall come back to the table at once," her mother ordered, appearing at the doors. "I'll not have you raising questions over dinner with your strangeness."

"Oh Mama, how could you do it?" Emelyn said, turning to face her. "My promise was made to you in private."

"And its terms shall be met quite in public. But shall I ever understand you; why as a girl you were positively raving to be married!"

"And you refuse no eager gentleman his address; I am drowning in acquaintance Mama, but those I fancy are never enough for you."

"Is that what you imagine?" her mother balked, drawing near. "But that is not true my dearest; why I should never have objected to that cooper, had he been but of able fortune."

"*That cooper* has a name. Fitzwilliam Arkwright is as worthy a friend as any gentleman I've met."

"Yes very well, we shan't rehearse it. But there were others whom the both of us liked; that young baronet by example, Sir Thaniel Gliffton. Vanished without a trace did he not? You cannot blame me for that."

Emelyn rolled her eyes "I'll allow Sir Thaniel was charming, if overly curious of our history, but he did not relish a lady's opinion."

"Oh must you find fault with *every* man born of Adam!"

"But how could you say it? When you know your part in driving them off."

Mrs. Morley sighed. "We have accepted your unaccountable attraction to tradesmen and scholars, but they must be of suitable means, especially now."

"I know that Mama; you remind me at every turn," Emelyn said. "But what is the urgency? Can we be any worse off now than a year ago?"

Her mother picked at her daughter's dress, heaving with a dramatic sound. "Oh my beautiful darling . . . there has been a turn in our fortunes, and again for the worse."

"What do you mean?"

"I might have spared you the news, but we are forced to let the house in town; we shall go without the London season I'm afraid. Your father drew up a contract with one Mr. Townsend, whose family shall be settled in the week, and with none but the servants to welcome them."

"So we are to lease Ledgefield after all," Emelyn said vaguely. "I suppose I shan't miss the narrow halls and dim light of it . . . but why now? Was there not great profit expected by the new ships to Boston?"

"Well you're welcome to ply your father for the accounts. When it comes to business you might as well be the favourite son."

"Oh Mama, you know it's only because Deacon takes no interest."

Mrs. Morley puffed her lips. "Be that as it may whatever we have to spare shall be put to your dowry; to be executed in the month I should hope."

"In the month! But that's impossible; are Sarah and Isabelle not just as keen to marry?"

"They are penniless in your wake my dear," her mother said, "with no prospects, and no settlement of their own, not until by your union we are preserved."

"You would guarantee me to Mr. Loganbrek sight unseen," Emelyn marvelled.

"Oh don't be dramatic. Of course you shall meet the man first, and take care to know him a little, before judging him over-weighty or tedious."

"Or old," Emelyn murmured, turning to watch the fire.

"Don't mumble my dear," her mother said loudly. "Now we shan't lock you in a tower, and your father will not command you, but if you've any love for your family you will keep your promise; you are to be married before midsummer."

"My promise was for this to be my last season at home," Emelyn said, her eyes going wet as she watched the dancing flames. "I've until twenty-first of September have I not? There is time yet for me to choose for myself . . ."

Her mother made an exasperated noise. "And you'll forgive me if my confidence in your choosing has eroded to nothing. In fact I sometimes wonder if you don't pick your gentlemen out of spite."

"Spite!" Emelyn repeated, rounding on her. "What on earth have I to be spiteful about?"

"Well I'm sure I don't know! Even as a child you were too oft in your own world, but ever since your debut you are *changed* my girl; we've all seen it, and every year the more. Sometimes I look in your eyes, and I cannot find you."

"I'm right here Mama . . . I've only grown up."

"It is more than that. What happened to you that night, your debut at Daulton House?"

"Nothing happened, I danced," Emelyn said, walking to the windows as she recalled the breathless thrill of her first ball six years past, brought nearly to ruin by the aggressions of a regrettable nobleman, and gazing through long crimson drapes into the sleeping dark a flash of memory pierced her mind: deep clouded sky, cold breath on her skin, a piercing sting at her throat; was it not there the woman in black had found her, but then surely she was more than a dream . . .

Mrs. Morley adjusted a book on the mantel, eyeing her daughter. "Nothing happened, are you quite sure?"

Struggling to decipher the memory Emelyn shook her head, staring through the windows.

"Well you must recall how the Prince of Wales attended you," her mother continued. "A royal suitor at only seventeen! But of course you refused him."

Emelyn closed her eyes. "No Mama, Prince Frederick's offer was never of marriage; I think you deliberately misremember."

"Then we shall forget the prince," her mother said, coming closer, "but you are still the Belle of Brighton, and with the three of you on the market together the dignity and reputation of Hastelbrook hang in the balance."

"Very well," Emelyn droned, batting the crimson drapes. "I shall meet Mr. Loganbrek without complaint, and try to keep an open mind. All I ask is your patience."

"Oh we have been *very* patient with you my girl," her mother said. "Tomorrow he shall make his address, and henceforward you will not inflict him with suspense, but correspond promptly; you do write such beautiful letters!"

"I will try, but how does one answer so much repetitive simpering?" Emelyn complained. "His sister professes to write from the privacy of her apartments, but I shouldn't wonder if he dictates from her lap."

"Oh don't be clever," her mother said curtly. "Now I shall be good enough to tell our guests you've retired with a headache, though in truth it is your mother with a headache. Go and rest as you like my dearest, for tomorrow we shall require your full glory."

"Yes Mama." Emelyn curtsied, and swishing past she made her way back to the main hall, passing by the grand Morley family portrait, which towered austere and solemn over the wide great hall hearth. Her mother's footsteps followed, and Emelyn quickened her pace, mounting the stairs with a mind to read in her room, and lock the door.

Chapter 2
The Prime Article

Sunday June 5ᵗʰ

That evening Emelyn sat at her dressing table picking at the bristles of an ivory hairbrush, clad thinly in a linen shift, a diaphanous undergarment that hung loose to her ankles like a long chemise. Before her on the table lay a ribbon-tied package with a letter, but one of several presents she might receive on such a night, delivered of hopeful gentlemen seeking her partnership for dancing.

The rewarding if arduous process of donning a ball gown she had repeated many dozens of times, but under the expectation of impressing Mr. Geoffrey George Loganbrek Emelyn felt a heaviness of distaste for the entire business.

Shannon Breda, her bonneted lady's maid, waited behind her for the brush while a younger maid stood by, wielding a white cotton underskirt by the inside, as though expecting her mistress to jump through it.

"Must hurry now miss," Breda said.

"Yes of course," Emelyn said, handing back the brush, and skipping the letter, already unsealed and approved by her mother, she tore into the paper wrapped gift, spilling out an emerald scarf, fine silk edged with tassels of cream, to be worn about the arms or draped over the shoulders. "Lovely," she sighed. "From Mr. Loganbrek I suppose," and she opened the letter to read as Breda unloosed the fiery autumn tresses of her hair:

> *'Madam,*
> *Despite vastly prosperous horizons before me, which I humbly submit must elevate my estimation in the hearts of all whom I address, my mind's eye finds no fondness but in looking*

back, to wait upon the memory of she whom I relinquished two summers past under the cherry trees: a species of wood the sight of which I can no longer abide. I pray that you are well and content, and do not ask you to think of me as you wander the gardens of Hastelbrook with the enclosed stole of silk about your arms, yet still I am,

Your true and onetime friend,
M.B.'

"Who is M.B.?" Breda asked, twisting up Emelyn's hair to prepare for her dressing.

"Meriton Bowtree; I can't think why he still writes to me," Emelyn said, standing to brace for the ritual.

"Very good miss."

Emelyn tucked in her elbows, squinting as the smaller maid thrust the underskirt over her head and wrestled it down to her waist, tying it smartly and repeating the steps twice over for a pair of soft taffeta petticoats. Selecting them from where they lay on the green canopy bed, Breda held up slender hard-panelled stays and Emelyn slipped her hands through the shoulder loops, pulling the garment to her front and turning for the maid to encase her torso and lace up the back. The pressure increased, pulling her shoulder blades backward, and Emelyn winced, holding a deep breath to keep the compress of her stays at bay. Breda selected pins from a small case, and the second maid pulled the laces tighter yet, yanking from behind to elicit a gasp as Emelyn steadied herself against the dressing table. The maids pinned a rigid stomacher panel of gilded rose under her bosom and fit over her head the fourth and last of her skirts: a heavy gown petticoat of red satin, modest hoop sewn within for a more rounded shape. Emelyn breathed high as she could and reached back for the sleeves as they wrapped her in the final layer: a lavish gown of embroidered crimson, pulled around her body like an open robe and pinned against either side of the stomacher, presenting an elegant united bodice. The little maid adjusted her elbow sleeves and pinned up the train of her skirts, and Breda circled her mistress, making final adjustments as Emelyn stood waiting with her hands at her stomach.

Her hair was tied in careful loops atop her head, with a few strands loosed to frame her face, and the young maid brought a folding box of jewellery as Emelyn perched on the chair, squirming to temper the fit of her bodice. "Oh these I seldom wear," she said, watching as the maid presented her with several options to adorn her collar. "If you would fetch the other box from the top shelf."

"Sorry miss," the maid curtsied quickly and was about to shut the lid when Emelyn bid her to wait, a glint of blood red catching her eye.

"Yes miss?"

Emelyn's pulse raced as she studied the necklace— a slender chain of gold mounted with teardrop diamonds about a gilt pendant centred with an enormous ruby of otherworldly beauty. The item was an anonymous gift, and had been left under her nose on an outside table two years past. Finding it too scandalously precious to speak of, and fearing what society gossips would make of it, she had tucked it away, keeping the jewel a secret, even from her mother.

Never had she mustered the courage to wear it, except alone before the mirror, but somehow she felt that tonight must be different. "Yes, the big one, that ruby necklace there," she said, sitting up tall, and she watched in the mirror as the little maid lay the jewellery across her chest, pulling it closer to fasten the clasp. The pendant shimmered wildly in the firelight, and for a moment Emelyn had a mind to snatch it off, dreading the questions that would follow, but she stayed her hands and gripped the chair, stretching her leg for Breda to roll on her stocking.

With stockings cinched above the knees, leather heeled shoes fitted and tied, Emelyn stood from the chair, marvelling at the opulent ruby decorating the neck of her reflection, even as she pondered where on earth one might find such a stone.

"Radiant as ever," Breda praised. "But the necklace, why it's fit for a queen miss; never have I seen the like!"

Emelyn covered the pendant with her hand. "Thank you Breda. The gloves?"

Her lady's maid blinked as though released from a spell, signalling her subordinate. The little maid appeared at Emelyn's side with gloves for the party, a fine pair of white silk with dark ribbons at the edges, pulled just past the wrist.

"Quintessence miss?"

"Jasmine oil," Emelyn said, accepting the prompt bestowal of a tiny glass phial, and after dabbing the opened tip against her neck she returned to the mirror for a great straining breath, accepting a fan of scented sandalwood. "You may tell her I am ready . . ."

Her mother was approaching from the wide doors to her own rooms, moving quite consciously in a fine mantua of deep purple, chin up and expression stern, with peacock feathers in a colourful scarf over the knot of her hair.

"I began to wonder if you'd ever come out," Mrs. Morley said.

"I'm sorry Mama," Emelyn said, hand at her heart to conceal the necklace. "Perhaps if Mr. Bowtree hadn't written me a letter; I'd rather you did not permit gifts from gentlemen I've refused."

"Should I have stopped it at the door and injured the poor man all over again?" her mother scoffed. "Nay my dear, and you will keep all such presents in future, now that your sisters are to have your allowance."

"They're not to know it's from me," Emelyn said quickly, "and I wish you would speak plainly about our circumstances. Is Morley Maritime in trouble?"

"I counselled your father to sell off his interest years ago," Mrs. Morley said bitterly, "but always he hesitates," and she interrupted herself with a gasp, catching sight of the ruby. "What in mercy's name is that?"

"An anonymous gift, from the green garden party, two springs ago," Emelyn said, lamenting she'd moved her hand.

"But I see why you never wear it," her mother puffed. "It cannot be real my dear; French fakery with a chain of pinchbeck I shouldn't wonder. You must take it off at once."

For a moment she thought to seize the opportunity, but something within her would not permit retreat, and Emelyn shook her head, touching the ruby again. "No Mama, it is quite real I assure you; ruby bordered with diamonds, and the chain is gold. If we've come to such necessity as you say, perhaps I should have it appraised."

"Certainly not," Mrs. Morley said, staring with wonder. "It can only be Mr. Loganbrek to have lavished you with such a gift . . . we shan't insult him to ransom it."

"I'm certain t'was not he."

"Either way," Mrs. Morley said, "if it is real as you believe, we must be sure to use it to best advantage."

"What advantage?"

"We shall publish it a gift from Loganbrek. And on the odd chance it was not, I daresay your unknown benefactor will come forward with all haste."

"Really Mama . . . Mr. Loganbrek wouldn't send so much as flax ribbon without withering sermons on its worthiness."

"Nevertheless he must have the credit," Mrs. Morley said, leading her along the rich red carpet of the upper hall. "In this way we shall flatter his vanity and ignite his jealousy besides; brandish your charms my dearest and I daresay he'll present you a gift even finer."

"Perhaps he'll present me with a different gentleman . . ."

"You may leave that satirical attitude here with me," her mother said, turning to descend the stairs. "Now it is Sarah who shall start the minuet . . ."

"So I'm not even to open the dance?" Emelyn asked with dismay.

"Mr. Loganbrek does not care for country dancing; he waits upon you with a large company of friends, outside by the fountains."

"He does not care for dancing!" Emelyn laughed. "Oh Mama, could we be any more ill-suited to each other?"

Mrs. Morley sighed, stopping to seize the edges of her daughter's bodice, adjusting it downward. "My wilful darling," she said, "we shall talk in circles until the new year if you have your way. But the time for your interview has come."

"Very well, I shall rush to meet him," Emelyn said, staring past her mother as she readjusted her bodice.

"And when you do, remember to speak to his interests, and with deference," Mrs. Morley added. "You've strange turns of thought my dearest, that is to be avoided. We do love your fanciful stories, but with Mr. Loganbrek you must keep such wit at an agreeable distance."

"And how does one apply distance to wit," Emelyn muttered, feeling a weight of reluctance as she turned to resume her descent.

The butler of Hastelbrook, Mr. Eugurt, a dignified elderly fellow much her father's senior, escorted her to the doors, and the footmen threw them wide. Distant tones of a minuet wafted from the ballroom, the night fluttered breezily cool, and Emelyn paused to drink it in, admiring the watery eye of the full moon through the clouds. With each passing year it seemed to her the dark grew ever more pleasant, and not for the first time she wondered if a raucous dance in the gardens by moonlight wouldn't be a great deal more fun.

She guessed Mr. Loganbrek must be somewhere across the wide chalky gravel of the drive, ensconced among a large and boisterous company mulling about the twin marble fountains that guarded the entrance to the maze. Emelyn's father waited at the landing on the stairs, dressed in long coats embroidered with silver, a pristine white cravat under his long wig.

Rimmed with gold in the flickering light, the elder Morley's spectacles rose on his cheeks as he smiled, offering his arm. "Here we are my dear," he said, and she took his wrist, concealing the jewel with a modest hand as they descended.

"So I am to fall directly into his arms," Emelyn said, "and under a full moon, how auspicious."

Her father's expression was warm, if tired. "Emie my dear, I know your mother's insistence taxes you, but her alarm is not without cause."

"All she's told me is we're to rent Ledgefield house. Is there some new enemy to our fortunes?"

"Just a spot of business my dear; we'll not trouble over it now," he said, slowing as they approached the group, "nor shall I have you pressed to like this Loganbrek person, but we only ask you allow the gentleman a fair shot."

"Yes Papa," Emelyn said, envisioning for a moment life as a married prisoner in the cold misted hills of Scotland, where the last wolves yet roamed, certain to feast on young ladies who enjoyed walking at night. "I suppose it's too late to forswear the meeting and write to him a thoughtful letter?"

Her father chuckled softly. "Come," he said, squeezing her hand, "if after tonight you cannot bear the poor fellow, you may write to him as much as you like."

In her mind's eye, Geoffrey George Loganbrek had become a reliable subject for caricature, only increased by his sister's Herculean attempts to obfuscate the matter of his eccentric nature and appearance—praising the dashing masculinity of his laugh, or the stately poise of his buttons. Emelyn had rather hoped her estimation would improve by encounter with the man himself, but the sight of him standing between the fountains, bouncing on his toes and rubbing his watch chain dispelled any such illusions. Of ponderous raindrop figure, with green frock coat over the straining bulge of his gilded amidships, Mr. Loganbrek stood in rounded trousers with polished buckles on his shoes, his fist high on his side. His countenance was knobby and round, shining between the mane of his full bottomed wig with bacon-faced glee.

The entourage gave way, excepting a tail-wigged lackey in dark livery, who stood with a distasteful expression, as though he rather smelled something. Emelyn mourned the sight of him, for this could only be Mr. Loganbrek's valet, the presence of whom meant the lot of them would be quartering in the village, and probably stay for the week.

"Mr. Loganbrek at last," her father offered in greeting, bowing low. "Welcome to Hastelbrook; I trust the evening finds you well."

The corpulent Geoffrey George Loganbrek drummed his fingers

on his chest with a hearty laugh. "My dear Morley!" he crowed. "Delighted to be in attendance, and might I just say, I've never held with those who impugn Hastelbrook's design. That marvellous clock face peering down from the garret, and I believe that was an old sextant over the ballroom? But I'm in shipping myself! Such jaunty asymmetry smacks of courage."

Emelyn felt her father's embarrassment.

"Right you are sir," Mr. Morley said, looking up to the strange granite sculpture high over the ballroom at the peak of the west wing. "The sextant has largely fallen apart alas, but this and the clock were the choice of my grandfather, and I'd not see them moved."

"You honour your line sir," Loganbrek answered, puffing with a breath. "A man must be judged for more than the lay of his house."

"Perhaps the manor's outward appearance bewilders," Emelyn interjected, unable to wait for introductions, "but I think you'll find the interiors answer every question of elegance."

Mr. Loganbrek trained his beady focus upon her, his eyebrows raised.

"The staff's hidden corridors run the longest in Sussex," she added.

"Yes my dear," Mr. Morley said, squeezing her hand.

"And our greenhouse holds all manner of exotic plants, from twinflowers to banana trees . . ."

"Yes my dear, quite right," Mr. Morley said, squeezing more firmly.

"By the light . . . I am struck blind!" Loganbrek declared. "Can this stunning fair, this most beauteous advocate of the estate be she, the *Belle of Brighton*?"

Mr. Morley cleared his throat, raising his daughter's fingers as she curtsied. "May I present my eldest daughter, Emelyn Elizabeth," and he passed her hand to the expansive gentleman, who took it at once, bowing to smell her glove.

"Jasmine oil . . . most fetching, my dear Miss Morley," Geoffrey George began, "it is a peerless honour, to acquaint the most delectable fruit of the county at last!" And he strained with a flourish for another bow.

"Mr. Loganbrek, I am at your service," Emelyn replied.

"Splendid, now you must take the air, and rely on our good footmen to attend you," her father said, and she gave him a look as he turned to leave.

"But the breeze is fine," the eager Loganbrek enthused, offering his arm, "shall we begin our intrepid perambulation, into the bowery maze!"

"By your leave sir," Emelyn said, "though before we walk, shall I thank you for the gift of this pendant, a prize beyond all expectation," she said, touching the ruby.

Mr. Loganbrek blinked as he smiled, his small eyes widening at the jewellery. "I do confess, fair maid, I am at a loss. It was not I who sent you this gift, but some other admirer, and of no small means!"

"No gentleman has come forward," she said. "We had therefore assumed it a product of your own boundless generosity. I shall remove it, if it offends you."

"Oh do not dream of it!" he exclaimed, grinning broadly. "It sparkles over the cloven cream of your bosom as the very spear of Apollo."

"Very well sir, as you wish of course," she droned, looking into the dimly lit mouth of the garden labyrinth, and spotting from the corner of her eye the darkly clad valet yet unmoved.

"Thank you Quinson," Loganbrek said, and the squinty fellow bent low, his eyes fixed upon the necklace as he receded out of sight.

"And how fares your dear sister?" Emelyn asked, turning to face her obligation.

"Yes indeed," Loganbrek answered, watching the rise and fall of the ruby pendant as she breathed.

"Your sister," Emelyn said louder, "Miss Poppy Loganbrek, how is she?"

"Aha! Quite so," he said, amending his gaze. "She is in Edinburgh."

Emelyn closed her eyes for patience, and the pair of them turned together to walk, leaving the fountains behind as they entered the maze. "And how is Scotland this time of year?" she inquired, thinking of wolves.

"The country beautiful as ever, if cold for the last buds of spring," he said, plucking a single waxy leaf from the wall of green as he looked upward. "Now I've never seen a boxwood of such prodigious elevation, it must be twice the height of a man, and more!"

"Yes we've the tallest garden maze in the county."

"But tell me, is it true a young woman once vanished here within, never to be found?"

"That young woman was never given a name," Emelyn said. "I've been investigating such rumours as long as I can remember; it's only a story I'm afraid . . ."

Fractured light played over the hedges, cast from lanterns dangling on their chains or mounted high in the lush walls, and Emelyn felt a smile as she inhaled the pleasing scents of earth and hedge, tickled to think if she but dashed away he would catch no trace of her, for she knew every inch of the maze, which sprawling deceptively vast had a tendency to intimidate visitors. They took several paths and turns, a pair of footmen following twenty paces behind, while Mr. Loganbrek made liberal use of the air, crooning her praises in both prose and verse:

"By brunette beauty soft of duty a man might seize the day. By blonder fair of golden hair a boy might have his way. But better said to court a red-head with marital bouquet, as wild flame grows warm and tame within a hearth to play, where other shades are sure to fade and quickly burn away!"

"That is lovely thank you," Emelyn said, hoping this poem to be the last.

"Of course, of course . . . Now on the matter of your gentlemen suitors," he went on, "I really must extol the virtues of age and wisdom, for men yet poor in years only gallop after beauty, proving themselves changeable as the wind, whereas we gentlemen of experience and fortune esteem your womanly charms with sober reverence."

"And all the more after drinking," she remarked, finding the usual joy of the paths quite vanquished at his presence. "Mr. Loganbrek I do apologize, but I must plead a chill. Perhaps just a bit farther."

"Of course Miss Morley forgive me! I forget the delicate sensitivities of the fair sex," he twittered. *"The cold to me were but a knave, I crow to winter's froth behave! But fear no rain nor wind nor wave."*

Emelyn clenched her jaws to suffocate a yawn, and walking a few steps ahead of him she stopped at a green hedged wall.

"But these meandrous foot paths are a delight!" he cheered, squinting upwards.

"Well, we've missed the turn for the pavilion," she said, yearning to free her precious maze of him. "Returning that way we might look over the lakes for an easier walk back, but if we continue here . . ."

"Oh let us forge ahead!" he interrupted. "Take my arm and we might slip our pesky minders, what say you?"

"They are too well trained for that sir," she said, keeping her arm to herself. "Now, follow me if you would," and she led him on, increasing her pace.

Mr. Loganbrek mopped his brow as he wobbled behind, the distance growing between them. "I do not walk for my own pleasure," he coughed with a laugh. "Perhaps your hand for a kiss might fortify my constitution!"

"Nay gentle sir, we are obliged to honour my boundaries," she called back, "lest you think your sister's letters have won you special privilege." And she laughed with the fun of the chase, rounding one corner after another, listening for his reply. But Mr. Loganbrek made no response. The greenery came to an abrupt halt, and she looked around, finding herself alone, nestled between towering walls of boxwood on three sides.

"Just here! Right then left and right again!" she shouted, amused to have lost him so easily.

There was a thrashing sound, as though an animal had crashed through the hedge, and Emelyn retreated to the corner to look, spotting no sign of Mr. Loganbrek, nor the footmen. A shadow made her turn, and she gasped to find a pale skinned woman standing not five paces away, shrouded in hooded black.

"It's you!" Emelyn gaped at her, fixed in terrified fascination as the woman grinned, drifting closer, her eyes void as night . . .

"Help! Help here!" a footman cried, and the woman vanished.

"Wait! Don't go!" Emelyn pleaded, searching about her.

There was a wheezing cough from the way she had come, and the sound of her heavy footed follower rumbling with curses.

"What is it? What's happened? Help me up you loafing laggards!"

Some minutes later a distraught Mr. Loganbrek perched heavily on the edge of one of the entrance fountains, attended by the footmen as Emelyn stood by. The gentleman sat with knees wide apart, lamenting his ordeal as he slurped brandy for his nerves.

"Of all the misadventures that ever man befell," he complained, "to be struck down by a shock, with guts of iron as I have? But it must be the effect of the lights, how they play in the mist."

Emelyn stared at the faceless angel in the fountain, which lifting its weathered bowl shimmered as water plumed from within, toppling over its edge into the pool. Panting with nervous breath against the cage of her laces she deliberated over the haunting encounter, holding herself to be neither drunk, nor ill, nor faint; indeed her faculties were awake and keen as ever. But there could be no other explanation— her dark visitant was no dream; the woman in black was real.

Though uninjured, Mr. Loganbrek had been found at first quite unconscious, having taken a fall in his pursuit. "But I've never collapsed in my life," he blustered, snatching a second brandy from his attendants. "I tell you I felt as though I were staring into the deeps of a bottomless well, with the most compelling sense of falling down into it! In fact," he laughed, "I fancied at first I was looking into someone's eyes, but black as coal oil they were . . ."

"Perhaps you'd care to rest a while?" Emelyn asked, reaching to nearly touch his shoulder before crossing her arms.

"Oh Miss Morley sweet and true," he said breathlessly, sweat beading on his brow. "Your concern touches profoundly, but rest assured, you'll find my people among the hardiest in the realm."

Unsure how to respond she allowed him the reluctant charity of her hand. "Good . . . thank you."

"Shall we fetch you anything else sir?" the footman asked.

"You must leave me to the tender care of this most enchanting and capable Samaritan," Mr. Loganbrek replied, puckering his lips for her hand.

"Thank you," she repeated, removing it just in time, "but if you'll forgive the delicate sensitivities of the fair sex, I fear I must recuse myself, to recover . . . ere I join you for the party."

Mr. Loganbrek made no attempt to stand, but nodded with a wink as she curtsied her goodbye. "Of course, most fetching fair," he gushed, addressing the footmen with great volume as she took her leave. "Mark how beauty walks! *Belle of Brighton* indeed; *Belle* of my very soul!"

Emelyn walked as quickly as she dared without drawing attention, passing the front doors and rounding the corner of the house to enter the eastern courtyard, making her way through the kitchen gardens to the side entrance. The handsome first footman Adam Comberland trotted after her, catching up as she reached the humble door to the kitchens.

"May I be of assistance Miss Morley?"

"No, Comby, thank you," she said, "and if you tell my mother where I've gone I shall have your head."

"Wouldn't dream of it miss," he said with a smile.

The door opened on stairs descending to the basements, where lay the manor's expansive kitchens, larders, craft rooms and servants' dormitories. Reaching the bottom Emelyn came to a landing before an arch to the kitchens proper, where she paused to appreciate a door to the thin back stairs at her right. Their steep ascent was one she'd often escaped to as a child, exploring networks of narrow corridors that wandered all through the house, hidden between the walls for servants to perform their office without being seen.

Finding her abruptly among them, the kitchen maids stopped their tasks to curtsy, but Emelyn bid them pay no attention, passing by the great walk-in hearth and through the staff dining room to slip into a dimly lit pantry, where she leaned on the thick table to breathe. By the distant roar of it the party was at full tilt, promising another assembly of mirthful chaos as guests flooded ballroom and balconies, those arriving by special invitation mixed with those from prosperous farms and minor estates about the county, with any number of their curious friends. A few of these were bound to test the watchful footmen, stealing away to nose about where they weren't wanted, pleading ignorance always, when they were inevitably caught detecting for secret passages.

Gasping to imagine whether the woman in black might have snuck into the house under cover of just such a gathering, Emelyn retreated to the darkened corner of the pantry, opening a tall cupboard door to shelter behind it, where covering her mouth she stared with wide eyes into the grain of the wood. That this haunting visitor should exist outside her imagination was at once impossible and intriguing, for she'd the strangest conviction the ghostly woman had set upon her before, that like a biting serpent she had pierced her throat, though she could recall no horror in the embrace, but rather a profound and terrible exhilaration . . .

Servants flashed in and out of the kitchens, and Emelyn remained very still, watching a low burning lantern over the cutting table and holding her breath at every sound of footsteps. Fingers of memory crept back to her as though at the behest of some outside force, and the realization dawned that she'd not only encountered the mysterious woman before, but had spoken to her, though she could remember naught but a single word of what had passed between them: *Vaela*. Her name was Vaela.

A little housemaid popped into the pantry, squeaking at the sight of her. "Beggin' your pardon miss! I'm just down for the firewood canvas. We're to heap the fires; the night bein' unseasonable cold as it is."

Emelyn nodded, watching as the maid wrestled a small canvas tarp from beneath a crockery cupboard and paused, as though unsure whether to spring upon her duty or wait for permission.

"Oh I'm sorry," Emelyn said. "I don't mean to interrupt. Abbie, is it?"

The maid curtsied. "Addie. And if you'll forgive my sayin' it miss— the staff, well, we wish you ever so much happiness . . . but we'll be sorry to see you go we will."

"Thank you Addie, but I'm not promised yet," Emelyn said quickly, "nor can I promise to *be* promised . . . much though my mother disagrees."

Addie did not respond, but curtsied again, swishing out of the pantry.

Someone broke a dish, and a wafting smell of cheese reminded Emelyn of the substantial suitor she'd run away from. "Bear up Emie," she muttered, dabbing her eyes with a kerchief. But there was nothing for it; upstairs the cumbrous posture-making Mr. Loganbrek would be waiting. Still, the riddle of the woman in black demanded answer, and she was nearly resolved to return to the maze alone when a burst of footsteps made her jump.

Isabelle leaned through the door, her fuss of blond hair in girlish loops for the party. "Not the pantry again! When you disappear Mama conscripts *me* to dig you up."

Emelyn swiped her cheeks. "Because you're not afraid to run in the house."

"Are you crying Emie? What's wrong?"

"Nothing at all . . . but everything is different now," Emelyn said, staring into the flickering lantern.

Isabelle groaned. "You say that every time you finish a novel."

"I do not." Emelyn sniffed. "And you needn't have troubled. I shall be up when I'm ready."

"Your pursy dumpling is on the veranda, but is it true he fainted from walking?" Isabelle asked, strolling around the table to the cupboards.

"I don't know," Emelyn said.

"Well, what do you think of him?"

"He's a happy smarming pettifog, who stares down my neck . . . and you will not repeat that."

Isabelle giggled, and opening the cupboard doors she cooed with pleasure to discover pineapple glazed sweet rolls. "Well whatever he is, he must be in love with you," she said, selecting one from the tray. "He's casting sonnets into the air for all to hear; he'll be singing afore long . . ."

"He is free to sing all he likes, and those are for breakfast," Emelyn said, her mouth watering at the smell. "Pineapple is very expensive."

"Well I've had quite enough of peaches," Isabelle said, peeling back the paper to pop a piece in her mouth. "And I'm sure we can afford as much *pineapple* as we like, whatever that is."

"No Bell, I promise you we cannot. In the natural course of our finances there are peaks and valleys . . ."

"Yes, and business is grand," Isabelle said thickly, chewing with relish. "Papa has restored our pocket money didn't you hear?"

Emelyn sighed, retrieving her fan from the table. "I am happy to hear it, now you may tell Mama you could not find me."

"Tell her yourself," Isabelle said, picking slivered almonds off her pastry. "Sulk until I finish my treat if you like, then you must come up."

"I'm not sulking, though I should prefer to be left alone."

"Oh I almost forgot," Isabelle said, lamenting a dropped morsel. "But you'll never guess who I saw dancing . . . do you remember Mr. Bowtree, who wept so bitterly when you rejected him under the cherry trees?"

"Of course I remember. He's just sent me a present in fact . . . but he's not been invited, Mama would never."

"You forget his sister is my croney." Isabelle winked, carefully sliding the tray of sweets back in its place. "Merina has come for the party, and he is her chaperone. Therefore, you shall follow me to the ballroom, or I'll imply to him you've had a change of heart."

"You would not dare."

"Shall we go and see?" and with a cackle Isabelle fled the pantry.

"No!" With a charge of panic Emelyn dashed after her. "Bell wait!"

The back stair was dimly lit by wall mounted candles, climbing all the way from the basement landing to the wide second floor corridor, which ran the length of the house, making a lofty bridge over the main hall before plunging between rooms to its termination at the railing overlooking the ballroom in the west wing. Bursting through a concealed door in the wall Isabelle won the top with a cry of triumph as Emelyn caught up to her, rounding the corner onto the maroon carpet and catching her sister by the wrist.

"Stop it!"

"I thought you're afraid to run in the house," Isabelle panted, squirming to free herself.

"Really Isabelle!" Emelyn snapped, eyes shining as she released her. "You are not to threaten me, with Bowtree or anyone else, do you understand?"

Isabelle frowned, scratching her arm. "I wouldn't really tell him you ninny." Her eyes widened. "But where in the Danish hoards have you come by that necklace?!"

Emelyn pulled her aside, glancing at the handful of guests down the hall. "Lower your voice! It was a gift . . . anonymous."

"Anonymous? Well I shall never have such a present," Isabelle said, her mouth trembling. "And if I don't bring you back I'm forbidden to dance, and shall have nothing left but to go to my room forever."

"Oh Bell . . ."

"You bid me forget John Lawford, and there is no one else!"

Emelyn exhaled a long breath. "Did he not flee to escape his arrest?

Is that really the sort of person to set your heart on?"

"John Lawford would never flee without a word, he would not! He must have come to a bad end . . . Have his enemies murdered him?"

"That is ridiculous," Emelyn said. "If he cared for you truly he'd have faced his accusers with honour. But it is a blessing— his character is revealed before any harm was done."

"It's not a blessing!" Isabelle insisted, stamping her foot. "That wretched Mr. Cavendish baited my John, he must have done!"

"Bell hush," Emelyn said, taking hold of her shoulders. "Of course you're free to think of him if you like, I cannot stop you. But I know you shall find better. As for Mr. Loganbrek, whether I abide him or not is no one's concern but my own."

"Well I can't see why you don't just refuse him, if you hate him so," Isabelle said, wiping her eyes. "You refuse everyone."

"That's not fair . . ."

"But you've turned down so many, some of them *quite* handsome, with wealth and gentility to match. And none stand accused of attacking our solicitor at a party."

"That is all very well, but it's how you *feel* in a gentleman's company that matters most. True romantic connection should lighten every hardship, make every moment apart like an age . . . and ages together like a moment."

"Hell's bells Emie you read too much," Isabelle grunted. "I require naught but living enough to do as I like, and a good deal of culture. But *you* are never practical, and you shall languish alone until you learn to be so."

"And you're to lecture me, after falling over a scape-grace?" Emelyn asked hotly.

Isabelle's face crinkled, threatening tears, and Emelyn seized her hands. "Oh Bell don't . . . I'm sorry. I only wish Mama would not play you against me. Of course you must be allowed to dance."

Isabelle pouted with a sniff, waiting for more.

Emelyn released her. "Oh go on then . . . lead and I will follow you."

"Thank you Emie," Isabelle chirped, rising on her toes to kiss her sister's cheek. "But not too closely," and she turned to flit down the hall.

She disappeared through a boisterous group of young fellows under the sharp eye of an attending footman, and clearing her throat Emelyn smoothed her gown, straightening her back to rejoin the party.

Navigating past jovial guests and alcoved statues, she smiled with polite excuses as various gentlemen of vague acquaintance addressed her, finding the glorious ruby pendant ample excuse to solicit her attention. "Thank you," and "Enjoy the party," she said, continuing on her way.

Stepping out onto the gallery above the ballroom she hurried along the wall, passing by glances and greetings to squeeze through gaudily dressed couples and those leaning over the railings to watch the dance below: ladies and their gentlemen bobbing to the music as they traded sides for a spirited rigadoon.

At the south end of the gallery through an arched doorway, past columns supporting the old garret balcony above, there opened a grand veranda of tiled stone, large enough for thirty people to take the air and enjoy luxurious balcony views of the gardens and lakes beyond. Whispering through the crowd Emelyn stopped to peer between the columns, espying the long powdery wig of Mr. Loganbrek as he stood chuckling between party lanterns that dotted their way around the semicircular railing. Leery at the sight of three empty chairs set behind him, she was about to retreat when she was accosted by her mother, who taking her daughter's elbow guided her to a solitary sofa.

"Your eyes are red my darling, are you feeling unwell?"

Emelyn shook her head. "No Mama, I'm fine . . . but must you send Isabelle to hunt after me like I've run away?"

"The servants won't cross you my dear," her mother said, "how else shall we impel your return?"

"The necklace is not from Mr. Loganbrek," Emelyn said flatly.

Mrs. Morley tilted her head to peer toward the veranda. "Really . . . No matter, the man is clearly besotted; but I hear you charmed him into a dead faint!"

"I did no such thing. He collapsed quite on his own."

Mrs. Morley clicked her tongue. "Chasing a girl through the hedge is a young man's game," she said. "Now he may not be of strapping health, but I daresay he is the very wealthiest gentleman to seek your favour; he's been honourably diligent in his affections, and I am encouraged to report has all but promised investment in the business!"

"Has he indeed," Emelyn said, smiling for a jovial couple as they passed. "But I hope you don't imagine that bears on my decision."

"Well perhaps it should," Mrs. Morley said, teasing at her daughter's hair. "I was embarrassed to hear you startled away from him like a bird, so at the very least you *will* apologize, and whether he's an offer to make or only empty words, you will hear him out."

"Very well I shall apologize, though he is ridiculous."

"And hear him out," her mother repeated, accepting a letter from a footman's tray, which she puzzled at.

"How curious," Emelyn stalled. "Post at this hour? What is it?"

"Nothing to excuse you I'm quite sure. Now to it my dearest; you will present yourself gently, seek amends for your inattention, and if he makes you an offer, for the love of your family I expect you to consider very carefully your answer."

Emelyn took a step, but anxiety clutched in her chest, and she turned back. "Wait . . . Mama must I really see him again? Can you ever imagine I'd spend my promise on a man beyond even Hogarth's ability to caricature?"

Mrs. Morley hissed with frustration, coming to take her arm. "We have come to the edge my girl," she said, her voice strained with displeasure. "Your father would conceal the worst of it, but I've never seen him so distraught, and it frightens me. Therefore you will tuck your shoulders back and return to your gentleman, the same who with a stroke of his pen might deliver us."

Emelyn swallowed hard, and leaving her watchful mother behind she dragged her feet to the veranda.

"Good even sir," she said, fiddling with her fan as she made her approach. "I trust you are in better spirit."

Geoffrey George Loganbrek turned with a happy noise. "My radiant lady returns!" He heaved into a bow. "I am quite recovered myself, as you can see," and he executed a casual lean on the rail, his fist on his hip as he perused the depth of her neckline.

Emelyn gave him her shoulder, looking over the dusky gardens below. A gentle fog had rolled in, casting the hedgerows in sharp relief against the misted paths between them. "Thank you for waiting," she said.

Mr. Loganbrek tittered behind his fingers. "Oh for a vision such as yourself, a trifle. Now, but have you ever heard your own praiseworthy mention, in William Popple's account, *On Persons Notable*?" And he grinned with tension, as though he must recite the lines or explode.

"I know the indelicate rhyme you speak of; I should prefer you not repeat it."

The gentleman deflated with a mournful sound, but recovered quickly, brandishing a wide smile. "A lady well ripened in poetry is well harvested in matrimony," he quipped. "But we shall never get on Miss Morley, if you do not savour the sweet salt of the poet's tongue."

Emelyn grimaced. "Well . . . perhaps you're right," she said, and seized with a sudden daring to know whether the woman in black might be watching still, "but would you fancy a return to the maze Mr. Loganbrek?"

"Oh I think not," he said, looking rather pale. "Night and fog have descended in treacherous union; I dare not test a woman's well accounted fear of the dark."

"How very considerate," she said, staring into the lakes.

"You must guide me to bestow upon you a gift," he said softly, leaning to linger his gaze, "one as will rival this extravagance hanging about your collar . . . You have but to name it."

"To answer would require some consideration," she said, snapping out her fan to block his view.

Mr. Loganbrek squeaked, coughing to repair his voice. "Then *consider* Miss Morley! You must trust your covetous desserts to my keeping."

"If you please sir, I am not seeking presents," she sighed. "There is no obligation between us; I could scarce behave more selfishly, than to demand you improve upon such a jewel."

Mr. Loganbrek dabbed his neck. "Oh come now Miss Morley, you cannot but apprehend it is *love* that would stir me to such expenditure."

Emelyn blushed, lowering her fan to snap it closed. "Mr. Loganbrek, we hardly know each other," she said, watching as he took her hand for a kiss, "will you pretend to love me at our very first meeting?"

His gaze attending every part but her eyes, the gentleman cleared his throat, standing tall as he was able. "Oh but hark," he said wryly, and raising arms over his head he performed a double clap like a maestro. "Dearest Miss Morley, you are acquainted well enough with my epistolary devotions, but basking now in the exalted glow of your company, I find your manifold charms multiplied beyond measure; my resistance is vanquished!"

Three slender fellows in dark coats with white ruffles sprang onto the veranda making for the chairs, and Emelyn stared as they snapped to their seats, eyes cast down and violins at their necks. The musicians burst into a serenade, and Mr. Loganbrek took her hands, trembling downward as he lowered his weight into a kneel.

"Dear me but oh! Where to begin," he burbled. "May the nine Muses guide my elocution . . ."

Emelyn's chest tightened to find her mother still observing from the hubbub of the gallery. "Please sir," she interrupted, "not yet; we've had scarcely a moment together . . ."

"Emelyn Elizabeth Morley!" Mr. Loganbrek beamed up at her.

"What is time in the face of truth, for true as the face of heaven I must have you for my own, though your beauty burn into my eyes like the sun!"

Looking down at his knobby round face, alight with the same expectation she'd seen in many others before him, Emelyn determined to forego her usual course of flattering apologies, and move straight through to her departure. "Thank you sir," she said, taking a breath as she retreated her hands. "I am honoured, truly, alas I think it better if we exchange letters as friends; now if you will excuse me . . ."

"But a moment Miss Morley!" he said loudly, struggling to maintain a grin. "You must realize, sailing from India under such hazardship, it was only the promise of your esteem that maintained my spirits . . ."

"Well I'm sorry for your *hazardship*," she said, "but there was never such a promise on my part, except to abide this meeting, which I believe has run its course."

"My dear madam," he spluttered. "Would you deny a poor fellow before he's asked?"

"Only to spare us both; as you have not yet proposed, I needn't ravage your hopes with my answer."

The musicians stopped, and Mr. Loganbrek wobbled on his knee, threatening to capsize, but she grabbed his elbow, helping him to stand. "Shall I speak to your parents perhaps?" he asked, chuckling with effort. "Perhaps my generous intentions are unclear . . ."

"Not at all sir," Emelyn said with a curtsy. "I can only hope my reply is as clear to you as your intentions are to me," and not daring to check the windows for her mother she set off, reaching the stairs at the west end of the veranda that cornered the house.

"I've been warned of your wintery ways Miss Morley, and I'll not be deterred!" he cried, the tap of his heeled shoes following, and stopping at the top of the stairs he belted out William Popple's familiar lines:

"Miss Emelyn Morley played dice, won dear mother's beauty by thrice, leaving nothing for sisters, little bell and thin ginger, but to trail behind her like mice!"

Groaning at the words Emelyn gathered her skirts, descending as quickly as she might, and reaching the drive she slipped past the front facing doors of the ballroom. The mist played about the gardens as music rang out in joyful measure, and looking to the darkling sky she resolved that she must have the truth of it; she must find and speak to the woman in black, tonight.

Chapter 3
The Sympathetic Darkness

"Why Miss Morley! This is a merry meeting."

Arming herself with a smile Emelyn stopped, turning to behold a delicate blond wigged gentleman emerging from the ballroom doors under the veranda. "Mr. Bowtree. How are you?"

Slenderly handsome in coats of stormy grey, her onetime suitor Meriton Bowtree doffed his hat as he approached, his eager blue eyes sparkling. "I am well madam, I thank you," he said brightly, "though a lesser man might deplore of his fate . . . having been once in your favour, henceforth to be known only as the brother of your sister's friend."

Emelyn cleared her throat, finding his self-effacing over-earnest demeanour just as she remembered. "And how is dear Merina? Where is she?"

"Dancing I suppose," he said. "Forgive me, Miss Morley, but might you have received the little trifle I sent up for you, with my note?"

"I did sir, though I'm not sure it's appropriate. I might have expected you well married by now."

Mr. Bowtree nodded, seemingly caught between speech and laughter, despite the anguish in his eyes. "There was a young lady, a flaxen haired beauty with eyes green as yours, but she languished in my neglect, for my heart could not manage it . . . And what of yourself? How can the Belle of Brighton yet find herself unaffianced?"

"I really could not say, but I'm happy to wish the best of luck to us both. Now if you will excuse me . . ."

"I was just speaking with your uncle," he said, stepping sideways to catch her, "but Geoffrey George Loganbrek seems a rather tawdry hopeful does he not? I was certain you'd acquit your promise with a handsome duke, or a prince."

"Were you indeed," Emelyn said. "Then I suppose the whole

county must be aware of private conversations between myself and my mother."

"Oh I meant no offence."

Emelyn sighed. "I'm not offended Mr. Bowtree, but it's not fitting we should be speaking, and I would like a walk to myself. I really must bid you goodnight."

"Tarry Miss Morley, half a moment!" he implored, keeping up. "You must know, in these twenty-five months apart I have contrived, nay even rehearsed a dozen speeches, a hundred epigrams in your honour . . ."

"I wish you had not . . ."

"And yet, here now beside you, with but a dog's chance in the ocean of winning you back, my words fail me . . ."

"One cannot mistake your sincerity," she said, continuing to walk, "but I think it were better plied in different company sir."

Mr. Bowtree made an affronted noise. "Do you mock me madam?"

Emelyn stopped, and turning to face him she cast about for a gentle response, finding none.

"I say do you mock me Miss Morley?"

Vacantly she blinked at him, sure of nothing but that the woman in black must be pursued, and the fellow before her got rid of.

"Can it be lost on you that my fortunes have advanced tenfold since our last meeting? Will you answer?"

"I am surprised sir, by your address," she said, finding it ridiculous that she should refuse two such offers on the same evening. "As I recall every question between us was settled."

Mr. Bowtree gave an incredulous laugh. "Oh yes! When you took up with that cocksure Sir Thaniel Gliffton, who then dropped your acquaintance without a word. Well done."

"Was I ever unkind to you?" she asked, feeling a stab of anger. "I think you forget yourself."

"So it is confirmed! I must rise no higher than one more heart trampled in your wake, one more notch on your blade."

Emelyn rounded on him. "Mr. Bowtree we did try each other's company, if you remember, and we are no match! What can you ask of me now?"

"What can I ask," he echoed unhappily, stepping back from her. "Nothing at all I suppose; what does the water ask of the wind that freezes it? Perhaps I hoped my agonies might only find a patient ear . . ."

"I am sorry for your agonies," she said, "but as your heart is not for this *flaxen beauty* you describe, mine is not for you. I say again goodnight!"

For a moment he was silent, watching as she resumed her way. "So I am to be *good-nighted* thus, like a stranger," he called to her back. "Forgive me Miss Morley! I shall remove myself in a trice," and turning sharply he marched back to the house.

With an angry groan Emelyn resumed her way, and entering the cherry walks west of the maze she rounded a vine covered trellis, putting her back to a large statue of Saint Francis. The night breezed cool, and there she stood a while, feeling quite suffocated, until a pursuing footman appeared at her side, raising his lantern with concern.

"My lady bids you return presently miss," he said. "May I light your way back?"

"Thank you Percy, no," she heaved. "I should rather order you to breathe my laces," and she bent over to catch her breath, noting his blush of alarm. "But do not worry, I wouldn't dare."

Percy cleared his throat. "Will you not return to the house miss?"

"I must have a walk to myself," Emelyn said. "You may tell my mother I was obstinate."

The footman bowed his exit. "Very well miss . . ."

Watching him tread back up the hill Emelyn dug her fingers into the front of her bodice, catching the edge of her stays and pulling ferociously. Some of the laces stretched and she took a magnificent breath.

Keeping hidden from wandering couples among the trees she sheltered behind a bushy row of scarlet geraniums, their dense blooms shielding her path until she could hurry from the cherry walks to disappear into the maze. The hedges were so tightly pruned as to block out nearly all the light between them, the lanterns overhead casting eerie shadows in the mist, and dashing through the paths she reached the old gazebo at the back, where guided by cloud tattered moonlight she plodded carefully down the steps on the far side. The shallow stair sidled its way down along the wall, which was thickly draped in trumpet honeysuckle, their pale flowers troubling in the wind.

The thrill of her defiance lent exhilaration to every step, and aquiver with nerves she left the stairs behind to pick her way further along the wall, sheltered beneath the overhanging hill. High above, outside the boundary of the maze grew the tallest elm on the property, that from which her brother had fallen as a boy, to the ruin of his legs . . . A low stone bench by a lamp post gave her pause, and she sat for a rest, perched betwixt great fronds of love-lies-bleeding, their weeping tentacle blossoms gleaming red in the moonlight.

The woman in black's name returned to her, and for some time she sat very still, daring herself to call it out.

"Vaela," she spoke at last, making fists in her lap. "You are more than a dream; I know in my heart we have met before . . . Will you not reveal yourself to me?"

There was no answer, and swallowing hard she scanned the night blue-greens of the surrounding garden shapes. The white cobbled path ran away from her feet to thread its way down between the lakes, where it was consumed by banks of fog drifting over the water. Straining for the slightest sound she looked up, watching wisps of cloud as they dragged across the stars. Frogs hummed and croaked, punctuating the natural score of cricket song and wind rustled plants, but there came no sign of the woman in black.

Nervous moments passed, the drowsy lakes lapped at their borders as the ancient oak across the water shifted against the sky, and the recklessness of her errand began to come clearer. "What am I doing?" she asked aloud, and rising from the bench she was just making her way back along the wall when a soft, silken voice spoke behind her.

"You remember me . . ."

With a start Emelyn turned to find the same woman from the maze standing by the bench, cloaked and hooded as before with a dark robe beneath, split at the plunge of her pale neck. She was coldly beautiful, taller than Emelyn, with raven hair hanging thickly about her shoulders, and eyes that glinted silver as though possessed of their own secret light.

"Please, do not disappear," Emelyn entreated, palms forward as she strove to master her fear. "Vaela . . . I mean you no harm."

The woman raised her hands just alike. "Nor I you, Emelyn Morley."

Emelyn's breath caught in her throat as the woman slipped close, catching her about the waist. Ebon nails clicked against the ruby pendant. "You wear the necklace," Vaela breathed. "I'd begun to fear you did not like it . . ."

"It is beautiful . . . Was it you who left it for me?" Emelyn asked, feeling a strange and familiar fascination, as though a dream long interrupted might now continue. "But you must be more than a spirit . . ."

"I am flesh and blood as you are," the woman said, her silver eye passing close to Emelyn's own as she sniffed at her softly.

Emelyn trembled. Soft lips brushed her neck, and at the touch of slender fangs she meant to cry out, but cold fingers stopped her mouth.

"Hush," Vaela said, her expression tinged with sadness. "I am bound to protect you . . . you must never fear me."

Hidden memories, even those from her earliest childhood, began to stir. "What are you?" Emelyn inquired, shivering with the conviction that these same silver eyes had once peered at her over the railing of her cradle. "But you cannot be . . . *vampire?*"

"So your kind has taken to calling us, but I prefer my name."

Struggling to recall what she'd ever read of the night stalking drinkers of blood, Emelyn stared at her. "Did you kill Philip Denlund?" she asked, heart pounding at the question.

"He was rotten."

Vaela's presence perplexed and intoxicated, like warmth in her body with ice on her skin, and Emelyn squirmed for release, her mind reeling. "But the necklace . . . I cannot repay you."

"Oh but you can," Vaela replied, and touching her chin she coaxed back her head.

Feeling a breathless compulsion to offer her throat Emelyn obliged, and the stars flashed as the bite pierced her neck. Hot pain split through her, and she gasped, but the sensation diffused, spreading to a pulling itch of pleasure as the vampiress swallowed her blood . . .

It seemed not a moment later the bond was broken; the cold fangs withdrew, and wetting the hurt with her tongue Vaela lapped gently.

Its tenderness slipped away as the wound healed, leaving only a subtle, listless weakness, and Emelyn sagged in her arms, soft and insensible. "Shall I become vampire . . . as you are?"

More rosy than pale after the nourishment, the vampiress licked her teeth with a grin, releasing her to stand on her own. "No little one, not unless I were to drink you to the point of death, and feed you of my own blood, before the end."

Emelyn embraced herself, atremble with curiosity. "But have I not known you, since I was a child?"

"Yes," Vaela said. "I have watched over you all your life. Long have I wondered . . . whether you would grow strong enough, to remember me."

Emelyn's emotions tangled within her, and she backed away, her pulse throbbing. "But what have you done to me? Why do I feel I shall bare my very soul to you?"

"We are bound by blood," Vaela said. "Relinquish your pain . . . confess it to me."

Emelyn opened her mouth to speak, and soon found herself airing her every burden— the impending spectre of her family's financial ruin, which little she understood, and the impossible expectation set upon her to prevent it. "But I never imagined we should come to such extremity," she finished at last, swiping her cheek, "or that my future would be ransomed to atone for it . . . I might have married better years ago, but was I too proud?"

"Do not blame yourself," Vaela said, watching her closely. "It is the loss of your father's venture, those ships bound for America."

The words fell from her mouth, but Emelyn struggled to understand them. "What? The new frigates? But you are mistaken, they've only just set out; it's been scarcely a month!"

"You must have the truth of it from your father," Vaela said, taking Emelyn's hand to remove her glove. "You needn't be sentenced to repair the sins of your forebears . . ."

"I cannot abandon them," Emelyn said, watching as the vampiress brushed her palm with a delicate claw.

"They do not deserve you. Great signs attended your birth."

"Great signs," Emelyn repeated. "Can you refer to the ground shaking beneath the house, on the night I was born. That is naught but a village story."

"Not a story, a portent," the vampiress said, scowling as she spoke. "Hastelbrook was built over a sacred place: an ancient chamber buried deep, long ago. Without you it cannot be opened."

"A hidden vault beneath the house?" Emelyn clarified. "I grew up with these rumours; there's nothing deeper than the family crypt under the library . . ."

"The vault is real," Vaela said, fading back a step, "though I must say no more of it now, for I answer to others, just as you do . . ."

"What others? Wait you're not going!" Emelyn insisted, and rushing to grab Vaela's hands she found them warm. "Please . . . but the vampires I've read of are shambling corpses that attack without thought, and sleep in the earth in their graves. How is it you are so different?"

"Shambling corpses. And have you ever seen a troll under a bridge? Not every superstition is worthy of comment."

"But I scarcely believe my eyes, even as you stand here before me," Emelyn said. "Will you not explain to me who you are; where you've come from?"

Withdrawing her hands from Emelyn's grasp, Vaela removed her hood. "My name is Vaela Audette de Masseine," she said, her face glinting in the pale light. "I was born in France, mortal as you are now, in a castle on the river Vienne in 1528, to a family of crumbling nobility. I came to this country with another, nigh a century ago."

To exist for two hundred years in so unchanged a state . . . it was a thing quite beyond her reckoning, and Emelyn felt a terrible fatigue on her behalf. "But you look scarcely older than I am. You cannot be thirty!"

"I was twenty-nine," Vaela said, her gaze darkening to black. "But youth is not only in body; it is found wherever hope yet masters regret. You are better at being young . . . than I was."

A feeling of sorrow hung in the air, and Emelyn swallowed with a frown. "You said we are bound by blood; what do you mean by it?"

"Let me show you."

There was a surge of sensation, as though they were moving at impossible speed, and Emelyn startled with a cry, finding herself much farther from the house. Vaela lay her down in a bed of soft grass among blooming purple cranesbill, lowering to kneel beside her.

"What's happened?" Emelyn asked, her head spinning.

"Every year our bond is renewed," Vaela said, baring her fangs to puncture the tip of her own finger. "But tonight you have proven stronger than I might have hoped . . . I begin to think you will awaken completely, to the power of my blood in your veins."

"What does it mean?" But Emelyn could not wait for the answer; she parted her lips, a wild thirst surging within her as she recalled with needful ecstasy this same moment repeated time and again, as far back as she could remember.

Vaela turned her finger, and a single drop of blood landed on Emelyn's tongue. The vital fluid lit through her like fire, and the stars above blazed into new being, waking the heavens as they painted the night in luminous colour.

Emelyn shivered in wonder, finding her dark visitant to be the most majestic and beautiful creature she had ever beheld. A mad desire to possess and protect her took hold, and she repaired to her knees, grabbing the vampiress about the waist. "You cannot leave; but I feel your sadness. Have you no one to care for you?"

Vaela laughed softly; her voice rich and sweet. "You are only drunk on my blood," she said, stroking Emelyn's cheek with the back of her nails. "This frenzy of it will fade."

"I don't want it to fade," Emelyn said, half in a daze as she stared over her shoulder, squeezing her close. "I don't want to forget you again."

"You will not forget me, not anymore," Vaela said, gently freeing herself from Emelyn's grasp. "By and by, I believe you will remember all that has passed between us. My blood will quicken you; your senses, your strength, even your passions will increase, until you master them . . . I ask only that you make no report of me to your kindred, for it would put you in danger."

Emelyn nodded, and the vampiress took her about the shoulders and beneath the knees, lifting her as she stood. Again came the sensation of moving on the wind, and Emelyn was laid down on soft grass in a different place. The lanterns had been relit, the green walls of the hedge towering overhead in the murky light, and she felt as though the sky were below her, the ground above. For a moment she wanted to fall from the earth and tumble into the stars, but the sounds of night lulled her mind and the desire for sleep began to grow. A hooded shadow leaned close, and she felt the touch of soft lips on her brow.

"Goodnight, Emelyn Elizabeth . . . I will see you again soon."

"Wait," Emelyn whispered, grabbing into her cloak. "I dream that you lead me by the hand . . . There is a midnight road in the mist, beyond an iron gate . . . but where are we going?"

For a moment Vaela was quiet. "To the dark citadel," she said, "to Saunmoor . . . but I hope not for some while yet."

Making little sense of the words Emelyn tried to hold on, but the shadow vanished, her eyes drifted closed, and she slept.

■■

Many miles east of Hastelbrook, in the downs of Kent there lay a densely forested valley, where under the bandaged sky, in the broken glimmer of the full moon's light two weary men sat on fallen trees for benches before a sputtering campfire heaped high with rags, boxes, and various sundries they had unearthed. The ground about them was perforated with shallow holes, marking a disappointed hunt for treasure.

The younger of the two was a lanky fellow with nervous hands, who sat holding in his lap a weather-beaten book, acrid with the smell of earth. "Mr. Stanwick," he sighed, "these pages are little more than paste; can you imagine we'll find proof of *the city of the dead,* herein?"

His elder was a thick, sturdy man, his salty beard tucked in his collars, his coats dark with the recent rain. "Come now Mr. Havid," he said, licking his lips. "Do your father's memory proud, there must be *something* to it . . ."

The close forest creaked around them, moaning low on the wind. "I never followed his path," Mr. Havid said. "I'd never have believed in vampires . . . were it not for the night I found him, drained to his end."

Mr. Stanwick poured from a jug into a pair of tin cups, passing one across. "Tell us again sir, of that night . . . the night you saw an immortal and lived to remember it."

"There's little to tell," Havid said quietly. "In the attic window over my father's body freshly still, there crouched a man in black. He was little of stature, short bearded like a gentleman of the continent, with one eye dark as ink, the other dead white . . . I'll never forget."

"And what were his words to you?" Stanwick asked, hunching with eager attention.

"*Do not waste your life as he did,*" Havid quoted. "*Do not seek that which will not be found* . . . and then he was gone. And I swore it off. I'm no hunter Mr. Stanwick."

"Aye but you could be. Let this be the adventure to prove us both!"

"Adventure? I've lost my shop, my coat is threadbare, my boots are patched, and I am very tired," Havid complained. "I'm only here on your promise of reward, should we find something. But I should much rather we'd waited for dawn."

Mr. Stanwick poured himself another. "Take heart sir," he said, "the boundary between living and dead be thinnest under a full moon; best time to search. Anyway this be the place I'm sure of it; the very site I heard the voices, singing like mournful angels they were, with a discord of strings and drums a poundin' as like from deep in the earth . . ."

"But was that not during the day?" the sullen Mr. Havid asked, sipping his rum.

"Aye, the bluebells bright beneath my feet."

"Then it was only gypsies you heard," Havid said, crackling gingerly through the pages of the book as he squinted in the dim light. "Ah, well here's a legible bit . . . *1725, September. I have escaped my faithless captors. Bethlem Hospital it is called; I will never go back* . . . Bedlam? Is the author a madman? Who is he?"

Stanwick leaned forward with interest. "What should it matter; read on."

Mr. Havid cleared his throat to continue. "*The entrance is lost to me, the fortress melts away as a dream, and I can find no trace of it. Even the great red eye of her cathedral begins to fade from mind. But my dread queen must never breach the vault of Hastelbrook, lest the six thrones of Saunmoor fall to ruin, lest the coming storm consume us all . . ."*

"Ha!" Stanwick interjected. "I'll tell you who our intrepid author must be sir, a man what seen the city of the dead and lived to tell it. Baron Dramen shall pay handsomely for these notes, and whatever else we find."

"So he writes . . . of the *queen of vampires*," Mr. Havid said, his face pale. "And this *Hastelbrook*; but is there not a great house in Sussex by that name?"

"Aye, the family Morley," Stanwick said, pausing to down his rum, "their daughter quite a renowned beauty what I heard. I should say our luck has turned."

Tearing out the few lucid pages Mr. Havid stuffed them in his pocket. "Then let us be off; I for one shall be happy to see the taproom again," he said, and raising his drink he froze.

Stanwick was on his feet, but Mr. Havid sat very still, the edge of the cup at his lips . . . as without a sound a dark figure had joined them, sitting by his side.

"Stand fast fell spirit!" Stanwick yelled, brandishing a silver cross as he levelled his pistol.

Fighting the shock of his fear Mr. Havid turned to regard the stranger, who struck him at first as little more than a man, clad in black from boots to high collars, even to the silken cravat at his neck, with long ebon hair hanging to half obscure his youthful face. Bright silver eyes met his own and Havid found himself fixed in place as surely as if he were held at the point of a spear.

Without expression the man began to speak, his voice low and soothing. "Trespassers . . . The music you heard was but the echo of the festival of Sanziene, where we honour the dead and the coming of spring; the voices of our queen and her handmaids are not meant to sound beyond our borders . . . a momentary lapse of her will."

"Who are you?" Mr. Stanwick demanded, rattling with obvious nerves.

"I am Morion, eldest son of the queen's blood," the man said. "I know your business here; I have come to offer you a choice."

The stranger's gaze shifted from silver to brown, and Mr. Havid dropped his mug, feeling abruptly enchanted, relieved to find the man welcome company.

"Creature of the night," Stanwick growled, pointing the pistol, "You will answer my questions, for you are in the presence of proper vampire hunters."

"Please Mr. Stanwick, let us not be hasty," Havid said, sweating into his shirt.

Morion reached down, selecting a stick to toss into the fire. "Vampire hunters? I find you poor specimens; you will never leave these woods."

"Cross and chaplet shall keep us safe enough!" Stanwick barked, flushing with courage as he aimed the gun. "You shall tell us of your cold queen, and the man who escaped her clutches, and this, the book he's left behind, or I shall put a silver ball in that princely face."

The vampire chuckled softly. "You are but passing shadows; my queen is real."

"Please Mr. Stanwick, we are yet unharmed," Havid submitted. "Lower your weapon, let us hear the choice he would offer us!"

"Too late for that," Mr. Stanwick replied, beads of sweat on his brow as the pistol shook in his grip. "But here's a prize Lord Dramen should pay for most handsomely . . ."

Morion's silver eyes flicked upward. "I've got the whip hand of you," he said softly.

"Wait, please!" Mr. Havid implored, raising his hands.

"Nay sir, he means to have us," Stanwick said darkly, his finger on the trigger. "Unless we have him first . . ."

The pistol fired, but the vampire was not there, and Mr. Stanwick jerked from the ground, lifted into the air from behind. With a brutal crunch he shook, eyes agape as a bloody wheeze escaped his lips, and Mr. Havid watched in horror as the vampire lord pulled his hand from deep in his victim's back. Released from his killer Stanwick crashed into the fire, coming to rest broken and still.

Havid turned to run but found himself planted against a tree, the vampire holding his head by the chin. "The crucifix!" the young man whimpered, digging it out of his coats.

"There is no veneration in your devices," Morion said, his eyes pure black. "They are but copies of copies, casual ornaments girding a sinful soul."

"Mercy!"

"Forget the other, you must answer for yourself . . . vampire hunter. But if you mean to fight, or to flee, I will rend you apart and leave you in the fire."

Hot tears wet his cheeks, and Mr. Havid swallowed his voice, struggling to recover it. "No!" he blurted. "My father was the hunter. I am but a humble man of trade . . ."

"And what is your trade?" In the vampire's gaze there was none of the earlier welcome, but only a cold weariness.

"I am a shoe . . ." Mr. Havid caught his breath. "Shoemaker! I am a shoemaker."

Morion relaxed his grip, scowling as though in thought. "A shoemaker," he said. "Men's or ladies?"

"Oh," Havid said, blinking rapidly. "Well, both sir; I have been working at the craft since I was a boy, since my father squandered all our living on the hunt, finding never so much as a vampire's boot."

Morion grunted with something of a smile, setting him down. "Then behold my offer, shoemaker. In exchange for your life, you shall be nevermore seen in the world of men, but serve the remainder of your days behind the wall, under the absolute rule of your queen. Make your choice."

"Then I am not to be devoured?" Shaking to his teeth the beleaguered young man dropped to kneel, clasping his hands. "There is nothing left for me here. Please, I will go willingly, I will serve!"

The vampire lord pulled him to his feet, and Mr. Havid found his back once more to the tree. For a terrified moment he thought the immortal had slashed his throat, but a wild burn of pleasure slipped through his body, and he realized the creature was drinking his blood.

"And now my own blood you must take," Morion said, releasing the bite as the mark of it healed.

Mr. Havid tried to speak, but his attacker's hand clapped upon his mouth, and he tasted a delirious salt, its metallic tang flashing through him like the breath of a furnace. The trees above came alive, waving their tangled arms as the sky ignited to the horizon, its white fire burning into his eyes until all the light went out . . .

Blinking furiously against the blindness he shrieked with alarm as the grass vanished beneath his feet, replaced by hard packed earth. The space was open and cold, the sounds of the forest quite different, and he collapsed as the vampire dropped him, finding himself on an unfamiliar road. Unmistakable notes of a strange and haunting refrain drifted on the wind, accompanied by thin and ghostly cries, as of disembodied voices wailing in wordless lament. Edges and shapes began to return, and looking about him Mr. Havid found the land sloped down to either side of the road, vanishing in lakes of fog that swam about the legs of ancient trees. Rising ahead of them stood a monstrous gatehouse of stone eerily lit by high rounded windows, its chasmal maw gaping over a spiked portcullis of spear-capped teeth poised to drop. A massive wall curved away from the gatehouse to either side, vanishing in the mist to encircle a vast inner bailey, beyond which towered a mountainous fortress the like of which he had never imagined, its craggy spires rising deep into the sky like the claws of a forgotten god.

With a soft chuckle the vampire pulled him to stand, gesturing to the wide tunnel under the portcullis, which lit by duelling flickers of iron torches descended a long walk to the inner gate, through which Mr. Havid espied what looked to be dim and dancing lights.

"Welcome to Saunmoor," Morion said. "Behold the citadel of Umbremar."

"It's real," Havid whispered. "But how . . . how should we not have seen it from the camp, from the road, even from Braborne, where we set out?"

"It is the power of her will, that closes your eyes to it," Morion said, his face sinking with despair. "But the queen's resolve is lately tested, by some secret affliction . . ."

"Secret affliction?" Mr. Havid repeated. "Can it be the queen of vampires has taken ill?"

"We do not take ill," Morion said, his eyes flashing. "The genesis of her suffering eludes us, but to your fate it matters not. Now, you must enter of your own free will . . . and do not stare overlong into the lights."

Chapter 4
Friends and Strangers

Monday June 6th

Emelyn came to gradually, finding herself reclined in a softly lit space, surrounded by her family. She lay in the south end of the drawing room, reposed on an aqua settee embroidered with a dramatic scene of ocean voyage that she had imagined herself part of as a child. The room was arranged with lounges and couches, little tables for cards and games by the windows, with frivolous books shelved in the walls or lingering on chairs. Her mother took note as she stirred and came to sit at her side, fanning her daughter as Isabelle watched with Sarah, who clutched a printed pamphlet to her chest. A young man with slicked black hair stood at Emelyn's head, slouching against a pair of well-worn crutches— her older brother Deacon, aged now twenty-eight.

Her encounter with the vampire came rushing back, and Emelyn touched her neck with a flinch, finding no trace of the bite, though a drained and ebbing euphoria promised the experience was real . . .

"Oh thank heavens, she awakes," her mother breathed. "Thank heavens my darling I was at my wit's end. It's nearly morning!"

"So she's swooned her way out of another proposal then," Deacon said. "She's a regular adept."

Distant music rose from the ballroom, cheerfully banging on as though she'd never left, and Emelyn squinted her eyes, bringing the ceiling into focus. "Please they're not playing the rigadoon again," she said.

"Now you've torn your laces, and for not the first time you've lost a glove, careless girl," her mother chastened. "Your gown is a privilege my dearest."

"I'm sorry Mama, I could not breathe."

"If I was to injure such a gown I'd be shipped to the colonies," Isabelle remarked.

Emelyn closed her eyes at the light tickle of her mother's fingertips scratching troublesome spots on her bodice. "And your hair is a mess," Mrs. Morley fussed, picking bits of grass from her daughter's head. "You should not have slipped the footman! We must all of us take care in the dark," she instructed, glancing over her shoulder, "lest we follow Emelyn's example and become lost in the hedge."

Emelyn's eyes popped open. "Me, lost in the hedge maze? You do not know me Mama."

"Well if you'd not raced yourself out of breath, you would not have collapsed, and we needn't have raised the alarm."

"Perhaps if my bosom weren't crushing into my lungs," Emelyn grumbled, laying a forearm over her face.

"Deacon excuse us," her mother said, and Isabelle shook with giggles.

"Just leaving Mother," he said, turning on his crutches to plod out of the room.

"Do remember your dignity in front of your brother," Mrs. Morley chided.

Emelyn knit her brows, pleasantly puzzled that Loganbrek's name was yet to be raised. "For our next engagement I shall trade my stays for jumps."

Mrs. Morley laughed. "Certainly not my dear. Soft jumps for the party? They improperly address the cone of your waist."

"The gentlemen are not looking at my waist Mama," Emelyn said, speaking under her forearm.

"There is nothing so inelegant as a young lady with sagging posture," her mother said sharply. "Fully boned stays make for proper bearing, and move your arm I cannot see you!"

Emelyn relented, uncovering her eyes to rub her hand over the embroidered back of the settee. "Very well . . . but you should know Mr. Bowtree accosted me by the veranda, and I am exhausted. So if you mean to wail at me for Mr. Loganbrek, I'd as soon have it over."

"I've no interest in wailing at you. You refused him. What more is there to say?"

Emelyn scowled at her. "Is that all? Shall I not be punished for hastening our destruction? Shall I not pack my things?"

"Ever the dramatic," her mother said with a frown. "You might remember your sisters learn by your example."

"They're not children Mama."

"Look here," Sarah said, stepping forward to give Emelyn the pamphlet, but their mother hissed, startling her to retreat.

"No dear, not yet!"

"What is that?" Emelyn asked, watching as Sarah hid the paper behind her back.

Mrs. Morley smiled. "Emelyn Elizabeth my dearest girl, I have decided we shall no longer trouble over Mr. Loganbrek."

With a cautious thrill Emelyn sat up. "Have you really? But I'm not sure I believe you; has he surrendered his suit?"

Her mother leaned back with a little laugh. "Oh I was foolish to think you could ever accept such a man; you would have run away from him."

"Very possibly . . . but is he not to stay for the week? How shall I avoid him?"

"By avoiding him my dearest," Mrs. Morley said, unable to stifle a grin. "Of course he will persist, and I've no doubt make his intentions plain in a letter before he departs, which you have my permission to throw away unread, for I fear any response at all would only encourage him. As for his direct attentions, I shall deflect them . . . What matters now is that a man generously superior to both Bowtree and Loganbrek has presented himself."

"Really? And who is he?"

Mrs. Morley gasped for joy as though she'd been holding her breath. "He is a lord my dear! But we shall give you a clue," and she snapped at Sarah, who extended a stiff arm at once, pamphlet in hand.

Emelyn accepted the printing, puzzling from the text to her mother and back. "*The Adventures of Captain Lord Van Croft*," she read aloud. "What can be the point of this?"

"Why, you read these stories when you were a girl!"

"Yes Mama." Emelyn sighed with impatience, "and what have I to do with it now?"

Mrs. Morley tapped the pamphlet. "Do you recall the letter I received, just tonight as we were talking? But you are to meet the very man!"

"Captain Lord Van Croft?" Emelyn repeated. "Mama there's no such person."

"Oh there most certainly is! Captain Van Croft is the Bloodhound of His Majesty's navy, a title of which I'm sure we're all aware. Doubtless he has been drawn from his adventures by word of a great beauty to be found right here in Sussex."

Emelyn blinked at her. "The *Bloodhound of His Majesty's Navy* is a real captain? But he cannot be . . . how could any man be so lucky in the office of war?"

"Lord Van Croft is no common gentleman," Mrs. Morley said. "He is a lord of the Hanoverian line, a wealthy cousin to King George himself, so they say, and by all accounts remarkably handsome. Oh my dearest are we not saved!"

Finding no response Emelyn scowled at the pamphlet.

"Do you know he once called out three men in a single evening to avenge a lady's honour," her mother enthused, "vanquishing all three!"

"That is only a story," Emelyn said, flipping through the booklet. "Yes here we are page nine: *A Matter of Manners* . . ."

Isabelle tittered with a laugh, covering her mouth, and Sarah shushed her.

"Authors exaggerate my dear, it is only expected," Mrs. Morley pronounced. "Be that as it may, the captain promises to call upon you before the party Saturday next, and forecasting happy developments he means to return the following week!"

Emelyn stared aghast. "So a heroic character from my childhood is soon to arrive, and I shall have a week to fall in love with him . . . oh Mama it is too ridiculous!"

"Ridiculous is it?" Mrs. Morley flushed. "Well should I ever expect such ingratitude! I permit the snubbing of Mr. Loganbrek, even after your encouragement, which must bring upon us no small embarrassment . . ."

"*Encouragement?*" Emelyn laughed with surprise. "For Mr. Loganbrek? But my letters offered not a word of it! I might as well have been listing the price of grain."

Her mother stood from her chair, eyes shining with emotion. "You will mock every effort I make on your behalf!"

Emelyn leaned to catch her hands, marvelling at her distress. "Wait Mama, don't be angry; if you can produce this captain I will meet him, of course I will . . . I'm only surprised."

"Well," Mrs. Morley nodded, rubbing Emelyn's knuckles with a frown. "I'll not deny it's all rather sudden, but desperate times my dearest, as they say . . ."

"Mama, may we go?" Isabelle inquired.

"Of course my girls."

"And me?" Emelyn said hopefully, feeling a swirl of dizziness as she rose to her feet. "I am very tired Mama."

"Yes my beautiful darling," her mother sighed, looking her over. "To bath and bed before anyone sees you in such a state, and you may tell Breda if I find any bits of nature in your hair, she will be out on her ear."

Hair brushed to the point of soreness, Emelyn tried to relax in the late bath, her head swimming with drowsiness. Breda hummed softly, bundling her hair to dry as the water began to cool, and Emelyn settled back in the tub, shutting her eyes.

With a rush the press of Vaela's fangs returned, and she jolted.

Breda startled at the splash. "All right miss?"

"Yes . . . I must have dozed," Emelyn said, touching her neck.

Wrapped in fresh linens she adjourned to her bedroom to perch at the dressing table, examining her throat in a hand mirror to find one side as smooth as the other, while Breda tied back the corner drapes to turn down her blankets.

Emelyn retrieved her journal from its locked drawer, determined against her fatigue to take down something of her encounter with the vampiress:

'There can be no doubt. I have confirmed she who watches me from the darkness is a living vampire, which I believe in my heart I have always known. Her name is Vaela Audette de Masseine, and it was she who murdered Philip Denlund. This revelation should terrify but I feel nothing for the man, brute that he was.

Vaela took of my blood again tonight, and in a wondrous heightened moment I tasted hers; she maintains the bond between us is renewed and strengthened every year, but to what end? She tells me its power will awaken within me, though I little apprehend what that means. I must remain vigilant, and discover in all haste whether her terrible prediction regarding the fate of our ships has come to pass.'

Breda presented a silken nightdress, and changed for sleep Emelyn climbed into bed, shivering beneath the covers. Twitching her feet she watched the fading embers in the fire, half wondering if her mother's manic celebration of the captain and his pamphlet had really happened. Her eyes closed, and she imagined there came a dark presence, alighting on the wall just outside her window. But perhaps it was Vaela, come to watch her sleep . . . There was a strange and settled comfort in the thought.

Outside Emelyn's window, between grand torches where the drive met the road, a late carriage rolled to a halt among its parked fellows, and scarcely waiting for the door a young man burst from the vehicle with a laugh. White wigged in sky blue finery, he dashed across the crunching stones for a knot of exquisitely dressed ladies, who chattered amongst themselves in gaudy gowns before the carriage house, a two-storey timber-framed outbuilding with lime-rendered walls over brick, for the Morley stables and carriages. One of the women left the group, hurrying past the garden maze fountains to meet him; he crashed against her, and she laughed, leaning her curtsy to dodge a kiss aimed for her neck.

In sea green hooped skirts, her generous bosom powdered beneath a swept up wig of curls, the woman swatted playfully at the fellow's face. "Hershel Foster you absolute scandal! But however do I find you here?"

"Loretta Louise Pembrook," her young paramour replied, pulling her close to nibble at her ear. "I'd not let mother stop me; of course I promised her you'd never attend the party . . . and yet here we are, cheek to cheek in the carriage pool of Hastelbrook; but can you not see why it is the talk of the county, with its dark edifice so grandly peculiar."

"Grand enough for plunder, my dear Mr. Foster," she giggled, smacking him lightly with her fan. "Now we must sally inside, for I dare not trust your wandering hands . . . unless of course you've brought the map?"

Hershel grinned. "My sweet creature," he said, drawing a slender roll of parchment from his coat, "I have it by the hand of young John Lawford himself!"

"You found him!" she squeaked, bouncing in her bodice. "The Devil's Inn? Or was he at Tom King's? What did I tell you!"

"Yes my sweet, he's been bending every ear that will listen, for a price. Hastelbrook rumours abound, and Lawford has the very best: there's said to be treasure hidden beneath the library, and old Mr. Morley too blockish to find it out. In fact Lawford was shown to the very entrance, a secret door done up as a book case; just now the room should be empty and quiet for the party."

"Oh what fun; we must design our way in!" Miss Pembrook said, biting her lip as he returned the map to his pocket.

"Not here," he warned, eyeing the other ladies, "too many likely vultures; we shall plan our intrigue by the hanging lanterns of the garden labyrinth."

"Really sir," Miss Pembrook said, nose in the air as they entered the maze together, "if you mean to ravish me I shan't know you . . ."

"Nor I you," he said, taking hold of her arm. "But tell me my dear, have you yet acquainted the *Belle of Brighton*? Is she as . . . diverting as I've heard?"

"Well, she is awfully pretty, everyone says so," Miss Pembrook huffed, watching the suspended lights as they passed underneath. "Alas I've not had the pleasure to meet her; the poor thing retired early."

"I do hear she's a witty odd goose," he confided, "You know after her brother fell from that old elm, it's said her father wanted nothing so much as another son, and all but raised her as such."

"Well, these people can't belch up a word without praising her," Loretta said with a pout. "She must surely be prettier and wittier than I am."

"My Dear Loretta, I daresay you've fuller *wits* than she," he chuckled.

The boxwood closed in around them, and he stopped, turning to press her into the green. "I do believe we're lost my lady luscious, certainly deep enough for dark business . . ."

"You're naught but a thirsty trap," Miss Pembrook protested, her eyes drifting closed as his lips seized upon hers for greedy kisses.

"If we but distracted the footmen with your wares," he murmured, suckling his way down her neck as she heaved, "I might sneak my way into the library . . ."

"I've heard Miss Morley wore an astounding ruby necklace tonight," the lady said breathily, her temperature rising. "You won't find it, but you might swipe a bauble or two for me . . . for our trouble."

The wind rustled through the hedgerows, and gripping his moaning partner by her softness Mr. Foster froze, stunned to hear a second female voice, just on the other side of the hedge, mocking the lady's noises of pleasure.

Miss Pembrook gasped, evicting his hands from her stays. "There's someone there you great mump!" she chided in whisper. "We must leave at once!"

Hershel shushed her, and they breathed together quietly to listen. The voice had stopped, and watching the angry heave of his lady's breath he was about to continue his siege when with a shriek she was yanked away, vanishing through the hedge wall with a bristling crash.

"Loretta!" he cried, standing agape in the silence that followed.

Finding the damaged hedge too dense to step through, he fought the prickly twigs and broken ends of it, thrashing with a curse as he caught a snag, cutting his hand. "Nine hells and damnation!" he spat, pulling a kerchief to clench in his fist. "Loretta! My love you must answer me; have you fallen?"

"Hershel Foster," a female voice spoke just behind him, and turning with a start he beheld a woman, robed and hooded in black. Staring with eyes dark as coal her beauteous face was empty of expression, and no sooner had he taken her in than she snapped him up in a crushing embrace.

"You are not welcome here," she snarled.

In a rage of terror he seized her throat, squeezing with all his might. But beneath her fair skin was only the illusion of softness, as though he meant to strangle the trunk of a young tree.

"Cease your struggling," she said, her voice worming into his mind like a wave of drunkenness, and parting her lips the woman brandished slender fangs, plunging into his neck.

The pinhole stars seemed to laugh at his plight, quivering in the sky as she supped, and by and by he could no longer discern whether it was pain or pleasure coursing through him, until she threw back her head with a soft gasp, holding him close as though he were a rare and cherished thing.

"You will not remember this night," she said, trapping him in her gaze as he sagged in her arms, and reaching into his coat she plucked out the map.

The world flickered with sudden motion and the ground crashed into his side as she dropped him like a sack. Groaning against the pain in his ribs he rolled to find Loretta Pembrook trembling beside him, heaving with panicked breath, her sleeves torn and bare shoulders rent with scratches.

"Please Hershel please . . ." Miss Pembrook puled like an infant. "Do something!"

"Emelyn Morley is under my protection," the vampiress warned, standing over them. "You will leave this place, and never return."

His vision wobbled, and Mr. Foster opened his mouth for a plea but the vampiress bid him to irresistible sleep . . .

"As for you, rotten little mercenary," Vaela said, sprouting her fangs as she crouched beside the terrified woman, "when you return to your filthy plough house I suggest you keep your tongue, lest they find you for a madwoman . . . for you shall remember *everything*."

Miss Pembrook raised her hands, squeaking in protest, and lifting her chin the vampiress lurched upon her, fastening to her neck with a growl. The young lady squealed with a sob, her voice trailing into a moan of rapture, and with trembling arms she embraced her attacker, holding her tightly.

After drinking some moments Vaela released the bite with a contented noise, lapping the little wound until it sealed and vanished.

Miss Pembrook mumbled insensibly, staring into the dark of her eyes, and the vampiress rose to her full height, glaring down at her. "Go now, crawl back to your rented coach, and do not stop before London."

■■

Tuesday June 7th

"Slugabed!" Isabelle shouted, crashing atop her elder sister.

"Bell stop! I'm awake." Emelyn puffed hair from her mouth as Isabelle clung to her side, peering over her shoulder.

"You've been in bed near two days. You must have drunk out of your wits on Sunday. Are you sick?"

"No Bell, I never did and I'm not sick," Emelyn said, eyeing her sidelong to find Isabelle's hair brightly busy with ribbons. "What do you want?"

"Come down and see."

Happy notes of Sarah's practice at harpsichord tingled through the house, and having donned a simple morning dress and pinned up her hair, Emelyn sat by her little sister's direction in the small parlour. Before her a polite milliner's daughter from the village unfolded a standing box of tape ribbons and lace, which Isabelle was determined to try in Emelyn's hair, having already bedecked her own with as many adornments as it could accommodate.

"Mama says we may keep only those we like best," Isabelle said, selecting slender white and blue samples from the open wings of the box. "So we must like best as many as possible."

Emelyn nodded, indulging a yawn.

"These little fillets with roses," Isabelle said thoughtfully, studying a few satin examples, and leaving a small heap in Emelyn's lap she let down her sister's hair for practice.

The milliner's daughter smiled, and Emelyn smiled back, growing drowsy at the delicate pulls and twists of her sister's fingers, until the slipping sound of tying ribbon grew violently loud, and she twitched, scowling into her lap.

"Hold still," Isabelle said.

The long weight of Emelyn's hair was braided into a single tail, and too tired to protest she waited patiently as Isabelle marked the length of it with fanciful bows of every style she liked.

"We've gilt and silver as well," the girl offered, opening a mirrored panel in the box.

Isabelle responded, but Emelyn did not hear as there came a thunderous gale, with a rattling like the windows would shatter, and she leapt from the chair with a start.

"Have a care!" Isabelle protested, picking fallen ribbons off the floor as the noise died away.

"Is it happening?" Emelyn gasped, watching the window. "Did you not hear that?"

But the wind was again silent and soft, gently rustling the shrubberies outside.

"What did I not hear?"

"I don't know," Emelyn said, striving to remember the bond of blood Vaela had described. "Nothing I suppose. I must speak to Papa."

"He's out walking," Isabelle said, grabbing Emelyn's shoulders to sit her down again. "But first you must let me fix it."

Weeded of its myriad ribbons, the fire of Emelyn's hair was tied up once more. She returned to her room, fetching a hat with the green scarf from Mr. Bowtree, which after trying on in the mirror she left on the floor, selecting another before departing. Dodging busy footmen and housemaids she made her way down as they prepared for the party outside.

The brilliant sky was brave and blue, clear but for a few patches of cloud slipping away over the trees. Descending the hill Emelyn found her father walking the grounds by the lakes, swinging a stick as he strode, and she increased her pace to walk by his side.

"Emie my dear!" he hailed, blinking at her in the sun.

"Hello Papa," she said, taking his arm. "I needed a moment, away from the buzz of the house."

"Parties all the long week; how shall we bear such fun," he said. "Your mother would invite the whole London season, if ever she could."

"And they may yet come," Emelyn said, watching the path as they walked. "Tales of Hastelbrook grow taller every year."

"So it would seem," he said, gazing into the distance, "but so large an attendance is not without social perquisites, even if they only pretend to friendship . . ."

"Not all of them pretend," Emelyn said, steeling herself for the question. "But Papa I must ask after the ships, those we had built lately at Portsmouth. They are bound by now for America are they not?"

Mr. Morley frowned. "We'll have no talk of shipping here thank you. Now, I am told Margaret Mettles is to join us, escorted by her cousin Elton; I suppose he must be older than I remember."

"Yes . . . he's sixteen now, old enough to protect the ewes. But you must tell me, what of the ships?"

"We are terribly fond of your friends of course," her father said, "Miss Mettles in particular."

Noting a marked strain in his voice, Emelyn sighed. "Well, I should have no patience for anything without Mags to confide in."

"Quite so," he said, patting her arm as they mounted the little bridge over the neck of the lake.

Whistling a country tune he stopped to admire the placid water, and reluctantly Emelyn resolved to press him no further, at least not under so lovely a day.

"But I do hope arrangements are being made for Mrs. Denlund," she said. "She mustn't be evicted on account of a husband who, being murdered, cannot work."

"Mr. Denlund's death was accident, not murder," Mr. Morley said firmly. "As for his wife, I've no plan to levy a distress for the lease. Hastelbrook is her home, I hope for many years to come . . ."

Emelyn watched him. "And Reverend Dowlich, he will review what charity the parish may provide?"

"Yes my dear, which I daresay shall go further without the expense of Denlund's gin."

"Good," Emelyn said.

Just along the bank south of them the massive oak tree creaked in the wind, its sprawling lower limbs thick as gnarled trunks of lesser specimens, brushing the ground as they swung upward to reach a golden-green effulgence of canopy, larger than any other hardwood on the estate. "How old is the climbing oak?" Emelyn asked. "It looks quite the same as in great-grandfather's portrait."

"Yes, by old Samuel Bastian Morley's account it was here before the first manor house was built; I daresay it's one of the eldest in the country."

For a moment she imagined the tree was watching them, and looking up into its gnarled limbs she thought back to the day her brother had fallen from the great elm. Deacon had been six at the time, and she scarcely old enough to sit upright on the blanket. There were no pictures of the memory left to her, but the terrified sound of his cry was seared in her mind. "Why could Deacon not have climbed here that day . . . instead of the elm."

"He wanted to impress you, his baby sister whom he loved beyond reason," Mr. Morley said, patting her arm again.

Emelyn nodded, staring into nothing as they continued their walk.

By dusk her energy was much restored, and happily she changed her simple white gown for a confident robe a la Francaise of gilded lavender, centred with cream and gloves to match. The party swelled loudly as ever, and with the ruby necklace gleaming once again against her bare collar she slipped through the crowd seeking after her dearest friend, finally catching sight of a bright lemon gown beneath familiar close-knotted curls.

Margaret Farah Mettles, a charming bright eyed brunette of twenty-two, had just gone through the north doors, leaving the ballroom to descend a pair of wide steps to the towering indoor gardens, which dominated the northwest corner of the house.

Emelyn pursued, and reaching the garden room she breathed in the fresh damp scent of exotic greens and tropical flowers as she checked through the rows. Narrow iron stairs wound their way up along the outer walls of glass, pausing at landings where great ivies and fronds draped over the railings, and looking up she could just make out the stars through the faceted dome of glass high above.

"There you are!" she said joyfully, finding her friend at last under a Brunswick fig tree, examining the buds.

Margaret gasped at the sight of her. "Em!" she cried, catching her embrace. "On my soul such a necklace!"

"Thank you," Emelyn said, releasing her with a smile. "I am quite taken with it. I've half a mind to wear it every night . . ."

"Well I would," Margaret said, her eyes aglow.

"But you've not been waiting long?"

"We've only just arrived," Margaret said, beaming at her. "Grandmama sends her love, and *stridently expects* you will attend the shooting party on Thursday a week; we shall have games and all sorts.”

“Of course she needn’t ask.”

“And you must dance with cousin Elton tonight; he is concerned for you to know he’s a man now,” Margaret said with a smirk. “But Emie, has it really been a month? How are you?”

“I feel like I’ve been to Crusoe’s island and back,” Emelyn said, glancing at the guests who peered down at them from the surrounding balcony above. “Let us come outside and I shall tell you all.”

The octagonal carriage park fountain behind the house was sheltered by vine-covered walls of latticed white under a low roof, the vines thick with blooming sweet pea which lent Emelyn’s lengthy confession a sense of privacy, improved by the fountain pool itself, wherein a little cherub babbled water from his horn to soften the sounds of traffic. Margaret sat on one of four curved benches around the fountain, her mouth agape as she listened.

Emelyn talked on her feet, working her way through the unfortunate saga of Mr. Loganbrek, to Lord Van Croft, the pamphlet hero soon to make his address, coming finally to the woman in black’s visitation. “But I am not afraid of her, odd as that may be,” she finished at last, picking at the cherub’s upturned face. “On the contrary, I might say her very presence is a tonic.”

“*Vampire!*” Margaret exclaimed. “And it is she who’s given you this, this enormous ruby pendant . . .”

“It was she. Of course I’ve never seen such a jewel, but in size and lustre I cannot help comparing it to the gem atop my great-grandfather’s cane, in his portrait . . . Do you remember it?”

Margaret shook her head.

“Well, it’s only similar,” Emelyn said. “His cane was buried with him.”

“All right . . . but really Emie, when you say vampire, do you mean *vampire* literally?”

“Yes Maggie I do.” Emelyn sat, taking her friend’s hands. “Vaela has been at the edge of my thoughts for so long; I think I even contrived a little figure of her, to go with the others in my baby house when I was a girl, and now I am to find she’s not only real but has appointed herself, or been appointed by others, to watch over me.”

“Others? What others?”

“I don’t know, nor do I understand her purpose as yet. She speaks of a vault beneath the house, though I scarce believe it; nothing of the sort has ever been found."

Margaret opened her mouth, as though searching for the words. "Emie I would die before I betray your secrets, but you must forgive me; this is all a bit . . . scarebug is it not?"

"Not at all! In fact I believe you might have seen her yourself; my first ball at Daulton House, do you remember?"

Margaret made a sharp noise, covering her mouth. "But I do remember! You said you espied a woman through the windows, watching us from the edge of the park."

"Yes!"

"But . . . oh my dear Em," Margaret said, her expression pained, "do you recall . . . when I followed your point, I did not see anyone."

"Yes Mags, she hid herself in the shadows, until I went out."

"Or perhaps you are the only one who can see her?" Margaret asked gently. "But have you not always relished sneaking into the dark, even when we were small?"

"And what should that matter?"

"We're grown now," Maggie said. "And I know how you've longed to escape . . . this pressure to marry a king's ransom. I know you want to be seen for more than, that is I know you long for . . ."

"For what, exactly?" Emelyn interrupted, feeling cold. "For a gentleman to know me a little, before talk of our wedding night? That is an entirely different topic Mags."

"I only meant I know you wish things were different, like in those stories you love to share . . ."

"Do you think I've invented her?"

"No of course not! But I know your mother can be an absolute harridan . . . oh Emie anyone would understand."

"Understand what? She was here Maggie! I was in her company only two nights past."

Margaret cleared her throat. "Well, you might at least bring the matter to Doctor Bayten."

"No!" Emelyn rebuffed. "Vaela must remain a secret. I've only told you because our trust is absolute. I've known you all my life; have I ever confused imagination with reality?"

"Of course not," Margaret said. "But you must consider that imagination, or even madness, would be rather easier to swallow than . . . vampires."

Emelyn laughed, covering her face. "I'm sorry Mags . . . I've put it all upon you with no warning. I'll not fault your suspicion, but if I brought you to meet her, there could be no doubt."

Margaret blanched. "Meet her? Certainly not! How should I ever sleep again?"

"But she is not a monster. Vaela is nothing like the superstitions we've heard."

"You're quite sure she will not murder you and drain your blood?"

Emelyn looked into the fountain. "She has tasted my blood, but she would never harm me, I know that now . . . She is cold and yet warm; terribly strong but also soft. And now that I know her for certain . . . I cannot imagine nightfall without her."

Margaret grimaced. "All right Em, I can hear no more tonight on the subject of vampires. Try me again tomorrow; I'll be here all week. Now might we talk of *anything* else . . ."

"Certainly," Emelyn said, watching her with a grin. "Dear sweet Mags forgive me; shall we go in for a glass of fortitude?"

"Splendid," Margaret said, standing from the bench.

■ ■

Wednesday, June 8ᵗʰ

Under a sour haze of coal smoke and fog, bits of papery soot wafted on the wind, blowing into a darkened courtyard to snap at linens draped along the washing lines. Here a young boy with troubled curly hair lay clenched up against the cold, head swimming with drink as he sheltered under his hat in a door well. Overhead rose creaking tenement walls, the buildings squeezed between Cross Lane and the mud black banks of the Thames. Eight other children lay nestled together nearby, damp stone for their beds as they huddled beside a long fusty water trough that bisected the abject yard.

A jostling light pole stumped around the corner, and the boy in the doorway peered from under his hat to behold a bulldog-faced watchman surveying the yard. "Tallie Denship!" the man cried, looking to a second storey window. "I've come to salute thy lips!"

The shuttered panes squeaked open, and a thin faced woman in frilly bonnet leaned wantonly over the sill. "Why Mr. Gowder," she chirped.

"But where's your head sir, comin' round on so dark a night. Brought me some clink have you?"

Watchman Gowder grinned with a bow. "As it happens there were two broad-pieces in my pocket, and all for you my dove . . . only, just on my way I peeked in at Tom King's to make it double, and who should I find but that sharping Jack Randall dealing the cards; well I thought the better of it, but he gives me the eye and I'm not a man to retreat . . ."

"Oh bugger off Cuddy!" she shouted, her face pointed with contempt. "Lost it all have you? Well paint me surprised."

"Tallie my dear! I'll see to my debt; always do don' I? Come on then, give us a quick roll!"

"No coin no cram!"

"Don't close up!" he protested, rubbing his nose as he looked over the foundlings. "But I see seven, no, all nine of your darlings asleep on the cobbles? What you done then, let out their rooms to fund your drink?"

"What's it to you if I spice my tongue?" she retorted. "I share the diddle good as I get; look here, a dram of geneva on no supper and sleepin' like angels. Don't even know they're out of bed do they!"

"Dast you cheat the parish?" the watchman puzzled, adjusting his hat. "Drawing alms for a charity house while ye turf them out of their beds? The warden would crack your head if he knew; shall I bring him round?"

"You don't scare me Cuthbert Gowder! You couldn't care a mite for the little wretches; now you'll pay for my touch like all the rest, or crawl away home."

"Tallie my tender tail!" He grinned with cracked teeth. "Let the warden sleep I say; all what needs doin' is you quench my thirst."

"Not till cows eat crows!" she spat.

"What's that my duck, shall I come up?" he laughed, his smile faltering as the woman vanished from the window with a gasp, slamming the shutters.

Feigning sleep through half-lidded eyes, the boy in the doorway watched as dark shapes slipped into the courtyard from the river side, quiet as death.

"Tallie!" the disappointed watchman called, sloshing dirty water from the trough as he gave it a kick. "Tallie Denship I'll give you to count o' ten, or I'm for the warden!"

There was no answer . . . but the sound of heavy chains clinked in the gloom, and with a start the lantern armed watchman turned. "Halt there by the king's law!" he charged, fumbling a pistol from his belt.

The shadows did not respond, stirring just beyond the light, and wide awake now the boy clutched his knees, murmuring a half-remembered rhyme as he trembled. *"The chains if ye flee, the chains if ye stay, the Lurkmen are come to take thee away . . ."*

"Who goes there!" watchman Gowder barked, pointing his weapon about.

"Surrender the little ones, or take your last breath," a low voice spoke, and at the edge of the light there appeared a silvery gleam; a snarling lion-headed cane clacked on the ground as its bearer stepped forward: a tall man shrouded hat to boots in faceless black.

"People snatchers is it? Hold fast or die where ye stand!" came the watchman's answer, but no sooner had he spoken than ropes of metal sprang out of the dark, lashing the pistol from his hand. A hooked chain snagged the lantern pole, crashing it to the ground; the steel cane flashed, and clenching his eyes the boy clapped hands to his ears as the assaulted watchman shrieked in horror. Muffled impacts echoed in the night, a body collapsed, and a hush fell over the courtyard.

Soft boots crunched closer, and the lad sprang from the door to run, tripping over his steps, his head spinning round with the gin, but a gloved hand caught his wrist, and captured in a blanket he was lifted in the masked man's arms, catching bleary sight of the other children snatched and bundled the same.

The boy muttered in protest as the man carried him to a high covered wagon, passing him to another who stood in the back.

"Sick?" the second man asked.

"Sick with gin, the lot," the first said. "Get them all in."

The shadowy figures leapt to running boards alongside the wagon as a wool tarp was drawn across the gated end, their leader ducking inside to slouch with his cane on a low bench at the back, and with a whip's crack the wagon lurched forward, pulled on wide padded wheels by great strong steeds. Frightened from their alcohol addled sleep, the stupefied children blinked in the dark as they jostled, four girls and five boys clinging tightly together.

"Is it the Lurkmen?" a terrified boy whispered.

Soft-shoed and snorting, the massive hack horses broke into a charge, dragging the vehicle at precarious speed as it weaved between slower trundling carriages and startled coachmen, flashing down Parliament Street for the long road south.

"Ammy?" the youngest girl sobbed, and one of the others found her hand, warning her to silence.

"Who are you?" the boy who'd been sleeping in the doorway asked, holding steady his voice. "What you want with us?"

"You may call me Mr. Lorris," the sitting man replied. "I am a teacher. Now, who among you is eldest?"

"It's me sir; I am," the same boy answered. "I'm eleven . . . this week."

"Good," Mr. Lorris said, his voice the only sign of him in the rattling dark. "What's your name then?"

"They call me Grey sir . . . on account I don't know my right surname. Miles Grey."

"Well Mr. Grey, there's a sack here with meat, bread, and bottles of milk. You're no good to us half-drunk and starving, so you must give it out fair to the rest. Come to my voice . . ."

With a nervous gulp young Miles Grey felt his way forward to accept the bag, and after careful sorting and shuffling the children were deep in unexpected suppers, slurping milk, crunching cured bacon and gobbling bread with grateful noises.

Moments later, his belly full and head no longer spinning, Miles helped one of the smallest with his milk. "Where are you taking us?" he ventured.

"Home," Mr. Lorris said, knocking the floor with his cane. "By the blood of the queen, to Saunmoor."

"The blood of the . . . Queen Caroline?" a girl asked, her voice trembling.

"Nay, I speak of the Dire Lady, Pazoa Qiminossa, our immortal queen beneath the mountain," Mr. Lorris declaimed. "Now Mr. Grey, if you would collect the bottles . . . the lot of you must rest for the road."

Chapter 5
The Worthy Gem

Friday June 10th

For many a guest at Hastelbrook there was no finer example of its grandeur than the vaulted ballroom. With engaged columns half submerged in white walls and gold edged frescoes, the room was ringed with a long rectangular balcony, the walls rising to a prodigious height, lifting the crenellated roofline of the west wing higher than any other point in the house, save the dome of the garden nursery behind it.

Admiring the spacious vast of the room as he stood at the edge of the floor, the unremarkable Mr. Goodman Codgrass clutched his hat with both hands, training his gaze on the crystal bloom of a flint glass chandelier overhead, one of three. Clerk of Hastelbrook parish and proprietor of the Stafford House Inn, he struck a starkly humble figure to the sharp immaculate dress of the dancing couples on the floor.

Swallowing as he watched, Mr. Codgrass took note of the eldest Morley daughter as she clapped and twirled, engaged in a vigorous country dance, a brilliant ruby pendant such as he'd never seen sparkling over her neckline. The gaiety continued around him, and so enthralled was the clerk that he did not hear the first footman's voice until he was nearly shouting.

"Goodman Codgrass!" Comby tried again, snapping in the man's face with a white glove. "Mr. Morley will see you now, if you'll follow me."

Built for gentlemen with a mind to lounge, smoke, and talk of the world, the map room was appointed with high-backed chairs and a roaring fire, trophies of the hunt and exotic items in glass cases: masks, horns and tusks, with bone-carven tools and talismans. Long wigged in his narrow high collared coat, Mr. Morley stood muttering to himself by the fireplace, brandishing a schoolmaster's rod which he tapped against a wide leather etched map of the islands hung above the mantle.

Mr. Codgrass stepped into the room, jumping as the footmen shut the doors firmly behind him.

"Codgrass my good fellow," Mr. Morley greeted, swishing the rod to lay it against the hearth, "cherry brandy I think," and he poured his guest a glass from the near decanter.

"Thank you," Mr. Codgrass said, hat behind his back as he accepted the drink. "Well my lord, I come first about Toomey's farm. Lost fourteen merino sheep he has."

"Fourteen? Wandered or stolen?"

"Nay sir, slaughtered in the night; left all in a great pile they were."

"Good God man," Mr. Morley said, pouring a brandy for himself. "Has he anyone to accuse?"

"Tom Bennison the distiller, but he already been sent up, and for poaching on his land."

"Another mystery unwelcome." Mr. Morley rubbed the bridge of his nose. "The good rector and yourself are free to investigate, but I've not the time."

"Very good sir," Codgrass said, scowling into his brandy, "now as to repairs of the main road, the stone carts have refused delivery, on some matter of my lord's credit . . ."

Mr. Morley sighed, removing his spectacles. "After three and twenty years with the same surveyor I might have hoped for a little more faith."

"Yes, of course sir," Codgrass said, knocking back his glass and setting it on one of the trophy cases, "but there is another matter, to wit the body . . . of our late Mr. Denlund."

"I've heard the worst of it," Mr. Morley said with a grimace, "poor devil wounded under the arm, must have bled out in the rain. Murder most certainly, though I've assured my family it was only accident, and it must be circulated as such."

"Aye sir, Doctor Bayten and I are of the same mind. As for the body, it were to be interred on Sunday, but the reverend instructed it be laid to rest with a stake of iron through the heart, which I thought a grievous injustice upon the widow."

Mr. Morley grunted, interrupting his drink. "Dowlich is of the old country. Of course I'll permit no such desecration."

"Just as well sir, but now I find there shall be no burial at all."

“What’s that?”

“Well sir, some city folk came and took the body away. Paid Mrs. Denlund handsomely, so I heard, but she’ll not speak of it.”

Mr. Morley set his glass on the desk with a frown. “Men from the college of barber-surgeons I should think. We cannot stop a grieving widow from selling her deceased, much as I would discourage it.”

“But it weren’t only the murder sir,” Codgrass said quickly, squeezing his hat, “nor the sheep slaughtered. There be new complaints of animals goin’ strange. A pair of my Devon cattle gone missing, and folk are whisperin’ again of old apparitions, the lady in black, and bright eyes in the dark . . .”

“Now that I will not abide,” Mr. Morley said sternly. “Occultists and treasure hunters have been making ominous fantasies of Hastelbrook for generations. In truth we need look no further than poachers and thieves, which abide in every parish, not just our own. As to the murder, Philip Denlund was generally despised; it might have been any one of his enemies.”

■■■

Giggling with Margaret as they shared a secret bottle between them, Emelyn stood by tables of refreshments among fire-winking legions of candles in golden stands, her head gratefully light with the wine. “I danced with Elton for *you* Mags,” she said, scanning over the crowd. “I’ll not sacrifice my toes for anyone else.”

“But he knows the steps I swear it,” Margaret laughed with a wince. “I’m so sorry Emie . . .”

“Don’t be; he’ll make a fine gentleman,” Emelyn said, giving her arm a good natured squeeze. “I’ve partnered with many unsteadier feet I’m sure.”

“Is that Mason Barlowe again?” Margaret observed, watching a sharp-featured young man with powdered hair as he laughed with his friends. “I know you know him; you must introduce us.”

“I’ll do no such thing,” Emelyn said, turning to look over a colourful tray of glazed cakes. “He’s a vapouring bravo, and I’ll not be parted from you.”

“You managed well enough without me for a month,” Margaret said. “Though when I do return I find you either mad or haunted . . . and I should like neither."

"Nor I," Emelyn said, feeling rather more sober.

"But I don't mean to make sport of it . . ."

"Not at all." Emelyn rallied, draining her wine.

The ladies shared a few moments of silence, until a starry eyed gentleman stopped to offer Emelyn his hand for the dance, which she promptly accepted.

Smiling vaguely as the movements commenced her mind returned to the spectral moments of Vaela's attention, and it seemed hardly a beat later she was nodding to her partner's eager bow as the music stopped for applause.

"Dare I impose upon you for the next?"

"Thank you sir, but I must plead your mercy," Emelyn said, giving him a curtsy, and after noting Margaret was partnered she caught sight of the darkly dressed valet of Mr. Loganbrek watching from the balcony. Feeling not a little irritated at his insistent gaze she bid her gentleman goodbye and made her way back to the peace of the garden room.

Margaret's scepticism echoed in her head, and stopping to pick at the leaves of an areca palm, she began to wonder whether she'd told her friend too much, when the sound of argument caught her ears. Approaching the near doors to the map room, she made out her father's harsh tones as he spoke to a man she guessed to be Mr. Codgrass, the village clerk.

"Zounds man, tell them whatever you like!" Mr. Morley pronounced, *"you understand that without a timely financial restructure, road repair shall be the least of our troubles . . ."*

"Restructure sir?"

"Recomposition of the debt," her father clarified. *"Our doom Mr. Codgrass, is that I find myself the victim of my own caution. I meant the corridor to Boston to set us right, and now, impossibly, myself and the partners have not a plank to show for it."*

"Then . . . shall the land tax be in question sir?"

"A thousand was put by for the year," Mr. Morley said, his voice thin and tired. *"But now even this must be turned over to the trustee, with all we can spare. You may be called upon, to assemble the tenants, if things go sour."*

"How's that sir?"

Mr. Morley made a small, hopeless sort of sound.

"I require ten thousand pounds, Codgrass, to stay proceedings against us. Otherwise I stand to lose everything . . ."

"But there's no justice in that sir," the clerk protested. *"But I can't imagine*

how the ships should be lost all together. Was it an act of war? Pirates?”

“I can only argue the unforeseen, an act of God. But the truth . . . well, I’m certain you’ve heard the rumours, which as a man of reason I cannot accept.”

At this Emelyn was struck, and searching her father’s words she missed what came next, until Codgrass agreed to delay further business until called upon.

“You must take home a bottle of frontignac, and a basket for Mrs. Codgrass with our compliments,” Mr. Morley said.

“Thank you sir, much obliged to you . . . I’ll just go back through the ballroom shall I?”

Alarm pounded in her chest as Emelyn backed away from the opening doors, and the slouching, small eyed figure of Goodman Codgrass startled to attention at the sight of her. “Lovely as ever Miss Morley!” he declared, blushing into a bow, and squashing his hat on his head he rushed to make his exit.

Watching him leave Emelyn bid Comby wait to shut the doors, and swishing into the room she presented herself with a curtsy.

“Hello Father.”

Hiram Morley turned to face her, his expression slack. “Emelyn my dear! Should you not be dancing?”

“I *have* been dancing,” she replied. “Please Papa, I must have it. Our ships bound for America; are they truly lost, it is confirmed?”

“Good heavens. Who’s told you this?”

“Never mind. Is it true?”

Mr. Morley massaged his forehead. “It is.”

“What, all of them? How is it possible?”

“I’m sorry my dear . . . we’ve little report, beside tall tales and nonsense.”

“What nonsense? But you must have heard something!”

“Certainly,” he said, pouring another brandy. “There is word, but only of unaccountable weather over the Celtic Sea, black storms holding fast against the wind.”

“That is absurd.”

Mr. Morley sucked down his drink with a gasp. “Superstitious flummery,” he said, turning the glass in his hand. “Nevertheless, we cannot deny six ships set sail, and six are lost.”

“But ships and cargo, were they not insured?”

“There was measured coverage,” he said wearily, “balanced against the risk. Any one ship’s loss we might have endured . . . but I was foolish.

I never should have taken such a gamble."

"Such a gamble?" Emelyn repeated. "And who on earth could have predicted all six ships lost!"

"Who indeed." Mr. Morley summoned a smile. "But I drew up the contracts myself, and it is to me the investors look for explanation. Fear not my dear . . . your father will sort it out."

Her face was hot, and Emelyn touched the ponderous ruby at her throat, approaching as she reached back to unfasten it. "Papa, you've neglected to admire my necklace."

"Oh forgive me," he said, pinching his spectacles for a closer look. "Well by Jove, I've never seen such a stone; and does the poor fellow parted from it find your favour?"

"The *poor fellow* has not revealed himself . . . or herself. We shall sell it, against whatever demand is most immediate," and loosing the chain she took his hand to place the pendant in his palm.

Mr. Morley blinked, turning the crimson gem as he studied it. "By gad it must be the heaviest jewel I've ever . . . but this is too princely a thing to trade for common guineas," and he took her hand to return it.

"Nonsense," she said, pushing it back to him. "Perhaps it might fetch ten thousand, or near enough."

Her father frowned at her. "My dear Emie . . . have you been listening at the door?"

"Yes, your dear Emie was listening at the door. But could it not buy us some time to negotiate? I really must insist . . . You will sell it won't you?"

Mr. Morley raised his chin. "No my dear, if anyone deserves so pretty a jewel it is my eldest daughter."

"Please Papa, I shan't go to pieces over a single piece of jewellery, however grand."

"You may rest assured," he said, pressing it into her hand, "there are yet avenues untried, and I will see to them."

Emelyn frowned. "And if they are not enough?"

"Never mind," he said. "I'll not see you distressed over debts you had no part in contracting."

"Papa . . ."

"You will keep the jewel, and there's an end of it," he said. "But tell me, this Captain Van Croft fellow, who tramples down poor Mr. Loganbrek, inviting himself with scarcely a notice . . . Will you see him?"

Emelyn stared at him, and with a sigh she headed back for the doors, stuffing the jewel in her pocket. "I suppose."

"Your mother is most insistent that you do; I hope you will indulge her."

"Yes," she said, turning to face him again. "I will meet him, though I cannot promise what I'll find."

Her father nodded, and leaving with a curtsy she slipped through the doors into the garden room.

A bold plan took shape, and mounting the broad steps to the ballroom Emelyn touched the place on her collar where the heavy pendant had lain. "Nay sir," she muttered, "I'll not require your permission to sell my own things."

The musicians on the corner stage had changed, and to the sounds of violin, flute and harpsichord many partners raised their palms to begin the dance anew. After working through two quick glasses of claret Emelyn went up to her room, where she returned the grand ruby necklace to its box, exchanging it for a more modest chain of silver with amethyst gemstones, before returning to the ballroom in search of her friend.

No longer dancing, Margaret stood with a group beside her young wallflower of a cousin, the tousle headed Elton, who at sixteen looked younger still. The pair of them listened as two stuffed gentlemen in pastel coats traded laughs, one of them being the handsome Mr. Barlowe, whom Maggie had earlier inquired of. Between the men stood a tall and willowy young lady, her shock of blonde hair bundled high over a gown of green. Upon approach Emelyn discovered her to be a onetime childhood playmate, whom she knew now only by wild reputation.

"Emelyn!" Margaret beamed, raising her glass.

"Maggie!" Emelyn answered, taking her arm as she turned a happy face to the others.

"Miss Morley," a flushing Elton greeted, giving her a bow. "I should apologize for my missteps."

"There's no need," Emelyn said. "You only kept me nimble."

With a giggle the tall blonde bestowed her attention. "Oh bless us at last, it is Miss Morley herself; does she not positively stun the senses! Will you not give us a turn Miss Morley?"

"Another time perhaps," Emelyn said, reacquainting her dislike for the lady.

The blonde smiled before continuing. "But my dear, were you not just wearing the very largest ruby in the kingdom, or did I imagine it?"

"Largest in the kingdom? I think you imagined it," Emelyn said.

There was a pause, and Margaret cleared her throat. "May I present Miss Urania Blinnley, whom you'll remember from summer parties at Candlewood, and Mr. Mason Barlowe I believe you know, and this is Mr. Callum Wincott Esquire."

"Miss Blinnley, of course, gentlemen," Emelyn said as they exchanged bows and curtsies. "I hope the ball is to your liking."

"Who could refuse an evening at Hastelbrook," Mr. Barlowe answered, sipping his drink as he regarded her, "that enigmatic estate where anything might happen . . ."

"Yes quite," Miss Blinnley said. "But I am to be called Mrs. Urania *Wincott*, if you please."

"Mrs. Wincott-to-be my sweet," the bright-eyed Mr. Wincott corrected, speaking to Emelyn. "We are to be wed in August you see . . ."

"You shan't stop me using your name," Miss Wincott-to-be tutted. "But how fortune favours me, that I should be married before the *Belle of Brighton* herself, and two years younger!"

"Then perhaps my gown should be the colour of envy, instead of yours," Emelyn said, happy to retort, "but I recall you were often in green as a girl."

Miss Blinnley swirled her drink with pursed lips. "Such sweet memories," she said, smiling for the group. "Miss Morley and I were playfellows you see, until we quarrelled most viciously. But I'm afraid I dug soot out of the scuttle, and smudged it on her face."

"You never did!" Mr. Barlowe cried, tilting back for a laugh.

"Oh yes," Miss Blinnley said, "though I daresay the poor creature had her revenge, terrifying me in the dark as she did . . ."

"Did I? I don't remember it," Emelyn puzzled, finishing her wine. "Then I hope you will forgive me and accept my congratulations; an auspicious match is not easy to find."

"Fiddlesticks," Miss Blinnley said, addressing her fiancé. "I'll wager every fellow in the county has made his address. But she is much too mysterious for them, are you not Miss Morley?"

"Well I've not had the pleasure of meeting *every* gentleman in the county," Emelyn replied. "Perhaps you'd care to recommend, from any I might have missed?"

A mortified pause followed.

"This is the very highest ballroom in Sussex," Margaret announced. "Shall we take the view from the balcony?"

"I should like that," Elton said.

No one else answered, and a blushing Miss Blinnley snapped out her fan while Mr. Wincott stood very still.

"How now Miss Morley," a wry faced Mr. Barlowe said, "what do you say to this young pretender aiming to excuse King George of the job; shall Prince Charlie reignite the Catholics?"

"For that I should defer to Miss Mettles," Emelyn said, smiling at Margaret. "I do not follow politics as she does."

"How like a beautiful woman!" Barlowe laughed, trampling Margaret's response. "Even were rampaging Jacobites at the door Miss Morley would find no interest in politics, for it must affect her kind least of all."

"My kind?" Emelyn bristled. "But of course it's not beauty that keeps us from political discourse."

"Yes I daresay it's *interest*," Miss Blinnley said, "or rather the lack of it."

"Naturally," Barlowe chuckled, "as they are without proper education, ladies have no use for public office."

"A man's circular reasoning," Emelyn said, feeling a flush. "We cannot hold public office without proper education, but are prevented education because we cannot hold public office," and she missed her reach for another drink as Margaret shooed the footman away.

"In any case," Maggie said loudly, "certainly there are nearer threats than rebel Catholics."

"Such as?" Barlowe asked.

"Are we not alarmed to hear the city is rife with murder and vanishings like no time in our history?" she said, addressing the group. "I put it to the night gangs, particularly the Mohocks."

"The Mohocks haven't been heard from in twenty years," Barlowe scoffed.

"I'll differ there sir," Emelyn put in. "Wearing sashes or masks of red, in name at least I've read they are haunting the streets once more."

"And the Lurkmen," Maggie continued, "who steal solitary children off the streets after dark . . . if you believe in such things."

"People snatchers, and corpses washing up on the Thames is nothing new," Mr. Wincott said. "I daresay little has changed for murder and disappearance but the accounting of it."

"Is such a topic appropriate for gentleladies?" Miss Blinnley exclaimed.

"I don't believe it's a matter of accounting," Margaret persisted.

"Far more children go missing than adults, and so many at night."

"Sold into transportation no doubt, to the colonies," Mr. Wincott said.

"Or eaten in the dark, by the haunted queen of Saunmoor," Mr. Barlowe said, raising an eyebrow.

"Really Mason!" Miss Blinnley scolded.

"But if the Lurkmen exist, let us hope they snatch papists," Barlowe added. "Now Miss Morley, shall we forget such sober talk and try the floor?"

"Thank you sir," Emelyn said, pulling gently on Margaret's arm, "but I daresay Miss Mettles is more accomplished than I at the contredanse, and I am due for a rest."

"Yes I see. Very well then Miss Mettles, shall we?" Barlow offered his elbow, and Margaret obliged, laying her hand on his arm.

Left to conversation with a silent Elton, the blathering Miss Blinnley and her apologetic swain, Emelyn said as little as possible, enjoying the soothe of the wine as she observed Maggie in steps with the jaded Mr. Barlowe. The candle lights were softer now, and she wondered what it would be like to see Vaela dancing among the others, gowned all in black, and whether everyone would stop to marvel at her, or carry on oblivious to the predator in their midst.

"Thank you so much," Margaret said, and Emelyn startled to find her returned.

Mr. Barlowe bowed, and the party bid each other polite farewells.

"You were right Emie, he's a contemptuous peacock," Margaret confided, leaving her cousin behind as she guided Emelyn to a soft bench by the grand south facing windows, "and I left you with Miss *Nearly-Wincott*; I'm sure she was unbearable . . ."

"Oh let the yellow chandelier say what she likes," Emelyn said, dropping to sit. "But I can't think what she meant, that I terrified her in the dark when we were girls, do you remember it?"

"I remember the soot on your face," Margaret said, sitting beside her, "and didn't you mean to splash her with your chamber pot for answer? I'm only glad the footmen put a stop to it."

Emelyn covered her face. "Not my finest hour, but I never understood why she hated me so."

"Envy I expect," Maggie sighed. "You carried yourself like you had a secret better than our company, but it didn't bother me; you and I could talk absolutely for hours."

"Well . . . I suppose I did have a secret," Emelyn said, staring at the grand chandeliers as they cast icy shards of light over the crowd. "Though it still feels like a dream. In any case now that you've heard it, I confess to feeling rather exposed . . . But you won't tell anyone will you?"

"And what should I tell them?" Maggie asked. "That my best friend in the world speaks to vampires? No Emie, I won't be telling them that," and her eyes fixated on Emelyn's neck. "Where is your ruby necklace?"

"I've taken it off," Emelyn said, touching the silver choker at her throat. "I mean to sell it, and perhaps buy us some time . . . before I am to stuff a husband into my bed."

Margaret leaned against her with a chuckle. "Such things you say. But can prospects really be as bad as that? Is your father's business in trouble?"

Swallowing her answer Emelyn looked up to find the same valet, Loganbrek's Mr. Quinson, leaning over the high balcony to watch her. "Mr. Loganbrek is easy enough to avoid, but his weird valet is ever staring," she said. "Perhaps he wants an audience."

"What? Now?"

"Now," Emelyn said, and squeezing her friend's hand she left the bench, tracking Mr. Quinson as he retreated along the railing, slinking past the music room to disappear onto the veranda.

Climbing the steps Emelyn made her way back along the balcony, slipping past the columns and into the welcome cool of outside. "Quinson I presume," she said, coming to join him as he stared over the night softened gardens below.

"Miss Morley," the valet greeted, swatting the air as he stooped low. "Your servant."

"I have been puzzling at the reason for your attention. I've not seen your master in the ballroom, but perhaps you've a letter for me."

"How perceptive; Indeed I have mistress, penned in his own hand. But some might find it cruel, that after promising your attentions you should eschew his company, without giving your answer."

"I answered him plainly," Emelyn said, extending her hand. "Still I expect this letter is a proposal, perhaps containing those embellishments he had not time for at our last meeting?"

"I would not know, of course," he said, reaching into his coat to withdraw the letter, which he handed over with an obsequious grin.

"Well, either way I shall answer him now if you're willing to wait."

"I do wait upon your convenience, but to sweeten the bargain I am instructed to advise that my good master will offer you two hundred guineas a month for pin money . . .”

“Thank you,” she said, not a little diverted to imagine what she’d do with such a sum. “Wait here and I will return directly.”

“A moment!” the valet said urgently, arresting her exit with a theatrical gesture. “If you will indulge this poor servant a moment more . . . I could not help but notice the radiance of your jewellery these past evenings, which I see now is missing from your fair collar, exchanged for this pedestrian affair,” he added, wrinkling his nose.

“*Pedestrian?*” Emelyn said, taking offence. “Thank you sir, what of it?”

“But so grand a ruby as you lately wore, wherever did you come by it?”

“That necklace was a gift.”

A flicker of relief shown in his face. “Might I assume you had it of Sir Thaniel Gliffton, baronet?”

“No sir, not from Sir Thaniel. But you must have heard he vanished two years ago, just before I received the necklace in fact.”

Mr. Quinson nodded gravely. “I did hear as much . . . and how strange, given the common opinion that he was a most ardent admirer of yours.”

Emelyn blinked against the buzz in her head, stuffing the letter into her pocket. “I don’t follow your meaning, but if you are seeking gossip I’ve nothing to add.”

“But the wayward baronet is found mistress, would you not care to know what became of him?”

“Sir Thaniel is found? So he was abroad I suppose,” she said, a little stung that the one man she and her mother might have agreed upon had disappeared without so much as a note . . .

“Well Miss Morley,” the valet said slowly, seeming to relish the moment, “as it happens Sir Thaniel Gliffton never left his estate, but was found in his own mausoleum, quite dead.”

Emelyn gasped. “Was Sir Thaniel murdered?”

“Most certainly,” Quinson said, watching her closely, “which does afford his final romantic entanglement a certain intrigue.”

“There was no entanglement I assure you.”

“My dear lady you misunderstand,” he said. “You see, the most precious jewel in his collection was a grand ruby necklace of gold, to which he added a halo of teardrop diamonds. I had the privilege of witnessing the jewel myself, at a party to which my master was invited. Now imagine my surprise, to find the very piece sparkling across your bosom.”

Her blood raced, and recalling Vaela’s claws ticking against the ruby, Emelyn wondered if the vampiress had a hand in Sir Thaniel’s fate.

“So if it was not his gift to you, it must have been stolen, do you see?” Quinson inquired, blinking rapidly.

“No sir, I do not see,” Emelyn said, unwilling to accept that Vaela could have killed the charming baronet. “But even if it were the same stone, perhaps he sold it.”

Quinson laughed heartily, a disquieting, cackly sound. “Sold it? Oh no Miss Morley he most certainly did not. The case is simple, we’ve a noble gentleman murdered, his most precious property stolen, and now there shall be a hundred witnesses to its home round your neck . . .”

“Are you accusing me?” Emelyn asked, an icy tension rising in her stomach. “What do you want Mr. Quinson?”

“The ruby of course.”

Emelyn gaped at him, appalled to find herself caught up in the very sort of blackmail she’d read about in penny novels. “You’re joking.”

“Nay, Miss Morley,” he said, his smile disappearing. “I will take the necklace, and in return I’ll spare your part in this sordid tale.”

“But I have no part in it!”

“Bring me the jewellery, or I shall address myself to Mr. Morley with the truth.”

The thought of her father accosted with such a story after the tragedy of the ships was impossible. “I told you sir, it was gifted to me . . .”

“Alas I do not believe you, Miss Morley.”

“It was gifted to me,” she repeated, “and I shall prove it.”

“How?”

“I will introduce you to the person who provided it. Then if still you are not convinced, I will turn it over . . .”

The odious valet gestured forward, smiling broadly. “Very well Miss Morley, lead on.”

Guiding him outside, and across the drive to the burbling fountains by the labyrinth entrance, she paused for a breath, staring into the dimly lit centre alley of green, which led to a deep archway of stone, marking the most direct route through the maze.

“Well?” he asked. “Do we enter? How delightfully covert.”

Emelyn nodded, and flanked by dense walls of boxwood they walked, her heart hammering as she gazed down the central path, half expecting the woman in black to appear at any moment.

"Oh my, but we are alone Miss Morley." Mr. Quinson chuckled. "Yes . . . I think I see; you mean to buy me off with scandal of a different sort. But really madam, do you imagine the charm of your flesh worth more than Sir Thaniel's pendant?"

The abrupt offence lent her courage, and she thought to slap him in the face, but only smiled as they continued walking. "I've no intention of seducing you Mr. Quinson," she said, feeling oddly afraid for him, "though I begin to wonder if this was a mistake . . ."

Quinson came to a stop. "No more games Miss Morley; produce this benefactor of yours if you can; either way I will have the necklace!"

The bones of her bodice grew tighter with every breath. "I do not have it," she said, feeling at once fearful and ridiculous, to have imagined the vampiress would intercede.

"Do you take me for a fool?" Quinson snapped. "Have you lost it this very hour? You must realize grubstreet pamphleteers would sell their children to print my story!"

"Enough!" she panted. "You shall have it tomorrow . . ."

"Tomorrow you're damned," he said, "bring it here by dawn, or I shall reduce the Morley name to ashes," but turning to leave he expelled a sudden sound, as though he were choking. There was a shadow behind him, and for the briefest moment he was lifted from the ground, before vanishing in the gloom.

Emelyn looked round in horror, finding no trace of him, and breathing through the shock she turned to dash deeper into the maze, the mist dampening her skirts as she ran. "Wait!" she rasped, her back and sides aching against the press of her stays. "Vaela please . . . for mercy's sake don't kill him!"

There was no sound but her own voice, and heaving with panic she began to stagger, slowing until she could go no farther, clutching at the hedge to rest. But there was not enough air; the little branches cracked in her grip, giving way, and she collapsed with a moan as the lights multiplied around her, and went out . . .

Chapter 6
A Matter of History

"Wake up little one . . ."

Coldly familiar, a protective sense surrounded her as Emelyn opened her eyes, finding herself in Vaela's arms, being carried over the bridge between the lakes. "Are you kidnapping me?" she asked.

"Only for a moment," Vaela answered, bearing her toward the woodland border away south of the house.

The crashing voice of the sea drifted to meet them. "I can walk," Emelyn said.

The vampiress set her down, taking her hand, and together they made their way through the brush toward the cliffs over the channel.

Shivering with nerves Emelyn clenched her jaws, girding herself for the query. "Mr. Quinson, the valet . . . have you killed him?"

"No, it wouldn't look well."

"Yes I quite agree," Emelyn said, feeling a rush of relief. "And . . . Sir Thaniel Gliffton. I don't suppose you know of him, or his fate?"

"Your heart burns with questions," Vaela said, moving a branch as they passed beneath it. "Let us look over the edge together, and I will answer them as I can."

"But you did not harm Mr. Loganbrek," Emelyn said, unable to wait. "I suppose then, vampires do not always kill?"

"I prefer to prey upon those who are rotten."

"Meaning bad . . . irredeemable," Emelyn said, watching her as they walked.

"If you like."

The grass surrendered to grey rocks beneath their feet, trees and scrub broke away, and a striking view opened before them. Below and beyond stretched an endless deep, flickering in flashes of white as the wind curled the waves. Wanting to feel the sheer height of it Emelyn ventured closer, leaning to peer down, but her shoe slipped, and she startled to find herself back in Vaela's arms, twenty paces from the edge.

"Sorry!" Emelyn gasped, panting as she held on tightly.

"Never walk here alone," Vaela said, and for several breaths they shared the view, until Emelyn spoke again.

"Will you explain to me precisely, why you are to protect me?"

"You are the Chosen Child, whose coming was foretold," Vaela said.

"But why? For what am I chosen?"

"The prophecy is not mine to understand, but our queen believes you will deliver her, and her kingdom . . . from its doom."

"What? How?"

Vaela twitched, as though to shake her head, and squeezing Emelyn close she kissed her forehead.

The gesture was comforting, if unexpected, but at a gust of wind a shiver ran through her, and Emelyn curled her toes. "Vaela, what is the prophecy? What am I to do?"

For a moment Vaela's expression turned to anger, and she adjusted her grip. "*Vampires*, as you know us, come into being each with a particular gift. Mine is to sense the truest depths of the heart, and yours is the surest, the strongest heart I have ever felt. That is all the proof of your value, that I require."

"The strongest heart? Well I'm not sure such a thing can be measured . . ."

"And yet it can be."

"But I know nothing of Saunmoor . . . and even less of your queen, whom I should tremble to imagine. How am I to understand my part in this?"

"Do not let it weigh upon you, you must conduct your life as though nothing is changed."

"As though nothing is changed?" Emelyn balked.

"Yes, Emelyn, your daylight world must continue as it has. Your people are not to know of us."

Grateful at least that Vaela's presence dulled the frantic edge of her thoughts, Emelyn swallowed, her mind drifting back to Mr. Quinson's ill-fated blackmail, and the demise of the baronet. "Sir Thaniel Gliffton," she said. "If you've watched over me all my life, then you must have seen him. Was the ruby necklace once his own? Had you anything to do with his death?"

The vampiress looked out over the long churning sea. "Do you know, the deepest water is eternally black; not even the brightest noonday sun can reach it."

"No . . . I did not know that."

"Nor did you know Sir Thaniel," Vaela said. "The truth is he deceived you, hiding mercenary interest beneath wit and flattery. A great many young women he brought to ruin, many estates he plundered of their secrets, but here was his greatest prize: the ruby necklace, which he stole to serve his own vanity, embellishing the pendant with teardrop diamonds. It is an heirloom of your family."

"An heirloom?" Emelyn marvelled. "Then however did it come into his possession?"

"He took it from the grave of your great-grandfather, Samuel Bastian Morley."

"So it is the very gem from the portrait, mounted in the top of his cane?"

"The same. Sir Thaniel imagined himself heir to an esoteric order founded by your ancestor, a band of Rosicrucians determined to profit by Hastelbrook's mysteries. That brotherhood is long extinct, but knowledge of the jewel was passed down to him."

"Then he only wanted treasure," Emelyn said, feeling a twinge of disappointment. "He dug it up, and you killed him for it."

Vaela's eyes glinted silver. "I challenged him to return the stone of his own free will; in the end he forfeit his life for greed."

The wind brushed cold, twisting about them as Emelyn huddled in Vaela's arms, gazing out over the sea. "And the ruby itself, how did so precious a jewel come to Samuel Bastian Morley?"

"I cannot say. But I do know that you mean to sell it . . . a pity."

Emelyn shivered again. "You heard me speak to my father?"

"As I hear even your breath when you sleep."

"Do you? And did you hear . . . my confession to Margaret?"

"Yes."

"Forgive me," Emelyn said quickly, her heart racing. "I never meant to betray your confidence; she is my truest friend in the world. She will tell no one I swear it."

"I will not touch her."

Emelyn caught her breath with a nod. "I promise to better keep your secret . . . but have you ever revealed yourself to others in my life, perhaps to an insufferable blonde girl when I was a child?"

"Not that I remember, but I am not the only one watching."

Abruptly Emelyn recalled Sarah's fright. "And who else is watching? Not a monstrous man with burning eyes . . ."

Vaela nodded.

"Who is he? What does he want?" Emelyn asked, rattling with nerves.

"Do not fear him; he only listens, as he has done since your grandfather's grandfather was a boy."

"For so long? Is he listening now?"

"Perhaps. He could hear the beat of your heart through a thunderstorm, but he is not to hinder you, or yours."

The waves broke against the cliffs, and Emelyn trembled in a vengeful gust, holding on tighter as there came a sinking feeling that this dreamlike visitation was soon to end.

"I must return you to the house," Vaela said, her dark eyes glistening.

"Will you take of my blood tonight?" Emelyn asked softly, tingling to think of it.

"Yes," Vaela breathed, meeting her eyes, "only a sip . . ."

The light of the fire danced on the ceiling, and Emelyn blinked to find herself lying in bed, the ebbing sounds of party rising about her, mingled with crunching wheels and hoof beats of departing carriages outside. Pulling the blankets to her mouth she stared into the deepening night through the bay windows, finding the gown she'd worn fluttering like a ghost by the open panes.

"It wasn't a dream," she murmured, unable to account for how she'd returned to the house. "It cannot have been . . ."

"Your gown was wet miss," Breda said, dousing the last candles on the dresser.

"What time is it?" Emelyn asked.

"Quarter to one."

Breda shut the door behind her, and left alone in the shadows Emelyn sat up, striving to delay the tempting enchantment of sleep, at least long enough to amend her journal with the ominous tidings Vaela had shared . . . but the ember light from the hearth grew invitingly dim, and too drowsy to write she lay down again, frowning at the sight of Mr. Loganbrek's unopened letter on her desk. All sense of Vaela's presence would fade by morning, and she would spread her arms to be costumed for breakfast, and again for the afternoon, and finally in grand fashion for the fateful meeting with one Captain Van Croft.

Saturday June 11th

Much too early Breda creaked open the door, and nursing a wine headache Emelyn threw a pillow at her.

Sleeping away the morning, it was nearly noon by the time she dragged herself from bed, and Breda set upon her at once, preparing her for a cold bath after which she assisted her mistress into a white day gown florid with green, coiling her hair back tightly, garnished with a cap of lace.

"Dinner is to be served at one o' clock miss," Breda said.

"Thank you," Emelyn replied, sitting at her desk to study Mr. Loganbrek's letter, the edges of which she found had been decoratively singed. The overcomplicated seal was stamped with what looked to be a one-winged eagle attacking several ships, and turning it to the front she found 'E' for 'Emelyn M' swirling itself into a frenzy to nearly bully the rest of her name off the paper. With a sigh of fatigue she took a gilded letter opener from its case, but touching the tip to the seal she paused.

"Mr. Loganbrek's valet waits for you in the foyer miss; very unhappy he looks."

"Does he indeed," Emelyn said, staring into the fire as she struggled to imagine how Vaela might have left the man. "I suppose he's come for my answer . . ."

"Shall I open it for you miss?"

"If you like," Emelyn said, handing over the letter and opener.

Breda was just digging the blade under the wax when Emelyn stopped her. "No," she said. "Burn it."

"Burn it?" Breda startled as her mistress snatched the letter from her hand.

Walking to the hearth Emelyn tossed it into the flames, watching the eager light dance about the paper until the overwritten pages were consumed. "You may tell them I am coming down," she said.

Mr. Quinson sat hunched like a beggar on a bench by the front doors, head bowed with nervous hands clasped in his lap. "You must forgive the intrusion!" he gasped, creaking to his feet as Emelyn approached. "My good master should very much like to know, that is, if you've considered the sentiments expressed in his letter."

Emelyn looked him over, finding the man all but vanquished with fatigue. "I have," she said. "You must thank him, and tender my decline."

"Very good," Mr. Quinson said, his eyes drooping. "Shall I bring him your note?"

"You may relate my words. There shall be no further response, written or otherwise."

"Ah." He nodded, pulling a kerchief to wipe his brow. "Very good."

"It would seem you've undergone a change of heart," Emelyn observed. "Are you quite well?"

"I am . . . I've had," he stammered, blinking as though confused, "the most terrible nightmares; I woke in a wretched state, robbed of both rest and memory . . ."

"Am I to understand you remember nothing of our exchange on the veranda, or outside?" Emelyn inquired, feeling a curious pity for him.

The valet twisted his hands together, flinching as though afraid his own thoughts might do him harm. "Forgive me," he said. "I recall only shadows . . . I must beg to sully your home with my unworthy presence no longer."

Emelyn frowned at him. "Very well, but you shall take the calash," she said, snapping for the footman. "You're in no condition to walk."

Sitting in the parlour window, she watched as the ashen Mr. Quinson was assisted into the open two-horse hooded carriage, where he collapsed in the seat like a man about to expire. "Vaela . . . whatever have you done to the poor man?"

"What poor man?" Isabelle asked, surprising her as she approached the bench with a book.

"It's nothing," Emelyn said. "Mr. Loganbrek's valet is sick."

Midday dinner was set at a long table in the lower gardens, covered in white and festooned with painted vases of brightly coloured flowers. Emelyn was relieved to find her disappearance from the party was not at issue, though she could not yet remember returning to her room. Mrs. Morley appeared well distracted by a group of friends over the meal of glazed partridge with French beans and artichokes, and passing over meat pies and jellies Emelyn minced through her plate, speaking only to Margaret, whom she discovered had met her on the way back to the house.

"I did wonder at your state of mind," Margaret confided, "you seemed half in a daze, but are you feeling quite yourself again? You do look rather pale Emie . . ."

"I saw her," Emelyn said in a hushed voice.

"Who?" Margaret asked, and eyes widening she covered her mouth. "Oh no . . . not your vampire!"

"Hush Maggie, as I told you I'm in no danger."

"Well . . . I'm glad of that," Margaret said, eyeing her as she forked her partridge.

With their duty to the table fulfilled, the pair of them were just setting out up the hill when Mrs. Morley called for their return.

"Yes Mama?" Emelyn said warily, coming to her side.

Coaxing her daughter close enough to whisper, Mrs. Morley took hold of her wrist, smiling at her ear. "I've spared you the embarrassment of a scolding," she breathed. "But you have snuck away in the dark for the very last time my dearest, it isn't safe! Shall we lock you in your room for the party?"

"I didn't . . . I'm sorry Mama," Emelyn said with a flush, smiling for the other guests as her mother released her.

Hiking arm in arm back to the house Emelyn and Margaret stopped in the drive for their goodbyes.

"I shall see you at Dhorings Park very soon," Margaret said as they reached the carriages.

"Yes, and I shall have more to tell you," Emelyn said, accepting a cheerful embrace to see her off, before making her way inside and down to the kitchens.

Undisputed authority on all things comestible, Hester Roggel, Hastelbrook's cook, was a stoic, red faced woman with strong hands and a quick temper. Spotting Emelyn over a thick table spread with demolished vegetables, she wiped her brow and laid down her knife, setting off for the larders.

"Hello Mrs. Roggel," Emelyn said, hurrying after her with a basket. "I am going to the bookshop, and I'd like to bring something to Marta Denlund and the little ones, on account of her husband's loss."

Mrs. Roggel waved her into the storeroom and began pulling items from the shelves. "Weren't no loss miss," she said. "That man got his deserving; it were the darkness what took him."

Seeking rather to avoid the topic, Emelyn waited as the cook loaded her up with a half wheel of cheese, rounds of bread, a heavy side of bacon, biscuits and jam, with a sleeve of large almond cookies. "And just some of the fresh rolls, if you please."

Moments later she was blinking in the bright sun, seated in the returned two-horse carriage as it trundled down the hill to the village. "Lockmartin's, thank you Horace," Emelyn said, squinting in the breeze as she held her hat.

The main road split wide around a little copse of trees, with the charming freehold cottage of Doctor Bayten to her right, and the grandest structure in the village, the Stafford House Inn run by Goodman Codgrass, on the other side. The inn common room was crowded today, as often it would be, made use of not only for lodgers but village meetings and auctions, and once a gallery for Isabelle's blink of a passion for painting.

Lockmartin Bookseller, which rested just next to the inn, was a favourite shop and the only place Emelyn cared to visit with regular frequency. The happily hearty Warrick Lockmartin, a literary scholar self-determined to be a direct descendent of King Edward the Confessor, was today as always smart vested over billowy shirt, with round spectacles for his round face. "Well met Miss Morley!" he greeted with cheer. "New play from Dodsley, *The Toy Shop*, and fresh copies of Henry Fielding just today."

The dusty shop was tall, if narrow, with a roaming ladder to reach the high volumes and stacks of books on the floor by the shelf corners. Admiring his silverpoint portraits, which hung above the desk behind him, Emelyn presented Mr. Lockmartin a buttered roll, which he accepted gratefully, toasting her health with a cup of tea. "No plays for me today," she said, "but have you anything of the old legends hereabouts? You must know them as well as anyone; any odd tales I've not read?"

"More than tales of late I'm afraid," he said. "If you've heard what's befallen parish livestock; a dozen sheep slaughtered and many missing besides."

"That's awful. Is it poachers?"

"I rather doubt it, but we shall leave the dailies to conjecture; Mrs. Bayten's pamphlet shall have a thing or two to say about it."

"But what else, has there been word of storms sinking shipping in the Celtic Sea?"

"Dangerous bit of water that. But can't say as I've heard aught on that account."

"And what of the vault beneath Hastelbrook house; do you know the rumours?"

"Has your family not a secret crypt under the library? Never seen it myself."

"Yes we have, but no . . . the vault is said to be deeper, underneath."

"Then you know more than I miss, though I'm old enough to remember that earthquake, October of 1712, the night you were born if I don't mistake."

"Yes," Emelyn sighed. "But I know you're a man of historical study; if I ask of Saunmoor, is there anything you might tell me?"

Lockmartin rattled his teacup. "*Saunmoor?* The fabled kingdom of the dead?"

"Yes."

"Well . . . tales go back to the eleventh century, as I understand. Danes had all but overrun the country; it was monks fleeing into the wilds of Kent who first made record of haunting voices on the downs. They named the place Palucantus, the *swamp of songs*. The name *Saunmoor* derived therefrom I suppose. I might have something or other, but shall Miss Morley turn her keen apprehension to lore of the occult?"

"Just a curiosity," Emelyn said. "Is there not some dismal poetaster who writes oft of it?"

"You're looking for Lord Cumberstone." Mr. Lockmartin climbed down from his desk to cross the shop floor, whereupon he set to rifling through a pile of pamphlets, and the mixed stack of old books underneath. "An alias of course; any number of dark and deplorable things have been put to his credit. The name goes back centuries."

"I've heard as much," Emelyn said, knowing well that Cumberstone, though widely read, was seldom spoken of in good society.

"I cannot imagine your parents should approve, but here's a start," Lockmartin said with a smile, producing a small printing of *Bequeath the Grave*, a collection of works by the scandalous poet.

Emelyn cracked open the book, and moving further down the shopkeeper picked up a faded picture-work for children. "*Dark Down Totter Town,*" he said. "Cumberstone again, children's stories, if you've the stomach for them. And you might try this . . ."

Gingerly she accepted it, untidy manuscript pages between folio covers.

"An old book of records," he said, "letters mostly, concerning missing children from Middlesex, Southwark and London Town. Do you know the story of the Lurkmen?"

"Does not every English child," she said, tucking the others under her arm as she studied the book. "Boys and girls who defy their bedtime are snatched by faceless men in the night, and stowed in their ghostly carriages, never to be seen again. But if it's true I should wonder at there being any children left at all.”

Lockmartin chuckled. “Well, it’s said the Lurkmen ride out from Saunmoor, stealing foundlings who shan’t be missed, and offering them up to the dark queen . . . it’s only stories of course,” and he accepted her selections to wrap them in brown paper.

Emelyn watched with tentative excitement, feeling she’d rather acquired something forbidden, and bidding him goodbye she smiled as he promised to add the charge to her family’s account, though she knew he wouldn’t.

A short albeit bumpy drive later she reached the Denlund cottage at the end of a plain row, and dismounting the trap she crossed a little brickwork courtyard cluttered with tools and sundries, stopping to knock at the door. Wearing a plain black dress, hair kept tight under her bonnet, Marta Denlund answered with a happy gasp, wringing her hands in a dish cloth.

“Miss Morley!”

“Hello Mrs. Denlund,” Emelyn said, brandishing the basket. “May I come in?”

Accepting her guest into the kitchen, Marta rushed to pour the tea as Emelyn placed the food on the table, waving at a pair of very young girls who peered at her from the bedroom doorway, one head above the other.

“Come here darlings,” Emelyn said, unwrapping the cookies to hand them one each. The children accepted them gratefully, nibbling with concentration as they retreated to the other room.

Marta took a cookie for herself with a gleeful shrug. “Ever so kind miss.”

“I am sorry for your loss,” Emelyn said. “I should like us to help against the expenses; burial and such, if you’ll permit it.”

“Burial? Oh no miss, men from the Company of Barber-Surgeons come to collect him. Very keen they were, finding him a special case, paid me four guineas they did. I couldn’t say no on account of the girls.”

“Really? Are the anatomists after subjects so far from London?”

“I can’t say miss; all I know is my Philip never saw a pack of cards but he’d lay down a shilling. There were long debts to see to, and I was happy to do it, though we’ve little enough left over.”

“My dear Mrs. Denlund if it was only the money . . .”

Marta’s eyes were soft with fear. “It weren’t only that; I saw a woman in black at the window, not a week before . . . He never believed it, but my husband came to bad ends, it were she what portended it.”

Emelyn swallowed, amazed at her guess. "You need fear no dark omens. What's important now is to see you through this."

"Thank you miss," Marta said, smiling faintly. "It don't escape me we shall have some harmony in the house now. I only tremble to think . . . what must have befell the poor sot."

"Well," Emelyn said, striving not to imagine it, "you and your girls are safe."

Marta cleared her throat, rubbing a spot on the table. "I'll hope you understand miss, when the lease comes due . . . I couldn't hide a farthing but he'd drink it up."

"You'll not be cast out; my father will see to it," Emelyn said firmly, and she placed her hand over Marta's on the table. "More harmony in the house."

Marta nodded with a tearful smile. "Right you are miss, of course."

With a parting embrace Emelyn bid her farewell, and after a pleasant drive up the hill she returned home with her new books which, being that she was too restless for reading, were left on a library table for later study. That afternoon she waited in her dressing room before the mirror, staring at her reflection as the maids prepared for her introduction to the looming Captain Lord Van Croft. The first strains of music seeped through the walls, and she sighed as Breda divided her hair into tails, pinning them up in imitation of ocean waves, while the younger maid armed herself with the first layer of petticoats, ready to pounce.

At last the dressing was complete, and Emelyn stood rigid as a splint, clad in a low cut blue and white patterned gown that split over a silky white stomacher with shimmering skirts underneath. Heaving for breath, she adjusted her comfort as Breda related her mother's instructions. By design the gown had been selected to recall the rolling sea for the delight of the captain, who would await her arrival in the large library west of the foyer— which she was to approach expressly by way of the south parlour, to avoid his first catching sight of her by the interior windows.

"I'll have the trim if you please," Emelyn said, and the little maid obliged, tucking a lace border across her bosom to fortify Emelyn's modesty as she donned a selection of earrings— brilliant platinum backed opals.

Breda's usually stern face softened with a smile. "Sparkling like crystal miss," she declared, wrapping the final piece about the neck of her mistress— a webbed chain of silver mounted sapphires.

Emelyn pulled white gloves to her elbows, and reaching into the pocket gaps through her skirts she was surprised to find only a thin layer of shift between her fingers and legs. "Wait, you've forgotten to tie on my pockets underneath."

"Your mother has said no pockets."

"No pockets? Why on earth not?"

"I'm sorry miss."

Emelyn found her brother waiting at the bottom of the steps in the grand foyer, leaning into his crutches as she descended. "Good evening Deacon. Are you to join us in the library?"

"I am not," he said. "You are to meet the man alone, excepting the footmen."

"Am I to meet him alone? Well if Mama wants a wedding tonight I must change my gown . . ."

"We can only hope Lord Van Croft wins you so easily," Deacon said, shuffling closer, "if any man is good enough to coax you down from your tower."

"Why should he coax me down? Why can't he come up?"

Deacon rolled his eyes. "Yes have your fun; I know you only speak so to cover your nerves. But if you're ever to catch so lofty a fish, you must take the matter seriously."

"I've never taken a lofty fish for granted."

"Well you might check your forays into the dark for a start. You can't be waking up in the hedge; you're not a child anymore Emie."

"I shall take it under advisement," Emelyn said. "Now if you'll excuse me I am to throw myself at a sea captain."

Tremulous with guessing after the man she was about to meet, she made her way to the south parlour, pausing to settle her nerves as she looked about the room. The parlour was warm and pleasant, with soft benches under the windows and flowing drapes of crushed gold that ran from the ceiling to pour down the walls, perfect for hide and seek, though not for many years now. Before her a high arched hallway exited through the north wall, running a short way to the closed doors of the library.

Squaring her shoulders, Emelyn was about to start in when her mother snatched her arm, pulling her back with a hiss.

"Ouch!"

"My dear wake up!" Mrs. Morley scolded. "You cannot mean to charge the man down unprepared!"

Emelyn flushed. "Is that not precisely what you wanted?"

"Oh my dearest," her mother said, "my sweet girl, I understand it is highly unusual, moving from one to the next so quickly, but with the demands of his station we are fortunate the captain is here at all; he shan't even stay for the party."

"Then why have you accosted me?"

Her mother clutched her arm tightly. "He is yet youthful and strong, but Lord Van Croft is thirteen years your senior; he is not only a captain but noble titled twice over, and well used to being in command. He has requested your individual company, and your father is satisfied that he is a man of honour. We shall therefore allow him to acquaint you without our interference, that things might take their natural course . . ."

"*Their natural course?* You cannot expect him to propose this instant?"

"Oh fie, you *must* make an impression," Mrs. Morley said. "You will present meekness and sweet amenability. He must forget every other young lady who seeks his address."

"Shall I faint at the sight of him? What if he neglects to catch me?"

Her mother made an irritated noise. "You must take the matter seriously! You will smile with bright eyes, and do not follow yourself in conversation, but listen more than you speak . . . and we've no need for the lace."

"Mama!" Emelyn gasped as her mother pulled the lace border from her front, wadding it in her hand.

"We must bring all your attractions to bear," Mrs. Morley observed. "One of the most eligible men in the Empire stands in our library, and you will do your part."

"Have I not followed your every instruction?" Emelyn asked, swelling with impatience.

"You must understand," her mother said, "Lord Van Croft is of an austere and unforgiving reputation; it is not only your beauty but your tenderness, your blushing delicate nature, that shall win him over."

"My blushing delicate nature? But this is the first I've heard of it."

Mrs. Morley adjusted her daughter's necklace. "As I recall you were not so insufferably clever as a girl."

"Yet that is precisely when I spent long hours reading of Captain Van Croft's adventures, and would have thrilled myself into a swoon to meet him. Oh Mama, are we ten years too late?"

"Must we live and die by your satirical tongue? I only ask that you meet an exalted man with ease and charm befitting!"

"Well if you mean to put me *at ease* I am decidedly not," Emelyn said, fidgeting with the slits in her skirts, "and why have you forbidden me pockets?"

"Emelyn Elizabeth we cannot have you fussing in your pockets, as you do when you're nervous."

"I don't," Emelyn protested. "But if I'm nervous it's only your cryptic warnings making me so."

"Oh my sweet radiant darling." Mrs. Morley kissed her cheek. "You have nothing to fear of course. You must go to him now, and strive to enjoy yourself. And do remember he is a peer of the realm, to be addressed always as *my lord*."

"Yes Mama, I do understand titles," Emelyn said, feeling not a little anxious as she walked through the arch, clutching her fan. Two footmen waited, and standing tall she took a deep breath as they pulled open the doors.

Chapter 7
Captain and Cooper

The library was a grand room, with two floors of books and a railed walk supported by oaken pillars. Emelyn tarried in the doorway, resolving not to be daunted by the gentleman before her, who stood facing the far shelves, his nose in a book. Lord Van Croft looked every part as described, very tall and broad of shoulders, clad in a magnificent coat of royal blue trimmed with gold over charcoal breeches and white stockings. His dark hair was pulled into a tail tied with ribbon, and he wore a jewel encrusted rapier slung low on his belt.

"Miss Emelyn Elizabeth Morley," the footman announced. "Lord Jonathon Van Croft."

The captain did not turn, but recited from the pages before him, his voice low and strong: "*Neck arching white in last despair, veins pounding blue in Samael's prayer. Blood blushes red to meet the air, as breaking claws and slaking fangs twist down upon her mortal pangs . . .*"

"I beg your pardon my lord," Emelyn said, surprised to hear him quoting the book she'd just purchased. "I think you'll find reading Cumberstone aloud is tacitly discouraged in polite company."

"Your father shows great indiscretion," the gentleman crowed, snapping the book shut as he stared into the wall, "allowing unmarried girls to read such tripe."

"Is marriage a protection from bad poetry?" Emelyn asked, bewildered to begin in such a way.

"Virtue is its own protection," Captain Van Croft stated, raising an eyebrow as he turned to regard her.

He was alarmingly handsome, from the deep brown of his eyes to the strong angles of his face, sun tinged and stern.

Silence hung in the air, his colour rising as did hers, and snatching another book from the table he scowled at the binding. "Your countenance and figure do not disappoint," he said, replacing the book. "You are a vision, Miss Morley."

"Thank you my lord . . . And how do you find Hastelbrook?"

"Stuff Hastelbrook," he said, approaching to clack his heels for a bow. "There is but one reason to be caught this close to the stink of Brighton, and I stand before her."

"A bereft compliment, but I will allow it," she said.

"And I marvel to give it," he replied. "Through oceans of disappointment the winds have brought me to you at last . . . the most beauteous Belle of Brighton."

"Beauty is a happy chance of birth," she said, and noting the musky scent of him she wondered if it was not that of oiled ship decks and spiced rum.

The captain laughed heartily. "Does madam tire of such praises? Nay Miss Morley you must accept them with grace, for never have I seen so lovely a shore."

"There is more to a country than the shore my lord . . ."

"Then I must venture inland, to penetrate her defences."

Emelyn held her breath with a smile, determined to get her footing. "Well my lord," she said, looking to her skirts, "great pains have been taken that my presentation might remind you of the sea . . ."

"In the words of Brome," he said, his gaze fixed on hers, "*the novice youth may chance admire your dressings, paints, and spells, but we that are expert desire your sex for somewhat else . . .*"

Nonplussed Emelyn snapped out her fan. "Even my fan bears a scene of the sea, but I imagine a naval man tires of water, does he not?"

"Water? The open ocean is not water Miss Morley, but brine. Those who drink from the sea die of thirst."

Emelyn fanned herself. "Yes of course."

"Now I am told you've read of my adventures," he said, gripping the hilt of his sword and flashing it from the scabbard to catch it in the other hand.

"I have, yes, I did that is, when I was younger," she said, giving him space as he swatted at nothing and brought the blade to his lips.

"Excellent," he said.

"Though I daresay your exploits are seasoned with dramatic licence?"

A shadow of anger crossed his face, but he recovered with a

chuckle. "To which do you refer?"

"Surely you've not vanquished *legions* of pirates? Or at the Battle of Cape Passaro; can it be true you captured a ship alone . . ."

"The swells were treacherous, breaking our angles. Mine was the only rope across, but I could not let her escape; I killed a dozen at least before the dogs were at my side."

"I see," she said, imagining the blood-washed decks of a Spanish frigate, strewn with her slain defenders.

"Does it fascinate you?" he asked, offering her the grip of his sword. "Should you like to know how it feels, to push your blade through a man's heart?"

"Not especially . . . But you must have other stories, being a man of the world, where those concerned still live at the end?"

Lord Van Croft slid the blade home with a clink. "Certainly Miss Morley," he said, and stepping closer he took her hand, pulling it to his chest as though for a dance.

"Excuse me my lord," she said, failing to retreat. "I think perhaps you've mistaken me . . . for someone familiar."

He released her with a grin. "Tell me, how do you dispose of yourself after reading such scandalous bilge as Cumberstone?"

"Do you mean how else do I spend my time, or how do I carry on thus transformed by reading him?"

"Both, and neither," he said, offering his arm. "Tour the room with me, and answer how you will; your voice diverts like sweet music, whatever the words."

"Whatever the words, I see," she said, accepting his escort for a turn about the shelves. "I suppose I could share that I read not only fictions, but enjoy history, geography, modern languages and medicine, as well as fruitful study of maritime business, news of the exchange, and whatever I can get from London."

"Your mercy madam! Take care to leave room in that beautiful head for womanhood."

"Is womanhood at odds with these things?" she posed, bracing for argument.

But the captain dismissed it with a wave. "By Jove what a pair we shall make . . . for we are fated for combination you and I."

"Are we? I really couldn't say my lord."

Van Croft left her to walk to a tray of crystal resting on a corner table by the rolling ladder. "Do you deny it?" he asked, decanting the brandy to pour himself a glass. "But we are paragons of the species, towering among insects. What more would you ask, to make a pair of us?"

Emelyn stood where he left her, fiddling with her fan. "I'm not sure that's meet to answer sir; we have only just met."

"Yes, and by sight and sound of you alone I am undone. King and queen we would make, were the world as it should be."

"Well, before any talk of coronation I must learn of your family, and your home, and precisely what sort of man you are."

"How refreshingly direct," he said, pausing for a sip. "My broad estate lies in Shropshire, the castle Vivere Gloria. Surely you've heard of it?"

"It might have been mentioned in one of your adventures . . ."

"A proud fortress, realized far beyond its twelfth century foundations," he said. "Of course the house and grounds are in want of a wife's administration. As to family, I am the third Viscount Van Croft and fourth Baron Clearmont. I've a living uncle with a stake in my affairs of shipping, and a younger sister who yet lives on the estate. Five frigates sail under my banner . . . including my own, the Long Dragon; more than 250 guns in all."

"Five frigates in your command? Are you not then a Commodore?"

"In time of war perhaps, but it is my commission as captain that I hold dearest of all; my crucible. The other titles I might surrender, but never captain. I would not expect a lady to understand."

"We do not all understand alike," she said, feeling his gaze as she strolled along the wall, stopping at the table to stack her books. "I find no fault in holding one's passion above land and rank."

Lord Van Croft sipped his drink and sucked through his teeth. "Damned if I wasn't advised to find you extraordinary . . . and so I do."

"Then I find your advisors of sound character," she said, warming to the flattery.

"As to what sort of man I am," he continued, throwing back his brandy and clapping the glass on the tray, "I bless those fortunate enough to earn my good will. My allies are many, my friends are few, and my enemies, well . . . while they live they live in fear."

"And when your enemies run out," she said, watching as he made his way back to her, "do you not pause to enjoy more civilized pursuits?"

"There is but one civilized pursuit on my horizon," he replied, drawing near enough to crowd her against the books. "Now I must ask, have you ever been kissed?"

"I dare not answer," she said, glancing at his mouth. "I am twenty-three my lord; if I say no you will think me naïve. If I say yes you will think me immodest."

"Your gift of tongue," he said. "But I hope you are as gifted in knowing when to be clever, and when to demure."

"I should say that depends on my audience."

Lord Van Croft laughed softly, leaning close. "Tell me, sweet Miss Morley, have you any doubt I shall conquer you?"

Emelyn turned her head, and flushing with heat she found her indignation, stepping around him. "I wonder my lord," she said, making an appropriate distance, "is it true you mean to neglect the party and take your leave before the dance? I am expected to sing with my sisters, as it happens."

The captain stepped closer. "I'd love nothing more than to acquit your desire for my company, but I've affairs in Brighton which cannot be put off."

"Yes, very well," she said, feeling both relieved and annoyed.

Without warning he snatched her hand for a kiss, and she dropped her fan. "But by the fetching heave of your breath, it is clear enough I will be missed," he said.

"Is it?" Emelyn tested her hand, but he held it fast. "Though as I need air to live you mustn't put too much stock in my breathing."

The footman by the doors gave a loud cough, and Van Croft flashed him a look like daggers. "Have you not a coach to chase somewhere?"

"And we may leave the poor footman out of it," Emelyn said, trying her hand again. "He's only to protect me from aggressive sea captains."

Van Croft grinned. "My dear madam, I might warn you I am not to be ranked among those grovelling fops ever seeking your fancy."

"Should I rather rank you among the brittle self-serious sort?"

They stared at each other, her hand in his, and for a moment she thought him building to rage, but the captain released his breath with a sigh, his expression softening. "Forgive me Miss Morley," he said, his grin fading, "rarely do I find myself so affected," and taking hold of her fingers he began to loosen her glove.

"That is my glove sir."

"You must allow me this token," he said, peeling it down from her elbow to wrist. "You shall be my fire haired Helen of Troy, and I your Achilles."

"That is not quite the story," she said, watching as he pulled the glove from her hand.

"With this in my care," he said, folding the article to tuck in his pocket, "I shall count the moments, until next I hear my name on those sweetest of lips. You are worthy of no man less than myself."

"I see . . ."

"Alas you must settle for the attentions of insects, until I return."

"Then I shall be careful where I step."

The captain kissed her hand again, pinching her bare skin in his teeth, and straightening up tall he knocked his boots for a bow, turning sharply to take his leave.

Emelyn leaned into the table, gripping the edge as she watched his exit.

"All right miss?" the footman asked, returning her fan.

"Yes Timothy," she said, puffing her lips. "If you would fetch me some water . . ."

Minutes later Mrs. Morley rushed to her side as Emelyn sat at one of the study tables, perusing a book of maps.

"Oh my precious daughter, but I should say you've done very well, very well indeed!"

"Thank you Mama," Emelyn said vaguely.

"And what do you think of the captain?"

Emelyn took up a quill pen from the desk, brushing her face with the feather. "I hardly know . . ."

"Nonsense; the man is desperately charming anyone could see it. He cannot have failed to impress you."

"He is very attractive, and articulate," Emelyn said thoughtfully, "and I daresay cocksure as an emperor; it were as though he jumped right off the page . . . and he bit me Mama."

"He bit you?! Oh he didn't."

"He did," Emelyn said, showing her hand, "and he insists on crowding me; he stands too close."

"Is that all?" Mrs. Morley huffed. "Lord Van Croft is cousin to King George; he must stand where he likes. Come now my dearest, it's no mark against you to concede he is the very best of the lot, the uttermost paragon of gentlemen!"

"He must be, he said so himself."

Her mother frowned, leaning against the table to stare at her.

The silence grew uncomfortable, and Emelyn raised her brows, looking over a map of New Guinea.

"Emelyn Elizabeth you shall be four and twenty this year," Mrs. Morley said at last. "You have toyed with every season, but there shall be no more of it. The time has come for you to plant your feet and see to your duty."

Emelyn focused on the book before her, turning pages which might as well have been blank. "I know that Mama."

Mrs. Morley reached over to shut the book. "Yet you carry on as though the world were only here for your amusement. Can it be possible that even Lord Van Croft were not enough to distract you?"

Taking up the ostrich quill Emelyn ran the cold feather between her fingers.

"Is that your answer? Not a word?"

"My answer is . . . that wherever he is, *whomever* he is," Emelyn said, her eyes going wet, "I should hope that I save him, as he saves me. And there shall be no secrets between us."

Her mother took the quill, tossing it away. "My darling naïve girl we are not waiting for one of your storybook characters."

"Van Croft *is* one of my storybook characters!"

"And if you're thinking to cast him aside as quickly as the others I must disappoint you, for we shall tolerate no such caprice!"

"I am not casting him aside . . . neither will I promise here and now to marry him."

With an exasperated laugh Mrs. Morley took her daughter's hand, squeezing it tight. "Emelyn my dearest no one is asking for your promise today. And how have you lost another glove; are you eating them?"

"He took it, for a token."

"Oh I see, well that is . . . very much different," Mrs. Morley said with a happy flush. "Now I shall leave you to your thoughts, but do not forget you are to open the dance, and then you shall sing on the balcony with your sisters, in particular the duets we discussed."

"Yes Mama," Emelyn said, sipping her water.

Late afternoon bled into evening, and eager to quit her oceanic ensemble Emelyn emerged from her dressing room reconstructed for the ball in a gown of deep shimmering red, square necked with chains of gold gleaming in the high twists of her hair. Longing for Margaret's advice, she was left to ruminate without her, swallowing down competing impressions of Lord Van Croft as she struggled to imagine herself beside such a man for the rest of her days.

Music rang out for the dance, and squelching her nerves she summoned an enduring smile, resigning herself to the business. She led the minuet, stomped and clapped for a vigorous bourée, and spun round for the gavotte before curtsying her exit to take a turn about the room. The clamorous voices and colours blended around her, and carrying two half glasses to discourage conversation she tarried by the grand windows, peering up at the changing sky. Distant lightning split the heavens, and she recalled with a shiver the edge of the cliffs, the cold shelter of Vaela's arms, the icy wind in her hair . . .

A small neatly bearded fellow, masked and coated all in green, stopped to offer his hand with a feint, snapping his fingers to produce a rose. Emelyn smiled at the trick, setting down a glass to accept the flower.

"My dearest where is your head?" Mrs. Morley flustered, bursting upon her as the man vanished into the crowd.

"Yes Mama, I haven't forgotten," Emelyn sighed, and after finishing her drinks she left the empty glasses with her mother to make her way across the floor and up the stairs. Swishing along the balcony she found her sisters in the common space before the veranda, Isabelle staring impatiently while Sarah sat behind her at the small triangle harpsichord, and quickly Emelyn took her place by the railing overlooking the ballroom.

"You're lucky we waited," Isabelle said, coming to join her, a violin tucked against her neck.

"Thank you Bell," Emelyn replied, freezing with joyful dignity as a hush fell over the crowd.

Rapt faces turned upward, Sarah started in on the keys, Isabelle joined in with strings, and holding the rose at her stomach Emelyn began to sing. A popular tune of lyric longing, *The Midsummer Wish* captured her audience, and as her gaze wandered to include the room she found a handsome familiar face amongst the crowd: a man she'd acquainted not two years past . . . the son of a cooper.

Music hummed through the hall, and Emelyn gave them several ballads in both English and French before Isabelle rested her instrument to sing beside her. Together they performed country duets to the delight of the assembly, until after finishing the last notes of *Hero and Leander* the sisters clasped hands for a bow amidst applauding laughter and tossing of kerchiefs, with a few stately gentlemen tapping their canes in approval as the man she'd recognized raised his glass, receding into the throng.

Returning downstairs to seek him out, Emelyn was obliged to stop for a flattering group of ladies, captained by a sturdy brunette gowned in umber, whom she knew to be the recently wed Olivia Weatherton, made Countess Grahamsby. Introductions came quickly, Lady Grahamsby capturing Emelyn's hand as the others delivered fawning praises.

"Brilliant Miss Morley! Such a performance!"

"Oh dear, thank you so much," Emelyn said, accepting a narrow glass of port from the footman.

"But your voice is absolutely angelic," Lady Grahamsby said. "Such clear attendance to the music; like yourself I find melody of paramount importance, regardless of pronunciation."

"Thank you," Emelyn repeated, a little stung.

"Now we old crows quite enjoy the mysterious air about Hastelbrook," Lady Grahamsby continued, "a welcome distraction from the predictable elegance of town, but I was quite surprised to learn Lord Van Croft has paid a call. He can only have appeared for you my dear of course; now you must tell us, how did you find him?"

"Without difficulty," Emelyn said, nursing her drink. "He was in the library."

Lady Grahamsby made a fussy sort of noise. "Well! Then I suppose the captain's intentions are secret . . ."

"I have only just acquainted him," Emelyn said, swirling her glass, "I cannot speak to his intentions."

"Oh I am relieved to hear it," Grahamsby answered, gloved hand over her heart. "For I should warn you against too great a hope. Van Croft is notoriously difficult to catch; it's well known he's broken several engagements."

"Has he? Then I must be grateful we're not engaged . . . But how is Lord Grahamsby?" Emelyn asked, seeking a new topic as she scanned the crowd.

"Oh I must tell you, the dear man means to open a hospital in Southwark, to assist the gin-addled poor . . . they say the city has never known such vagrancy; the lower people die and disappear at an alarming rate."

"Pernicious ebriety, first to last," one of the other ladies tutted. "But Miss Morley, perhaps your father might open a charity school, here in the parish?"

"Unless the timing would put him in difficulty," Lady Grahamsby said quickly, reaching out to her. "But I was astonished to hear of your father's junior partner, arrested on account of his debts."

"I beg your pardon?" Emelyn said, unable to hide her surprise. "I've heard no such thing."

"Oh yes," Grahamsby followed quickly, taking Emelyn's wrist to speak closer. "Poor fellow wagered against his family's business, which is to be sold off all to pieces now, I expect. The banks have called him for no less than twenty-five thousand. He'll be languishing in the Marshalsea 'ere the month is out."

That the newly made countess, a woman Emelyn once found less than equal, could be in possession of such intelligence before herself, was infuriating, but there wasn't a moment to respond before Isabelle broke into the group, seizing Emelyn's other arm.

"Excuse me ladies, I must have my sister."

"Why Miss Isabelle, such rapturous violin, so ably done," Lady Grahamsby flattered, clapping on the heel of her hand. "Would I were more musical myself!"

"We can't all be beautiful," Isabelle said hotly, pulling Emelyn away as the countess coughed.

"She said musical, not beautiful," Emelyn said, following her sister to the eastern exit.

"Olivia Weatherton is a fig-headed fussock," Isabelle replied.

"No Bell, she's Lady Grahamsby now."

"Well she's nothing to me," Isabelle said, leading her sister between a pair of sentinel footmen to the quieter atmosphere of the empty small parlour.

"Bell stop pulling; what is wrong?" Emelyn asked.

"Is it true?" Isabelle demanded. "I was just behind you Emie, is it true?"

"Is what true?"

"Has Mr. Ashworth, has Papa's junior partner been arrested for debt?"

"I don't know Bell, but I should fear it is true."

Isabelle sniffed, her eyes going double with tears. "Then we shan't be spared," she said weakly. "We shall be put out of the house, we shall be destitute!"

"No, Bell, it cannot be as bad as that, I shall speak to Papa."

But Isabelle grimaced, suddenly wracked with tears.

"Heavens, Isabelle you must exert yourself!" Emelyn said quietly, turning her away from the crowd. "We shan't *lose* Hastelbrook, whatever our fortunes . . ."

Isabelle shook her head. "It's John Lawford," she sobbed. "He's been seen! He attended a party at Charwell manor in Shoreditch, hosted by that vile Lord Dramen; but I don't understand it!"

Emelyn groaned, yet coming to grips with Lady Grahamsby's alarming news. "Well, Mr. Lawford was bound to turn up somewhere was he not?"

"But then he must be out of all danger," Isabelle protested, her eyes gleaming. "He has time for parties, but no occasion to write to me?"

"Bell, he should not be writing to you at all, nor you to him; you were never engaged."

"My notes are hardly secret; Mama approved every word. I was only worried for his safety! And did I not give him a lock of my hair?"

"Come, come sit down," Emelyn said, and preparing her best protestations of sisterly support, she coaxed her to a powder blue bench by the parlour windows.

For some time Isabelle carried on, dabbing her eyes as she wavered between anger and tears. "And did he not stare at me with every aspect of love? And how I indulged him, leading him hither and thither, stealing away to every corner of the house, to share all I knew of it . . ."

"What should he want with every corner of the house?" Emelyn asked.

"Of course he talked of ghosts, and hidden chambers. But I wish there *were* secret treasure, for now we shall lose everything!"

Dissolving into tears once more Isabelle leaned on her sister as Emelyn sighed. "No my dearest, you mustn't think it."

"But I hear the most awful things of Lord Dramen," Isabelle said suddenly, wiping her eyes with a sniff, "that he welcomes indiscreet gentlemen and fallen ladies for midnight routs."

"Then we shall keep you and your good name away from them both," Emelyn said, embracing her shoulder. "Come now, we shall forget Mr. Lawford together."

Isabelle frowned. "Forget him as you like Emie . . . I cannot."

Emelyn kissed her cheek. "Well, for now you must think of dancing; you dare not deny your despondent partners."

Satisfied Bell's spirits were reinforced, if not so much improved, and forbidden by her mother to set so much as a toenail outside unaccompanied, Emelyn made her way up to the veranda balcony where she leaned on the railing, staring into the churning fountains below. The split of the moon swam through the clouds, and wondering at the extremity of change Vaela had brought about in the would-be blackmailer Mr.

Quinson, she found herself longing to know more of the vampiress, and the unbridled freedom she must enjoy, stalking the dark streets of London alone and unafraid, the subject of fear rather than its object.

As though in response the memory of tasting Vaela's blood hummed within her; vibrant notes of *Gray's Inn Masque* shimmered through her body, resounding from the ballroom like the entire house were made of glass. Yet even in this heightened moment her recollection of the vampiress was but faint, as elusive as it was certain . . .

A pleasant masculine scent caught her notice, and she turned to find a gentleman beige coated with ivory cuffs advancing from the gallery. Approaching the lights of the railing he inhaled deeply, sweeping off his three-cornered hat for a bow. Country handsome and warm of expression, he was a man she recognized at once: the son of a cooper, whom her mother would never approve, Fitzwilliam Arkwright was tawny brown of hair with eyes of hazel, fit and strong, certainly younger than the captain, if not so egregiously tall.

"Miss Morley, it is most joyous to see you again," he said, gesturing with his hat. "But we met at Dhorings Park some time ago, it was in the spring if you remember."

"Yes, Mr. Arkwright of course," Emelyn said happily, recalling their first encounter on a sloping green hill two seasons past.

"I've come for business in Sussex," he continued, "but upon hearing of an assembly at Hastelbrook I was delighted to attend; you sing *most* beautifully . . ."

Emelyn dipped for a curtsy. "I thank you sir, though I have been warned my pronunciation is wanting."

"Nonsense," he said, clutching his hat to his chest. "If there is any discrepancy, it is the French who must change, not yourself."

Emelyn smiled, feeling a blush. "Tell me sir, might you be wearing clove oil, with balsam, and a touch of rosemary perhaps?"

Mr. Arkwright blinked in surprise. "Indeed madam, you've a most discerning sense."

"It is a lovely scent."

"I should say," he said, pausing to swallow, "I am most gratified to meet you on your own, that my imprudent scheme to make it so shan't be needed."

"And what scheme was that?"

"I was resolved to scale the ivy to your window," he said, "until realizing I'd never be the first to think of it, and would feel foolish climbing the wall with a pack of gentlemen.”

Emelyn snorted into her drink, amused to imagine it.

“Forgive me,” he said quickly. “Wanting for impression I fall to humour, it is a pernicious habit.”

There was a polite silence between them as she glanced over the grounds. “Mr. Arkwright, I should enjoy escaping the house, just for a walk about the drive . . . if you would be so inclined.”

“It would be my honour,” he said, offering his arm.

The two of them descended the steps, leaving the house by the wide ballroom doors to make their way along the crushed stones of the drive, several other couples behind and ahead of them. Only the barest sprinkle of stars peered through the grey woollen sky, but the air was invigorating, and together they walked, speaking of many things as Emelyn reaccustomed herself to the ease of his company.

“Correct,” he said as they rounded the east corner by the kitchen gardens. “Arkwright Cooperage was my father’s concern, but the steering of the ship has now passed to me. We do a fair business, certainly with Morley Maritime, and with the navy in particular, though trade is trade I’ll not deny it.”

“I’ve nothing against trade,” Emelyn said, “nor boxing. But do you still fight at Marylebone Gardens? I may have inquired, after our last meeting.”

“Did you indeed . . . Yes, my first match was ten years ago now; I was seventeen.”

“And how did you fare?”

“I fear I slept through most of it.”

Emelyn grunted with laughter, covering her mouth.

“Though I was told the other fellow did very well,” he said wryly.

“And have you managed better since?” she asked.

“As it happens, I found defeat not to my taste, and have been fortunate to avoid a relapse.”

“Oh yes I see, well done.”

The repartee went on, and Emelyn was provoked to airing even her most ill-advised childhood pranks, delighting in his responses, which teased without taunting, until Arkwright paused his mirth as she stopped for breath by the low stones of the cemetery wall, her ribs sore with humour.

“Mercy I’ll burst my stays,” she chuckled. “I didn’t *decapitate* my sister’s dolls; I only took their heads out of revenge for her tattling. I always meant to give them back.”

"But a morbid inclination, you must confess; and to bury them! You're quite sure this is the place?"

"The very spot," Emelyn confirmed, tapping the ground with her foot. "But when I returned they were gone, all three . . ."

"Then you must bury their bodies in the same earth," he said gravely, "or their spirits will never know peace."

Emelyn closed her eyes with a sigh, feeling quite content with his arm as they resumed their walk, and looking away from the house she found even the cemetery charming, a green park of grey stones seasoned with fallen blossoms from Elizabeth apple trees growing among them.

"The eldest daughter of *Haunted Hastelbrook Hall*," he mused, looking to the sky. "What else has she got up to; what else has she seen I wonder."

"I've never seen a ghost, if that's what you're after," she said. "Not even when my brother locked me in the crypt under the house . . ."

"A rite of passage in your family, I'm sure. What else?"

"Well there's little more to tell," she said, thinking of vampires. "Perhaps I filched a few saucy novels, or beguiled Margaret Mettles to swim in the lake, ruining both our gowns . . . I might have slipped away now and again at dusk, particularly to Candlewood, the nearest estate to our own. I liked to lead the Bermont children in games of pretend, or hide until I was caught and driven home in the night, much to the delight of my parents."

"Yes I'm sure it was. And your governess, but she spent her keep on gin I'll wager . . . or switches for correcting you?"

"Gin. I could outrun her."

"But if these are the secrets you confess, I shudder to think what you're keeping," he said, and as though sensing her hesitation, "Candlewood Court let me see . . . the house is vacant now is it not?"

"Alas yes," she said. "Many years it's been; the lovely Mrs. Bermont took suddenly ill, and they moved away. She died apparently, poor creature. But how I loved that house . . ."

"And do you walk there still, in the dark?"

"No sir, I'm sure I would find it dismal," Emelyn said, and after sharing his gaze she glanced away, watching the wind wrestle through the treetops, before checking his eyes again. "Though I confess an affinity for walking after nightfall," she added, and feeling the energy in her own words she looked about them with a happy sigh, "the sky and trees and land stitched together; every sleeping colour made equal in the dark . . . It's an enchantment, where imagination sees farther than the eye, do you not think? And one can be anonymous, out of all judgment and expectation."

"I've never imagined darkness to be so agreeable," Mr. Arkwright said. "I must learn to better appreciate it."

Emelyn nodded and they walked in silence, until by and by stopped to address her.

"Miss Morley, I wonder if you would allow me to call upon you?"

"I would," she said, and taking his arm again she continued walking beside him, finding even in silence his company was a warm and natural pleasure, whatever her mother thought of him.

The white stones of the drive crunched under their feet, and as they passed the little path that wended between low wall mounted torches into the cemetery proper, he halted.

"But that's a strange light is it not?"

"Which?" she asked.

"Just there, at the top of the hill among the trees."

Emelyn followed the point of his finger, and her breath caught in her throat. High up the hill beyond the farthest headstones, near the bramble choked way to the overgrown cistern there was a broad darkened shape just at the tree line. In the upper portion of the shape burned two lights round and white, like hollow eyes peering down at them. "Oh no," she whispered, feeling suddenly laid bare, as though whatever it was saw only her . . .

"I have heard some animals reflect light in their eyes," Arkwright said, "but none should be ever so large . . . is it a trespasser? Two lanterns perhaps?"

"I daresay it is; come let us return to the house," Emelyn said.

They walked briskly in silence, hearing not a sound beyond their own footfalls, though she dared not look back.

The hairs on her neck tickled as they rounded the corner with haste, and breaching the ballroom doors they returned to the bright and merry buzz of the party. Eschewing the crowd she brought him through to the dimly lit garden room, that they might peer from the safety of the grand north facing windows up into the cemetery.

"I see nothing," Arkwright said at last, putting his hand over hers as she clutched his arm. "Perhaps we imagined it?"

Emelyn squinted at the tree line, leaning close to the glass, and it seemed all at once there could be no better proof of Sarah's ghoulish sighting, or Vaela's words: *I am not the only one watching . . .*

Arkwright spoke again but she did not hear. "Miss Morley?" he repeated. "Surely your father must be apprised?"

"No . . ."

"Have you witnessed such a thing before?" he asked.

"I have not," Emelyn said, glad that he stood yet very close to her, despite a few peering folk on the green draped balcony above. "But I would be most grateful if you speak no more of it, to me or to anyone."

"I'd rather not even speak of it to myself," he said, glaring into the cemetery.

Leaving the windows behind they ascended once more to the veranda, sipping fresh glasses as they shared a far less eerie view from the front of the house, looking out over the lakes which glinted like crystal in the dark. Emelyn gazed into the distance as Arkwright watched her. The festivity carried on with joyful volume behind them, lights and shadows dancing on the railing . . . and at last she turned to face him. The gentleman did the same, and their apologies collided.

"Good sir," she laughed, "let me," and Arkwright clenched his lips with a nod. "It was selfish of me," she said, "to demand your silence when I can occupy my thoughts with nothing else."

"I've fared little better," he said. "Perhaps an investigation by daylight would answer, I should expect them to find signs of poachers, or trespassers at the worst . . ."

Emelyn stared through him as he spoke, and thinking of Vaela she resolved to commute her fear on the matter.

". . . leaving little to be frightened of," Arkwright concluded, "I'm quite sure of it."

"You're right of course," Emelyn breathed, returning to the happy event of his company.

Arkwright all but crushed his hat as he regarded her, and she felt a swell of affection for the man, so determined to assuage her alarm despite the obvious struggle with his own. An almost manic desire to seize him for a kiss bloomed in her breast and she turned away, leaning on the rail.

"Are you quite well?" he asked quickly, touching her back.

Emelyn held her breath, her skin tingling at his touch. "I am well enough sir," she said, releasing a long exhale. "And such being the case, I find myself determined to rejoin the dance before it concludes."

"Then let us atone for these wasted moments, if you'll have me," he said, turning with her to the house.

The ball was wonderful distraction, and though Mr. Arkwright was obliged to turn with a few other ladies over the course of the dance, Emelyn was pleased to find he would not take his eyes off her. Thunder rumbled beyond the walls, and that the company might find their carriages before a deluge, the final number was called for.

With the ball drawing to a close Emelyn concealed a terrific yawn as ladies and gentlemen applauded their musicians, and after many smiling farewells she deliberately lost sight of her mother, before allowing Mr. Arkwright's escort to the foot of the stairs in the grand foyer.

"Well . . . I could say this evening has been every part an adventure," he said, taking her hand.

"Most certainly," she said, her knuckles prickling as he kissed them goodbye.

"I must ride early tomorrow, for Dhorings Park," he said, "but I should very much hope to see you, perhaps at the shooting competition, Thursday next?"

"I was planning just the errand," Emelyn said. "Miss Mettles is my dearest friend, and Lady Dhorings of course."

"Very good. Goodnight Miss Morley," he said, giving her a smile as he bowed his leave.

Dreamy moments later Emelyn slipped on her night dress and buried herself in the blankets, hurrying the maids to douse her candles and tend the fire. The stoked embers crackled, and she rolled to her stomach, barricading with pillows to block the flickering light. She was just beginning to drift away when the delicious scent worn by Mr. Arkwright returned to mind, and with a murmur she squeezed the pillow, recalling the aggressive attraction she'd felt for him on the balcony. The thought of it roused her to wakefulness, and quitting her bed she fetched a little dropper of clove oil from her toilette and unlocked the desk to pull out her journal, finding as well that something of the terrifying sight they'd shared had to be put down:

'Saturday June the 11th,

Sarah's vision, like my own, is now proved beyond doubt. And though I am warned not to fear him, the hulking man with glowing eyes is an apparition I should dearly hope to catch no further sight of. If not for the agreeable effect of Mr. Arkwright's company, and the diversion of our conversation, I might well have searched back into the maze for my dark visitant, that she should better excuse to me the presence of such a monster at Hastelbrook. Though contrarywise I dare not offend her, she whose tender acquaintance I am ever more convinced has been the most important of my life.

And still, when we are apart I almost disbelieve in her. I want her more familiar than a dream, and yet she never is, except when I stand in her gaze beholding her. Is not that the very definition of hallucination? But vampires do walk the earth, they must. Mr. Arkwright saw the lantern eyes as well as I did, Mr. Quinson was undeniably afflicted by Vaela's power, and even Mr. Loganbrek ran afoul of her. Therefore until I learn more of her kind what am I to do but accept that she is both real and remote?

As for Mr. Arkwright, I may say with unreserve that his attendance was a most welcome respite from my mother's curated appointments. He is by turns interesting, humorous, thoughtful, and gallant. In form he is handsome, active and pleasing. I shall scent this page with a few drops of clove, to remember him to myself, and honour our meeting, which I hope is but the first of its nature.'

Here she paused to bite her lip, recalling her contentious meeting with the captain, whose brash and swaggering presentation belied the arresting beauty of his person.

'As for Lord Van Croft, I daresay he's the sort to bear mention of no man but himself, and though he is Arkwright's equal, perhaps even his better in face and figure, I'm at a loss for what to make of him. Our conversation was not easy, the air between us hot and difficult. I must also find fault with him crowding me so close, like the storybook navy man who's been too long without the sight of a woman; a gentleman should know better. Still, I will confess some attraction, though perhaps it is only his stoking my vanity, that leaves me selfishly to wonder what he will say to me, when next we meet.

Thus am I equal parts curious and hopeful, though the contrast between Fitzwilliam Arkwright and Jonathan Van Croft cannot be overstated. Accounting for rank, wealth and humour I muse to think, ~~were I a bigamist, I might by their combination find for myself a lovely triangular match.'~~

This last line she crossed out, and slumping back in her chair she stared at the pages for a few moments before unstopping the little bottle of clove oil, which she tapped to drip its essence on the paper, breathing in the aroma with a sigh.

Thunder grumbled overhead, and after packing away the journal and locking the drawer Emelyn returned to her bed. A soft rain muddled her thoughts, soothing her to sleep . . . and soon water ran from fine bristled brushes down the sky over the bed of crimson blossoms in which she lay, wondering when Mr. Arkwright might knock on the window, and whether she should be too sleepy to hear it, and thus robbed of a kiss. The image of the handsome Lord Van Croft swam again before her, and she thought perhaps he would be a gentler man if he captained a great white swan, drifting across the lake between towering hooded statues, blissfully unaware of ghostly lantern eyes looming out of the dark ahead of him.

Chapter 8
Night Business

In the sleeping city of London, off the broad way of Thames Street, in a rented room crowded with lavish furnishings too good for the house, the Right Honourable Magistrate Taffram Brule sneezed into a kerchief, rattling the bed. A round bulbous faced man of reluctant middle age in untucked shirt and breeches, Brule lunged to grab the comely caramel skinned woman at his side as she leapt from the bed in disgust.

"I'll have none of what you dragged in 'ere if you please!" the woman decried, naked buttocks to stockings as she flitted to the corner dressing screen in only her stays, snatching a silken robe from the standing mirror.

"It's only the damp," the heavy gentleman groused, wiping his nose. "Now bedevil that garment; one more beast with two backs!"

"I'm finished sir," she said, cinching the robe at her hips. "Call in the afternoon tomorrow, if you must have it."

"I'm for the Old Bailey all day," he bemoaned, and heaving to his feet he snatched a long curly wig from the bedpost.

"And when do you arrest them what murdered my brother, and nearly meself?" she asked, holding the neck of her robe as she combed her fingers through unruly ebon hair in the mirror.

"Now you mention it," he said, standing behind her as he buttoned his vest, "I rather fear that vengeance you so desire has already come to pass . . ."

The young woman took a great frock coat from the chair, holding it for his arms. "Meaning what sir?"

"Your wayward brother . . . he threw dice at Redmarkle House by the water, did he not?" the magistrate clarified, donning the coat.

"That's right, until those red sash butchers killed him for his debt."

"And split your head like an Indies coconut for interrupting," he chortled, straightening his cuffs.

"I paid all I had; another week we was promised, and the animals struck me down for my protest! I tried to walk home, but I'd not the strength . . ."

"And so collapsed in the alley like a wet sack, to bleed your last. Yes Miss Kinsin it's one of my favourite stories; you lay like a lump until the *barefoot ghost of King Street* came upon you, preserving your life by her supernatural power."

"She's no ghost sir, though she disappears like one when she has a mind . . ."

"Well then, what is she?"

"She's real as you straining my floor," Lanie Kinsin spat, "a lady pale, cloaked in black. Some she helps, and some she harms . . . but I should have died that night I promise you that."

"And what did you expect, coming between men of the Mohocks and their owe," Brule grunted, labouring to engage his belt. "The most notorious gang of London is not to be toyed with."

"They should be rottin' under the pavers every last one!"

"Shall I remind you, you'd neither scratch nor scar from their attack," Brule said, raising his voice. "It never happened Miss Kinsin."

"On my eyes it did! The lady in black cured me of my injury, just as I told you."

"I don't say you've invented her, not entirely," the gentleman said, lifting his chin to tie a frothy white cravat under his neck. "Likely she's some wandering bat from Bedlam or Bridewell. I can tell you if she's aught to do with what happened at Redmarkle's that night, she'll swing for it," and he sat heavily on the unmade bed, creaking back to wrestle his feet into heeled shoes.

Miss Kinsin crossed her arms. "All right, so what's this *revenge already seen to* rubbish?"

The magistrate rested his hands on his knees, chewing his lip. "It was a post boy made the discovery, Redmarkle's door banging in the wind, blood-soaked nightmare inside. Gold and jewels all taken, only the silver left behind."

"Really? And the Mohock men murdered?"

"Hacked to the marrow," he said grimly. "None escaped, excepting a young domestic; poor girl hid herself in a trunk. Seven sturdy lads gone to their judgment, done in most brutally; sword and dagger by the look of it, and clear enough they were outnumbered."

"Sword and dagger? Claws more like . . ."

"Claws! Don't be stupid girl; whatever gang it was, the Mohocks will see to it they drink the river. Your *lady in black* hasn't murdered seven men, but if she's out there 'haps she saw something. You should pray the law finds her before they do."

"The law don't concern such as she," Lanie said, "creature of the night as she is; healed my skull with a bite, like fire burning and soft feathers all together . . . woke up safe at home I did."

Rising with an impatient groan the magistrate took her shoulders, biting at her cheek as she squinted. "A bite was it?" he murmured. "Am I to find your guardian angel for a vampire?"

"And what if she was?" Lanie pushed herself away from him. "You've heard the tales same as I. And that'll be hands off whilst I see only three guineas on the table."

With a sigh the magistrate tossed a pair of coins on the table by the others and caught her again, groping aggressively. "Your sharp-toothed lady shan't protect you from me . . ."

"Who's to say," she shot back, striving to hold him at bay. "Easy you soupy lout!"

The magistrate breathed against her neck as he felt into her robe. "I believe only in what eyes can see, and what hands can squeeze."

She fought against his grasping. "You'll have no favours from me! I know you sir, a justice who don't quit his bed without he's bribed to do it; well I've other culls to see to; you must clear off."

Brule smiled, knocking into her face for a last kiss. "Must I indeed?"

Miss Kinsin pulled away, wiping her lips, and leaning down she snatched his hat off the floor. "Perhaps I do better bringin' my case to Lord Dramen himself; I know you're tucked in his pocket. 'Haps he'll believe my story."

The magistrate sneered. "I daresay he would," and turning to the table he took one of the two guineas back, "But you're a fool to try, and you're wise to forget you ever heard of Redmarkle's, if you'd keep that pretty face fit for custom."

"Yes of course sir, anything else sir?"

"You'll not speak Lord Dramen's name again, or I'll have you pilloried for slander."

"By your will sir," she said with a smile, and finding him distracted in the looking glass she turned over the hat to spit generously inside. "I'll sleep well enough knowing the Mohocks got good as they deserved, snivellin' like babes I should hope."

Narrowing an eye Mr. Brule surveyed his reflection, making final touches. "I should take care speaking so; one never knows who is listening."

Miss Kinsin handed him the hat. "Here you are Your Worship . . ."

Turning to face her he snapped the article on his head with a leer. "Tomorrow I'll thank you to writhe more and talk less," he said, reaching to touch her face. "Do remember it's your body I hire, not your tongue."

"Tomorrow I have an appointment," she said, swatting his hand. "If it turns off you might see me at the window, you might not."

"Oh I think I will," he said, tucking a sovereign down her neckline. "There's a good little trull."

The Quarter Royal brothel rested in a dreary corner of the lane, and stepping outside Magistrate Brule returned to the shelter of his sedan chair in its covered box, opening the door and dropping to sit. A sullen looking link boy bearing a torch walked ahead to light their way, while two sturdy men lifted the box by long poles fore and aft, trudging forward with the weight of it as Brule fussed with his coin purse, jamming it inside his coat. "Home you slugs! By way of Oxford Street," he commanded, muttering a curse as he shifted for comfort, "and mind your path, the stones will be slick."

The journey was plodding, the creaky bounce of the chair making him drowsy, and they'd just come into sight of the Oxford Street lanterns at the far end of a narrow alley when the chair lurched forward and rocked back, dropping to the ground with a bang. The torch light fizzled as the link boy scampered off, and for a moment Brule sat listening, his eyes wide.

Fearful shock gave way to irritation. "Bollocks!" he cursed, and after rattling the handle he swung open the door. Stepping out with a kerchief under his nose he shrieked in terror, finding the front man face up in the running wet of the alley, his head marred black with blood. The second fellow lay behind, torn straight through his garments, stone dead as the first.

Like tines of steel long bony fingers seized his throat from out of the dark, and the magistrate gurgled in disbelief, lifting until his feet pointed desperately for the ground. Scarcely visible in the watery light, the bald head of a monstrous man dressed in black came into focus before him. Grinning like a pale puppet, the man's empty sunken eyes took on a ghostly brilliance, and Mr. Brule squealed like a stuck boar, shuddering in his attacker's grasp.

"Hush Mr. Brule."

The magistrate slackened, his mouth hanging open as he stared into the light.

"I grow tired of waiting, tired of watching," the voice sounded, its timbre unusually soft, with faint guttural notes as though holding at bay an animal rage.

"Mercy!" Brule managed, atremble to his fingertips.

With a grating growl the monstrous man shook him. "Whom do you serve?"

"I . . . I serve king and parliament!" Brule burbled, gripping the chalky wrist, which he found cold and hard as stone, like the arm of a weathered statue.

The long fingers, clawed like daggers began to squeeze. "Lying slug, who is your master? The truth!"

"Dramen!" Brule squeaked, kicking the air, "the baron, Lord Gadoric Dramen!"

"What does he want with us?"

The horrible grin split wider, baring cruel fangs, and the magistrate whimpered, mesmerized in the burning focus of the man's gaze. "It is power that Dramen craves! But we have no proof of your kind, of your queen! Without it we have nothing . . ."

"You would drag Saunmoor into the light . . ."

"For the glory of the Order, but I am only a servant!" The magistrate shivered as the hand pulled him closer, the scent of death wafting from teeth like blades of bone, and he spasmed as the creature spit blood in his face. The oily liquid found his tongue, the bitter burn of it inducing him to violent shudders . . . until the hellish voice spoke again, stilling him at once.

"In shallow words and shallow deeds you will continue to serve your baron. In heart and mind you will serve me."

Something took hold within him, like icy claws squeezing his very thoughts, and Mr. Brule sagged, his eyes popping. "I will obey . . . my master."

"Hear my first command: behind the George Hotel in Crawley, beneath the old cistern, search while the sun shines; there shall you find the proof Lord Dramen seeks."

With a lash of wind the burning gaze winked out, and blinded by darkness, too distraught for the burden of his own weight, the magistrate buckled on his feet, crashing to the stones with a cry. Floundering backward he searched desperately about him, but there was only the faintest glimmer of lantern light, shining on the wet street where the monstrous man had stood.

■ ■

In a long basement mortuary room on Great Chapel Street, beneath high blacked windows, hanging candles with mounted mirrors struggled to keep the shadows at bay, as a sober pair of long coated gentlemen hovered like crows over the embalmed corpse of Philip Denlund. The deceased lay naked to the waist upon a heavy butcher block table, its edges nicked and gashed from long years under the anatomist's knife.

"There can be no doubt," the thinner of the two spoke, a long faced doctor in wiry wig wearing the gloves of a surgeon. "Here is the mark of the violence," he said, addressing his portly counterpart as he lifted the corpse's arm. "And I have tested the femoral vein; dry as desert bones it was. Death was deliberate causal, not accidental; as clear a case of vampire attack as I've seen."

The second fellow, round and bespectacled in academic periwig, shook with humour as he looked up from the wound. "Really doctor . . . *vampire* attack? Shall this be your excuse for the delay?"

"Professor Borm," the doctor said. "If you've changed your mind you're free to wait for the next. But I should be grateful the blood drained has assisted his preservation; ice and alcohol would not be sufficient, not after so many days."

"Shall I be grateful?" the heavy professor balked. "Perhaps it is you who should thank my need being so desperate as it is. And how shall I undertake to explain *vampire attack* to my students?"

"Tell them whatever you like; the body's dry and fit, just as you asked," a third man spoke up, quitting his lean on the wall to approach. Comely and a good deal younger than the other two, he wore fine embroidered coats, his sandy hair tied back under a cornered hat.

"The lad speaks true; you'll get nothing so undamaged from the resurrectionists, not lately," the doctor said. "We're infested with grave robbers Mr. Borm, and as you well know they're not coming to market."

"Yes, very strange that." The professor dabbed his face with a kerchief. "But if the man was murdered I must have the paper for it!"

"He looks peaceful enough now," the youth put in, wrinkling his nose. "The smell not so bad as it might be . . ."

"The documents are in order," the doctor said, turning to one of the hanging lights to aim the lamp. "Now might I remind the both of you, these rooms are secret, so if you've no other questions I should very much like to have him back in the ice well."

"Not quite yet doctor, if you please," a woman's voice called from the little doorway at the far end of the room, and the men turned with a start.

Gowned in black with high choking collar, an imposing crucifix adorning her chest, the handsome sharp-featured lady came into the light, blood red flowers in her dark bundled hair.

"Good heavens a *woman*, here?" Professor Borm puffed.

"Keenly observed," she said, coming to the table.

"Ah Miss Winter at last," the young man said, cracking a grin.

"John Lawford you beautiful scoundrel," she chuckled, lending the youth her hand, "how good of you to attend."

"It's lovely to see you again," he replied, leaning to kiss her glove, "but I'm sure you're not a day over twenty-five!"

"I've been twenty-five for ten years my dear boy," the lady clucked. "Now what have I missed?"

"Gentlemen may I present Miss Ariana Winter," the young Mr. Lawford announced, "dangerous as they come she is; godchild of the Marquess of Crennock, and lieutenant to Lord Dramen's interest. The doctor was just confirming this poor sap was drained of his blood."

"It is an honour madam," the doctor said, giving her a deep nod. "If you serve Baron Dramen it must be you I am to thank for the cadavers."

"You must thank Dramen's merry men," Miss Winter said. "The Mohocks are happy to devise a body when none may be found."

"Hullo!" Professor Borm said loudly. "I'm a legal anatomist; I'd prefer not to hear such talk . . ."

The lady bumped the professor aside, gasping with delight as she seized the dead man's arm, lifting it to examine the puncture in his ribs. "Oh this is perfect!" she exclaimed. "See how the lower holes are wider, and shallow . . . the mandible fangs are not as sharp as the upper, serving to anchor the pinch of the lips . . . not a drop spilt."

Employing his lens the doctor leaned in with an appreciative sound, while the distressed professor rubbed his hands together. "Have we all gone mad? In twenty years of anatomy not once have I come upon a victim of vampires, for all the hysteria!"

"That is because our immortal enemies are careful," Miss Winter said, snatching the doctor's lens for a closer look. "Most who die of the vampire's bite are never tried for exsanguination, as the wound is erased by some unknown means. An unmarked corpse, even drained of blood, looks very like any other."

"Unless examined for blood pooling on the earth side," the doctor said. "But I wonder, why should the wound in this case be visible?"

"Perhaps the attack was interrupted," Miss Winter said, pressing her fingertips to the injured flesh, "and see here the spacing of the teeth; I might guess our vampire is a female . . ."

"Or a child," Mr. Lawford suggested.

"Impossible," Miss Winter said. "They have not the strength for undeath."

"Undeath! Nonsense the lot of it," Mr. Borm declared, "or how has this man failed to rise from this table and drink our blood?"

Mr. Lawford chuckled as Miss Winter rounded on the professor. "I will pardon your ignorance," she said, bearing down as he retreated. "But dear Professor, even were a vampire to drain you to death this very moment, unless your final act were to drink the creature's blood you would never rise as one of them."

"And by what fell witchcraft have you learned such a thing?" Borm demanded, swallowing hard as he bumped into the shelves, rattling dusty implements of glass.

"Years ago my family were tenants of Lord Crennock," she said softly, standing close enough that he was obliged to avoid her eyes, "until the blood drinkers slaughtered my parents, and the marquess took me in as his own. For eighteen years I've studied these predators, therefore I speak of science dear Professor, not witchcraft," and reaching into her pocket she produced a small loop of leather with three teeth strung upon it, each long and slender, sharply pointed.

"I suppose you must tell me these are vampire fangs," Borm said, gesturing in apology as he slid away from her.

"The *devil teeth*, the upper left, taken from three drinkers of blood in Moldova," Miss Winter said, "even now these are capable of puncturing hardwoods with ease."

"Well I've no use for pressing teeth into hardwoods," Mr. Borm said, taking note of the doctor as he swaddled the corpse in long wraps of linen. "I'm in for twenty-five guineas, for a body supple and exsanguinated, though I might have hoped for fresher."

"A long and dedicated subscriber you have been," Miss Winter said.

"Let us see you back to the street," and with Mr. Lawford following the three of them made their way through to the stairs leaving the doctor behind to pack away his tools.

"Twenty-five guineas, for vampire attack," Mr. Borm complained as they reached the top and stepped out into the steep-sided alley, shutting the low door behind them. The gutter trickled under their feet as rain played on the stones, with only a few weary lights glinting from high windows above.

"Now Mr. Borm," the lady said, "as we have transacted in good faith, and you are under contract to receive cadavers of no one else, we shall say adieu."

"Madam if you please," the professor objected, nudging his spectacles, "all this vampire fuddery rather gives one pause. I begin to think it were time I dissolve our contract and look elsewhere."

"Oh sir," she said with a pout, "but the commerce of anatomists such as yourself is only in support of our sacred cause, that being to purge all Britannia of night hunting monsters and their sympathizers."

"You're a politician madam, but I've little interest in vampire folklore. Never has there been the slightest proof to answer for it . . ."

"But you alone are given the special arrangement of first refusal. If Lord Dramen were to hear of your ingratitude, well, we mustn't even think it."

Mr. Borm blinked with wide eyes. "Are you threatening me madam?"

"I will concede the circumstance is unusual," Miss Winter continued, taking his arm, "let us provide the corpse with a return of ten guineas, to soothe your distress."

The professor glanced about him. "Ten guineas refunded me? Very well I accept," he relented, smearing the rain from his face. "And you must give Lord Dramen my compliments."

Miss Winter released him with a smile. "Then you may expect your subject in the morning as agreed. We shall even sheer away the bite if you like, to save you the embarrassment of explanation."

"Yes, good, but not too deep," Mr. Borm said, puffing with breath as he pressed a broad hat over his wig, and raising his shoulders against the rain he left the shelter of the eaves to splash down the alley for the street.

Blinding the stars in endless grey, the sky was heavy, and Miss Winter wiped her face with a huff, watching the professor as he disappeared around the corner.

"Do *we* not need the body, for the very proof he spoke of?" the young Mr. Lawford asked.

"Denlund's murder deepens the intrigue of Hastelbrook to be sure," she said. "But his corpse is only proof to the converted. Any competent surgeon could drain blood and contrive wounds very like the bite we just witnessed."

Lawford narrowed his eyes with a nod. "I see, yes of course. But surely the teeth you collected . . ."

"Don't be stupid. Vampire fangs decay to dust within minutes of their demise. These are wolf's teeth."

"They fooled that fellow well enough . . ."

"We shall need more than wiles," she said, beginning to pick her way along the building, sheltering from the rain. "Without tractable evidence of a living vampire we have nothing. But tell me John, when was it I saw you last; February was it?"

"Yes madam," he said, following behind her.

Not twelve paces later a sheet of water blocked her way, and Miss Winter stopped with a curse. "I should like to hear your side of it," she said, turning to regard him. "In service to the brotherhood you were to learn what you could of Hastelbrook; the Morley crypt in particular, and what lies buried beneath it, were you not?"

"I was."

"And what did you find?"

"I found the eldest Miss Morley to be a beautiful prude," Lawford said, leaning with a disdainful sneer. "She would have none of my charms, but the youngest I dazzled easily enough, Miss Isabelle. Smart little thing she was, told me of a way down through a hidden door in the library, though I never saw it."

"You never convinced her to secret you inside? Did you not see the floor of the crypt for yourself?"

"No mistress, as I'm sure you've heard, I had not the time," he said, scratching at a chip in the limestone plaster.

"Because an ill-advised confrontation with their lawyer compelled you to flee," she said, looking at him with pity. "You struck the man with a bottle."

Lawford shrugged. "The white livered ass had it coming; I only bruised him. Anyway old Morley keeps the key out of sight; Isabelle could not obtain it. And her elder sister mistrusted me from the beginning, I couldn't breathe a word in Bell's ear but Miss Emelyn Morley was near enough to hear it."

"A ready host of excuses," Miss Winter said, "but really John, to boast in coffee houses of the vault, which we've yet to prove, and buried treasure. You even drew up a map did you not? And this you sold, to anyone with a sovereign who would listen."

With a laugh Mr. Lawford crossed his arms. "What's it matter if I make a coin or two; your lot never paid me, despite what was promised."

"You were not paid because you did not deliver."

"Right. Well, no harm done. The drinking idle love a good tale of Hastelbrook, and I gave it to them."

"But you should have kept Lord Dramen's name off your lips. You've caused him no small embarrassment."

"Great gad madam, has he not accepted my apology? If I mentioned him at all it were only to make my pitch respectable; he must know I meant nothing by it, his son and I being best mates as we are . . ."

Miss Winter glared at him, fidgeting with her gloves. "Nevertheless, after the disappointment of Sir Thaniel Gliffton, it's gone hard for us that you failed so dismally."

"The baronet was a peacock, wasting himself on Miss Morley, who don't live but to spurn a man's address."

"You poor fool. I suppose she saw you for the child you are. Ah well, in any case it would appear Sir Thaniel's covetousness cost him his life, and the treasure of the ruby necklace is lost. I'm sure there's a lesson there somewhere."

"Perhaps not to steal a priceless jewel and fly off the tongue about it, lest you find yourself murdered," Lawford said with a chuckle. "As for the vault, like as not there's nothing to it."

Miss Winter tilted her head. "You really are a simpleton; the Morleys have been protecting its secrets for generations. And here I hoped you would prise *something* of use from your time among them, but just as Sir Thaniel before you . . . you learned no more than we might have guessed."

Lawford smirked at her. "Once you found keener use for my talents than sneaking and spying."

The lady smiled, adjusting her gloves. "Those days are long past."

"Then what am I doing here?" he posed, looking around with distaste. "I cannot go back to Hastelbrook, much as I'd like it. Isabelle's a little rapier she is; we had a laugh. I nearly wrote to her you know, despite your ban."

"Well I suppose it doesn't matter now," Miss Winter said

thoughtfully, checking the alley round about them. "By her desperate letters it's clear you provoked a great attachment. Perhaps you will write to her after all, and make my introduction."

"Whatever you like madam," Lawford said. "Now, as the lady Ariana Winter needs no protecting in the dark, I'll be off home, unless there's some other way I might be of service?"

"No John, not anymore," and crossing her wrists she drew a pair of silver blades from her gloves. The knives flashed and the young man spluttered in disbelief, grabbing his throat as he stumbled into the wall.

"Lord Dramen forgives you," she said coldly, rinsing the blades in the rain as her victim staggered a few steps and collapsed, face down in the drenched stones.

The water rushing beneath him clouded darkly, and Miss Winter sheathed the weapons inside her gloves, watching as he twitched his last. "I am sorry, you beautiful wayward boy; it was not to be helped," and grimacing at the rain she turned to dash through the spillage toward the end of the alley.

Chapter 9
Rising Blood

Sunday June 12th

With shutters thrown wide the grey light of morning filled the room as Emelyn perched at her dressing table, hair spilled about her shoulders as she recalled the previous day's encounters. The stern and challenging presence of Lord Van Croft contrasted sharply with that of Mr. Arkwright, who despite being the captain's inferior in rank and situation was certainly his better in conversation.

At the pleasant reminiscence of Arkwright's company, Emelyn giggled here and again, until her lady's maid began to laugh softly along with her.

"Don't Breda, or I shan't be able to stop."

"I'm that happy to see you in high spirits miss," Breda said, setting down the brush to gather her hair for a bun.

"I suppose I am," Emelyn said, her smile fading at the encroaching memory of the walk by the cemetery, and the glaring lantern eyes . . . A chill wind made the curtains dance, and she rubbed her arms with a shudder. "Close the window," she said.

The Morleys took their breakfast in the smaller sky blue dining room, overlooking the gardens through broad south-facing windows. Mrs. Morley in powder green gown and shoulder cloth sat at one end of the table, opposite her husband, who wore a blue morning coat, his face in May's *London Magazine*. For their part the sisters were dressed in front-laced gowns of simple embroidery, with Emelyn perched between Sarah and her father, across from Deacon who wore black.

The breakfast porridge was sugar boiled oats in milk, served beside fluffy cloud eggs and bacon, with raspberry tart on the table. Aside from

Emelyn calling for more cinnamon the meal began in customary silence, until Mr. Morley found something of interest.

"This George Hadley fellow has published a full account of the trade winds," he noted. "I shall have to send for a copy."

"Wonderful dear, that will be useful," Mrs. Morley said, smiling wistfully as she spooned yolk out of the baked puff of her egg. "I was just thinking, I must take the girls to morning prayers today. I daresay their books are gathering dust, save Sarah's of course."

Emelyn glanced at her sisters. "Really Mama?" she asked, hovering over a bite of porridge.

"But hardly anyone goes," Isabelle said, stirring chocolate into her coffee. "I daresay the Reverend Mr. Dowlich gives them nightmares."

"Then perhaps they've something to hide," Sarah suggested.

"Well, Mrs. Bayten goes to chapel thrice every week," Mrs. Morley went on. "I understand she is lately returned from Ireland, and I should prefer she have our news firsthand, for she knows everyone if she knows anyone."

"What news?" Emelyn inquired.

"Only that the esteemed Lord Jonathan Van Croft has paid you a call my dearest, and means to do so again!"

"Gossip spreads better than butter," Deacon remarked.

"Oh Mama really," Emelyn said, resting her wrists on the table. "If we're only going to bluster for Clara Bayten's pamphlet, I'd find it smaller sacrilege to take my prayers at home."

"Emelyn Elizabeth, I am assured you especially will benefit from the sermon," Mrs. Morley said sharply. "After breakfast I expect my girls in hats and shawls by the door. We shall return following dinner with the Baytens, for we are sure to be invited."

Emelyn salted her eggs with a sigh, thinking of the grim and gloomy reverend at his pulpit.

"And I am for shopping after," Isabelle said, slurping her coffee. "I must have some new things for week's end. The rain is stopped; I shall walk back on my own."

"Not today dear," her mother said. "Dinner and straight home; we shall drive up together."

"Must we really? But why?" Isabelle protested.

"The late Mr. Denlund," Emelyn guessed, breaking a piece of bacon as she wondered precisely how Vaela had dispatched him . . .

"Poor fellow's passing was no accident, mark my words," Deacon put in. "And whoever's done him is still lurking about."

"Nonsense," Mr. Morley said, turning the page. "As magistrate of the parish I can tell you with all confidence Denlund's death was accidental, with gin largely to blame I shouldn't wonder."

Sarah gaped at her brother. "Deacon . . . you're not suggesting he was *murdered?*"

"Of course not," Mrs. Morley tutted. "And we shan't speak of murder at the table."

"Every rumour starts somewhere Mother," Deacon said, glancing at his younger sisters, "and that rumour is of a woman shrouded in black, glimpsed about the village on the very night. Perhaps the old tales are true; are we haunted after all?"

"Thank you Deacon," Mr. Morley said, rattling his paper, "but ghosts have little interest in Hastelbrook, largely because they do not exist."

"Right you are Father," Deacon said, smirking at his wide-eyed sisters, "though even in London you'll hear talk of such a woman. I fancy I've dreamt of her once or twice, peering in at my window . . . Perhaps she's not a ghost after all; perhaps she's a witch, or a vampire."

Emelyn choked on a swallow and burst into a fit of coughing, spilling her water as she set it down.

"Good heavens!" Mrs. Morley fussed as Sarah thumped her sister's back in alarm.

"She's going to drown at the table," Isabelle said with a laugh.

Red faced, Emelyn shook her head, her fist at her mouth as a footman leaned in to mop up the spill. "I'm fine," she croaked, gulping her sister's water.

"A woman in black!" Sarah whispered close. "Could she be the same you described to me, from your dreams?"

"No of course not; it amuses Deacon to frighten us," Emelyn wheezed, having another sip.

Mr. Morley looked over his family with a frown. "Now look here," he said, smoothing the paper, *"Silent Siege on the Liberty of All London and Westminster, Gangs on the Rise: Murder and Disappearance stalk the Streets, surpassing every Plague of the Age; not since the Great Fire has the City slept in such a Terror.* There my dear Morleys, be it city or country exaggeration only sells papers; *every plague of the age* indeed."

"You see?" Emelyn said quietly, addressing her sister.

"Any way the Lamp Act is sure to pass," her father continued, "and the city streets shall have lights until dawn."

"We should put lamps round the back of the house," Sarah said. "The cemetery is too dark . . ."

"Those reports of crime are no exaggeration Father," Deacon went on. "It's the Mohocks, men of quality who wear masks of red, taking to the streets to prey on their lessers, men and women both. They've brought every rival gang to heel, thriving by the support of treacherous lords seeking chaos, so it's been said."

"Said by whom?" Mr. Morley asked, eyeing Deacon over his spectacles.

"I've read it, people are saying it," Deacon insisted, wiping sweat from his face.

"Are *people* saying it? Dear me it must be true," Emelyn said, and she caught her brother's napkin as he threw it at her.

"You are looking especially pale my boy," Mrs. Morley interjected. "You mustn't strain yourself."

"Strain myself? I'm sitting and talking mother," Deacon said, accepting his napkin as Emelyn tossed it back to him.

"That's quite enough nonsense for one breakfast. Good morning," Mr. Morley said, by which he meant goodbye, and slapping his paper on the table he stood from his chair. "I shall be in my study."

Emelyn looked up. "A word, Papa."

"Certainly my dear."

Mr. Morley's office was in the southeast corner of the house, opening from the long gallery adjacent to the small library. His windows were narrow and tall, with burgundy drapes and gold embellishment, a great oaken desk set before them, facing into the room the better to conduct business. Her father sat at his desk, a wide bound ledger spread open before him. "Ah, excellent," he said, looking up as she entered. "We've matters to discuss."

"I am going to town," Emelyn said quickly. "Tomorrow I think, to call on Ledgefield."

Mr. Morley removed his spectacles, looking them over. "Are you indeed?"

"I must collect what things I've left there," she continued, "and welcome our tenants," she said, meeting no response but his quizzical expression. "I understand no one has been to see them. We shall divert to Dhorings Park on the way back; it's naught but five hours from Southwark."

"That may be difficult my dear," he said, squinting through the lenses to check his work, "we were hard pressed already, to think of sparing you the good carriage on Thursday."

"You shan't be without it; I'll hire the stagecoach to London."

"You mean to stay with the Fallworths?"

"Yes, I'm sure Uncle will be delighted; I wrote to him this morning. I shall depart from thence for Dhorings early Thursday."

Her father leaned back with a frown. "I do not relish the thought of you travelling public, with none but Breda at your side."

"I mean to take Comby as well," she said, thinking of the ruby, and how best to proceed.

"So, your poor sisters left behind; they won't be happy."

"To miss a day and a half in the city? Oh Papa they'd be insulted. Sarah and Isabelle require a week at least."

"I daresay you're right," he said. "Now! I am looking over the books; Cavendish can manage the office in town well enough, but I may require you to step in, for affairs of the parish, if I am called away."

"Called away?" The gloating concern of Lady Grahamsby echoed in her mind.

"It is only a precaution," he said, turning over a document. "Now the tenancy, as of mid-year rents . . . we find thirty-four cottages, nine houses of trade, six farms, and let me see . . ."

"Papa, is it true? Has Mr. Ashworth . . . your junior partner, been arrested over the lost ships, for his part in the debt?"

Mr. Morley twitched as though wounded, his eyes focused on the ledger. "Ashworth borrowed far over his means for the venture . . ."

Emelyn was incredulous. "Are we not in precisely the same situation? How much is our owe?"

"You needn't trouble over it. I shall negotiate with the trustee, who represents our creditors, and I trust that we will come to terms."

"When? When do you mean to leave?"

"I have given myself a week to prepare the records. And, if I do not return from London promptly as I should like, I must leave an administrator I trust."

Swallowing hard she stared at him. "Promptly as you'd like? You're speaking of debtor's prison. Will you scoff at the sale of my jewellery Papa, even now?"

"Now and always." Mr. Morley was polishing his spectacles. "I'll not be reduced to pawning my child's property."

Crossing her arms Emelyn glowered at the high office walls, with their legions of colourful books, near every one of a nautical subject. "And if you are taken by the bailiffs, should we not be turned out of the house?"

"No," he said emphatically. "There would be an allowance for you all, to occupy the second floor . . ."

"*Occupy the second floor?*" Emelyn repeated. "Until when? Can you mean the estate would be broken up, and sold off?"

"It is too early to fear any such thing," he said sharply. "Please my dear, we must anticipate hardship, but I've every hope the trustee will see reason; we've a great many depending on us after all . . ."

The notion of being abruptly destitute, ruined in both name and fortune, had never occurred to her, but it seemed now quite distinct, and Emelyn took a sharp breath, wondering what evidence she thought she had for dismissing Isabelle's concern. "I've told Marta Denlund to rely on us, that the parish would not let her girls go hungry, and shall she be thrown out for our debts?"

Her words seem to cow him, and Mr. Morley hunched over his ledger. "We must pray such is never to be, for Mrs. Denlund nor any of our tenants."

That her father could so dedicate his life to an enterprise, and in the end it come to nothing . . . the idea was maddening, and she wanted to blame him for the lost ships, for the pressure upon her to marry, for amounting to less than he ought to be in the world. Yet in this bitterness of disappointment, there was too a captivating determination that Hastelbrook must *never* be lost. To sell the necklace was a start, but it would not be enough.

"You forget the possibility of my engagement," she said, feeling suddenly cold.

Mr. Morley replaced his spectacles. "Can you mean Lord Van Croft?"

"Yes Papa, who else."

"Well, he's a worthy fellow to be sure," he said thoughtfully, "rich as Midas, and handsome if ever a man was, but do you like him? He's never the sort of partner I imagined for you . . ."

"And you never talked of being locked away for debt. Perhaps the time for imagining is over."

The clock ticked as he looked at her. "Well I am certainly in no situation to advise you," he said, employing a ruler to mark lines on the page with pencil. "I will notate my ledgers, that you should make better sense of them."

Emelyn gripped tightly one of the books, resolved to demand ten thousand for the necklace in London, and not a farthing less. "I must go to chapel," she said, blinking to discover she'd scratched the binding of *A Great History of Naval Sacrifice.*

"Of course. Good morning my dear," he said with a nod, minding his papers.

Pulling the office doors closed behind her she returned to the checkered floor of the long gallery: a vaulted room wherein the Morleys kept their largest paintings and works of sculpture. Here exquisite model ships sailed velvet seas in glass cases, while erect suits of plate armour stood silent sentinel between Greek statues: lounging figures half draped, captured in pearlescent Parian marble. The candlelit gallery was darker than it might have been, owing to the lack of windows, with the room being oddly placed between her father's office and the corner library on one side, and the vast main dining hall on the other. Of the attractions her family had collected, one object in particular had always drawn her interest, and Emelyn walked to it now, half in a daze to think her father could be clapped in irons for his debts.

The haunting piece before her was an oversized bust hewn of obsidian, a hooded head with smoothly hunched shoulders, the carven black of its cowl completely concealing the face. Though certain to be very ancient, having been unearthed by her grandfather's grandfather, it was of indecipherable origin, and thus deprived of historical context was of little practical value. As long as Emelyn could remember the statue had been strangely comforting to her, despite superstitions among the staff . . . Often she would dream of it, though in the adventures of her sleeping mind it was not a mounted bust, but a towering completed form, and appeared always with another— identical sculpted figures hooded in flowing ebon cloaks, but markedly different than Vaela; they were tall and ethereal, looming like giants.

She placed her hand atop the hood, just as she had ever since she was tall enough to reach. The cold smoothness of the stone seemed to make the very air more agreeable, calming her disquiet as she followed a hairline crack with her fingers, pondering who might have carved it so long ago.

A low draught tickled her skirts, and collecting herself with a breath she tapped the statue on the head. "I must find a hat," she said.

The church of Hastelbrook Minister was set apart from the village, the expansive green churchyard cordoned from surrounding forest, with a sprawling cemetery round about, sheltered under the eaves of despondent willow trees. There were several dozen for the service, and Emelyn took her place along the family pew between Sarah and her mother, with Isabelle at Sarah's right. The ladies sat with clasped hands and were promptly greeted by the sour faced minister, who stopped at the end of the row, gesturing with his fingers for them to rise. The Reverend Ivan Dowlich was never seen but in his heavy robe and white tippet scarf, grey hair cropped short under a square Canterbury cap. As first officer of the parish and incumbent rector with a living of three hundred a year, he commanded great authority in the village, even serving as justice of the peace when Mr. Morley was indisposed, and though Emelyn had grown up accustomed to his dismal sermons, the urge to seek shelter from his disapproving gaze was as present now as it had ever been.

"Mrs. and my dear Misses Morley," the reverend greeted, smiling in such a way that his thin mouth appeared smaller. "I should hope to find your presence a sign of contrition, heretofore supported by a better attendance?"

"Certainly sir, we shall make every effort I'm sure," Mrs. Morley said, leading her daughters in a curtsey.

"I urge unmarried ladies to pay *special attention* today," the clergyman advised, his voice low and dry. "We shall discourse on the patient rewards of virtue, of duty, and the eternal perils of casting them aside, with a particular emphasis in the evening prayer service," he added, staring at Emelyn.

"We can only hope to better ourselves by your wisdom," Emelyn said, fixing her smile.

A syllable of laughter escaped Isabelle's lips, and Mrs. Morley shushed her.

"The shadows of sin grow long and deep," Dowlich said gravely. "Pray yet these moments, as we prepare for the divine word," and he turned with a swish, floating his way down the aisle.

"My girls you will show proper respect or face him again for evening service," Mrs. Morley warned.

"I was every part in earnest Mama," Emelyn said, sharing a glance with Isabelle.

"Quiet if you please," Sarah said

The Reverend Mr. Dowlich took his place at the pulpit, scowling over the congregation like a bird of prey watching for movement, and with a gesture he signalled them to rise for the opening prayer, a verse from the Gospel of John. This was followed in solemn tones by the exhortation:

"*Dearly beloved brethren, the scriptures moveth us in sundry places to acknowledge and confess our manifold sins and wickedness . . .*"

Emelyn's focus wandered, though she was called back to attention for the Lord's Prayer and a recitation from the Psalms, after which the congregation sang out the Litany responses, before hearing the Collect for the day and readings from Acts on Saint Barnabas the Apostle, which led into the sermon.

"Our Lord above clothed Adam and his wife in naught but the garments of duty," the reverend began, "and when by misguided mortal will this duty was put off, the first children fell from immortal bliss to sinful despair, its infernal weight hanging about our necks to this self-same day."

Dowlich's voice was like the distant roar of the sea . . . and Emelyn thought again of the ruby necklace, wondering wherever it might have come from. A long blink threatened to carry her off, and she sat up straighter.

"It is in abject surrender to the burden of duty," the rector continued, raising his voice, "that we find hope to redeem our wretched state, to protect those we love from the darkness at our door. Foremost, to every daughter of Eve let me enjoin: it is only in the unblemished chrysalis of virtue that a woman makes herself worthy of the Lord's sacrifice here on earth. She must ever strive for humble solicitude to God and king, to husband, to father, to brother, to children 'neath her care, if she would keep her feet on the rising path from perdition . . ."

Finding herself scowling Emelyn fixed her expression, striving for pious contemplation . . . but the air was warm and there came upon her a soothing temptation to doze. The reverend droned on, with few words of encouragement or inspiration, and so she took to cataloguing every draft by taking note of which candles danced or flickered. These she'd counted several times over when at last Dowlich lifted his arms, bringing the sermon to a close.

The Morley women knelt, and at Sarah's prodding Emelyn joined them as the minister led his flock to recite the General Confession. The service thus ended, and shuffling into the centre aisle Mrs. Morley and her daughters joined the throng making their way out.

Emelyn caught sight of Mr. Dowlich moving in parallel along the wall, looking as though he very much wished to speak with her, and she quickened her stride. Leaving her family behind, she glanced sidelong to see him matching her pace, and feeling a tickle of alarm she redoubled her steps, swishing through the outer doors just before he reached them.

Walking quickly along the charming cobbled path to the road, she inhaled the crisp open air as the wind heaved in the trees. After a safe distance she turned to find the frowning reverend still in the doorway, and with a smile she stopped, waiting for the others to catch up.

"My dear girl whatever is your hurry?" Mrs. Morley asked.

"Nothing Mama, I wanted the air," Emelyn replied, waving in greeting as a petite woman in simple dark colours rushed to join them.

"Ah Mrs. Bayten, how are you?" Mrs. Morley asked, welcoming the newcomer with open arms.

Known across the county for her well-circulated pamphlet *The Country Squire*, which covered every topic from cricket matches to the competent seasoning of cold meats, Clara Bayten struck a bright and earnest figure, with large eyes under a broad-brimmed hat. At twenty-six she was eight years her husband's junior and, by her oft repeated confession, had always been resolved to marry a country doctor.

"Oh my dear Morleys!" Mrs. Bayten said breathlessly, beaming as she clutched her hat. "Can it be I've not seen you all since midwinter?"

"We welcome your return," Mrs. Morley said cheerfully. "But how fares your uncle, and your dear nephews?"

"They're grown into little gentlemen, long as French beans," Mrs. Bayten said, "though my poor uncle is dull as ever. He's just completed his river boat, which I've no doubt he shall name *The Conveyance*."

The women laughed together, trading happy embraces, and after answering a few more questions of her journey and a brief lecture on the wretched state of those she described as the *Irish Catholic landed poor*, the young Mrs. Bayten pressed upon Mrs. Morley with an ecstatic invitation for noontide dinner, which was promptly accepted.

Coming to Emelyn's side Clara took her elbow as they set out, walking ahead of the others. "I never see the Morley women but they are positively bursting with elegance," she said happily. "If the Spitalfields run dry of silk we shall lay it squarely on your account."

Emelyn smiled briefly, watching the dappled light on the path.

"But tell me, my dear Emelyn, for I did rather wonder at your dashing out of chapel so quickly . . . have you some labour of guilt to confess? If you do I must have it."

"Not at all, I only hurried that he could not request me for evening service, which had I refused would invite him to gossip."

"He might have asked your mother, but then he knows you for the real prize . . ."

"And I daresay *one* lecture of such profundity is enough; now I must practice prostrating myself for a husband, that I'm ready to drop when he appears."

Clara laughed. "And it's never too early to pray for three in four children boys . . . But really, how is it I return from abroad to reports of sheep slaughtered, cows missing, murder in the village?"

"Spring has been very busy," Emelyn said, eliciting another laugh.

"Philip Denlund, but I remember him; can it be true he was found killed in the log yard?"

Strangely Emelyn wished she had been there to see it. "It may have been accident, who can tell," she said, watching the sky as they turned down the lane.

Clara Bayten scrunched her face in disgust. "Poor fellow died owing his doctor's bill," she said. "Ah well I never liked him. But you've some happy tidings to share I think . . . Have I not heard an august lord of the navy paid you a call?"

"Captain Jonathan Van Croft."

"And what do you think of him?"

"I don't know what to think of him," Emelyn said. "But you may rest assured Mama will speak of nothing else at dinner."

"Oh but I am on tenterhooks," Clara said with a bounce. "Can it be our illustrious Miss Morley is in danger at last? You are my favourite beast; I cannot imagine the fellow fit to tame you!"

"No, nor can I apparently, nor can anyone," Emelyn answered, feeling in little mood to make sport of it. "But have I really been out six years? What on earth have I been doing?"

"My dear Emelyn fret not; you don't look a day over twenty! Anyway, love takes us where it finds us, and you of all ladies *must* be married for love; the *Country Squire* is counting on it. But always remember patience must have her due. You know ever since I was a girl I was determined to marry a country doctor."

"Were you?" Emelyn chimed.

One of the larger cottages, the home of Mr. and Mrs. James Bayten was of smooth white limestone framed in oaken beams beneath a peaked roof, with the parlours and kitchen below, bedrooms and small library above. Reaching the door with her mother and sisters Emelyn wrinkled her nose at a sudden smell. "Oh, you keep a dog now . . ."

Clara stood aside as the ladies entered. "Oh my, can you smell him from here? He stays in the back, the mangy ruffian. Mr. Bayten has contrived him a cozy little house in the garden."

Doctor James Bayten was a shorter gentleman, with receding hair and a light moustache. He welcomed the party with open arms, and soon they were settled at a lovely table under the covered porch by the enclosed back gardens. Brought by one of two staff in the house, the service was scorched loin of beef with rice and shredded potatoes beside boiled peaches in broth with sweet cheese, though Emelyn found she could scarcely eat a bite. The air was damp, and the smell of dog was very strong, along with another, blunter stench which she took to be a dead bird or something.

"June is never aught but peaches," Isabelle muttered softly, toying with her fruit as Sarah gave her a glare.

Though markedly excited on Emelyn's behalf, Mrs. Morley gave their host his due, asking after his travelling practice and his wife's printing, before at last proclaiming her news. "Our dearest Emelyn has met the Bloodhound of His Majesty's Navy!"

A great litany of questions followed, the answering of which proved increasingly difficult as the acrid smells grew heavier, and only after Emelyn had endured a thorough cross-examination did the table pause for breath.

"Well it would seem you've captured the notice of a great man," the doctor said, "a hero of the navy no less."

Emelyn's head began to swim. "Yes, so declares *The Adventures of Captain Lord Van Croft . . .*"

"I cannot imagine why they don't contrive a uniform for the Royal Navy," Clara said brightly. "But it must be blue; who could resist a navy soldier in blue."

"Seamen in the navy my dear," Doctor Bayten corrected. "Soldiers on land."

"Yes James, but *seaman* rather leaves something to be desired," Clara said, smiling at her husband, "where *soldier* evokes bravery befitting a commissioned officer, such as the captain."

"Though there's been no war for some time," Emelyn said, squinting as she rubbed her head.

"There are always pirates," Isabelle said, and Clara laughed in agreement.

"Quite so," Doctor Bayten said. "And when is the illustrious captain next to call?"

The sun was bright, but there was a stinging chill in the breeze, and

Emelyn gripped her arms with a shiver, lamenting that her cloak would not be fitting at table.

"What's wrong Emie?" Sarah asked, staring at her.

"But she's hardly had a bite!" Clara decried. "We must cease our questions and let the poor creature take her dinner."

The party laughed in agreement and Emelyn forked a bite of cold beef, pushing it into her mouth. Its flavour was smooth and savoury, but mixing with fouler animal notes of death and dog the scent was unbearable, and she coughed it into her napkin as her stomach threatened to revolt.

Doctor Bayten scowled with concern, looking her over. "I say Miss Morley, but you are positively off-colour; are you feeling quite well?"

Emelyn fanned herself with her hand. "It is only the smell," she said, wondering that the others seemed unbothered. "I don't mean to be difficult."

"The smell?" Mrs. Morley flushed, pinching her daughter's leg. "I'm quite sure she doesn't mean it. But your collar is sweating my dear; perhaps the doctor should have a look at you?"

Shaking her head, Emelyn winced as the kitchen maid set to clearing plates, the shrill sound of clinking flatware reverberating in her ears. Doctor Bayten's gulp of beer was like a boulder tumbling downhill, and without warning the sun flashed impossibly bright, the faces around her melting into the glare. A whirl of dizziness took hold, and she swayed, certain the table had begun to tilt.

"Stop!" Emelyn gasped, grabbing the edge to keep it steady. "Mama please, I must excuse . . . I must lie down." But the tilt was too steep, and losing her grip she slipped off the chair with a sigh, collapsing to the floor.

Mrs. Morley leapt to her feet. "Help me doctor!"

Carried upstairs by Doctor Bayten, Emelyn was delivered to the guest bedroom, though even flat on her back she could find no comfort, unable to lie still as her breath came painfully. Her mother fretted aloud as the doctor plied her with questions, while her sisters looked on from the foot of the bed, their faces fixed with worry.

"It's nothing I've eaten!" Emelyn moaned, scratching at her gown as Clara rushed to wipe her neck and brow with a damp cloth.

"It is very like a fever," the doctor said, "but she is not burning; rather she is quite cold."

Emelyn grabbed into her bodice and pulled, ripping open the laces amid gasps of horror as several hands seized her wrists. The inside of her garments tickled and scratched, and she could feel every fibre as it pressed her skin, irritating her wildly. Struggling against them she pleaded to be let out of her clothes, begging her sisters for help.

"What's wrong with her!" Isabelle demanded, clutching the footboard as Sarah frowned with tears.

"Help me hold her!" the doctor barked. "She's the strength of the possessed!"

Wheezing with laboured breath, Emelyn trembled as the hysterical voices began to fade, and she fell into a swoon, feeling as though a stampede of horses were rushing just past her nose. The fever dream plunged into a bubbly crystal glow, and she saw her brother laid upon hundreds of glasses of wine over a white table, raising his arm for a toast.

"Come Emie, we're drinking my legs," he said. "Come try before they're gone . . ."

The scene collapsed, buffeting her about in swirls of chaotic motion as shapes and colours dissolved and rebuilt again and again . . .

"Make it stop!" Emelyn begged, and as a strong hand grabbed her wrist she found Lord Van Croft looming over her.

"We shall consummate our union with a hundred witnesses to the act," he said with a grin.

"I don't want a hundred witnesses!" Emelyn protested, unsure whether she dangled by his grasp or there was a floor beneath her to stand on . . .

"Fitzwilliam Arkwright would be lucky to find three witnesses!" the captain retorted.

The bed rose to meet her, and Van Croft grabbed the back of her neck to tilt her head forward, raising a cup to her lips as she struggled ferociously, finding her arms and wrists strapped down at her sides.

"She wakes! She is hysterical!" the doctor called, his red face coming in focus.

"No!" Emelyn protested, turning away.

"Don't force her!" Isabelle yelled. "What is that?"

"My own electuary," the doctor said. "Tar water, pepper and groundsel; it will fortify her against the chill!"

"Get them off," Emelyn whimpered, quailing at the sight of her bare legs speckled with stretched and twitching spots, her skirts rolled almost to the hips. The doctor tried again to administer his concoction, but she shook her head vigorously, arching and raising her chin. "No leeches! Get them off!"

The doctor redoubled his efforts. "The bloodletting must take its course, please Miss Morley you must drink!"

Emelyn gurgled with a cough, spluttering as he held her nose to pour the syrupy vileness into her teeth, and the liquid fought its way down, thick and bitter.

"Emie can you hear me?" Sarah's voice implored, and Emelyn meant to respond but she stood now in a dark and dismal place. Rising before her was a wide staircase of stone, weathered and cracked, and slipping away just ahead, dragging up the steps, was a long train of silken red. Looking up she discovered a statuesque dark skinned woman in billowing diaphanous crimson ascending the stairs, her open hands at her sides, with slender nails stretched to pointed claws, her long ebon hair entwined in a golden crown, before trailing down her back.

Compelled to know her Emelyn followed, but at each step the climb grew more difficult, and at the top, lain upon a slab, she espied a young woman, red of hair and bare of skin, with rivulets of blood winding their way down her flesh to drip from the stone . . .

The woman's face was indistinct, and Emelyn tried to hurry, to catch the ascending queen, but the scene fell away, and she was in darkness. A pair of candles flashed into being, hovering in the air, and as she watched the flames grew dark, clouding downward like ink poured into water, until finding solid form they towered above her; two hooded figures carved in black. But their stone cloaks swirled like cloth, tenebrous as a starless sky; long fingers reached from beneath the sleeves, and she was about to go to them when she was embraced from behind.

"It's only a dream," Vaela breathed, holding her tightly.

Collapsing without a sound, the statues became candles once more, and somehow Emelyn knew they would wait for her. "Vaela! But I am nowhere . . . how did you find me?"

"I felt your distress," Vaela spoke in her ear. "You mustn't be afraid."

"But what is happening to me? Shall I become vampire?"

"No," Vaela said. "It is the power of my blood awakening within you, now that you have grown strong enough to remember me."

"I feel so terribly cold . . ."

"The bloodsick will run its course," Vaela said, "but the doctor's improficient poisons make it worse. Your body struggles against its heightened state; your senses are coming alive . . ."

"Don't leave me! I feel myself slipping . . . I shall disappear."

"Exert yourself, stay with me," Vaela commanded. "I will hold you until the fever breaks."

The vampiress moved to face her, and unable to stand Emelyn collapsed in her arms. Expanding like the petals of an ebon flower Vaela's cloak billowed about her, and Emelyn sheltered in its embrace, lying gently down in a sea of shadows. Dark waves drifted through her, settling her manic thoughts, and she felt herself lightly afloat, rising and falling with the undulating rhythm of a distant heartbeat . . .

"Open your eyes little one . . ."

Water splashed her face and Emelyn jolted awake to discover Clara Bayten dabbing her neck and collar, her expression the picture of joyful weariness.

"The chill is broken, she's warm!"

Like mist under a bright sun the fog in her mind evaporated, and Emelyn blinked to focus, finding herself still bound to the mattress, her garments soaked through, her body aching with exhaustion. Clara pounced on the straps to unfasten them as a tearful Isabelle rushed to her side, catching hold of Emelyn's head to kiss her face.

"Papa's gone home to make a conserve by Bayten's instructions, but you won't need it now!" Isabelle said breathlessly, kissing her again as Emelyn squinted.

"Gently!" Clara scolded, pulling Isabelle away.

Sitting up as her sister dashed out of the room Emelyn scratched the itching places on her wrists where the straps had been. "I am hollow with hunger," she said, her voice small.

At the anxious direction of her mother she was bundled in her cloak and helped to a little corner table in the library. Sarah watched her closely, and soon Emelyn was working her way through a porringer of cheese soup with bread.

"How long have I been out?" she asked thickly, resting between bites, "what time is it?"

"Ten hours or so," Sarah said, her eyes soft and tired. "It's nearly midnight."

"Midnight! Good Lord, I'm so sorry." Emelyn found the food as rich and rejuvenating as any she could remember, and she missed her mouth as Sarah interrupted her with another embrace.

Emelyn dropped a hunk of bread. "Sarah my love! I'm all right if you please."

"I know," Sarah said, nodding through fresh tears. "But we were so afraid . . . I thought perhaps you'd been cursed, or poisoned, and that you'd never come back."

Emelyn quaffed deeply from a mug of cider, feeling as though Vaela's sustaining presence was with her still. "You mustn't admit every frightful notion," she said, wiping her mouth. "I am perfectly recovered, only hungry, and tired."

"Of course you are," Sarah chuckled, wiping her eyes. "But if you only heard Mama bewailing the end of us; we thought you should die . . ."

"Mama must always guess the worst," Emelyn said, sopping the dregs of the bowl with her bread. "You should know better."

Sarah swiped her cheeks with a laugh as footsteps sounded on the stairs. "I should."

A short while later Emelyn accepted Clara's embrace at the door, promising never to so terrify them again, and fighting off her mother's advice she staunchly refused a stoppered vial of medicine, which the doctor insisted should be mixed with water and taken thrice daily to recover her strength. "Thank you I am quite content!" Emelyn declared with finality. "I'm only sorry to have been so much trouble."

Making their exit with grateful farewells, the Morley women woke up their driver and piled back into the open carriage. As a precaution Emelyn was crammed between her sisters on one side, lest she swoon and fall out, while Mrs. Morley spread herself comfortably on the opposite bench, treating her daughters to a lecture on the calamitous ruin in store, had Emelyn never recovered.

"We shall be ever *so* grateful, for her strength," Mrs. Morley exclaimed. "And Doctor Bayten . . . he dare not drench us over the cost; she fell ill in his house after all."

"That's naught to do with it," Emelyn mumbled, though she was too tired to argue, and as they pulled away from the cottage a wrath of sleep came over her. The calash rattled to a stop, and waking on Sarah's shoulder she found they were home. Through half-lidded eyes she saw lights in the dark, frantic lanterns approaching amidst hailing voices from the house.

"Say not that she is worse!" her father called, dashing to meet them.

"She is better, she is with us now. Timothy!" Mrs. Morley shrieked. "Wake the kitchen! Tea with brandy, and a bowl of hot panada before she puts head to pillow!"

"Lord bless you child; here we are, carefully," Mr. Morley fussed, helping Emelyn down from the carriage. "Has Bayten any more idea what came over her?"

"None whatsoever," Mrs. Morley said.

Leaning on her father with closed eyes, Emelyn gave weary assurance that all was well, refusing Comby's offer to carry her. "No thank you, I can manage."

"I'll lend her a walking stick shall I?" Deacon remarked, following behind on his crutches.

Tucked at last into her own bed, having rinsed the bready porridge from her mouth, Emelyn watched in a daze as the maids scurried about, dousing her lights and adjusting her pillows.

"Thank you Breda, it's perfect," and turning onto her stomach she melted into the mattress.

Chapter 10
Grave Words

Monday June 13th

Emelyn did little more than sleep away the morning, though by afternoon she was feeling at last much recuperated, if content to relax and read in bed, taking intervals at her desk to pen her correspondence: a letter she hoped would be the final *final* response to Poppy Loganbrek's pleading on behalf of her brother, and an exuberant note to Margaret anticipating their visit at Dhorings Park on Thursday.

The brief and mysterious illness, the *bloodsick*, as Vaela described it, had left behind a sort of crackling restless energy that played with her senses here and again, but which she trusted would resolve with rest. Her mother and sisters fawned over her recovery to the point of distraction, but the tea-laden attentions of Sarah she had not the heart to discourage.

"Any more tea and I shall burst . . . oh good, thank you," Emelyn said, accepting another bowl of chamomile at her bedside, this time with milk and liquorice.

"You must drink it every drop, until you're feeling better," Sarah said. "You're still a bit wan Emie . . ."

"I'm really not," Emelyn said, trading her half empty tea for the new one. "Now I must have the news from town, before Papa realizes I've taken his papers."

After reading the *Daily Courant* too quickly for any retention she found in the *Evening Post* a grisly description of two men murdered in the city, sheared of their faces and left in the gutter of Oxford street. Of no mind to dwell on it she returned to the books she'd purchased from Lockmartin's down the hill, picking up the heaviest: *Dark Down Totter Town,* the picture book by that grim and peculiar poet Lord Cumberstone. The verses were uneven and ghoulish, every noun in capital, the over-inked pages crowded with stylized towers and twisted trees, and turning to her place she found the silhouettes of children tottering through the gates of the bleak citadel of Saunmoor, never to return:

'Tall as Babel, broad as the Sea, ringed without the pitchbark Trees. Tackle Tumble Topple and teem, bending tending her crimson Dream, Tonight thirteenth to feed the Queen. Trouble Tremble Trample and scream! The Last of You, the Last of Me . . .'

"The children . . . sacrificed to a *queen of vampires*, in Britain," Emelyn said, struggling to imagine such a thing, and closing the book she ran her fingers over the cover— a faded woodcut of a monstrous black fortress, centred with a high round window like an eye painted red.

Retrieving her copy of *Bequeath the Grave* by the same author, she leapt back into bed, rearranging her lap of blankets before settling to read. The book was old, the pages crackling as she turned them, but flipping front to back she could find only cruelly clever poems of death and disappearance.

"Whatever am I looking for," she breathed, and selecting a page at random she came upon the very lines Van Croft had quoted, from a piece entitled *The Speaking Glass*, in which an apathetic mirror was entreated to recount the vampiric murder of its fallen mistress:

'Neck arching white in last despair,
veins pounding blue in Samael's prayer.
Blood blushing red to meet the air,
as breaking claws and slaking fangs
bore down upon her mortal pangs.'

'Yon witness mirror did espy,
Its lovely mistress in demise,
And if demanded to recall,
Must out her killers one and all,
Or if a single monster's kiss,
With burning eyes and drawing lips,
his image etched upon the pane,
could surely not but leave a stain?

But jaded looking glass replies
'Animal screams, a shadow spry,
Are all that passed my silver by,
I saw none of her shrieking fear,
But ruts beneath my lady's ear,
And blood abroad upon her chest,
as splayed apart she found her rest.

A wanton drab with breath of churl,
she really was a wasted girl.
Nay I'll not miss her painted wigs,
nor cullies, grinning pocky prigs.
Nor too her squeaming actress cries
for pursy bacon-bellied flies.

Yet true as furniture can tell,
when tonight she ope'd to sell,
and laid immodest glistering,
awaiting even's mystery,
came transpiration 'yond desire,
in wailing solitary fire.

But I no trace of custom caught;
no sight of man nor beast nor aught,
for tho' her wounds be deep as bone,
my vanquished mistress died alone.'

"How horrid," Emelyn murmured. "So the vampire bears no reflection . . ." A gust of wind breathed over the house, and after an eye-watering yawn she shut the book, glancing at the washed out sky through her window.

The afternoon trudged on, with the only curious discovery coming from the leatherbound folio, which comprised handwritten lists of those kidnapped in the city 1719-1729, of which there were hundreds, many of whom the writer condescended to blame on the Lurkmen: men who stalked the night garbed completely in black, snatching the unwary and unwanted. Inserted among the pages was a yellowed scrap of paper upon which was scribbled a well-known children's rhyme:

'When Frolic be spent an' Daylight is dead, and ye naughty Imps be caught out o' Bed, tap tap on the Window, Teeth at the Glass, Lion's Head glimmer, the Cane an' the mask. The Chains if ye flee, the Chains if ye stay, the Lurkmen are come to take Thee away.'

Resolved that Vaela must know whether stories of the Lurkmen were true, if anyone did, Emelyn finished her tea and laid down for another nap, which was promptly interrupted by approaching footsteps, and she rolled over with a sigh to watch the door.

The latch turned and Isabelle poked in her head. "Will you really be in bed all day?"

"No Bell, I've been productive," Emelyn said, turning the pillow to avoid a spot of drool. "But I am ready to disembark, if you would be so kind," and she pointed to the bell.

"Oh may I," Isabelle said, rolling her eyes as she pulled the rope for Breda.

Outdoors for a walk Emelyn was surprised to find she could smell supper all the way from the lower gardens, and after climbing back up the hill in a heady breeze she joined her family in the small dining room for lamb in cream soup with duck, though she was obliged to excuse herself twice during the meal.

"Oh my dearest, tucked in your room you convalesce through breakfast and dinner, and now you cannot keep still," Mrs. Morley observed.

"I've been drinking tea all day Mama," Emelyn said, returning to the table.

After supper the sun began to sink into the western forest, turning green woods to gold, and the wind came stronger as rain speckled the windows. Searching the grand library for anything that might illuminate the dark pre-history of Hastelbrook, Emelyn pulled down a great many volumes, though she found nothing notable among them.

"Good heavens my dear," her father said, entering the room with papers and pipe to find her sitting on the floor, surrounded by open books.

"I was just finishing," Emelyn said, scratching her forehead. "But I don't suppose any more has occurred to you, on the matter of the foundations?"

"There was a time I shared your zeal," he said, "as did my father and granfer before him. Alas, a secret vault beneath the crypt is romantic myth; would I'd never squandered real treasure looking into it."

"Well as I have no money of my own there's little danger of that," she said, closing and stacking the books. "But you hired an antiquarian did you not? Do you remember his name?"

"Certainly; Montgomery Gapplethorpe, of London, may he live in infamy. Though I confess at the time his knowledge was impressive, even infectious. Of course it ended in nothing; whatever he found he kept to himself."

"So he discovered something and withheld it from you?"

"Who's to say my dear; he held his peace for ransom, and I'd not pay him another shilling. I had him ejected for a charlatan, which I suspect he was."

"Perhaps," she said thoughtfully. "But there were others before him; was there not an order of Rosicrucians founded by Samuel Bastian Morley, precisely to unearth the secret of the vault?"

Her father marvelled as she lifted a large stack of books in her arms. "Heavens Emie be careful."

"Please Papa," she said, setting them easily on the table. "What of the Order?"

"A band of troubled gentlemen with time to waste," he replied. "I do cherish your interest in history my dear, but the less said of ours the better. I should rather have expected you glad at the prospect of leaving this drafty old fortress behind . . ."

"Hastelbrook is home," Emelyn said simply, marking her place in *Legends of the Isles Britannia* before setting it with the others. "You mustn't think me overeager to leave."

"Nor am I eager to see you go." Mr. Morley smiled, collecting the last of her books from the floor. "But I've every confidence you'll find yourself mistress of a house far grander, and warmer than this one."

"There is no such place Papa," she said, accepting the book as she sorted them for returning to the shelves.

Her father gave a wistful sigh. "Oh don't trouble. Comby will see to it, he knows the cases well."

Oncoming night digested the last gleam of dusk, and the family adjourned for quiet recreation in the drawing room, finishing with a game of bragg which Deacon won handily, owing to his unreadable knack for the bluff.

After returning the cards to their packet Mr. Morley took his paper to sit by his wife on the red sofa, the girls found something to read, and Emelyn sat at a little table by the windows, staring through darkening glass at the cemetery headstones, dim grey teeth sprouting unevenly from the rising ground. "We must be the only family in Sussex whose drawing room overlooks the cemetery," she said.

"We can't have it looking on cheery front gardens," Deacon said, sitting by the fire. "Hastelbrook has a reputation to think of."

"Well the orchard blossoms are lovely," Mrs. Morley said, sipping her drink over a copy of *The Country Squire*. "I've never heard a guest complain."

"They all whisper Mama," Sarah said, looking up from her book. "They think its ghoulish."

"Who cares what they think," Isabelle said. "The whole county comes to our parties."

Knowing well her father would say nothing until she did, Emelyn took a breath and addressed the group, describing her plan to leave tomorrow for town, staying two nights before calling on Dhorings Park. Her sisters, as she might have expected, were appalled to think of cutting such an excursion to only two days.

"How pointless," Isabelle groused. "One requires a *proper* stay for art and theatre. This week Mama? If Emie is only travelling by stage we might take the good coach ourselves. Mama?"

But Mrs. Morley paid no attention, busy contriving boundaries for Emelyn's departure. "The Fallworths must keep you always in their sights," she said, adding to her list. "The city is dangerous, especially of late. You are to keep indoors after sundown, and go nowhere without your uncle."

"Yes Mama," Emelyn droned.

"And you must treat the Townsends with every courtesy; they are a notable family, and we owe them a debt of gratitude, for leasing Ledgefield so quickly. It is good that you are to visit, as I'm sure I promised one of us would do. And I understand they've an eligible son near your age, though of course we attend upon Lord Van Croft, so you will not be distracted."

"It's seven hours to London at speed," Emelyn said, "I shall have little time for distraction."

"Good," her mother said curtly.

The Morleys settled to reading, the evening dwindled in thoughtful silence, and at ten o' clock Emelyn went up. Perched in a thin robe at her desk she let down her hair, preparing to have another look through the dreary texts of Cumberstone before time with her journal. The wind blew cold across the glass, and rising to shutter the window she imagined for a moment she saw Vaela's face, but it was only a trick of the bright half-moon, playing in the branches outside.

■ ■

Flashing along latticed alleys and wet running gutters near the river, Vaela stopped in a dreary lane tucked off the road, detecting the scent of mortal life approaching its end. A miserable groan sounded nearby, and there propped against the alley wall she found a sickly man wrapped and wretched, his waxen flesh marked with boils. Crouching before him Vaela caught his eyes in hers, smiling as she pushed the matted hair from his face.

"Is it my Mary?" he wheezed, his expression lit with wonder. "Is it my Mary alive again?"

"I will take you to her," she said, and mounting his lap she pulled him close, biting into his throat.

The midnight bells of Saint Paul's Cathedral rang out over the streets, and moments later Vaela swallowed the last of him as the man's embrace relaxed, his arms dropping to his sides. She closed his eyelids, and after laying him gently down she stood and opened her mouth to the sky, basking in the fresh prickling rain. A feral cat yowled at the sight of her, and she hissed in return, scaring it away.

"I find you well, my dear Vaela Audette."

Startling at a familiar voice Vaela turned to behold a tall darkly clad gentleman, his long silver hair tied back, a smile on his narrow lips beneath platinum rimmed spectacles.

"My Lord Simeon," she said, her eyes full and black as she beheld the vampire responsible for her immortal life. "You are returned."

"I am," he replied, drawing closer.

The vampiress bared her fangs. "You left before the Chosen Child took her first steps; you sent no word, not even in dreams . . ."

"I was away longer than I meant," he said, raising his hands to her face.

Vaela retreated a step. "Much has changed."

"Yes, I understand the queen is afflicted," he said gravely, bending his claws to beckon her closer.

"But *I* have changed," she said, tingling at the connection in their gaze.

"Let me see," he replied.

Vaela stood very still, closing her eyes, and reaching out he grasped her head, his cold fingertips spreading against her skin. Fortified at once by the true and steady sense of his heart, the vampiress stilled her senses, allowing his power, and like a silent storm profusions of memory surged into focus as he read her thoughts . . .

Twenty years roaming the teeming streets of London came back to her; every rotten soul she'd preyed upon, every innocent she'd spared, and all those between . . . Her maker's focus shifted, a bloom of light searching the shadows of her memory: her century of service to the hidden city of Saunmoor, and its eternal queen, Pazoa Qiminossa, grown fickle and strange as she suffered in secret.

Vaela felt the warmth of the Chosen Child, Emelyn Morley, in her redheaded infancy, heard the sounds of her laughter and tears as she grew into girlhood, caught the scent of perfume outside under the stars at Emelyn's debut ball, where Vaela had first revealed her name, had first tasted her blood . . . Lord Simeon's perception lingered there a moment before probing forward, finding the queen's hulking brother, Vorsadat of the lantern eyes, who lurked in the deepest hollows of Saunmoor and listened in the dark . . . and then there was a sparkle of red, the ruby necklace, and Sir Thaniel Gliffton, the thieving baronet who promised her destruction even as Vaela drank him to the last.

Back to Emelyn again, grown strong, and lucid, awake to the memory of the vampiress who watched over her . . .

With a snap the alley returned, and Vaela inhaled sharply.

"Your bond with Miss Morley is stronger than I should have expected," Lord Simeon said. "You have allowed her to remember you."

"On the contrary, she broke the spell of my blood on her own."

"And will you deliver her to her fate, when the time comes?"

Vaela met the challenge of his gaze. "No my lord, I will not. Even should the key be found."

Lord Simeon stared at her.

"Emelyn is my charge," Vaela said, her eyes gleaming. "I will protect her, even from the queen."

"Your affection betrays you; you use her Christian name."

"I do. I know her better than my own thirst."

"Well, my dear," Lord Simeon said, checking his cuffs, "you shall be heartened to know that Rome proved no closer to the key than London; Miss Morley's time has not yet come."

Vaela exhaled a long breath, staring at the platinum buttons of his coat. "So the vault remains out of reach; your errand was in vain."

"Not entirely." Her maker sniffed the air, looking about him. "But not here; let us discourse atop the cathedral, as we used to . . ."

Vaela followed him, and racing through the murky streets the vampires came to Saint Paul's in a flash, where they launched from the cloistered green of the churchyard to scale the wall like beetles. Reaching the top they sheltered among Corinthian columns under the grand dome of the cathedral, looking down over the spine of the south rise rooftop.

Chimney pierced buildings sprawled away before them, crowding to the river, and counting the myriad steeples jutting tooth-like into the skyline, the vampiress found more than a dozen had been erected since last they stood here together.

"I see our stone gallery remains the highest vantage in London," Lord Simeon observed, looking toward the busy bend of the Thames, "though the city bristles with spires and peaks anew; even my beloved Westminster Abbey has changed."

"They've been constructing its western towers for a decade," she said, pressing her cheek to one of the columns, embracing the cold stone.

"Nine popes have come and gone since last I was in Rome," he said, staring into the distance. "Under Pope Clement XII the Invisible College is quickened; rumour has reached them the queen of vampires in England grows weak."

Vaela scowled, watching the moon as it drowned under the clouds. "Is she in danger?"

Simeon looked down at the mist settled streets. "Not from mortals. But I am made aware that whatever oppresses the queen, is likely casting its shadow over her brother as well."

"Vorsadat is grown erratic," Vaela said. "He murders livestock, and he has allowed himself to be seen."

"Hastelbrook was his watch long before it was ours. On these matters we are wise to seek counsel."

"Counsel? With whom?"

"Dire Lord Tredavius; it was he who hosted my stay in Rome."

"The Old Man," Vaela clarified. "Is he returned to Britain? Has Pazoa lifted his exile?"

"She has not, but her affliction has stirred him to our cause, despite the enmity between them."

"You trust him?"

"He would not suffer me to search his mind; he guards his ancient secrets. But he will permit you should divine the truth . . . of his heart."

Vaela released the column to approach. "Am I to meet him myself, and be guilty of treason?"

"The queen must be protected, even from her own judgment," Simeon answered.

"Yet we are never to vex her, those were your words," Vaela contented.

Lord Simeon shook his head. "She is desperate for the key to the vault, but the Old Man has convinced me . . . she must never find it. He lairs at the uttermost end of Cornwall, through a cleft in the rock where the cliff wall meets the sea. You will know it by the chime of a bell; every night shall it ring until the new moon." Her maker grasped her shoulders, facing her squarely, and again the deep sense of his heart sparkled through her.

"You believe he will treat with me fairly," she said.

"He will. But rest you tonight . . . dawn comes early."

The night air swirled around them. Vaela's eyes glistened, and for some moments they shared in each other's gaze. "I am encouraged to sense your approval, but I do not require it," she said. "Emelyn is my purpose, and I would preserve even her estate, if I could. Her family's need is desperate."

Lord Simeon smiled. "It warms my blood, to see you so rekindled, after a century of despair. But to solve her father's debts would bring abrupt and undue attention."

"Yes, of course," Vaela sighed, turning to stand beside him.

"I am resolved to bookkeeping," he said, rubbing his hands together, "and then to haunt the southern roads once more. The highwaymen of Kent have grown fat and fearless in my absence."

Vaela nodded. A howl of wind swooped between the columns, whishing through her hair, and he was gone.

Invigorated by the sympathetic vibration of her maker's return, the vampiress stood like a statue, cloak rustling about her as she stared into the city. With a soft and steady sound rain whispered over the dome, and hopping to the peaked roof of the south rise she rushed to the far edge, stopping by a hunched gargoyle to peer over the railings into the dark band of Old Change street below. Huddled against the weather like mournful shadows, a few wakeful citizens led lantern eyed wagons down the road, and leaving them to their business she leapt from the rooftop to land in the churchyard.

Thoughts of her clandestine errand settled to a deep and nervous cold, and putting them aside Vaela dashed along Cheapside to the soggy corner of Friday Street, where behind a stack of rotting timber she loosened an iron grate to squeeze through the wall, entering a hidden space beneath the building. Seizing a metal ring in the floor she pulled open a panel leading still lower, and dropping through she landed in a crouch on the moth eaten carpet of a narrow earthen chamber. The walls creaked above her, and swatting at the dust she pulled woollen blankets from a heavy trunk, taking hold of the rusting lock and jabbing a single claw in the keyhole to coax it open.

The lid of the crate swung wide to reveal a hidden trove— gems red green or white glinting among chains of wrought gold, with various gilded treasures tangled among wearable finery and jewel encrusted dishes. Looking over the little hoard with fondness, she plucked a few pieces out of the heap. "Back to sleep with you," she breathed, closing the lid with a clank, and locking the trunk.

She leapt through the trapdoor, slipping through the narrow gap to the alley. The moon swam into the open sky to greet her, and pulling up her hood she bolted into the darkness.

■■■

Standing at the corner of Searle Street and Portugal, the ponderous magistrate Taffram Brule mopped his brow with a sigh of relief. "Longest play in the history of man," he muttered, scratching at his neck, where the little veins throbbed with blood thick as ink.

Across the pavers a boisterous train of men and women bustled from the gates of the Lincoln's Inn Theatre, their midnight performance of *The Happy Order of Pillage* having run its course. Pulling up to the crowd a great black night coach, of the preeminent Hack & Humble carriage company, came to its rest. One of the coach's rear lanterns shined red through coloured glass, and taking note of it the magistrate hustled across the wet street. Coming to the end of the carriage he made his way around, wiping the water from his face, and he just reached the door when it closed before him.

With a rapid clack of his cane he tapped on the wood, squinting into the thick window drapes, which shifted aside for a moment, and back.

"Mr. Brule, my prodigal worm," a low man's voice pronounced

from within.

"My Lord Dramen," the magistrate panted, "have you come yourself? But I only expected Miss Winter."

"The lady is here sir," the man in the coach responded, "we have the both of us taken the play."

The curtain flickered. "Good evening Mr. Brule," a silky woman's voice spoke from inside. "But you look like death; I wonder that you've managed to come at all. Should you not find a doctor perhaps?"

"There were no curing what ails me madam, but I am sharp enough." The magistrate coughed, folding his kerchief for another wipe. "Shall I come in then?"

"I think not," the man said. "I'll thank you to keep your malady du jour outside."

The magistrate leaned a hand on the coach for support. "Very well my lord, and how did you find the play?"

"An ode to those glorious days, when men of power were jolly well *expected* to take all they could reach. A fantasy Mr. Brule; those days are gone."

"Are they indeed," Miss Winter said, humour in her voice.

Brule nodded with a wheeze. "Very good my lord. But I do not relish speaking through the curtain, as you know I've sober business to discuss, and opportunity."

The woman gave a lusty sigh and the man in the coach cleared his throat. "Do not sport with my patience," he snapped. "We hear each other well enough. Speak."

"I've had a visitant, an informer," Brule said, quivering to recall the monstrous man with eyes of fire, who commanded him. "I'm to relate to you what intelligence I have been given . . . information as to whereabouts, the place where we must search, where might be found . . ."

"Yes? Hurried hells man, get on with it."

"A *vampire* my lord, a vampire female, where she sleeps."

There was silence, and the magistrate crumpled away his kerchief, fluffing a spare out of his pocket to dab the sweat from his lips.

"Good heavens!" The woman's voice laughed. "What sort of madling would tell *you* where a vampire nests? Did this *intelligence* come from a penny pamphlet perhaps?"

"Nay madam it did not!" Brule said, drawing out a silver flask, which he tipped back for a hard swig.

"Where then?" Lord Dramen asked sharply. "Where is this sleeping vampire?"

The magistrate capped his flask, tucking it away. "In Crawley my lord, the George Hotel; there is an old cistern. Of course I'd not believe it myself," he added, staring into the dark wood of the coach as his voice softened to murmuring, "but he tortures even my dreams . . . clacking his teeth in my head."

"What is this apothecary blather; speak up man!"

"Nothing my lord," Brule said, leaning on the coach. "I only await your instruction . . ."

There was some shuffling within, and whispers between them. "Of all the bloody nuisance," the baron responded with impatience. "Well I suggest you go to Crawley sir. Get the better of your insobriety and find me out something of use."

"But should I discover the vampire as I'm promised, what then my lord? What am I to do?"

"You must contrive a box, a coffin wherein to keep her," the lady said. "And a sturdy hearse to transport it would not go amiss. The box must be lined with silver, and banded with chains. A vampire is helpless in the day, but if you find the creature to be real, which I suspect you will not, you must bundle her tightly before extraction; no particle of sunlight must touch her."

"I will see to your expenses," Lord Dramen said, brushing aside the curtain to reveal the long frowning face of a middle-aged nobleman, maned in a periwig of charcoal curls. "Conscript what men you require. If by some miracle you return with a blood drinking immortal trapped in a box, I'll see you requited to the tune of a thousand guineas."

"Thank you my lord," Magistrate Brule said, and the carriage lurched forward, nearly costing him his balance. "I will see to it!" he called after them, blinking in the splash as they passed.

Chapter 11
Above and Below

Tuesday June 14th

'Vengeance swarms on Storm black Wings, Dark Queen wakes the Bane of Kings, six Thrones dance on Puppet Strings, cast She down to scrape and sing.'

Emelyn had discovered a scrap of cryptic lines inserted into one of the books, and other than chilling certainty it must speak of the queen of Saunmoor, she could make neither heads nor tails of it, and so resolved to spend the remainder of the morning with her sisters. The stagecoach had been sent for, requested to divert for the house as it passed through the village, a luxury most certainly, but her father was sure to tip the driver handsomely.

Sat in the parlour between her sisters for embroidery hoops, Emelyn looked on with envy at Sarah's progress: a gilded harpist with sensibly austere background. Isabelle's stitching was nothing to this, but even her aggressive florals Emelyn could not match.

For a while they sewed in silence, Emelyn's face fixed with concentration as she strove with red fingers to correct Vaela's solitary figure, undoing the damage of her previous session.

By and by Isabelle stood to stretch and wander. "I still don't see why you should bother going to town on so short an errand."

"I told you," Emelyn said, hissing as she poked her nail, "it's fallen to me to welcome the Townsends to Ledgefield."

"But it was your idea."

"I want to fetch my old things," Emelyn said, "and before the family is well settled."

"You've too many knots," Sarah observed, moving closer beside her. "You must group them more tidily underneath."

"It's a very complicated picture," Isabelle said, leaning over the back of the couch to peer at Emelyn's work.

"It's our garden maze under the moon," Emelyn replied, "and that is to be a hooded figure watching the house . . ."

"May I see?" Sarah asked.

Emelyn handed over her hoop, wondering whether Sarah would be reminded of the woman in the black.

"Is this the sky, at night?" Isabelle asked as she pointed.

"Yes Bell, of course it is," Emelyn said shortly.

"Don't be discouraged," Sarah said, rotating it right side up. "Embroidery is not your strongest suit, but we shall never have your mastery of drawing."

"Perhaps drawing on it will help," Isabelle suggested, and Emelyn moaned, covering her face.

"We'll fix it Em, don't worry," Sarah said, glancing at her stock of coloured thread, "but we'll need more Lyon silk; this is nowhere near enough."

After embroidery hoops the three of them took a stroll along the lakes, Emelyn walking in silence as her sisters devised how a too-brief trip to London should best be spent.

"You must sit for *Alcina* at Covent Garden, before it closes," Isabelle said.

"Better to see Polifemo, which I'm certain is still at the King's," Sarah rejoined. "Farinelli's voice will absolutely transport you."

"I cannot hear the castrati but I pity them," Emelyn said, tossing a smooth stone into the water. "For a boy to grow up unable to properly love, only that he might reach the higher notes . . ."

"You cannot pity Farinelli!" Isabelle cried, turning with a grand gesture. "He has more admirers than we could dream of. *Long live the knife!*"

Rolling her eyes Emelyn tossed another stone into the lake, staring as the ripples made their way back to her. "I won't have time for such things; I shan't even arrive until dark."

"And tomorrow?" Sarah asked.

"Tomorrow is spoken for," Emelyn said.

A little frog leapt from the reeds near her feet, and she jumped as it bellowed like a house creaking off its foundations. With violent clarity the sounds of nature exploded around her, and she crouched with a cry, covering her ears.

Isabelle looked back. "Whatever is the matter?"

The world receded to its natural volume, and repairing to her feet Emelyn puffed for breath, adjusting her hat. "Nothing, there was a bee."

By two o'clock the coach had arrived, a large and sombre affair. Fit for six inside with as many on the roof, it was all of heavy lacquered black pulled by a sturdy team of grey horses. Her father being squire of the parish, Emelyn was afforded a centre seat on the thick bench facing the back, with Comby and Breda at either side.

Goodbyes were short, and as the machine set out Emelyn could not help a sense of rising apprehension. "It's been three years since I've been to London."

"Yes miss."

"In my head I am ever the explorer," Emelyn said, "but I never *go* anywhere."

"You shall be in good company with the Fallworths miss," Comby said, glancing at Breda.

"And with you both." Emelyn smiled, taking Breda's arm as she thought of her uncle's warm reception, and of Ledgefield, and the antiquarian, and the jeweller, most important of all.

The journey was hard, and proved longer than she'd anticipated. So it was after plodding over pitted roads with many stops for crowded passengers to climb aboard or disembark, the time was nearly eleven when they arrived, road weary and sore, at the house of her uncle. True to form, the expansive Mr. Fallworth was delighted, and beside cousin Tynan, his smaller reflection, he welcomed his niece with all the fawning hospitality she could bear.

The Fallworths owned a hall house in Southwark where they stayed for the season, near a respected binders and cartography office of which Mr. Fallworth was the proprietor. The house was comfortable, sensibly appointed with a colourful abundance of paintings on every wall, great robust portraits surrounded by smaller oval framed satellites. Mr. and Mrs. Fallworth's open invitation had on many occasions been a great convenience, particularly as the cost of stocking and staffing the Morleys' house in St. James's Square became prohibitive, though even before the lean years Emelyn had more often opted to stay at home, preferring the familiar walls and gardens of Hastelbrook.

Mrs. Fallworth was yet ensconced with relations in Bath, but cousin

Tynan was no less enthusiastic than she might have been for Emelyn's news, and despite protests of fatigue she was obliged to sit up with them in the drawing room, explaining as much as she dared of her purpose in town over warm brandy, milk and biscuits.

"Frusk and Partners jewellers," Uncle Fallworth said. "They'll not steer you wrong. He may cheat the low folk, but he'd never dare it with gentry, and if you're wanting cash notes on delivery he's your fellow. Now what's this heirloom you speak of, shall I clap eyes on it?"

"Just some old jewellery. I am as well seeking an antiquarian, by the name of Gapplethorpe. Do you know of him?"

"Gapple-thorn?" he clarified. "Never heard the name; wouldn't know where to start. But we're for Skin Market fair tomorrow if you'd care to join us; oh it's a raucous entertainment. They brew a wonderful public punch, with musicians, games, and there shall be two or three competing plays this year."

"They even have dancing dogs," Tynan put in, smiling shyly at her.

"Dancing dogs, really." Emelyn broke a biscuit for dipping. "Alas, with only one full day I'll have little enough time to spare."

"Pity you cannot stay longer!" her uncle exclaimed. "My boy and I would keep you out of any mischief. You'll find nothing like our Skin Market festivities in Sussex."

"That is my prayer," she said, finishing her brandy.

Uncle Fallworth laughed. "Ah well, I shan't be surprised you prefer the country! Now off with you to bed; I cannot think how you shall find this fellow Grapplehorn, or what's his name, but tomorrow I might look in at White's club or Shakespeare's. Someone is bound to know something."

"His name is Gapplethorpe," Emelyn said, standing from the couch. "And thank you, but I'd never impose. You have your fair to attend."

"Then may I ask how you mean to find him? I know my niece well enough to say the city hubbub disagrees with her, and a lady shan't be seen in clubs or coffee houses."

"I shall ask our solicitor, in Bloomsbury," Emelyn replied. "I have business with him."

"Bloomsbury!" her uncle puffed. "But that won't do my dear, St. Giles parish is all gin shops and shifty lodgers; I'll not hear of you going without me."

"Uncle you forget I've been there before . . ."

"Not in years, and not without your father. Nay Miss Morley, you must send your man or wait for our return from the fair. And by the by, what has Mr. Morley given you for expenses? I must know precisely."

Emelyn flushed. "Plenty I'm sure; he gave me ten pounds."

"That will never do; twenty I've put by, find it on your dresser when you go up. And I will see you at breakfast!"

"Very well," she said, knowing better than to argue. "Thank you Uncle, goodnight."

Emelyn's apartment for the visit was smaller than her room at home, but no less charming, with a narrow bed in one corner and little brick hearth in the other. Breda attended her cheerfully, humming as she helped her into a nightdress.

"I hope the attic is not awfully small," Emelyn said, making twists in her hair for sleep.

"We shall have to share a room, miss, but it's clean and comfortable."

"Share a room!"

"I mean myself and Mrs. Beckstall," Breda said quickly, "the cook."

"Oh, yes of course," Emelyn said, staring at her in the mirror.

■■

Over the edge of craggy cliffs at the southernmost tip of Cornwall, a solitary figure clung to the sheer wall of the bluff, scaling her way down as the night black sea broke upon the rocks some forty yards below.

Vaela's cloak whipped about her, the briny gale stinging her eyes as she clung to the wet swept stone by the tips of her claws, waiting for the tide. Waves crashed against the cliffs, and the jaws of the sea relented but slowly, revealing a sheltered pool of white webbed calm beneath her. Just as Lord Simeon had promised, the far chime of a bell sounded through the wailing wind, guiding her way, and following its call she dropped into the heaving foam.

Leaping from the water she caught hold of a narrow seam in the rock half submerged; like a jagged wound in the face of the cliff, the crack plunged into the dark, wider at the base than the top and just size enough for her to slip inside.

Leaving the barrage of the sea behind, the vampiress squeezed herself along, the path growing tighter as she went, until surrounded by crushing utter darkness she could go no farther. Wedged chest to back between immovable immensities of stone, she bared her fangs with a hiss, finding she'd not even room to turn her head, though some ten paces distant she could see the way expanded again.

Exhaling completely she stopped the urge to breathe, eschewing its mortal camouflage, and sliding forward a few inches more she found herself painfully constricted. An unlikely fear crept into her mind, and she screamed in anger, scratching at the stone that she might shear it close enough to pass.

"You are thinking like a mortal my dear!" an elder man's voice echoed from far ahead of her.

"Let me out!" Vaela shrieked, gasping with involuntary breath, and hearing no response she retreated, grinding her body back the way she had come.

"Not that way," the voice called again. "Look above you!"

Clenching her teeth against the compression Vaela reached upward, and feeling open space she sank her claws to drag herself higher, discovering the seam gave way, wide enough to continue on. Her grievous abrasions ceased their throbbing, and gripping along the rock she came to a place where the fissure narrowed again, leaving no choice but down. An echo of dripping water punctuated the silence, and hanging from the wall she peered below, finding the crevice opened to a hollow flooded chamber some way beneath her. Releasing her claws, she dropped from the ceiling of the grotto, striking a jutting edge and flipping over to splash into the pool.

Bursting from the waterline to light on a dry shelf, the vampiress collapsed to sit on her hip, gripping her leg with clenched teeth as the brutal gash sealed and vanished. Her sopping garments lacerated and torn, she slipped from the rock onto the sloping shore of the subterranean pool, finding a split in the wall that continued the path, gently rising and broad enough to walk.

By and by the narrow aisle widened, cut smartly square and culminating in a door of faceted iron, yawning in welcome to the flickering warmth within. Crossing the threshold she found a small rectangular room, carved out of the bedrock with exacting precision and dimly lit by hanging candles.

The air whistled with the slightest draft, and Vaela puzzled to find the room appointed for comfort; centred with a blocky table and chairs, tastefully carpeted and ringed with shelves in the walls stocking books, tools, and various objects of carven wood, while a low arch directly across lead to a deeper hall, wearily torchlit and narrow. The table before her was host to a number of maps and charts, and recognizing age-worn plans of the citadel at the heart of Saunmoor she moved closer, startling as the door behind her boomed closed.

There in the corner stood an elderly gentleman, small of stature in sharp black coats with white collars, his thinning hair brushed back, peppery beard trimmed short. An obsidian ring hung from a chain about his neck, and looking up from his bow he beamed at her, revealing one eye the colour of wet coal, the other dead white. "Vaela Audette de Masseine," he declared, clapping his hands. "A peerless honour, to meet you at last. I've boundless respect for your maker."

The vampiress stood before him, drenched and irritated. "Dire Lord Tredavius," she said, bowing her head as she clutched the edges of her cloak. "Why should you endure such an impossible place?"

"Security in abundance," he replied, gesturing to the chair at the head of the table. "There is no other entrance my dear; everything in these rooms was assembled *en suite*. I've been sculpting their capacious charm since the mid-fourteenth."

"You've been in England, all these years?" she asked, lowering herself to sit.

Thin wrinkled and grinning behind his moustache, the elder vampire pushed in her chair, leaning close. "From here to Rome I make my home and everywhere betwixt."

"I risk treason by this meeting," Vaela said, watching as he reappeared at the opposite side of the table, "but Lord Simeon believes you would help us, and I am to test your sincerity." An icy draft swirled through the room, and she offered her hand.

"Naturally." Appearing by her side Tredavius obliged, and taking his knobby fingers in hers Vaela held them tightly, sensing the deepest currents of his unliving heart. Fifteen centuries of immortal existence, with all its weighted cares, triumphs and tragedies, flowed through her like a deep and conscious river. The sense impression of friends, foes and fears, and of the woman who held his affections even now, in the cold grip of her claws.

The vampire gentleman snapped his hand away. "That is quite enough, I think."

Vaela shivered, returning to the present. "Very well," she said. "I am satisfied you mean us no harm. Where do we begin?"

The vampire gentleman shifted to the far end of the table. "With the queen's affliction, of course," he said, pressing a glass monocle into the darker of his eyes.

"What do you know of it?"

"I know you are but a century in her service, and as such, perfectly unaware of what must befall, should this curse in any way compromise her power of will."

"Meaning her control, her ability to keep Saunmoor from the discovery of mortals."

"Precisely. This affliction, as I have it from Morion, robs the queen of her rest . . ."

"Have you spoken to Morion?" Vaela asked, blinking in surprise. "You put him at risk."

A subtle breeze listed one of the papers, a diagram of ancient plans, and Tredavius pinned it to the table by the point of his claw. "That which enervates the queen is out of all context," he said. "Morion understands this. He fears even the purest innocent blood may not sustain her against it."

"And you mean to come to her rescue. Are you not banished?"

"I am, but when my tale is done I shall hope to have made of you an ally, the better to return to her grace."

Vaela gripped the armrests, sitting back. "I can make no promise, but I will listen."

"Very good!" he said. "Now . . . *The Song of Saunmoor*, that epic poem of the dark queen's ascendance; do you know it?"

"I know you are the *Old Man* to which it refers, though I little understand your place in its story."

He rummaged through the papers before him. "For that we must go back a very long way," he said, "to the age of monsters at the edges of maps, when the world was a stranger to itself . . ."

Thus the Dire Lord Tredavius began his tale, describing his witness of the first sacking of Rome in the year 410 *anno Domini*. A covetous fascination had brought him thence, a desire to obtain the rarest treasure of Honorius, the defeated emperor. This was a black stone of immeasurable value, said to visit wondrous luck before doom and despair upon all who possessed it. Scorning its curse, the victorious king of the Goths had it placed in a sceptre, in celebration of his victory. But the black stone would take its price, and within months King Alaric and all his house were stricken dead. The dark jewel was shunned, buried with its owner and many servants in the bed of the river Busento, and there it rested.

"Until the night I dove in to fetch it out," he added, adjusting his monocle. *"That like in size a serpent's head, a living jewel darkest red, what once was black with cursed despond, should come to tempt the deepest fond."*

"So it was the Bloodstone you found," Vaela said, shifting in her seat, "the jewel of the queen's crown. Then it was you who gave it to her."

With a soft sigh Tredavius unearthed a faded picture; the stark portrait of a beautiful woman, rich bronze of flesh, with bejewelled ebon hair straight as pouring water and eyes like starless night, whom Vaela recognized at once for the queen, Pazoa Qiminossa herself. And painted in a diadem upon her brow was the Bloodstone.

"Long centuries passed, after the stone came into my possession," Tredavius said, brushing his claws over the portrait. "It brought me nothing, neither weal nor woe, but there settled in my bones a cold and damp I could not be rid of . . . until I found her. It was in the winter of 1013 you see, when word reached me of a kindred eternal, a dark beauty of Persian descent who, by some ingenious design had freed herself from the tortures of her maker, a brutal tyrant scourge known to be among the very worst of his age. With the aid of her first progeny she had reduced the monster to dust."

An eerie wind scraped through the hall to swirl about the little room, rattling the papers. "We never speak of him," Vaela said.

"Pazoa fled the continent," Tredavius continued, laying the portrait down before him. "With the first sons of her blood she crossed the water to Britannia, sleeping in old mausoleums, churchyard tombs venerable and forgotten. I tracked her closely, for her preternatural gifts were great, most notable among them an unerring sense of those deep and brooding places, where violent sorrows had stained the land, leaving traces to pool over millennia."

Vaela watched him as she listened, and with fingertips spread on the table her enigmatic elder explained how Pazoa, yet then a young vampiress, was called by eldritch whispers to the dense hills of Kent, to a ring of blackened wildwood crowning a rocky hill, a fell place that would suffer no living mortal to enter. At the centre of the knotted wood ancient burial pits plunged to an impossible depth, breaking into abyssal caverns over a subterranean lake. There submerged, the long forgotten dead did not sleep, but teemed in unrest, and by the lapping shore they thronged her. An immortal diamond sparkling among the nameless damned, by dominion of will Pazoa seized control of them, and raised a cadaverous isle from the black water, crafting atop it the first of her thrones, cast in bone. The dead swarmed to her service, and she styled herself their queen, commanding her newborn legion to lay the foundations of a great fortress.

"So it was building the hidden citadel became her *summa victoria*," Tredavius said wistfully, "as it became mine to assist her; but to earn her trust I was obliged to proffer a gift worthy of her notice: the black bloodstone."

Vaela crossed her arms. "And I suppose your appeal to vanity melted her woman's heart."

"No my dear, rather it was her heart melted the stone," Tredavius said, taking his seat, "for such arcana respond to her being; at her touch the hardened shell of it, dead with curse, dissolved away, leaving a flawless ruby gleaming red, which looked to pulse with life within. I wept at the wonder of it, and vowed that so long as I was a guest of Saunmoor, the Bloodstone would be a symbol of her reign. So it was I suited myself to her every whim, watching as she increased by the powers beneath us. But of late, all is changed, and I fear for her."

"Can her affliction be the jewel's curse, awake at last? But she lost it long ago."

The vampire lord shook his head. "The Bloodstone is not lost. You held it yourself in fact, the night you reclaimed it from an errant grave robber, to return the stone to Hastelbrook."

With a soft hiss Vaela stood from her chair. "The ruby necklace, the jewel that was buried with Emelyn's great-grandfather? *This* is the Bloodstone!"

Tredavius raised his hands. "Patience my dear, the object brings no harm; the curse is lifted."

"No harm? It was *you* brought it to Hastelbrook, knowing the queen must covet its return. Was it you who stole it from her?"

"It was, and the queen's suffering state has added courage to my conviction. She must never find it."

"But why? You loved her . . . I felt it, in the touch of your heart."

Tredavius frowned at the table, a distant longing in his eyes. "Now we come to it," he said. "I served her with a fever of devotion, and it was in seeking aught to kindle her regard . . . that I came upon a rare pitchbark oak by an overgrown lake, almost as though guided to it. And there, six hundred years ago, under a rising hill I unearthed the vault, which in those days lay beneath a Carthusian monastery. I knew at once it would command her fascination."

"But you could not open it."

"The Bloodstone beat like the heart of fire, betraying some

connection to the vault; we made bloody sport of the attempt, interrogating the monks as we fed upon them. In fearless defiance they only chanted at us, reciting in low tones *Regina intrat, Umbremar cadit, mortui surgunt.*

"The queen enters, Umbremar falls, the dead arise," Vaela recited. "And what do you take from it?"

"Not every mortal rumour goes amiss," he answered. "For seven hundred years the dead have been building at her command; if her control of them should ever be compromised . . ."

Vaela swallowed. "The dead would emerge, to roam the land and seek the living."

"To fracture the very course of human history."

"So it was a warning," Vaela said.

"Precisely, a warning that should the queen herself enter the vault; her kingdom would come to its end. By this she was enraged, but even her steely claws, hardened by the black sap of the unholy trees, could not injure the door."

The distant sea reverberated through the narrow hall. "So your gift ended in nothing," Vaela said. "The Old Man was left *dancing on the pins of her decry, as the fortress rose from roots to sky.*"

The elder vampire's moustache twitched. "Yes my dear, you know the very verse. Disposing myself to her use, I prosecuted the search for an answer, gathering books and antiquities for the grand library, while she raised her cathedral in the heart of the fortress, adding every century a new throne to her glory, each higher than the last. For a moment the room was quiet, and his eyes grew dark. "Ever the treasure beckoned her. Astrologers, antiquarians, sorcerers, seers and scribes; she was wooed by many false prophets promising the vault, each more useless than the last, until against all expectation a scholarly beggar I'd snatched in London town spoke of a prophetic dream, recalling our attack upon the monastery, of which he could not possibly have known."

"Isatio Radamus," Vaela said. "But I remember him, the dark robed sycophant ever at her feet."

"Pazoa uncovered at once his gift of prophecy, and by the slow administer of her blood he was forbidden to die, lest she be robbed of his gift. He was forced to record his every vision, to divine how we might break the vault," and clearing his throat the elder vampire recited the ancient lines:

'To vaulted dark a garnet dove, a Chosen Child born above. Disc of stone shakes Hastel home, root and bough turn north to south. Innocence

lies in draping blood, o'er faceless twain raised 'ere the flood. Emblazoned crimson stains the tree, her purest throat befits the key. Red embound drinks sanguine stone, by death of night the locks atone, and cursed tomb makes sun of moon.'

"These words intrigued her," he continued, "and for a time she was tender with gratitude, for the oracle I had found. We pursued the riddle together, one shadow chasing another. The Bloodstone was in our power, but the *Chosen Child* did not appear. Ages passed in the world outside . . . the Black Death bloomed and faded, an English king was beheaded and twice London burned, while within her timeless realm the prophecy defied us, and congruous disposition began to fray. The queen grew impatient, seeking some means to crack open the Bloodstone, for the power she believed to lie within. This I could not allow, and so, in the autumn of 1612, as she submerged herself in the black lake to commune with her legions, I stole it away, bequeathing the stone to a young shipwright, the founder of Hastelbrook, for the promise that it remain always on the estate, to the last of his line."

"A terrible risk," Vaela said sharply. "You put Emelyn and all her house in danger."

"Nay my dear; the vault dampens its very presence, and in the queen's cold logic, that I should hide the key by the door is inconceivable."

"And upon Emelyn's birth? You must have known she was the Chosen Child."

Tredavius smiled, his face aglow. "The earth trembled, the stone door turned, and by report of a servant, north to south the seal of the tree aligned, just as Radamus had described. Pazoa summoned me to court, demanding the Bloodstone's return, meaning to snatch the girl from home, for ritual sacrifice in the depths of Umbremar. I refused."

"And what is to stop you attempting the same on your own?" Vaela challenged, rising again from her chair. "Will you seek Emelyn's sacrifice, to breach the vault?"

"By no means," he said, shuffling through his papers. "For you see, on the night of her birth there was heard not only the shaking ground, but whispers, spoken far below."

Vaela sank into her seat. "Whispers? What whispers?"

"Sola coronam inveniet."

"Only she will find the crown," Vaela translated.

"Yes; but of course the queen is crowned already, and has been warned to come not near it . . ."

"Then what does it mean?"

"It means the vault has more to teach us," he said, slipping like a shadow behind her chair, "it means the Chosen Child must live, for I believe she alone will open the door. And now, I must taste her."

"Taste her?" Vaela asked, finding him very close beside her.

"I can read neither hearts nor minds, nor have I power over dreams as Vorsadat," he said, running a nail down her cheek. "Mine is to sense the story of the blood, to bear vicarious witness to every drop you have shed, touched or tasted, and Emelyn Morley's essence flows in your veins."

Vaela sat very still as he sniffed at her neck. His mouth opened, and she stopped his face with her hand, gently pushing him away. "Not my throat," she said, offering her upturned palm.

The Old Man wheezed with chuckles, taking hold of it. His teeth stretched to points, and with a snarl he crunched into her wrist.

The vampiress gripped the chair with a gasp, baring her fangs, as sensitive beyond its mortal genesis her skin crackled with pleasure, her veins throbbing at the sucking pull of his lips.

Grunting with delight the elder held firm, and she protested his squeezing tendril grip. "Enough, stop!"

With a spluttering cough he released her, hunching over the table as though near to collapse. "Magnificent!" he rasped, wiping his lips. "Heady sweet sharpness of life! I have never savoured such vitae; the Bloodstone is the key, but *she* will show us the way. I must return to the queen's favour, for though in her anger she banished him, I must pour over the scrawls Radamus left to us, and you must help me."

"You imagine I have some power against your exile?" Vaela asked, gripping the fading hurt as she rose to her feet.

"By this, Pazoa's most precious gift to me, you will," he said, snapping the black ring off its chain about his neck. "Like the Bloodstone, this ring bears a power of its own. Deliver it to her."

"And this will restore her trust?" Vaela asked, scowling at the obsidian band as she accepted it.

"It will buy me her audience, whereupon I shall curry favour by the revelation of her brother's treachery."

"Vorsadat . . . I cannot abide him," Vaela said. "But what proof could you offer of his betrayal?"

"I have observed him robbing graves for miles along the Thames; this the queen strictly forbade him."

"A minor infraction; he has been drinking the blood of the dead for centuries. He is inured to its poison.”

“He is not feeding on the corpses, he is collecting them,” Tredavius replied. “But I have more than this; he plots against the queen’s own children, he means to expose them . . . to mortals.”

Vaela stared at him. “How can you know this? Whom does he mean to expose?”

Tredavius grinned, and like a melting shadow he faded into the dark. “I am of no material use to you in exile,” he said. “I must return to her side. Have faith . . . Vaela Audette.”

Making her exit from the hidden lair the vampiress found the squeeze less harrowing, if only marginally more comfortable, and reaching the crashing edge of the salt sea she scaled the rocks, standing a few moments on the swept grass under a troubled sky by the edge of the cliff. Wet sand sparkled in the mist, lashing against her skin, and she closed her eyes, thriving in the wide open air for a breath, before vanishing the way she had come.

∎ ∎

Wednesday June 15ᵗʰ

The next morning Emelyn woke to find a severe silver sky outside her window, and anticipating a day of hard business she donned a high-necked gown of green with short gloves. Opting for a matching hooded cloak she went without a hat, standing in the hall outside her room as she entrusted Comby to have a card sent to Ledgefield announcing her intention to visit.

“I am obliged for breakfast with my uncle,” she said quietly, passing him the grand ruby necklace wrapped in linen, “but we dare not waste a minute. Straight to the jeweller you understand, and straight back.”

“Yes miss.”

“Cash or promissory notes,” she instructed. “Sight draft, payable to my father at once, not some future date. I want it settled today, whatever you can get. And no bullion, no coin.”

“You may rely on me.”

With a bow Comby was off, and Emelyn came down, finding her uncle and cousin already at the table for a hearty meal of black bread and roasted beef stew.

"Your good fellow is off in a hurry," Uncle Fallworth noted, dabbing his mouth.

"Just a spot of business," Emelyn said, watching as the footman filled her glass with a sweet scented wine.

"There is a charming market but a small walk from here," Fallworth said. "But you must wander no farther until we return; then I'm happy to join the search for this Dapplethor person."

"Gapplethorpe. Thank you Uncle, but you forget I must pay a call on our tenants at Ledgefield. St. James's Square is safe enough."

"Ah, quite right. But bring your man with you, all the same. You don't know the city as your sisters do."

"Of course."

"Cousin if I may," Tynan said, "perhaps you'll have time to watch my lessons with the fencing master this afternoon, and quarterstaff. I am told my progress is very good."

Emelyn smiled at him. "I've no doubt," she said, sipping her wine.

Breakfast ran its slow course, and ten o'clock found her standing in the foyer, waiting impatiently as footmen helped the men into their coats.

"Kiss me my dear, and bestow us a bit of luck!" her uncle said cheerfully, snapping on his hat. "I took four guineas at ninepins last year."

"Then I hope you win eight." Emelyn kissed his cheek, wishing them both a grand time.

There was yet no sign of Comby, and to soothe her restlessness she took to the library, where she found in her uncle's predictable collection little of interest. By and by she rang the bell for Breda to join her, and moving to the front parlour took her seat on a slender couch to hold open the book she'd selected on a whim: *The Gentleman's Adjunct: A Feasible Guide to Accoutrements for Every Social Diversion.*

The clock on the mantle ticked without any progress, and after some while pretending to read she set down her book as Breda did the same.

"Should I not go upstairs miss?" Breda asked.

"I don't want to wait alone," Emelyn said. "But I've not been stupid have I? Dispatching him with such a treasure in his pocket?"

"Comby's a clever one miss. He was raised here; he knows his way around the corners."

Emelyn nodded, picking up her book to try again. Time passed, and if not for the anxious beat of her heart she might have drifted off . . . but it was not until the tar pit of a passage extolling the fashion of nosegays and watch chains, that the world turned to nothing behind her eyelids, and she was just drooping into sleep when there came a knock at the door.

The hoped for footman had returned, having not only succeeded in his bid to sell the necklace at Frusk & Partners, but for more than the amount Emelyn had hoped for.

"Twelve thousand!" Emelyn marvelled. "Could he afford such a trade? Did he not negotiate?"

"It were like it enchanted him miss, the way he stared into that jewel," Comby related, presenting her the bills of exchange. "So I talked him up. No gold, no coin, but thousand pound notes on the Bank of England, made out to your father as you asked."

Emelyn accepted the cash, and unable to restrain herself she embraced him.

"Happy to do it miss," he said quickly, stiffening in surprise.

"Apologies," she said breathlessly. "Thank you Comby, very well done. Now with luck we shall find the antiquarian before dinner; but first the office of Mr. Cavendish."

"There's something else miss. On my way betwixt coach and jeweller I'll wager I was followed."

"By whom?" Emelyn asked, and pulling on her travelling cloak she caught a lingering glance between Comby and Breda.

"A dark imposing sort of fellow he was," Comby said, accompanying her down the steps to the street, "even through the crowd I could hear the tap of his cane."

Emelyn scowled at the thought. "But you sold the necklace and went about your business unmolested. Perhaps you were mistaken."

"Yes miss, perhaps I was."

With a piercing whistle the footman hailed a hackney coach, and in a moment they were off, driving a short way to the water before heading west on Willow Street along the river wall. Presently they came to the decrepit Old Barge House Stairs leading down from the wall to the riverbank, where Emelyn hired a wherry boat to paddle them across, taking the nearest of three beached close by. The scullers of the other two called out, promising to carry her faster and smoother, but she paid them no heed, requiring all her attention to climb unsteadily aboard the vessel she'd chosen. Three other passengers joined, with two men at the oars, and as the boat pushed into the rush of the Thames she recalled at once her preference for travel by land.

"Do ye know there be fifteen hundred wherries on the river

hereabouts these days!" one of the passengers offered cheerfully, seeming to take note of her discomfort. "Many hundreds of sail yachts and barges besides; that'll be the chop miss! The currents never been so fussy as they are now."

Emelyn nodded with a smile, pulling her hood close. Clear as day the river teemed with boats beyond count, and after a brutal fording in hard currents they drew near Dorset Stairs at the other side, grinding past several other vessels along the way, which the rowers employed oars to shove off, trading bursts of colourful language with the watermen. At last the little boat came to, and with a gasp Emelyn disembarked, accepting Comby's assistance on the slippery dock.

A Hack & Humble coach appeared almost to be waiting for them at the timber wharf above, and grateful to be off the water the pair of them climbed in with all haste.

The busy streets by daylight were as cacophonous as Emelyn could have expected. Working men and women bustled across the muddy road with little regard for their own safety as young boys banged on the carriage windows, jumping to peer inside. These the coachman drove off with threats of the horsewhip, while other vehicles trundled past dangerously close, their own drivers shouting at the heedless traffic to clear a path.

"I really don't miss the city noise," Emelyn said, smiling for composure as she jostled, her stomach yet settling from the water.

"Nor I miss," Comby said.

"Adam," she said, "I must ask, is there anything . . . romantic, between yourself and Breda?"

Comby swallowed. "No miss."

"And if I put the question to her, would she answer the same?"

"Yes miss," he replied, lowering his eyes.

"Then I shall speak no more of it," Emelyn said, leaning back. "But Mrs. Morley takes a dim view of such things among the staff, as I'm sure you know. You must be careful."

"Yes miss."

The Oxford Street office of Julian Cavendish, Mr. Morley's solicitor, was far less grand than Emelyn remembered; wedged tightly between two storefronts in ill repair, it resembled more a neglected bookseller than a proper legal office. Stepping down from the carriage, she was about to enter when a tired looking young woman, with the clothes and air of a domestic, tripped full into her. Comby caught the girl, yanking her away by the wrist, and after a brief exchange of urban pleasantries she huffed off on her way.

"Pickpocket miss; mustn't let them roust you."

"Of course, thank you," Emelyn said, catching her breath.

Mr. Cavendish himself, whom she remembered most for being oddly tall, was an austere squinty sort of gentleman, his long coats too snug for his slender frame, lending him the aspect of a respectable scarecrow. Entering with Comby at her side Emelyn found the room crowded with desks, one at either hand and the largest straight before her, leaving little room to access the cramped shelves beyond.

"Good day sir," she said.

The Morley solicitor stood in the back by a dingy little window, which he opened and closed by a crank as he scrubbed at what appeared to be soot stains on the glass. "We're two storeys above the back alley you know," he said, scrubbing all the harder, "and still they make a game of throwing things into my window. Ruffians!"

"Mr. Cavendish," Emelyn said, "I am certain you'll remember me, though it's been some years . . ."

"Miss Morley!" he exclaimed, turning sharply to face her, his eyes wide. "And Adam Comberland, if memory serves. To what do I owe the pleasure?"

"I am here for Morley Maritime," she said. "But I see your eye is better; a full recovery I hope?"

"I might have died as it happens, when that feckless knave lobbed a bottle for my head," he said, crinkling his mouth. "The doctor expected I should suffer bruising of the brain, but I've the luck of a Cavendish, and I suppose I have been adequately compensated."

Emelyn approached the large desk that stood between them. "By Mr. Lawford? Have you seen him?"

"Certainly not, but a magistrate, *The Honourable Taffram Brule*. A hundred guineas he gave for my signature, that I should pursue the insult no further. Now then," he said, rubbing his hands with a tight grin. "As you can see, you find us in some state of transition; this my desk here, and your father's there."

"My father's?" Beneath small inaccessible windows, Emelyn found the humble desk to her right woefully unkempt, laden with books and scattershot papers, with portraits of herself and her brother by the case clock.

"You'll forgive the disorder," Cavendish said. "The move from his office in the Square was abrupt. Upon my generosity I offered him this space, for meetings and business.”

“Meetings here? Do the partners not meet at the club, at White’s?”

“They do.” Mr. Cavendish nodded. “Regrettably, it seems your father’s membership is in arrears. But then as my own fees have not been paid for six months, I quite understand,” and he smiled again, squinting his narrow eyes.

“Well, I am here to remit monies for deposit on my father’s behalf,” she said. “Twelve thousand pounds sterling.”

“I beg your pardon.”

“I have it here,” she said, and unfolding her purse she took out the promissory notes. “There is an urgent payment to see to, is there not? To our creditors, on the matter of the lost ships?”

Mr. Cavendish blinked in disbelief. “Indeed . . . without ten thousand to the trustee they will administer.”

“And how quickly?”

“They have stipulated but two weeks, Miss Morley.”

“Then we’re just in time.”

“Perhaps, were I at liberty to accept it.”

“Of course you are,” she said, holding out the bills for him to take.

“I do beg your pardon, Miss Morley, but where has the money come from?”

“I’ve sold an heirloom, a rare jewel of my own property.”

Mr. Cavendish smiled, unmoved. “Alas, it would be highly irregular for me accept any such sum from *Miss* Morley, without her father present.”

“But the notes are payable to Mr. Morley, not myself.”

“Ah but I cannot vouch for the source of this windfall.”

“But I’ve just told you.”

Cavendish waved his hands with a grimace, as though to ward off evil spirits. “My reputation Miss Morley, is august. If you’ve sold property from your estate without your father’s knowledge . . .”

“Mr. Cavendish, I have only disposed of my own property.”

The lawyer grimaced again. “To invest in financial matters, a woman is obliged to do so in company, lest the bank refuse.”

“Then accompany me!” she said hotly, shaking the bills. “Act as my witness. Are you not empowered to conduct business on my father’s behalf?”

“Indeed Madam, therefore produce Mr. Morley himself, or his permission in writing, and I am happy to proceed.”

“This is absurd,” she protested, dropping her arm. “So I’ve no recourse but to store twelve thousand pounds on my person, until I return home?"

"I should put it in a strongbox, were I you," he said. "If lost, the jeweller may well refuse to replace them, fearing fraud."

Biting her tongue she opened her purse, sharply folding the bills to put them back, all but one. "You will take one of these, one thousand pounds. From it you shall deduct what you are owed, and pay my father's dues at the club."

Mr. Cavendish stared at her, tilting his head as though to consider, and taking the bill he scraped back his chair to sit.

"I should like a receipt of payment," she said, watching as he dragged up a ledger, wetting his thumb to crack it open.

"By all means," he said, peeling off the paper cap to open a bottle of ink.

Emelyn cleared her throat. "Will you not reconsider, for the whole amount?"

"Your father must be ever proud of your spirit," he said, pruning the end of a quill pen to prepare it for writing. "My heart goes out to your family, truly it does, though we find Morley Maritime in good and dismal company of late."

Emelyn watched him, wondering if he would ever dip the pen. "Good and dismal company?"

"Reports date back a year at least, but these three or four months other firms have fared worse than Morley Maritime, even the Royal Navy. The total must be some twenty ships lost, by now."

"*Twenty?*"

Mr. Cavendish nodded, his effected cheer sinking to a frown. "Whispers of heavy black storms which dissipate by day, only to reform at night, hanging like death over the sea away west. Rumours and nonsense I shouldn't wonder. The truth is pirates most certainly."

"Is it?"

"Who can say." He responded, scratching out the receipt.

Emelyn perused the document. "Thank you, but would you happen to know of an antiquarian hired by my father some years ago, one Montgomery Gapplethorpe?"

"Now there's a name I never thought to hear again," Cavendish said, giving her a quizzical look. "I remember him; off his perch I should say. If not for me the rascal might have taken your father for more than he did."

"Well, whatever he learned of the crypt beneath the house, he kept the best bits for himself. Do you know where I might find him?"

"Find him?" Cavendish chuckled uneasily. "Whatever for?"

"I've just paid your fees, Mr. Cavendish. If you know where he is I'll have it."

"Your pardon, Miss Morley, of course . . . If memory serves he owns a seedy little concern near Seven Dials."

"Seven Dials," Emelyn repeated with dismay, recalling it for one of the most troubled places in the city, if the *Gentleman's Magazine* was any authority.

"Of course you'll steer clear of it," he said. "Bloody riots not a week ago, two gin shops ransacked. And this week the parades; send your manservant if you must."

"What parades?"

"The *Mohock elections* they're calling them, hoodlums and footpads called out for a show of force. A great amusement I've no doubt, men masked in red with naught better than to bully the public."

"How diverting," she said. "Good afternoon, Mr. Cavendish," and she turned to leave, swishing outside as Comby held the door.

"I should abide the lawyer's advice miss," Comby said, taking her hand as she stepped up into the carriage. "I might go on my own to meet your antiquarian, and report back. I shouldn't advise bringing those bank notes."

"They'd be worthless in the hands of a thief," she said, nervously exhilarated as she took her seat. "We've wasted enough time as it is; we shall go together."

"Very well miss," Comby said, sitting across from her.

Chapter 12
The Men in Red

Emelyn knew St. Giles parish for one of the poorest in London, though she had never been, and the road through proved harder than expected. Twice they were obliged to stop for broken or abandoned vehicles in the way, which were only cleared by generous application of British pound notes, with one of the men attempting to change her good money for bad before Comby put a stop to it.

"Is there any manner of extortion they've not tried?" Emelyn grumbled, adjusting her comfort as they resumed their route.

"The sharpers know you for country gentry miss," Comby replied.

"Even hooded and cloaked?"

"It's a fine cloak," he said.

Emelyn said nothing more until the coach slowed to a halt amidst the chaotic sound of crowds and trumpets. "The parade?" she said, leaning to peer out the window.

Outside the scene found Mr. Cavendish as good as his word. A surge of men were marching past the doors, clogging the road as they swung their elbows and kicked up their knees. Many of these wore hideous red masks, with crimson belts or sashes, while out the other window she found a motley assortment of spectators, men and women ogling from windows or standing by the street, clapping along to the tuneless music.

"The wall side miss," Comby said, and climbing out away from the parade he took her hand to help her down.

"Is this Great Earl Street?" she asked, calling up to the driver.

"It's James ma'am," he answered, touching his hat. "Cross Long Acre, cross Castle, and you'll see the pillar at Seven Dials right enough, though were I you I'd go t'other way."

"Yes thank you," Emelyn said, handing him up some coins.

"Keep behind me," Comby said, directing her to walk away from the gutter along the wall as they made their way. "Don't let them have the wall of you."

"Don't let them what?" Emelyn hurried to keep up. "Why not?"

"Keep to the wall, lest we get knocked down on pretence and clean robbed."

Emelyn pulled her cloak tighter. "I'm sure you're aware plenty of highborn ladies visit the poor quarters for charity, and tending to the sick."

"Not so many as you think miss."

Ramshackle buildings sagged over the wet crowded street, the haze of innumerable kitchen chimneys dimming the sky, and Emelyn found the scene more vividly squalid than newspapers or novels had led her to believe. But to witness so many markedly sick with the burdens of poverty and addiction was incredible, their distracted wonder for the parade notwithstanding . . .

"It pains my heart; they are brave one and all," she said, crouching to leave several pound notes in the box of an unresponsive man with swollen watery eyes, who sat with a little boy asleep beside him.

"That's too much miss," Comby admonished, and reclaiming the bills he returned them to her, dropping coins in their place. "He'd be robbed the moment we're clear."

"You can't know that for certain," she said, folding the cash to tuck it hidden in the corner of the box. "Think of the child."

Comby sighed. "Go on then."

The air reeked of coal fires, smoke and soot, mingled with bodies unwashed and animal effluence, though she found the gin addled poor, as oft she'd heard them described, were in appearance as varied as she could have imagined. For every cadaverous wastrel underfoot there was here cheerful tradesmen tipping their hats in friendly greeting, there a whimpering bankrupt begging for sympathy, here ragged children running and shouting, there a flower girl sitting by her basket full with bright arrangements for sale.

"How much?" Emelyn asked, digging into her purse.

"Not here miss," Comby said sharply, pulling her along. "The man with the cane; don't look back I pray you, but he's there, not twenty yards behind."

"Is he following us?" she asked, aching to look.

"He is."

Beside them the parade carried on, men marching in red and Tory blue, many of them keenly well dressed. Emelyn stared at a large coach draped all in white like an elephant's ghost, with atop it a makeshift throne where sat a man dressed as a royal caricature, an enormous wig framing his long nosed mask. With silken gloves he waved and flourished, presently reaching into a bag to toss a large handful of gold coins over the onlookers.

The crowd surged like animals let out of their pens, splashing to the ground as they clawed and scrabbled after the money.

Emelyn held Comby's arm as the chaos unfolded around them. "Can the Mohocks really be Tories?" she puzzled. "But they're brigands; I can't imagine them royalist."

In a moment the little sparks of gold disappeared from the mud cracked street, and the greedy crowd receded. "We don't need to understand them miss," Comby said, keeping her from the curb as the draped coach continued on, the enthroned gentleman atop it waving and whistling to the throng that followed.

Behind them, forty paces back the way they'd come, Emelyn spotted their pursuer. Tall he was indeed, an intimidating figure, dark of skin and powerfully built, in clothes all of black, a cornered hat pulled low over his brow. A glint of silver caught her eye, and she saw in his gloved hand the cane, capped head and foot with the gleaming visage of what appeared to be a snarling animal.

"I see him," she breathed. "He watches us to be sure; he's not moving."

"Because we've stopped; he keeps his distance," Comby said, "I might swear we're on Great Earl now, or very near, but I've no idea where to find your antiquarian. Might be smarter we turn back miss . . ."

"We must be close; we shall ask directions," she said, pulling his arm to continue walking.

A quartet of men taking their leisure presented the opportunity. Wearing dress shirts and vests without wigs, two sat on a settle while a larger man leaned on the wall paring a potato. The fourth, the dandiest by his appearance, perched atop a barrel, his blond hair pulled back, his waistcoat finely tailored, a near empty bottle in his hand.

"I beg your pardon sir," Emelyn said.

The man tossed his drink, watching as it crashed in the street. "And I beg yours *Miss* . . ."

"*Miss* will do," Emelyn replied. "We are looking for a shop of antiquities, run by a man named Gapplethorpe. Do you know of it?"

The fellow took up a red mask from beside him, toying with it as he frowned. "What's the name again?"

"Grabapples I think," one of the men said, giving her a long leer. "But if you insist ma'am . . ."

"The name is Gapplethorpe," Emelyn repeated, feeling a flush.

"Grapplewhore says she?" the heavy set fellow spoke up, carving himself another bite of potato. "Oh he's not far miss . . . I'm sure of it."

The men laughed, and she noted weapons on their belts, cudgels and blades, with the man who looked to be their leader sporting both pistol and rapier. "Good afternoon gentlemen," she said, resuming her way.

"Gapplethorpe!" the blonde man cried, leaping up to block her way. "Why didn't you say so? Right this way miss, if you please." He gestured to his friends, and off they strode.

Comby stopped her as she tried to follow. "Nay miss, they're having you on."

The laughing men faded into the crowd, and Emelyn moaned with frustration, but the image of a towering cloaked figure pointing its arm over the parade caught the corner of her eye and she gasped, looking up to find it was only a branched lantern pole.

Following the point of its extended arm she peered across the street. "There! Gapplethorpe! I see it just across and three doors down."

Walking swiftly together they threaded through the parade as men strode past clapping and jeering, with one or two trying to catch Emelyn's hands for a jig. Comby put them off, and she increased her pace, winning the far side of the wide street with surprise to find the same four men they'd just met.

"The Honourable Robert Abbott Esquire," the man who'd been sitting on the barrel said with a bow. "Robert the Blade they call me, and these my free Mohock brothers. Now as we've led you safely across, we shall collect our fee."

"Your pardon sir, you led us nowhere," Emelyn said. "We crossed quite on our own. Now as we have our business I'm sure you have yours."

"Oh we've business right enough," the heavy one drawled, producing a garish red mask which he drew down to cover his face as another did the same.

"That's it clear off!" Comby said sharply, standing before her.

The men chuckled, one pushed him, and the confrontation broke into shoving. Emelyn's cloak tore as she wrenched it from a man's grasp, Comby heaved two of them back, another grabbed her bodily and she slapped the mask off his head, nearly knocking him over.

Red in the face, her attacker drew the club from his belt, bringing it to bear as Comby blocked her, though he'd scarce time to raise his arm before it connected, and with a hard impact he staggered, bumping into her.

Emelyn cried out, and the pair of them were flushed backward as the men bore down, forcing them through the trough of the gutter into a narrow bricked alley beyond. The man who'd struck first pressed forward, and catching hold of the offending club Comby lurched at him, cracking him with a hard fist.

The man yowled, dropping his mask, and Emelyn retreated to dodge another grab as Comby parried a swing, punching for answer before a cudgel struck his ankle, bringing him down.

In horror she watched as they proceeded to kick and mock him. "Wait!" she yelled. "Here . . . take it!" and digging out her purse she thrust what money she had at them, keeping back the thousand pound notes for her pocket.

Comby puffed with curses on the ground, holding his leg as the men regarded her, and the blonde Mr. Abbott gave her a smile. "Sure as the wind blows you're a rare beauty miss," he said. "But your man should know his place."

"Should he? You coward," she retorted, shaking with courage. "Take the money and harry us no more, or I'll see you in the gibbet!"

Abbott grabbed her arm; she tried to pull away, but his fist struck deep, sinking up and between her ribs. The pain was impossible, as like her lungs had been crushed, and collapsing with a croak she thought for a moment she would die, until ragged and strained her wind returned.

The villain ransacked her purse, and helpless to move Emelyn sat on her hip, wheezing as he snapped up the notes she'd dropped. Cackling and snarling the others kicked Comby all the more, and her eyes welled at the sight of him, curled up and broken in her defence. Their leader cast the torn purse away, pocketing the cash. "Now be a good girl and I'll not despoil your flesh, much as you'd enjoy it. But I will have these pretty baubles, your shoes I think, and this lovely cloak."

With no breath to protest she could only tremble as he fussed under her chin, unclasping the brooch her mother had given her.

Something moved behind the others, catching their attention, and she looked up to find a fifth man had joined them; taller than the Mohocks he was, with a silver topped cane leaning in his hand. By appearance she guessed him to be of African descent, though in age he was not to be placed, but somewhere between thirty and fifty.

The stranger fixed his sparkling eyes upon her. "Help us!" she wanted to scream, but it was no more than a whisper, tasting of blood.

"Perhaps I might be of assistance," he said, speaking to the men.

"Hoo it's a great Moorish valet!" one of them laughed.

"Your poor master's steered you wrong boy," the portly one said, snarling through his mask.

Emelyn shivered as their leader finished yanking the cloak from her body, and wadding it in his hand he got to his feet.

"On your way sir," Mr. Abbott barked, "you'll not meddle in Mohock business, not with Robert the Blade. 'Haps you've heard of me?"

"Not a whisper," the newcomer answered. "But I see no need to soil so splendid a cloak in the gutter. What say I buy it from you, twenty-five in five-guinea pieces?"

"Twenty-five!" Robert Abbott repeated with a laugh. "You've got yourself a cloak sir."

An urge to vomit struggled within her, but Emelyn pressed a hand to her stomach, watching with bleary eyes as the man in black tossed a coin purse to Robert the Blade, who snatching it from the air tossed him the cloak in return.

"Shall we ask him for a bit more?" one of those masked posed, brandishing his cudgel.

"Perhaps he'll buy her shoes for twenty-five as well?" another put in.

The stranger carefully folded the cloak, laying it atop a crate by his side. "She will be keeping her shoes," he said.

"Will she indeed," the thickest of the men said, stepping to confront him. "Ah so you're a smart one . . ."

Emelyn's eyes drifted to the ground. The pain pulsed in her guts, and a swimming dizziness threatened to rob her of consciousness.

A clack as of metal striking bone startled her awake, and she saw the thick set man careen off his feet, splashing into the gutter.

With yells of shock the others drew weapons. "Pink him!" Abbott shouted, but the silver cane swooped like a rawhide, parrying their attacks before its downward stroke dropped one head first into the alley pavement. The next lunged with a dagger, and the man in black slapped it free, spinning to catch his enemy in the chest, knocking him over the other into the wall.

The leader of her attackers drew his pistol, the hammer clicked, and Emelyn clenched her eyes as the gun fired. There was a curse of surprise, and daring to look she found his shot had missed. Robert the Blade dropped the gun, making to draw his sword, but the cane clipped him at the knees, and he caught it full in the chest as he fell, struck to the ground like numb timber beneath the axe.

With a flip of his cane the tall gentleman looked them over, as though checking his work. Three lay battered and still, while Abbott choked with a cough, rolling over.

"Whatever you are," he spat, wheezing with bloody lips, "you'll swing for this; your master will hear of it!"

The silver headed cane touched his throat, lifting his chin. "I call no man master," the man in black said quietly. "She whom I serve picked the bones of your ancestors."

"My father will have you!" Abbott rasped, flopping to his side.

"T'is a brave man, calls himself *the Blade* and invokes his father for protection," the stranger replied, and with a slack across the face he sent Mr. Abbott to sleep.

Crouching to look at her, their deliverer extended his hand, but Emelyn shook her head, pointing to Comby. "Please, please you must help him."

The footman was roused, and taking him under the arm the big man hoisted him up, before assisting Emelyn to her feet.

"I thank you sir, we thank you," Comby managed, wiping blood from his mouth.

Unfolding Emelyn's cloak, the man wrapped it about her, tying it at her neck as she leaned into the wall to breathe. "My name is Mr. Lorris," he said. "You are Emelyn Morley, and this brave fellow should be Adam Comberland, first footman of Hastelbrook."

"How do you know us?" Emelyn asked, watching as a vengeful Comby set to plundering the pockets of their enemies.

The dizziness had begun to abate, and sagging where she stood she listened as Mr. Lorris explained that he'd followed them from Sussex, having known of her journey to London even before she'd set out.

"Did you?" she asked, finding her breath at last as Comby returned her brooch, and the man's coin purse. "And why do you follow us?"

"I must apologize for the late intrusion," Mr. Lorris said, tipping his hat. "But I'm at liberty to say nothing more. You will learn what else you may from our mutual friend."

"Our mutual friend?"

"She who by her nature only appears to you at night."

Emelyn's eyes widened and she was about to speak, but he shook his head, putting a finger to his lips.

"Let us walk to your Mr. Gapplethorpe's shop," he said. "I shall wait outside, and see you safely from St. Giles. But best be quick about it."

The shop she'd crossed great misadventure to find was dimly lit, with greasy storefront windows and only a faded gilt marquee to record its namesake. Though her body ached, the idea that Vaela could know the man who'd come to their rescue set her curiosity ablaze, and leaving Comby in the care of Mr. Lorris, Emelyn slipped her torn purse in her pocket, now brimming with near a hundred pounds cash. The street was quieter, the noisy parade no longer in sight, and summoning her composure she pulled open the door to go inside.

Under a low ceiling dotted with an overabundance of lanterns, most of which were unlit, the antiquities shop was crowded with shelves and boxes warehousing odd collections of candlesticks, plate, books and old maps. In the far corner where the floor sagged was a recessed counter, behind which stood a vaguely familiar man, still as a statue. Montgomery Gapplethorpe had long and almost girlish carrot locks, though the top of his crown was bald as stone. Lit by a pungent tallow candle his face drooped with wrinkles, but his eyes were keen, gleaming under bushy red brows as he watched her.

"Mr. Gapplethorpe," Emelyn said, approaching the counter.

"Do mine eyes deceive me?" He raised the light to study her. "But there's a face one does not forget, the eldest Miss Morley! Some years it's been."

"Yes I was thirteen, when my father hired you to study the crypt beneath the house."

Gapplethorpe chuckled, a hoarse musical sort of sound. "But you forget I saw you just six years past, at the Brighton assembly hall, where your beauteous portrait was hung, and the legend of the *Belle of Brighton* came to be."

"Mr. Gapplethorpe," Emelyn repeated, skipping the anecdote, "it was not easy to find you and I've had a very trying day. I have come to learn whatever it is you withheld from my father, in regard to your investigation. I hope you know of what I speak. I am prepared to pay, for the information."

"Oh dear I see," he said quickly, and straightening up he cracked his knuckles with concentration. "But I kept nothing from him of course, except perhaps . . ."

"Perhaps what?" Emelyn slid a note marked for five pounds across the counter, which he pinned with bony fingers.

"I brought all my resources to bear, of course I did," he said, peering beneath his hand. "Deep under the crypt I made out a sound Miss Morley, I fancied at first it was a voice, or a whisper, and clearly after the scrape of stone upon stone."

"A voice? Could you make out the words?"

"Nay miss, I could not."

"Is that all? But you must have heard the earth shuddered beneath the house, when I was born . . . so they say."

Gapplethorpe raised his brows, peeking at the money again. "Yes well, I might have used my equipment to monitor hours, or even days longer, but your father showed waning interest."

"There must be more," she said, sliding him another five note. "What of the mysterious bust in the gallery, carved of volcanic rock, black hooded and faceless? I'm sure you've seen it. Could it tell us aught of the vault? Could there be any connection?"

"I remember it well." Mr. Gapplethorpe snatched the bill, grinning as he placed it over the other. "It was once the better part of a towering statue I've no doubt, and very old. But as to its importance . . . without even a sculptor's mark it has no pedigree, no history. I fear it is quite worthless."

Emelyn frowned; the tender spot between her ribs twinged with pain, and she rubbed it impatiently. "Yes, that much we've been told . . ."

Closing his eyes he gave a little shrug. "Then you know as much as I. But a word of advice . . ."

"Ten pounds of it I hope."

"T'would be a mistake, Miss Morley, to imagine that which lies buried beneath your home belongs to you. Whatever it is, it was there long before anyone thought to build on that hill."

"And how do you know this?"

"There is a clandestine order of gentlemen, right here in town, who study that very question, among others. On occasion I have had the pleasure of assisting them."

The blood taste had returned, and Emelyn swallowed. "A clandestine order you say, of Rosicrucians perhaps? Could it be the same founded by my great-grandfather, Samuel Bastian Morley?"

"Then you know of it; but yes the very same. They meet at the Devil's Inn, if you'd care to inquire, though it's no place for a woman, unless the sort to ply her trade at night.”

“I’m not afraid of a tavern Mr. Gapplethorpe.”

Wheezing with a laugh he shook his head. “Oh dear Miss Morley, the Devil’s Inn is no ordinary tavern. To find a lady of your . . . *qualities* on the premises, well it’s unthinkable.”

“My good sir, I’ve come for intelligence about the crypt, and what may lie deeper, so if you’ve none to give I’ll thank you to direct me to one who has, or return my money.”

Gapplethorpe’s smile melted away. “I’ll not betray my betters Miss Morley, but I shall give you the under-storey porter. He may find a thing or two to tell you, for a price. Thomas Attridge is his name.”

“Thomas Attridge. Where can I find him?”

“I do not know.”

Three pound notes slid across, and he absorbed them. “I know his daughter Penny works for a dressmaker near the water,” he said thoughtfully. “I can be no more specific I’m afraid.”

“Can you not? I’d be better off testing this Devil’s Inn of yours.”

“Oh do Miss Morley, do. I should relish hearing of it . . . You need only seek where Fleet Street dies at Ludgate, behind the old sawmill, ruined in the great fire. There you shall find the Inn, the haunt of those great and fallen, the headquarters of our benefactor.”

“Your benefactor?”

“He who watches over these streets, who leads the Order, who has revived the Mohocks and broken them to his will, though of course in public he must disavow them . . .”

“He is a lord?” Emelyn asked with surprise.

“Not telling, not for a thousand pounds,” he tittered. “But try the Inn, yes, take your beauteous person to that fox club of libertines, and you shall never come out again. They would love you to your end Miss Morley, and throw away the bones.”

With a noise of disgust she made to grab the money, but he snatched it away. “Is that all you have for me?” she demanded. “An under-storey porter, who I’ll wager knows nothing at all of Hastelbrook. Then I should find you a charlatan sir, as my father did.”

“A charlatan,” he repeated, a snarl on his lips. “But perhaps this little piece should convince you otherwise,” and reaching under the desk he withdrew a small object, slapping it atop the counter.

“A common coin,” she said dryly.

“This is no common coin, Miss Morley,” he said, finding his smirk as he presented it near the light. "Very old, bronze, and here, the obverse stamped with a woman's face, hair radiating about her, and note the laurel wreath upon her head, with the Latin inscription . . ."

Looking closer Emelyn marvelled at the regal profile, an exotic woman proud and elegant in beauty, with arcing letters emblazoned about her: ***PER SANGVINEM REGINAE***. "Per the . . . by the blood of the queen," she guessed. "And what queen is that?"

"The queen of Saunmoor, Miss Morley, the hidden kingdom of the dead. It is rumoured your very crypt bears some connection, to that most dreadful place . . ."

Emelyn swallowed, staring at it. "And what is on the reverse?"

He turned the coin in his fingers, and she found the depiction of a towered building, as like a cathedral, with a great round window like an eye, and, stars and crosses along the edge, and the inscription ***IN OCULO VMBREMARIS***.

"What does it mean?" she asked, unsure how to translate.

"In the eye of Umbremar," he said. "That being the dark citadel at the heart of her kingdom, if you believe in such things. A great cyclops eye, a window of stained crimson glass, watching over her subjects . . ."

"Fascinating. And how did it come to you?"

"It was left, as payment, with a few precious stones, on the night one of my working lads was kidnapped, taken in the dark . . . a boy of no mean skill as a tinker, but uncorrectable, despite liberal use of the strap. I suppose I had the better deal in the end, though the coin itself is worthless, a few pennies perhaps."

Recalling the red eye design on the cover of Lord Cumberstone's book, Emelyn steeled herself, and snapped the coin from his hand.

"What? Give it back!" he blurted.

"Shall I sir, after paying thirteen pounds for nothing but rumours?"

"That coin is not for sale!"

"But if worthless as you say, you should count yourself lucky trading it off so well," she said, pocketing the coin as he rushed around the counter to confront her. "Or shall I scream, and summon my gentlemen from outside?" she added quickly, holding her ground as he stopped before her.

"You would rob me in my own place of work," he said darkly, tensing his hands as though to attack.

"And you would cheat me, as doubtless you have many others," she said, stepping defiantly closer. "Have we a quarrel, Mr. Gapplethorpe? Shall I call my gentlemen in, to hear your side of it?"

"Take it," the antiquarian hissed, "and may it curse your days."

"Thank you. Good afternoon, Mr. Gapplethorpe."

The man offered no further protest, but spat and fumed as she took her leave.

Left both tense and exhilarated, Emelyn rejoined the men outside, and with a wave of his cane Mr. Lorris arrested a Hack & Humble coach.

"Will you tell me, do you recognize such a coin?" she asked, presenting it to Mr. Lorris.

He narrowed his eyes as if to think, and shook his head with a frown. "Cannot say as I do, Miss Morley."

"Really? You're certain?" she asked, disbelieving him at once.

But the coach pulled up sharply to interrupt, and he opened the door, tipping his hat.

Pocketing the coin, Emelyn insisted Comby step in first, and she held his hand as he did so, following after. Mr. Lorris bid them farewell, the coach started out, and sinking into her seat she folded her hands in her lap, the ache in her middle fanning the flames of her distemper. "No more boats, I could not bear it," she said. "We shall drive."

Comby adjusted with a wince, watching her with his good eye. "What did you learn of the antiquarian miss?"

"Very little," she said, feeling the coin in her pocket, a bronze piece the size of a guinea, and she thought to speak no more of the event, but on the thin hope that Comby might know the Devil's Inn, or the people Gapplethorpe had mentioned, she could not remain silent, and was soon sharing all he'd told her of Thomas Attridge and his daughter, as well as of the unnamed noble benefactor who purportedly had great interest in the legends of Hastelbrook, and kept the Mohocks under his thumb.

Comby listened intently, but by the vacant expression on his face she determined it was well and truly time to admit defeat.

"Well . . . that's that I suppose," she said, very much hoping the antiquarian would seek no reprisal. "I shall learn no more of it today, and I've brought quite enough harm, on us both."

"It were my duty to protect you miss," he said, "and I failed in that; if not for Mr. Lorris . . ."

"No." Grabbing Comby's hand Emelyn squeezed it, and without thinking she kissed his knuckles. She released him at once, turning to her window as her eyes went blurry. "Adam, you warned me of the danger, and I would not hear it. I am wretched with shame, for what happened to you."

"I'm only glad we're out of it miss," he said, crossing his arms.

For some while they rode in silence, and Emelyn wondered whether there could be any merit to Gapplethorpe's story of the coin, and whether Mr. Lorris had recognized it indeed, and opted not to tell her. But the pain in her ribs stole back her attention; to have sought for the antiquarian in such a place, with such an amount of money on her person, and with the bloody Mohocks on parade . . .

"If those men had found the jeweller's notes . . . eleven thousand pounds, I might have been kidnapped for ransom, forcing my father into much worse a place, than if I'd never left."

"*Dodge the aim, not the ball,*" Comby said, scratching the swollen edge of his mouth.

Emelyn sniffed, watching as they joined the slogging traffic to cross London Bridge. "I'm sorry?"

"That's how he done it miss, dodged the shot. Whilst firing a flintlock a man can't help his grimace; one anticipates the flash. So *watch his eyes, not his arm*, Mr. Lorris says."

Recalling the fracas Emelyn could almost hear the heavy thump of their rescuer's cane striking down their attackers. "It sickens me these *Mohock* men could be so bold in broad daylight; we can't be the first," she said. "Mr. Lorris fought like a demon."

"He fought like he were taking a walk. He could have delivered them to St. Peter had he a mind, but I suspect all four of the villains will live."

Emelyn cleared her throat. "I must change out of this ruin of a gown," she said, taking his hand again to place a wad of bills in his palm, "and you must have this, and be at your leisure, to rest and whatever you need."

Comby blinked at her. "Fifty pounds? That's five years' salary miss."

"Is it? For first footman of Hastelbrook? But I don't care, you must keep it."

"I'll not keep such a sum without suspicion," he said, handing it back to her. "Nay miss, I'll not take it."

"Ten pounds then. Here, I insist."

"Very well," he said, accepting the money. "I suppose after dinner, if you'll not be needing me I might look in on a strong drink somewhere."

"You've earned that at least," she said, and her eyes welled as she looked on his bruised face. "Comby if ever in future there is aught that you need, you must come to me first . . ."

"It were an ugly business miss," he said, "but I'll forgive your inexperience, if you'll excuse my going down quick as I did."

Emelyn chuckled softly, swiping her cheek. "Being as it was four against one I think you acquitted yourself with distinction."

"Four against two," he corrected. "Never thought I'd see Miss Emelyn Morley knock a fellow sideways; I'd watch it again if I could. And I should say you've a forcible ally in that Mr. Lorris. I do wonder what he's about."

"So do I," she said, marvelling at the thought. "Perhaps it was not a total loss, after all."

"Do you know what he meant miss, *our mutual friend?*"

"That is a question . . ." Taking out her kerchief she wet the corner, sitting up to dab at the swelling by his eye. "Comby, I must insist you tell no one what happened to us."

"Yes miss."

"Except Breda of course; she is a very good nurse."

"That she is miss," he said, smiling with closed eyes as she wiped the blood from his lip.

Uncle Fallworth was still about town, and Cousin Tynan in the park behind the house with his fencing master when they returned, the time being half-past two. A shocked Breda greeted them, stealing herself without questions as she took Comby's elbow to help him inside. The stairs were difficult, and gripping the railing for assistance Emelyn gingerly ascended to her room, appointing a maid to send down for bathwater. She disrobed before the mirror to examine her wound, finding a red and darkening bruise between her ribs, which Breda quickly spotted.

This Emelyn explained as her cold soak was prepared, speaking quietly of the trip to St. Giles and the attack, though details before and aft she omitted. The restful bathroom was cheerfully tiled, with a clean copper tub and bathing stove, woolly linen towels and indoor ferns.

"I can only be grateful it was no worse," she concluded with a wince, lowering herself into the tub.

Sitting on a stool beside her Breda took the handle brush to her back, scrubbing harder than usual. "I daren't imagine it miss, but if the pair of you had never come back I should be out searching the streets myself."

The cool water helped against the ache, if only for a while, and after the bath Emelyn retired to her room swaddled in linen, where she indulged a languishing look at the bed, before hiding the coin under her pillow, and bracing herself for the trip to Ledgefield.

"Must you really go miss, alone in your condition?" Breda asked.

"Yes I must call on them. It's the entire pretence for my visit . . . but you won't tell anyone I described it so. No one is to know what happened in St. Giles, excepting Comby and yourself."

"Yes miss." Breda unwrapped and dried her hair before helping her into layers for a clean gown of high collared white, though Emelyn found even the gentle lacing painful, and eschewing a bonnet she set out with her hair uncovered, bound up in braids.

Unwilling to cross by water she opted for the slower journey by coach, silently cursing her injury at every bump, and wishing more than once she'd added a hard kick to Robert Abbott's defeat.

Ledgefield was a narrow three-story townhouse in St. James's Square, shorter than its neighbours, like a pale child crowded between plump red brick cousins. Stepping gingerly down from the coach Emelyn looked up, and it struck her that even here her family's habit of spending for presentation, up to the utter edge of their means, was unmistakable: finely carved limestone blocks made up the street facing wall, with cheap painted timber for the window frames.

The coach had been obliged to let her off some way from the door, owing to other vehicles parked, and at the sight of people exiting the farthest carriage Emelyn realized it could only be the Townsends, arriving at the same time as herself. Indeed, no sooner had they touched the curb than a jovial woman with grey-brown hair called out.

"Are you come to see us my dear?" she inquired, waving with jubilant energy. "Can that be Miss Emelyn Morley, or do I very much mistake?"

Too far to respond without yelling Emelyn smiled, making her way toward them as the remainder of the family emptied from the coach. Beaming expectantly Mrs. Townsend stood surrounded by her bloodline: two young girls, perhaps twelve and six, blinking in the sun beside their brother, a curly haired young man not more than twenty, and behind them the patriarch, himself a curly headed gentleman with narrow eyes and a newspaper.

Emelyn was received with boisterous welcome. Mrs. Townsend did most of the talking, the girls curtsied, and Mr. Townsend consulted his pocket watch, contributing but one or two syllables while Emelyn heard of their trip to Piccadilly for shopping, coming home by way of the unfinished neighbourhoods of old Mayfair, which Mrs. Townsend deplored for an endless state of construction.

"I do not complain," she said, "but I've never understood why *all* the fields should be done away, with no fair at all; here we are fourteen years hence and not two in ten houses finished!"

"I remember the fair," Emelyn said, recalling raucous games, dancing and stage tricksters at the yearly festival.

Two footmen opened the doors, and Mrs. Townsend shouted for the girls, who'd begun to wander. Her son Bannister, whom she addressed as Banny, stepped quickly to Emelyn's side, offering her escort into the house.

"You must forgive my mother," he said. "She'll talk you off your feet if given room. But as far as the lease, we're positively in clover living in St. James's Square, though Mother misses the days of local bear-baiting and sack races."

Cruelly chained bears fighting their last against dogs was a spectacle Emelyn had blessedly forgotten, and busy recalling the blood and animal screams she neglected the handrail, twinging with pain as she mounted the front steps.

"It is good of you to visit us," Bannister said. "I have studied with ardour your portraits, particularly over the hearth in the drawing room, but your handsomeness madam, is beyond their power to capture."

Here a humble deflection was called for, but distracted by the discomfort in her middle Emelyn stuttered her response, thinking again of Mr. Lorris and his deadly silver topped cane . . .

The girls bounded upstairs, Mr. Townsend disappeared down the hall, and Mrs. Townsend took the housekeeper aside as footmen brought in the shopping.

"Well . . . I trust you find the house no worse than you left it," Bannister said.

"Oh it's lovely I'm sure, just as I remember," Emelyn said, her hands at her stomach as she regarded the entry hall.

For a few minutes more they conversed, whereupon she discovered her guess of his age to be correct. At twenty he was two years younger than Comby, haughty and erudite of speech, with slighter shoulders than she could register as attractive.

"I complete my final term at the Inns of Court within the year," he said. "My plan is to invest with East India; I have found both attacking and defending legal dissertations incident to affairs of trade to be most instructive," and seeming to sense her wandering attention he cleared his throat. "Is not your father in shipping?"

"Yes," Emelyn replied. "I'm sorry sir, but I really don't mean to impose; I've only come to collect some of my old things."

"Nonsense my dear!" Mrs. Townsend declared, swishing back to them. "To your good fortune we've not yet had dinner; you must stay of course. The freshwater sturgeon is not to be missed."

Dinner was served on white cloth in the dimly lit dining room, with its familiar walls of dark panelling oiled to a greasy gleam. Beside the breaded fish, which Emelyn found too salty, there was roast duck with ham and pigeon pies, and seasonal greens. The meal was fine, though unable to find her comfort she had trouble following the jumps in conversation.

"Your hand is ever at your stomach my dear, are you ill?" Mrs. Townsend asked.

"Just a minor complaint," Emelyn said, taking a large bite of salad to discourage further questions.

The wine was poured freely, even for the girls, whom Emelyn learned were named Mary and Vesper, aged thirteen and eight. Bannister, who sat next to Emelyn, plied her for news of Hastelbrook in such a way that she understood him to be ferreting out whether she was spoken for.

Cheerful sociability carried on thus, until convinced their guest suffered some malady brought on by travel over the impossible southern roads, Mrs. Townsend insisted they all adjourn to the drawing room for better ease. "You must take the most luxurious settee," she said, "and indulge my girls by drawing with them, just a picture, anything really! Their friends are far away, and we've had little enough female company."

Though initially numb to the idea, with pencils and drawing book in hand Emelyn found in it an opportunity, and as the girls sat beside her to sketch flowers and a bowl of fruit, she strove to depict what she remembered of Mr. Lorris's cane. An oddity it was without question, heavy of shaft, even iron perhaps, with bestial heads, leonine and feral, mirroring each other at either end. Of silver they must have been, or bright polished steel, with glinting gems in the eyes.

'Tap tap on the Window, Teeth at the Glass, Lion's Head glimmer, the Cane an' the mask . . .'

The poem returned to mind, and she was seized with an extraordinary notion: that if the *Lurkmen* existed, could not Mr. Lorris be one of them? Her heart raced, and staring at the drawing she pondered his words, which could only describe Vaela herself . . . *She who by her nature only*

"Dear me," Bannister said, looking over her sketch with a narrow-eyed show of critical admiration. "Articulate in both realism and menace; see, Mother, how she's captured it, as like a dream given form."

"Mercy me what is it?" Mrs. Townsend puzzled. "But that is a frightening thing; have you drawn a snarling lion from memory? A hunting trophy perhaps? Look George, is it a hunting trophy?"

Mr. Townsend grunted from a corner table, his face in the paper.

Emelyn folded the drawing for her pocket. "Just a fancy," she said, standing from the couch. "I daresay nothing so lovely as what your girls have rendered. Now, Mrs. Townsend if you will excuse me, I really must look into the storeroom, before I return to my uncle."

"Allow me to guide you," Bannister offered.

With candle in hand he led her down a closet stair, lighting several wall mounted lanterns. The room below was small, a simple storeroom separated from basement kitchens by a sturdy door.

There were trunks and boxes, covered paintings, and shelves along one wall thick with wrapped utensils, pottery, dry stores and even horse furniture. To one side stood a large covered shape, and pulling off the drape Emelyn marvelled at the familiar sight: a grand house made for dolls, nearly as tall as she was.

"My baby house," she said, smiling back at him.

"I should cover that up again, if I were you," he said. "Or risk my sisters having their way with it."

"Oh I don't mind," Emelyn said, and grasping the top edges she pulled open the front of it. The façade split in the middle, the wings of the little house swung outward, and its twenty-four rooms caught the light. The detail of each was exquisite, with tiny carved furniture, water silk drapery, worsted rugs and even miniature down stuffed pillows. There were people too, tiny wooden figures with embroidered outfits. Three girls and a boy for Emelyn and her siblings, with two taller figures for her parents . . . and one more, wearing a misshapen cloak stitched from an old glove. The sight of it made her gasp, and the memory came sharply back to her: as a child none would help her design the character, and so she had taken it upon herself to make the hair and cloak for her little effigy of Vaela, the woman in black from her dreams, which she would nearly lose by her mother's several attempts to discard it. But the diminutive figure was poorly crafted, unsatisfying to behold, and she recalled with relief that there was another likeness, a proper doll Vaela had given her . . .

"Forgive me, Miss Morley, but I must speak," Bannister said, watching as she closed and re-covered the dollhouse. "Seeing you here, radiant in the glow of the lanternlight, I am positively bumbazed to wonder how the Belle of Brighton should remain unmarried so long."

"I don't know what bumbazed means," Emelyn said, searching over the boxes.

"I am bewildered, baffled, bamboozled, Miss Morley . . . But it is a sin against nature that you should find yourself going on twenty-four, and yet without a husband."

Unsure how to respond she elected not to, sorting through boxes of old clothes they'd neglected to give away or sell on consignment, until she found at last the object she was looking for, a charming little dolly unlike the other moulded, painted examples she and her sisters had grown up with. This doll was soft and plush, with a charming face, ebon hair of yarn and a hooded cloak. The little stuffed vampiress had gone some way to easing the distress of losing her Queen Anne, which had been taken away after final warnings not to bring her outside. It was the night of her seventh or eighth birthday, when she'd found the mysterious doll propped up against one of the headstones, with a little note pinned to her cloak, which was with her still, just beneath in the trunk:

'I'm sorry you've lost your Annie, but I would love to play outside if you'll have me. I am easily washed and not afraid of the wet nor the mud.'

"How could I forget," Emelyn murmured, feeling a surge of happy energy.

"A doll?" Bannister chuckled. "Is that what you've come for?"

"It appears so," she said, and petting the doll's hair she wondered whether Vaela might have appeared, had the Mohock men deigned to attack at night . . . and what the vampiress might have done to them if she had.

"That sweet doll is dear to you," he said, studying her closely. "Miss Morley, if you'll permit my unguarded concern . . . have you any society with a man called Meriton Bowtree?"

"Meriton Bowtree? Yes I know him, not well."

"Can you be aware of how he's employed himself to slander you? Of course, I'll not believe a word of it . . ."

The wistful spell was broken, and Emelyn blinked at him. "Has he slandered me? How?"

"By publishing you for an icy wanton," Bannister said darkly, "claiming you provoked him to the very edge of matrimony, with no intent but to dash his heart *upon the rocks of antipathy*, and for your own amusement, as he maintains you've done to many before him."

Emelyn stood aghast. "He made suit to me, and I refused him. That is all. Has he really printed such a thing?"

"*The Succubus of Sussex* his pamphlet is titled," Bannister said quietly, drawing closer. "I read those hateful, misbegotten words and I thought to myself, where is her champion? Where is a man of principle, of scholarly acumen to print in her defence, to protect her from such lies?"

"And you recommend yourself," Emelyn said vaguely, appalled to think that even the bitterly disappointed Mr. Bowtree would stoop to such a thing.

"I would." Bannister swallowed hard, as though marshalling his courage. "I must exert myself, Miss Morley, to declare for you a most ardent admiration, even from my first glimpse of your beauty in the afternoon sunlight . . ."

"Mr. Townsend," Emelyn protested, squeezing the doll.

"Furthermore," he continued breathlessly, "I find no obstacle in your seniority of years, nor in the fiery cast of your hair; I cannot countenance those superstitions as would condemn it . . ."

"Thank you, but Mr. Townsend . . ."

"From men of such dissipated quality as this slanderer, you must be shielded," he said. "My family is of no small means, and myself of no mean training in rhetoric and elocution; I would rebut this Bowtree person, I would shame him into oblivion . . . if you would but permit me as the dearly devoted guardian . . . of yourself."

"Are you asking for my hand," Emelyn clarified, "here in the storeroom, upon our first meeting?"

Bannister was sweating, and smiled with some effort. "Miss Morley, you should never be made to fear such gossip, such grubstreet expostulations, nor would you, with myself as your steadfast companion."

Emelyn exhaled a long sigh. "Your character sir, does you credit. But I can assure you I've not come to London in the market for a protector."

"But surely Miss Morley, mature as you are, you must see the prudence of a qualified defence . . ."

"We are in exile from the city already," she said, "and by the time my family returns to Westminster, such tripe as Mr. Bowtree's pamphlet will be long forgotten."

"But are you not obliged to think of your future?" he entreated, watching as she mounted the stairs.

"I do, Mr. Townsend," she said, pausing for a painful breath halfway up, "and many other things besides."

"Dear lady, forgive me," he said, reaching out. "Do not say I have frightened you, I could not bear it. You must forget my indelicate address, please."

Stopping by the door she looked back at him. "You're not indelicate sir; your intentions are honourable, and we shall part as friends. But I really must return to my uncle before dark."

"Before dark? But sunset must be five hours away."

"The early traveller is never late," Emelyn said.

The wilted look on Bannister's face remained for the duration of her goodbyes, but she smiled nevertheless, fidgeting with the drawing in her pocket as the footman hailed her coach.

By half past five she'd reached her destination, and after finding Uncle Fallworth in the parlour for a quick greeting she rushed upstairs to check on Comby.

In the attic she found him clean and changed into fresh livery, lying propped up on his elbows, with Breda on a stool at his bedside, serving him broth.

"The clothes are down to the laundress," Breda said.

"Good. And how are you feeling, dear Comby?" Emelyn asked, noting his swelling had substantially decreased.

"Better miss," he said, "by cold poultice and the hands of an artful nursemaid. How are you getting on?"

"It smarts," Emelyn said, touching her stomach. "But I will live."

"And how did you find the Townsends miss?" Breda asked. "You've never met them before?"

"Only Father has met them," Emelyn replied, looking at the doll in her hands. "As for how we got on, they were lovely. Then their son proposed to me, and I left."

Comby put a fist to his mouth, coughing as he stifled a laugh.

"Yes I suppose it's all rather amusing," Emelyn said, pulling the doll's hood down and back up again. "But I wish he hadn't advanced himself. Mrs. Townsend is sure to mention it when she writes to my mother, and I shall be cautioned."

"You inspire passion miss," Breda said.

"Well." Emelyn took a deep breath. "We must leave early tomorrow; I must return to Hastelbrook, before Dhorings Park. We shall leave Comby off at the house."

"I'm strong enough to attend you at Dhorings miss," Comby said, sitting up straighter.

"Nay sir, I'll ask no more of you, and I must see the money into my father's hands directly. So tonight you must enjoy yourself," and coming to the bed she pressed another five pound note in his hand. "Keep it, spend it, or give it away. I insist."

Comby crinkled the cash. "Very well miss, I'll not argue."

"And you'll be careful tonight Mr. Comberland," Breda added, standing from her stool.

Outside his room the women paused in the hallway.

"He'll be all right, won't he miss?" Breda said, colour rising in her cheeks.

Emelyn touched her arm. "Comby is very strong. He knows his way around the corners, just as you said. Now I must apologize to my cousin for missing his fencing lesson . . . and then I'm going to bed."

Chapter 13
The Order and the Stone

Hunched over his desk behind wide glass cases at the back of the warmly lit shop, Meritus Frusk, of Frusk & Partners jewellers, blinked through the magnifier at the astounding piece before him. A greying, whiskery man of impressive means for his trade, Mr. Frusk had always prided himself on a hard bargaining temperament, and gazing intently into the red heart of the necklace— a ponderous ruby ensconced in gold, attended by teardrop diamonds, he could not help but presume it worthy to rival even the greatest royal heirloom.

"Twelve thousand faces of George," he said to himself, reviewing the transaction in his mind, a heavy price for this, the fairest piece of jewellery ever to cross his desk. But the partners trusted him to invest, after all.

"It might break us, shut our doors forever," he muttered, though as the entrancing glimmer reflected in his eyes he found himself of no mind to sell it. "However did *Hiram Morley* come by such a thing?" he wondered aloud, for to the best of his knowledge the Morleys of Sussex were of little report, excepting the sprawling curiosity of their ancient home, and the beauty of their eldest daughter.

"It's mine," he said firmly. "Everything else is trifles." The ruby glistened like crystalline blood in his hand, drawing him in, and staring into its depths he was absolutely resolved it must never leave his care . . .

The lantern burned low, and at an involuntary click in his throat he chuckled to realize he'd been holding his breath, thinking for a moment to have seen a shadow of movement in the depths of the ruby. "More precious than the finest carmines of Burma," he observed, adjusting the placement of the piece with slender tongs to better catch the light over its facets.

There came a knock from somewhere, which he ignored with a

snort. "But is there a cameo?" He said, wondering if he hadn't spotted a little scene carved into the gem.

The knock repeated and he startled, glancing at a tall clock by the shelves to find the time well after eleven. It could never be business so late, but any stranger knocking with his wife abed would have to be sorted.

"Coming, just coming!" he barked, pulling on his coat to creak across the floorboards as the knock sounded again. Opening a slide bolt to peer through the heavily reinforced door he beheld the figure of a woman in black, wild raven hair loose about her shoulders as she leaned against the railing, her hooded cloak matted with rain.

"I should hope you rap on my door by mistake!" he charged, taking immediate dislike to her untidy appearance. "I'll give no alms at this hour."

"Help me!" the woman pleaded, raising a bloodied arm before the little gap for him to see. "I am a gentlewoman, I have been robbed . . ."

Coughing at the sight of the blood Mr. Frusk roused himself to action, taking up a loaded pistol from its box on the counter, whereupon he set about unlocking the door top to bottom, pulling it open to reveal the unhappy visitor shivering on the stoop, clutching her arm. Her face gleamed youthful and beauteous in the porch light, yet almost reluctantly so, as though a heaviness of sorrow lay upon her.

"Are you in present danger miss?" he puffed, but scanning the dark thoroughfare of Cheapside he found it silently still, from where it changed to Poultry street in the east to the grand eminence of Saint Paul's cathedral, which towered over the rooftops away west, floating in the fog like a ghostly fortress.

The woman in black swayed where she stood, fine streams of blood running from her fingers to dapple the stones of the porch. "Please sir," she beseeched, her eyes cast down. "I am faint . . . May I come in?"

With ungloved hands and bare feet she struck a sympathetic figure to be sure, but there was too something unnerving in her presence, and for a moment Mr. Frusk thought to advise she seek the night watch, but the sight of her pale and shaking was past bearing, and a determined mercy welled within him. "You must come out of the weather madam, here . . ."

The woman grimaced, accepting his arm as she leaned into him, and helping gently as he might the jeweller guided her inside. "We must have you warm and dry now, and see to your hurt."

Stepping over the threshold she met him with a smile, her eyes flushing from doe brown to pure black.

"What is happening?" he managed, sagging in her embrace as an irresistible weakness came over him. The cool touch of her lips met his neck, and a sharp sting made him jump. For a moment he resisted, but the pleasurable heat of the bite spread through him like magic, and the smell of rain was in her hair . . .

Spluttering awake the jeweller found himself in a heap on the floor. "Dogdast it!" he exclaimed, jerking up to sit, a raw weariness in his bones. There was no one else in the shop, and clambering to his feet he staggered to the door to find it shut tight, every lock engaged.

"But was there not someone," he muttered, though he could little imagine visitors at such an hour, and picking his way to the desk he rubbed his eyes, dropping into the chair with an exhausted groan.

"A few more notes perhaps," he said, and adjusting the lantern he paused. There had been, he was certain, a piece of great value just here in the eye of his lamp, but he could not for the life of him remember what it was.

A quick perusal of his ledger found new transactions adjusted for the week, including recent purchase of several ornate necklaces totalling twelve thousand pounds sterling, which had in turn been quickly disposed of to various buyers on credit . . . persons of quality only vaguely familiar to him, but of reputation each beyond reproach. The item on his desk however, he would swear was of immense and singular aspect, something to be hid away, too precious to be resold.

"And left out of the books? Impossible. Nay, mad with lack of sleep like as not, you old fool," he grumbled to himself, rubbing his neck.

■■

The Hound's Hare was a lively little tavern, nestled in a low courtyard at the corner of Maid Lane and Thames Street but a few blocks from the Fallworths. The stout tables in the common room were peopled with the usual mix; gentleman scoundrels caroused with lusty working ladies over cards, while day-worn men of trade took solace in hot suppers and cheap spirits. At a corner table Adam Comberland had found his leisure, nursing a savoury ale he quite liked, and he was half resolved to order a third, when he looked up to find a darkly cloaked woman sitting across from him. Keenly beautiful she was, if pale, with hair of deepest black, her eyes strangely bright beneath her hood.

"Good evening," she said.

Comby swallowed to stifle a belch. "Hullo miss. I've not . . . I'm not here for company."

"Nor I."

"Shall I know you ma'am?"

"No. But I know you," she said, tilting her head.

"Who are you?" he asked numbly, finding himself locked in her gaze.

"My name is Vaela. You are Adam Comberland, and I think you have proven your mettle today."

Comby puffed for breath, striving to master himself, but her eyes were black as water at midnight, and he could not look away . . .

He woke with a splutter, finding himself in the misty alley behind the building, the woman's mouth locked to the bare knob of his shoulder as gently but firmly she denied his struggles. Strange immeasurable moments passed, and the rush of her feeding melted away as she released him with a sigh.

Slumping into the wall his heart skipped with dread. "Monster . . . *vampire!*" he whispered.

"Vaela," she corrected, tying the laces at his chest and straightening his shirt.

He tried to speak, but a finger to his lips stopped his words, and the iron taste of her blood met his tongue, warming his throat as an aggressive dizziness took hold, buckling his legs beneath him.

The vampiress pulled him back to his feet. "Stay with me, wake up," she said firmly, "and hear my command."

"Yes mistress . . ."

"Emelyn is my charge," she said, holding him close, "but I cannot see her at home in the day; henceforward you will watch over her, closely as you may without offending your office. Do you understand?"

"Yes mistress," he repeated, smiling vaguely.

"Very good," she said, tucking a folded piece of paper into his pocket. "In the morning you are to hide this note among her things, when you assist her trunks to the coach."

"I'm to hide the note in her things."

"Yes Comby. Now you must tell me what happened today. Tell me everything . . .”

<hr>

    Though the Fallworths kept very pleasant rooms for guests, and Emelyn's bed was warm and snug, the night hours crawled by too slowly, and thwarted in her pursuit of rest she surrendered at last to wakefulness. The fire was low, and after lighting a candle she set it by the mirror, untying her sleeping shift from the neck to examine her injury. In the dim light the bruise appeared larger, almost black, and not a little distressed she closed her garment. The writing desk promised some diversion, and carefully she lowered herself to sit, cracking open her journal.

    'Wednesday June the 15th,

    Bannister Townsend proposed to me today, coming to my defence against Mr. Bowtree's hateful pamphlet for an excuse. Perhaps I might have been kinder to Bowtree at home, but to take up public slander against me? ~~If I but had Vaela's power to correct him'~~

    Here she paused after crossing out the line. "If wishes were horses, beggars would ride . . ." The low fire spat as it settled, and after watching the crackling sparks a few moments she dipped her pen to continue:

    'Mr. Townsend is in every objective regard a worthy gentleman, and surely the very sort Mama would have foisted upon me, if not for the descending shadow of Captain Lord Van Croft.'

    Tempted to think of Mr. Arkwright, Emelyn wondered whether he was sleeping now, or perhaps reading by a cozy fire with his feet on a stool, unconcerned with Mohocks or vampires or pernicious suitors.

    'But of course Mama would rather contort herself in knots than speak well of a man I like.'

    Dragging her fingertips over the tender wound she knit her brows, nervous to ponder whether it was mending, or growing worse.

    'The jewel is sold, the money is won, but four men declaring for

the Mohocks attacked us in broad daylight. From now I think I shall believe everything I read about the deplorable state of the city. And can it be true the Mohocks are sponsored by a lord?'

Swallowing down the now familiar taste of blood she touched the bruise again.

> *'My body aches, and that Comby might have been killed, is unbearable. But Mr. Lorris, like an angel of war delivered us from our distress, and now I must find out if Vaela is acquainted with him, as he claims.*
>
> *Tonight I waited by the window for some while, but she did not come. It is now past midnight, and I must try again to sleep, though I'm certain to be watching the embers until dawn.'*

Slapping the journal closed she doused the candle and rose stiffly to crawl back into bed. Cool air swirled through the open window panes, fragile dreams lit upon her, breaking at every painful twitch, and after some while she fancied there were silver eyes watching her from the dark outside.

With a drowsy smile she gestured in welcome. "Come in," she muttered, certain it was another dream.

But in a breath the vampiress was sitting beside her, and if not for the immediately fortifying aura of her presence Emelyn might have screamed.

"You're hurt," Vaela said, her face sharp with anger as she lowered her hood.

Emelyn folded down the blanket and untied her shift, parting the fabric to show her. "It hurts the more when I'm anxious," she said. "Is there aught to be done for it?" but at a sharp sting she gasped, tensing to find the vampiress already upon her, snarling lips pressed to the bruise.

The wound rebelled with furious pain, but was soon depleted, leaving only a soft silken ease, like a warm and fluid embrace . . .

"Ohhh . . . How?" Emelyn marvelled, breathing deep.

Sitting up Vaela found the strings and tied her shift. "By the same power that repairs your flesh when I drink from your throat."

Testing the skin Emelyn found it strong and painless. "Bless you," she said, and rolling to her side she captured Vaela's hand, kissing and holding it close.

"Would I could stay while you sleep," Vaela said softly, and brushing her face with cold claws she paused, looking across the room. "Is that my doll, on the chair?"

"Yes. I found her again, and I remembered. I'm not sure I ever thanked you."

"You've taken good care of her," Vaela said, "better than yourself. You were very foolish today, tempting such danger beyond my power to protect you."

"I was foolish," Emelyn conceded, "and naïve; for all my pains I've learned little of the vault, unless you're moved to tell me more?"

"I am no closer than you are, to describing what lies inside."

Emelyn reached beneath her pillow and drew out the coin. "And there is this. Can it be authentic, a coin cast in the image of your queen?"

Vaela took it with a frown. "It avails you nothing, but yes."

"But I believe I dreamt of her," Emelyn said breathlessly, "when I was in the throes of the bloodsick. A dark woman crowned in gold, ascending a stairs before me. She climbed to an altar of stone, upon which there was someone laid, and I could swear she was . . ."

"Hush." The vampiress leaned close, slipping the coin back under her pillow. "In better times I shall hope to show you the beauty of my home, but for now you must trouble no more with it."

"Very well have your way," Emelyn said, seizing her hand again. "But how could you have known what happened to me today, except by Mr. Lorris. You must know him?"

For some while Vaela was silent, until with a relenting sound she answered. "He is captain of the Lurkmen, the queen's most able mortal servants, empowered each by a single drop of her blood."

Emelyn rested on Vaela's knuckles, adjusting her comfort. "So it's true . . . the Lurkmen are real. And why should they follow me?"

"When you roam abroad in daylight the queen's men will know it. But they are not to interfere with you."

"But I thank the stars he did," Emelyn said. "And do the Lurkmen ride out from Saunmoor, to capture children as the tales say?"

"Only those poor waifs who shan't be missed, forgotten foundlings born of predators and prostitutes."

Thinking to ask whether the queen devoured them indeed, Emelyn started to speak, but in conjuring the image she lost her nerve. "I can't imagine, but . . . I drew it," she said, interrupting herself. "The cane of Mr. Lorris, with a lion's head. It's there on the desk."

Vaela appeared by the desk, the illustration in her hand. "It's well done," she said. "The cane is a symbol of his office, passed down from his forebears.”

Emelyn reached out and the vampiress returned in a blink, sitting close beside her. “I have learned there is an Order of men conspiring after Hastelbrook,” Emelyn said, taking her arm again to hold it tightly. “They want the vault, and whatever treasure it holds.”

“Mortals are no threat to the vault. It is claimed by our queen; she will suffer no one else to plunder it.”

As Emelyn thought on this her eyelids grew heavy. “Then why has she not come for it?”

For a moment a shadow of fear shown in Vaela’s face. “Because the key yet eludes her,” she said, “and for that I am grateful. You must ask me no more tonight.”

Adjusting her pillow Emelyn closed her eyes again. “Fine. But you must know the Bodleian libraries at Oxford? Perhaps I might disguise myself as a man, and gain entrance . . . for research.”

Vaela sighed. “The atheneum of Saunmoor is older and deeper than any library in London,” she said, “but even there you would find nothing to elucidate the history of the vault. It is a mystery, even to us.”

“It’s not fair,” Emelyn whispered, her head growing light.

“Take heart little one.” Vaela said, leaning down to kiss forehead. “Your interview with the antiquarian was informative, more than you know. I have work to do.”

“Hmm?” Emelyn opened her eyes, but Vaela was gone.

■ ■

A new steady rain washed through the gutters of Buckingham Street, making its way south over the old pier into the black rush of the Thames. Just by the edge of the water stood a narrow warehouse, its lower windows flickering by the light of a single candle set inside near the wall, amplified by a cracked folding mirror. Three young women, in working dresses and bonnets sat close by on stools, stitching together pieces for sumptuous gowns of Spitalfields silk. Behind them sat four again, staggered to catch a bit of the candle as they worked with raw fingers to sew lace embellishments into the heaps of fabric at their feet. And still farther behind, crowded against tables stacked with bandboxes, hunched a wide half circle of six more young girls, straining to catch the very last of the light as they worked to embroider mantua sleeves and collars, each face mere inches from her needle.

Lady Lucille had been running her dressmaker's shop for many years, taking on poor girls who weren't afraid to work day and night through the season, many of them sleeping on the floor of the shop between shifts. One of these was Penny Attridge, a humble slip of a girl not yet thirteen, who sat in the farthest position of third-light, against the wide shop doors. The day had carried on eighteen hours now, and she startled from a dizzy swoon as a new candle flashed into the room. The girls paused their sewing to look up as their mistress entered from the stairs, clad in a woollen robe and nightcap as she held the light high.

"Well done girls," Miss Lucille said. "One last push, and we shall see the duchess and her daughters triumphantly finished! It is nearly two o'clock, and I've decided you shall have each an extra bit of bread and butter, with honey if you like."

"Miss Lucille," Penny Attridge entreated, raising her hand. "I was to be off early for me father's sake; I must go to him, if you please."

"The lamps have all gone out Miss Attridge," Lucille said. "I cannot allow you should walk home at such an hour, not through Durham Yard anyway."

"But I been feelin' terrible light in the head ma'am," Penny protested, rubbing her eyes as she leaned against the doors.

"You've been squirreling your food," Lucille said. "Don't think I haven't noticed. You're only dizzy because you haven't eaten. Now I suggest you do so, and then we must resume until dawn; we shan't be the shop to embarrass the Duchess of Rutland!"

"Me father got nothing to eat mistress," Penny said, standing from her stool as the others looked on. "They stopped his work on account of his coughing; I can be there and back in an hour, please!"

"This is not how you earn second-light Penny," Lucille warned. "If he's not eaten for a day he can certainly wait until morning."

"But I've promised!" Penny insisted, taking off her apron. "There's nothing for it mistress, I must go!"

"If you step into that alley you needn't bother coming back!"

With three rolls and a cold cooked potato wrapped in her apron Penny Attridge huddled under her cloak as the door slammed and locked behind her. Frowning into the rain driven darkness, she wiped her eyes and set off for home, keeping to the overhangs as best she could.

Splashing around corners she proceeded northeast into the wide lane of Durham Yard, lamenting the extinguished lanterns she passed, their candles having been cold an hour at least. She pressed on, stepping quickly past yawning gaps in the buildings, where a few wretched destitutes slumped or huddled. The rain came softer, and she tingled with fear at the sight of two men bearing a lantern, approaching down the lane ahead of her. Seeking a detour, she veered into a narrow alley strewn with bags and crates of waste from the local glassblowers, finding it a dead end, though the back wall of the factory was recessed and dry, kept perpetually warm by the furnaces. Penny crouched into the corner of the brick among upright pallets and bundles of rags left by squatters, holding her breath as she watched the end of the alley.

Soon enough the male figures began to slouch past, and paused. Penny lowered her head to hide her face as gruff voices argued, and one of them started toward her, bearing the light.

"You can't see me . . . you can't see me," Penny whispered, repeating the words as she pressed her forehead to her knees.

"Sovereign for your time love?" the man hailed, sloshing closer.

"Too grimy for games!" the other called. "Leave it alone."

"Is that rubbish I espy, or is that you poppet?" the first man chuckled. "I've got a bit o' Shrewsbury cake here; it's all yours for a chat."

He drew nearer, and then, with a sudden crash he was gone. Penny looked up to spot a contorted shadow tumble from the wall into the boxes as the lantern spluttered, lolling on the ground. There was a splash of fleeing footsteps, and she startled with a sob as a man's cry split the air, and was cut short. The steady wash of the rain returned, and a dark silhouette appeared just at the far edge of the light. Struggling to her feet with her bundle, Penny pulled her cloak tighter, straining to see through the haze as she prepared to bolt . . .

"Softly now, don't scream," a female voice spoke very close.

Mad with fright Penny opened her mouth to cry out, but managed only a whimper as she found the tall hooded shape of a woman beside her. The lady was clad all in black, but with no gloves, her bare feet drenched in the soggy sludge of the alley.

"I think your father works at the Devil's Inn on Fleet Street," the woman said, her captivating stare deep and welcome. "Does he not?"

Penny nodded. "Yes ma'am," she answered, finding her voice. "He's porter in the basements, and minds the furnace. But he's gone weak in the lungs by the smoke, and they've forbid him to work, lest he be contagious."

The rain settled into a gentle mist as they regarded each other, and the woman in black offered her hand. "My name is Vaela," she said. "Come now, I shall walk you home."

Leaving the guttering lantern behind they returned to the lane and set on their way, by and by stopping before an old boarded butcher shop.

The woman took a breath, looking it over. "Stay here," she said.

"But it's long closed ma'am," Penny said, holding her hand tightly.

"It isn't."

"Mistress?" Penny ventured, but she was alone.

Moments later the woman reappeared, and Penny caught the smoky scent of something wonderful.

"I know you've collected for your father," the woman said, "but you must eat," and she handed over a large, dried loin of pork.

Penny whimpered for the joy of it, her mouth filling with water. "Is it a smokehouse! How did ye know?" and she tore free a chunk, chewing the savoury crust of meat and swallowing with a groan.

The woman smiled, offering her hand. "Come . . ."

A few bites later a dimly glowing doorway yawned on their left, and at the sight of a frail, sickly man leaning in the frame Penny tried in vain to pull her escort to the far side of the street. "Mustn't pass this way, must go around," she implored, but the woman continued to walk, holding her hand tightly.

The man in the door made a gesture to someone inside and drew a long knife as they passed, stepping to block their path. "Now here's a pair of pretties," he said, grinning with brown teeth as he fingered the blade. "Hello my loves!"

The woman in black stopped, giving him a smile.

"No," Penny pleaded, sheltering in her cloak.

With scolding clicks of his tongue the fellow reached for Penny's hair, but the vampiress pushed her aside, and sprouting claws she seized into the man's chest, crushing him to the ground . . .

Penny startled with a jolt to find herself once again holding the woman's hand as they walked, the sound of distant cries and crashing glass fading in her ears like a nightmare slipping away. Before them rose shabby leaning tenements, and she puzzled as they climbed a narrow stair, drawing a key from her pocket to fumble at the lock.

The latch turned and Penny looked back. "Wait," she said, blinking at a spot of blood on her sleeve. "But what's happened mistress? Was there not . . . were there not men who set upon us?"

"Their lights have all gone out," Vaela said. "Nothing you need remember . . . You see, I have brought you home."

"You've brought me home," Penny repeated. "But please, will you come in?"

"I'd like nothing more."

The vampiress slipped inside behind her, finding the small room illuminated by a tallow lantern burning on the window ledge. The humble space was furnished with two chairs and a cooking stove, with a narrow bed in the corner, occupied by a lanky, ruddy faced fellow in soot stained shirt, his legs under a blanket.

Spluttering in shock at the sight of them, he lunged for the stool at his bedside, coming up with a pistol. "Penny my girl get away from her!" he barked, his face pale as he drew back the hammer. "I see your fine cloak madam; night hunting bawd you'll not have her!"

"Papa no!" Penny cried, brandishing the meat. "She saved me from some bloody pinkers she did, see what she's brought us!"

"She only wants you in her debt my lass!" her father snapped.

Vaela lowered her hood to address him. "Thomas Attridge. I've not come to corrupt your daughter."

"Then we can have nothing ye want," he retorted, levelling the weapon. "Now if it please you *my lady*, take back what ye brought us and be off, ere I make a hole in that fine robe!"

Vaela's smile faded as he shook the pistol at her, and in a blink she'd snatched him from the bed, lifting him against the wall as she caught his wrist. The gun clattered to the floor and the man blanched with terror, his feet dangling free.

"Don't hurt him!" Penny begged.

The vampiress locked eyes with her prey, pulling him close. "You must master yourself," she commanded, allowing him to sink until his toes touched the floor.

"Take me if ye must," he blubbered, "but spare the girl I beg of you!"

Vaela snarled, drawing him into her embrace. "If I wanted your daughter, I'd not have walked her home," she breathed, baring her fangs. "It is you I must have," and with a hiss she fastened to his throat. For several swallows the blood coursed warm, until releasing him with a shiver she wiped her mouth, looking to find Penny huddled in the corner, hiding her face.

The man started to speak but she caught his chin, pressing him to the wall to lick at his throat.

Shuddering with a moan he relaxed as the mark of the bite smoothed and vanished. "I'll not resist," he said. "Do what you will . . . Penny run girl!"

"Penny do not run," Vaela ordered, holding her father's face and sniffing at his mouth. "Silly creatures, I mean to help you," and releasing him into the wall she withdrew, pinching her lip with the tip of her fang. "Your lungs are strong," she said, kissing her fingertip to wet it with blood, "but you've an infection in your breath."

Moments later a recovered father and daughter sat on the bed before her, sharing the bread and potato as they finished the pork, sipping a jug of beer between them.

"There's fair magic in your blood mistress," he said, swiping his mouth. "My breath is come back to me, clean and easy . . ."

"Your daughter was discharged from the dressmaker's," Vaela said, reaching into her cloak and producing a handful of gold coins, which she pressed into his hand.

"Oh mistress!" Penny gasped, looking on as her father coughed in disbelief.

"Twenty guineas Mr. Attridge," Vaela said, crouching before him to take each of their hands. "See that your bellies are full, and your clothes mended, but speak of this to no one, for it would put you in danger. I will send instruction, that Penny may have lessons, to better her prospects. Tomorrow you must return to work."

"And what I ever done?" he asked, his eyes going wet, "angry sack like me . . . to deserve such as you given us?"

Vaela smiled. "But you haven't done it yet. You work as porter, you tend the furnace and watch the doors in the basement of the Devil's Inn. There is a brotherhood of gentlemen who take secret meetings there during the day."

Mr. Attridge squared his jaw, gripping Penny's shoulder as she clung to him. "Aye," he said, "gentlemen of quality, and for dark business if I don't mistake . . ."

"Who is their leader?" Is it Baron Dramen?"

"It is indeed, what I heard. I know that Lord Dramen by face, but I only ever seen him upstairs, never about the meetings."

"I wish to know more of their *dark business*," Vaela said, rising to her feet. "It will be yours to listen, and learn what you can, carefully."

"Are they your enemies mistress?" he asked.

Moving to the door the vampiress glanced back at the pair of them. "See to the duty I've given you," she said. "As for the furnace, use only new split wood, clean and dry; that basement is too small for burning coal . . . and take care of your father," she added, looking at Penny.

Penny nodded. The door clicked closed as Vaela stepped onto the landing, and breathing in the scent of the air, she vanished into the dark.

∎∎

Thursday June 16ᵗʰ

"You've locked your door miss! Shall I come in? Are you feeling better?"

Emelyn startled awake to find the early light of dawn filling the room. "Much better, Breda, just coming!" she called, sliding out of bed to greet the day.

Amazed to find her mistress's bruise healed overnight, Breda assisted her into a square necked day gown of sandcastle silk, coiling her hair up tightly anticipating a wide brimmed shepherdess hat, which Emelyn was keen to wear for walking at Dhorings.

Uncle Fallworth shook his niece's hand vigorously at the door. "You must come and see us again as soon as you're happily able!"

Emelyn kissed his cheek and bid him farewell, squeezing her cousin's arm before climbing quickly aboard for her departure. Comby was tired but content, the swelling in his face nearly gone, and his colour much restored. Their hired coach was of the special rapid line of Hack & Humble, and it being a great deal more expensive Emelyn insisted on contributing, though her uncle would not hear of it.

The resulting journey incurred only two stops for fresh horses, and the trip home carried off much more pleasantly than had the way up. By one o'clock in the afternoon the village of Hastelbrook was in sight, and a few impatient minutes later the coach pulled to a stop.

Emelyn leapt down from the vehicle. "Oh my happy fortress," she said, looking up to the stout granite walls of the house.

Mrs. Morley greeted them at once. "My dear Emelyn, were you not to go straight on to Dhorings?"

"We were obliged to return home again," Emelyn said. "Now I must speak to Papa."

"But how was your uncle, and the Townsends? You did see them."

"I did Mama, of course. Where is Papa?"

"Oh he's on business."

"Where?"

"In Brighton my dear; we expect him tomorrow. But the Townsends! What do we think of them? I very much hope they've not planned some great renovation, though your father insists they be given a loose rein . . ."

Relieved her father had not left for London, Emelyn answered as briefly as she could, recounting her visit with the Fallworths and the tenants, confessing no knowledge of their plans for the house, and leaving out Bannister's proposal. "Now I don't want you to be alarmed," she said finally, "but Comby came to grief at the hands of ruffians; that is why we've returned."

"Good heavens, how careless! How did it happen?"

"Not of his own doing; he was about errands . . . for me. Fortunately he is no more than bruised, and I adjure you to ask him no more of it; let him rest."

"Then you are to cancel your trip to Dhorings Park for his sake?"

"No Mama, I mean to set out at once. I only wish Papa were here."

"Well I'm sorry my dearest, we don't expect him before tomorrow. But will you join us for London?"

Emelyn almost laughed. "Thank you Mama, but if I never see London again I shan't mourn its loss."

"Oh what nonsense," her mother said, looking over the sleek black carriage they'd arrived in. "Dished wheels with iron hoops! How very modern."

Emelyn thought of her pocketbook, yet stuffed with cash, and the bank notes, and ensuing explanation, she must deliver to her father. "I suppose waiting another day shall do no harm."

"And you dare not forget," her mother added, "Lord Van Croft returns to us tomorrow as well, so we shall expect you early as possible."

"Lord Van Croft tomorrow! I confess it slipped my mind . . ."

Preparations were swiftly made, the grateful coachman was fed and watered, and Emelyn took a light dinner in the parlour before climbing back into the coach. Her heart hummed at the prospect of seeing Margaret, and fingering the coin in her pocket, she settled in next to Breda for the drive west, watching the green and yellow hills as they rowed past.

Chapter 14
Proof and Scandal

The palatial estate of Dhorings Park was home to the Dowager Countess Barteria Mettles, now Lady Dhorings, the wealthiest woman in the county and widow of the late Earl of Dhorings. Margaret Mettles was the dowager's last unmarried grandchild, her own parents having died when she was very young, and she'd lived at Dhorings Park in sheltered opulence ever since. Nestled on verdurous hills in West Sussex, the great manor inspired jealousy for many leagues around, owing in principle to its tiered gardens, centred with cascading water, which were cut each into the hillside like stepped porches over columns, and bordered at either hand by grand swooping stairs, which curved inward at the bottom of the hill by a gathering pool. Catching first sight of the estate was always a joy, and Emelyn leaned forward to espy its granite towers as they came into view precisely on schedule, two and a half hours journey from Hastelbrook.

A clear and cool afternoon found the expansive party gathered outside for the competitive shoot, some tenth of a mile downhill from the manor where manicured green faded to wide tufted fields, broken with white rocks and brambled scrub. Fifteen gentlemen in hunting jackets and cornered hats called out to each other, preparing to take their aim at an elaborate field of targets: high poles with stuffed birds, wood shields carved as deer and smaller as rabbits and foxes, all positioned at varying distances ranked by points for difficulty. Younger lads took up places behind the men, holding spare muskets ready loaded, while the ladies loitered nearby to watch, their parasols shifting and turning like so many restless pigeons.

Some way apart from them Emelyn took a languid walk with her friend.

"And the three ablest gentlemen shall be invited to return in August, and hunt the whole season long," Margaret explained, holding her arm.

"I love the park in Summer," Emelyn said, squinting under her hand at the far tree tops rippling in the Spring breeze, "the forest so peaceful, so expressive in the wind . . ."

Margaret hopped over a rock, before taking her arm again. "But is it true they feared you should die?"

"What? When?" Emelyn asked, recalling abruptly Robert the Blade's attack.

"You languished with deathly chill for twelve hours! Is it not true?"

"Oh that." Emelyn found herself chuckling. "T'was nothing Mags, really; the fever vanished as quickly as it appeared."

"That seems incredible."

"Well anyway, not the sort of thing I relish remembering under such a beautiful day."

"You're right Em, I'm sorry." Margaret nodded, twisting the parasol in her hand. "You know, Fitzwilliam Arkwright is there, among the gentlemen."

"Is he indeed," Emelyn said casually.

A whistle sounded, and in pairs the men began to fire; musket shots ripped through the air, cracking impossibly loud. Dropping her parasol Emelyn yelped in shock, covering her ears. The musket boys traded fresh guns for the shooters to fire again, and wincing at the skull rattling sound she collapsed to her knees, gasping for breath.

Margaret cried out in alarm, crouching beside her. "What is it? Emie what's wrong?"

"It's the noise," Emelyn breathed, forcing a smile as the echo of the guns died away, and for a moment she could hear the splinter and crunch of every bit of target as it broke away and hit the ground, while smatters of distant conversation drifted in and out as though spoken directly to her face. The inside of her ears itched horribly, and she rubbed them, startling to find spots of blood on her fingertips.

"Oh Emie your ears are bleeding!" Margaret gasped.

"Dammit," Emelyn groused, "I fear I must impose for new gloves."

Margaret produced a kerchief, dropping her own parasol. "Of course," she said, wetting the cloth in her mouth and catching Emelyn by the neck to scrub at her ear.

Emelyn winced as another round of firing commenced, though farther away. "I'm sure it's nothing . . ."

"We're going back," Margaret said firmly, turning Emelyn's chin to scrub the other side.

They'd made some progress on the hike back before noticing one of the men had broken from the line to fetch their parasols, jogging up the gentle hill to catch them. Emelyn closed one eye against the glare as she watched him, finding it was Mr. Arkwright most certainly, in a storm grey hunting frock over his ivory waistcoat, dark hair pulled back under his cocked hat.

"Miss Mettles, Miss Morley, but you look to have dropped your shade," he panted, catching up to hand them over. "I made as fast as I could, lest the blinding sun be the end of you."

Emelyn smiled at the familiar musk of his cologne. "Mr. Arkwright, we are in your debt. I shall recommend your valour to Lady Dhorings when we find her."

"The sooner the better," he said, touching his hat.

Emelyn rested the parasol on her shoulder. "We saw you take your fight to the targets. And how did you fare?"

"Just made my case for third slot of three," he confided, offering his arm. "May I see you up, to the shade of the gardens at least?"

"Thank you sir," Emelyn said, taking his elbow. "And congratulations on your place; I understand you're obliged now to return in August, for the infestation of partridge."

"I must do my part," he said gravely. "But I see you break ranks with the other ladies; shall I hope you mean to prepare a song for us?"

Emelyn's hands began to sweat in her gloves, and she smiled at him again. "If I am so disposed."

"Dispose how you will," he said. "I've been able to think of little else but your voice, since the ball at Hastelbrook."

It were as though she could feel the very pulse of his blood through their touch. "Despite my pronunciation?" she asked.

"Rather because of it," he replied. "I'll hear no one else."

Margaret cleared her throat. "Nor I, but I suppose we must have food, games and party before singing."

The inside of Emelyn's stays began to tickle and tantalize, very like she'd felt in the grip of the bloodsick, and a tremble of alarm fluttered through her. "Stop it . . ."

"Emelyn?" Margaret checked, taking her other arm as they walked.

"My dear Mags," Emelyn said quickly, distracted by the increasing beat of Mr. Arkwright's heart.

Navigating the immaculate green every step was more difficult than the last, and it required great focus not to stop and grab the man, to feel him against her . . . as too slowly the grand cascading gardens of Dhorings Park drew closer.

"Beautiful afternoon is it not?" Arkwright remarked, and Emelyn faltered with a gasp.

Margaret pulled for them to stop, her face concerned. "Emie! I fear she is not well; are you well? What is wrong?"

"I regret my jest about the parasols," Arkwright said. "But perhaps the sun overbears, we must get her to the house, quickly."

"Just . . . give me a moment!" Emelyn demanded, and releasing his arm she rolled her neck, striving to catch her breath. The air was warm and oppressive, and she began to think if she but tasted his lips . . . perhaps the heat within her would be satisfied. *Even your passions will increase . . . until you master them.* Vaela's words came startling back, and it was all she could do not to panic.

"Emelyn I'm frightened!" Margaret burst, her voice like a close and unwelcome bird call.

Emelyn leaned over, her arm tight across her chest. "Stop talking!"

The gentleman shifted where he stood, and desperate for any measure of calm she raised her eyes, allowing herself to look at him.

Arkwright's face was stern with worry, his hazel eyes tenderly affected, and breathing against her arm Emelyn found his gallant reticence the most alluring thing that ever was. With a relenting moan she straightened her back, holding his gaze as she came to him, and seeming to mark her intention he seized her about the waist, and kissed her.

Their connection was halting at first, but his lips fit perfectly, and Emelyn closed her eyes as Margaret shrieked, brandishing her parasol to shelter them both. For ecstatic moments the kiss was joined, and joined again, until with a breathless flush they parted, Arkwright retreating as Emelyn did the same, a wet tingle on her lips.

Mr. Arkwright snatched off his hat. "Miss Morley forgive me."

"No," Emelyn panted, the heat in her body ebbing at last. "I won't, that is . . . I'll not forgive what I would not be without."

"Excuse us, Mr. Arkwright!" Margaret said loudly, taking Emelyn's wrist and pulling her away. "Emie what is wrong with you!" she hissed.

"I don't know!" Emelyn lamented, glancing back as they hastened from the man's company.

The kiss lingered on her lips, the gravity of the indiscretion coming clearer as they reached the wide pool at the bottom of the garden tiers.

Margaret marched her in silence, and together they mounted the long granite stairs, hiking up the steps before crossing the drive to approach the eminence of the house. Turning back to look down at him Emelyn found Mr. Arkwright standing in the same place, crushing his hat to his chest as he stared up at them.

Escorted inside and swiftly upstairs, she was soon sat on a yellow chaise longue in a corner sitting room, hat and gloves on the floor, nursing a medicinal glass of Canary wine as her friend fretted, pacing before her.

"Perhaps it was apoplexy," Maggie suggested, "but he did kiss you, and you allowed it; perhaps hysterical paroxysm?"

"Oh will you stop guessing!" Emelyn rubbed her brows. "I'm not hysterical, only mortified . . . There is nothing wrong with me Mags."

"But there must be," Margaret protested, her eyes wet with concern, "you were bleeding at the ears . . . and then to see you in such a passion, such lack of restraint, like I'd never imagine in my friend!"

"Yes I know, I'm sorry Mags," Emelyn groaned, "but it was never my intention, after all I've only come to see you; I quite forgot Mr. Arkwright would be here."

"But I rather think we should avoid the party altogether . . . Should we not send for the doctor? If anything else were to happen . . ."

"No, Maggie, please," Emelyn said, fighting her nerves as she set down the glass. "I'll not have you afraid for me; I'm sure worse things have happened than a kiss . . . But there is more I must tell you."

"More?" Margaret asked warily. "Oh Emie anything but vampires."

"Shall you have the truth?" Emelyn tapped the couch for Margaret to sit beside her. "Or would you rather inflict me with every illness you've ever heard of."

Margaret inhaled with a nod, taking her seat. "You're right . . . Tell me what you will, and if I faint dead away let me sleep."

"You've already had the worst of it," Emelyn said, thinking it best to leave out the excursion to London altogether. "I really was not sick after all," and determined to keep the tale as pleasant as possible she described everything she knew, or thought she knew, of the power in Vaela's blood, how it could heal, what changes it had wrought within her, and that the freezing fever had only been the end of her body's resistance to its effect.

The cheerful light of afternoon faded to the mature glow of evening as they talked, Emelyn struggling to define the bond she shared with the vampiress, and promising her friend she would never become one herself, not unless she were to drink of Vaela's blood at the very point of death.

"How horrible!" Margaret exclaimed.

"No Mags, you need never fear such a thing," Emelyn said, and after fielding a few more squeamish questions she closed her story with some attempt to explain the incident on the hill. "So perhaps it is only that I am still recovering, but I assure you I am quite myself."

"But I saw the hunger in your eyes. When you approached him, were you thinking to bite his neck?"

"Oh my goodness Maggie no," Emelyn said, leaning back. "I've no fangs, no thirst for blood; I was contending with a sudden passion that is all."

"Contending very badly I would say," Margaret grumbled, "and he fared little better . . ."

"Yes all right," Emelyn said, striving for patience, "but the moment passed, and I'll not hear ill of him."

"Fine," Margaret said. "But if you are determined to come down you mustn't be seen anywhere near him, not tonight."

Reluctantly Emelyn agreed, and as the soft dim of dusk settled over the estate the party began in earnest, though after joining the happy throng she found she could not help feeling almost supernaturally conscious of Mr. Arkwright's location. The game room came alive with lights and laughter after dessert, and she caught his eye time and again as he sat for cards with a group of gentlemen across the room. The passionate frenzy within her had faded, and with it the titillating symptoms, but the desire to speak to him and settle what had happened came stronger as the evening wore on.

Distracting herself with table games and a relative parade of introductions, Emelyn drank some wine and laughed a little, holding the need to confront him at bay as she acquainted Margaret's younger friends, who with cousin Elton came to the estate but rarely. Prodded for details of her presentation to the king and queen on her debut, as well as what it had been to dance with the Prince of Wales at her first ball, she answered as best she could, balancing truth with fiction.

"Margaret's stories are ever so dull!" one of the girls complained.

"I only thought you should find out for yourselves," Margaret said, draining her wine.

The games played on, as continuing to account for Mr. Arkwright Emelyn was pleased to find him doing the very same: pulling his pocket watch as his eyes strayed over her person before finding the correct time, or turning with a contemplative look as though he'd missed something in the ceiling, and finding her again before returning to his cards.

New bottles adorned fresh table linens as empties were cleared away; cheerful music ushered the hours through, and sitting for Margaret's instruction on the finer points of *blackjack* Emelyn tilted her head, stretching to watch Mr. Arkwright as he leaned from his chair to fetch an errant card off the floor.

"And here you've seventeen," Maggie said, studying the table, "but there are too many low cards showing, so you mustn't risk hunting up another . . . Emie you're staring!"

"Hit!" Emelyn declared, returning her focus to the game.

The dealer drew her a ten.

"You must stop your eyes," Maggie scolded, "respectfully Mr. Arkwright keeps his distance; you must encourage him by taking no notice."

Flattering regard from the other gentlemen came in gusts, appearing under the pretence of advice, whether for cards, dice or assistance with her aim at paired billiards, and Emelyn had little peace before segregating herself again for a lesson at backgammon with Maggie.

"And I shall sit here," Margaret said, leaving open the chair facing the windows.

"Certainly," Emelyn said with a smile.

Losing every game in spectacular fashion, despite the recommendations of a chatty gentleman standing just close enough to include himself, her mind strayed from Maggie's tutelage, and Emelyn retained but little of the lesson.

"The game is five thousand years old Emie," Margaret chuckled, sorting the pieces for another match, "there's been plenty of time to learn."

"Not again Mags." Emelyn sighed, watching as encroaching shadow crept over the grounds, "you've quite finished me."

"Well I've not yet played hazard," Maggie said as they rose from their chairs. "Grandmama gave me a lovely set of dice. Shall we?"

"No thank you," Emelyn said, scanning the room. "Hazard is more rules than fun; I think I shall float."

Vibrant sweets like crushed flowers were brought in on silver trays, and promising Margaret her best behaviour Emelyn left the table to wander about, drifting on the currents of idle conversation. She found Mr. Arkwright igniting a stem reed pipe, standing a fair way off by the mantel, and checking for Margaret she started toward him, until looking up he met her eyes, and she lost her nerve, turning to accept a glass of wine from an eager young officer whom she'd earlier acquainted. The young man fawned with rehearsed pleasantries, and Emelyn nodded as she sipped.

"Do you mean to say you *have* toured the roses at Inner Temple, or you have not?" the officer puzzled, addressing the gap in her attention.

"I have . . . not. That is not since I was very small," she said, watching Mr. Arkwright as he laughed at a colleague's expense, before slapping the fellow on the back in apology.

"Did I see you stumble on the way up to the house, Miss Morley?"

Emelyn turned to find the unremarkable Shelley Browning, a smallish young lady she knew only by distant acquaintance. "I beg your pardon?"

Miss Browning shook her head, making a confused face. "I thought I saw you . . . Oh it's nothing I'm sure."

"I'm sure it is," Emelyn replied, feeling hot in the face, "excuse me."

But Mr. Arkwright, as far as she could gather, had stepped out. Patience was called for. The candles burned low, and failing to conceal her lack of interest in the speeches of others, Emelyn was left alone once more. Coming to stand at the windows she stared through the high glass between drapes of Turkish magenta, seeking distraction in the view: grand gardens painted in muted shades under the starlight as they marched away and down the open hillside out of sight. Her gaze skipped to the dark foam of the distant forest, and thinking again of Vaela she held her fan tightly to her chest, eyes wide to ponder how many vampires must exist in the whole of Britain, and whether they served the same vampire queen one and all.

"My dear Elizabeth you clutch that fan as though a frog might jump out of your bosom," an unmistakable voice pronounced, and she turned to find the Dowager Countess herself, the only person who addressed Emelyn by her middle name. Lady Dhorings was a robust and imposing matron, clad in a lavish gown of royal blue and silver, her explosive grey hair tucked under an enormous hat, well flowered and feathered.

"Your Ladyship," Emelyn said quickly, closing her fan for a low curtsy, and casting a final glance at the mantel she found Mr. Arkwright was not there.

Taking her arm Lady Dhorings guided her to sit at a lush mustard sofa with a wide view of the party. "I must concede," she began, tapping Emelyn's knee with a gaudy fan, "you look uncommonly fresh for someone white with fever only three days past."

"Four days past, Your Ladyship," Emelyn corrected, searching over the room, "and I was never white with fever; it was only exhaustion I'm sure."

"One is not strapped to one's bed for exhaustion," Lady Dhorings asserted.

"Forgive me Your Ladyship, it was a night I'd as soon forget; might we speak of something else?"

"Of course my dear!" the lady clucked, batting her knee again. "I only compliment your fortitude . . . the jewel of Sussex, your seventh season and yet unmarried! But I cannot think what sorcery you've employed to keep them away."

"Unfortunate choices perhaps," Emelyn sighed, her agitation growing to have espied no sign of the gentleman.

"There is nothing unfortunate about you," Lady Dhorings rebuffed. "Now let us hear of your family, and omit nothing, or I shall know it."

Speaking to every bit of Morley business she could think of, excepting financial matters, Emelyn talked of her parents and her sisters, confessing she'd little in the way of news for Deacon, who rarely left home. Fitzwilliam Arkwright remained stubbornly invisible as they conversed, and she began to fear he could think of leaving without a goodbye . . .

"Your BROTHER dear," Lady Dhorings repeated, "are there not renewed concerns over his health?"

"Renewed? Well I can't imagine where you've heard so," Emelyn said, trying to see around the boisterous group in front of them. "Deacon is as well as can be expected."

"Oh my dear Elizabeth where do you suppose you are? If I've not heard it, it isn't news. I had the dire report of Doctor Bayten himself; I assisted him in his investments if you recall, when my Roger was still wheezing about. There is no glamour in tin, but in quantity the stuff may amount to something."

Emelyn blinked at her. "Tin?"

"You understand the concern," Lady Dhorings said. "Hastelbrook is entailed my dear, and if, Lord forbid, your poor brother should perish before his time, that most unfortunate cousin stands to inherit."

"Charles Wellsea," Emelyn said. "We do not speak of him; I scarcely understand how we're related."

"By your father's great aunt, who was known for a greedy corner haunting flimsy, and Charles no better. A Wellsea is no Morley my dear; I've always said it."

"I'm sorry Your Ladyship," Emelyn said, feeling little desire to discuss the inheritance. "I confess I'm distracted; I was looking for . . . for

Margaret."

Lady Dhorings cleared her throat, signalling a change of topic. "There are little whispers about the room," she confided, "that Fitzwilliam Arkwright rather bumped into you on the hill."

The heat rose to her face and Emelyn swallowed. "No I don't know," she said, scowling at her lap as she smoothed her gown. "I can't imagine what that is."

"Yes I see," Lady Dhorings said thoughtfully. "But of course he is a capital gentleman by anyone's measure, so we shall skip these little whispers, and put our minds to whatever it is so obviously distressing you."

"Oh," Emelyn said. "Forgive me, it is nothing, truly."

"Aha. Well, whatever sort of nothing it is, I can see sitting here with me is the very worst remedy."

"Oh no, I couldn't say," Emelyn answered, feeling both impolite and ridiculous.

"Well go on my dear," Lady Dhorings said, shooing with her fan. "I daresay we can spare you a few moments."

Emelyn jumped to her feet with a gratified curtsy, setting off at once. Turning the corner her heart stopped at the sight of both Margaret and Mr. Arkwright standing across the enormity of the white tiled grand hall, speaking under the gaze of a lofty Greek statue. Maggie spoke with evident displeasure, while Arkwright leaned attentively, nodding as he listened. Catching sight of her the two ceased their conversation, and the gentleman gave a strict bow, turning to make his way down the stairs for the front doors.

Emelyn walked quickly, coming to her friend. "Maggie what have you told him?"

"Don't follow him, Emie please," Margaret beseeched, grabbing her arm. "You shall see him again when it is more fitting."

Emelyn twisted free but Margaret caught her wrist again.

"Emelyn stop! You must think!"

"Don't!" Emelyn pulled away.

The footmen opened the doors before her, Margaret trailing behind with protests, and Emelyn dashed outside, finding Mr. Arkwright just trotting out of the stable house on his steed. He paused on the drive at the bottom of the great fanning steps, and Emelyn gripped her skirts, rushing down to meet him.

"Miss Morley," he said, offering a smile, though there was sadness in his eyes. "I can only apologize again for my offence; a true gentleman would never have taken such advantage of your state."

"Whatever can you mean?" Emelyn asked, reaching out as his horse began to walk. "Wait sir, please . . ."

"I beg your leave madam," he said. "I'll not hector a woman I so admire; not where it should unsettle her recovery."

"My recovery? Please, if I might explain . . ."

"Your deportment is admirable sir," Margaret announced, coming to her side, "in light of the circumstances."

"Wait, please will you come down," Emelyn requested, and the gentleman swallowed, but he did not look at her.

"We wish you a safe road to Crawley of course," Margaret said.

"Miss Mettles, Miss Morley." Arkwright tipped his hat, and Emelyn watched in disbelief as he nudged his horse, launching to gallop away down the drive.

"Emie please come inside, it's colder than it should be, you'll catch a chill."

Emelyn stood aghast. "I don't understand . . . but was he angry with me? What on earth did you say to him?"

"Emie please," Margaret repeated. "You were too familiar; you are not yourself!"

Emelyn gaped at her, confounded. "My state? My recovery? Am I a madwoman?"

"Never!" Margaret offered her hand. "I only told him you were delicate of late, that you'd been very ill, which certainly you have."

"Maggie that is a lie! How could you say such things?"

"Emie he kissed you! Not your hand, nor even your cheek but a full married kiss! In clear daylight just up the hill from the shooting party; most of whom did not see but I'm quite sure a few of them did."

"He only kissed me to stop me kissing him first!" Emelyn insisted. "I daresay he wanted it as much as I, but how much worse if I'd been the one to," and she stopped short with an unhappy noise, infuriated to find herself making Maggie's argument for her.

"You see?" Margaret said, her eyes welling with sympathy. "Emelyn I love you like my own life, and you . . ."

"It was never your place to send him away!" Emelyn interrupted. "How ridiculous and girlish I must seem to him, now that you've robbed me of any chance to explain myself!"

"Emie can you not see it?" Margaret said miserably. "You are not well."

An arresting cold settled in her guts as Emelyn stared at her. "I am not well?"

"Look at everything that's happened; you need time Emie . . . you need help."

Emelyn's breath caught in her throat. "You don't believe me . . . You don't believe any of it."

"Oh Emelyn, I want to," Margaret said, crinkling her fan, "I want it more than anything, but vampires come to protect you? How could anyone believe such things? Can you not allow the illness may have affected your mind . . ."

"I spoke to you of Vaela well before I fell ill," Emelyn protested.

"Yes, but can you really be certain . . . you were not ill already?" Margaret asked gently.

Emelyn stifled the urge to scream, and breathing through her nose she pulled off her gloves. "I see now it was unfair of me, to confide in you."

"Don't say that."

Clearing her throat, Emelyn wiped her eyes with a fury. "There are dark things in this world Maggie, things we cannot explain. Take this for example!" and snapping out the coin she handed it over.

"What is it? What is the Latin?" Margaret asked, turning it over.

"The Latin . . . it doesn't matter. It's a coin, a bronze coin from her realm Maggie, from where she comes from."

Slowly Margaret returned the coin. "It must be an old trade token. But fifty years ago such things were common."

"Common is it?" Emelyn nearly shouted. "Immortal vampires are real, Margaret, and God knows what else; I have seen the proof of it. I cannot go back now do you understand?"

"I'm so sorry Emie . . ."

"You're sorry! You've no idea what it is, to keep my balance," Emelyn said thickly, wadding the gloves in her hand. "I am caught between dark mysteries I dare not speak of, and daylight catastrophes I'm meant to solve. I only ever included you for an ally . . ."

Margaret gave a little whimper. "Of course I am your ally, but will you not at least confirm that others can see her, your vampire? Perhaps if you took me to meet her after all?"

Emelyn raised her brows, folding the gloves. "Thank you for the gloves," she said, handing them over. "But she is not *my vampire*; I do not summon her at will . . . she comes to me when she likes."

Maggie accepted the gloves with a frown.

"And people kiss Margaret," Emelyn said, unable to help herself. "Not everyone who has a kiss is married."

"Well engaged to be married, I should think . . ."

"And in your little world Mr. Arkwright and I could never be so, because he is in trade."

"Have I ever said any such thing? But it's not as simple as that, you know it isn't . . ."

"Yes our estate must crumble to dust unless I marry up, how shall I forget!" Emelyn chuckled bitterly, glancing back at the fortress walls of the house. Silhouetted like paper dolls, the guests filled lighted windows with merry animation, and she felt just now more alone than she ever had.

"Emie, if there is anything," Margaret said, trying to meet her eyes. "If there is anything I might do, you know you have but to ask."

Sore with tension Emelyn crossed her arms, retreating to the wide granite stairs to sit. "I'll tell you what you can do," she said, breathing hard as Maggie sat beside her. "You may instruct your grandmother to write to Mr. Arkwright, to request he call at his earliest convenience at Hastelbrook, that I might apologize for the misunderstanding."

"Do you think that is wise?" Margaret asked. "Is Lord Van Croft not to see you again only tomorrow?"

"I am not yet married," Emelyn said quickly, elbows on her knees as she rested her head in her hands. "I am not yet engaged; there is no impropriety in speaking to Mr. Arkwright, and it may be the last time I see him . . . You will do this for me Maggie; I can ask no one else."

The air grew quiet as the women sat, Emelyn's eyes fixing on anything but her friend.

Margaret nodded, putting her arm about Emelyn's shoulders.

"I know you only intercede out of care," Emelyn said, prickling with annoyance at her touch, "but you are not my mother; one Mrs. Morley in my life is quite enough."

"I don't mean to cause you pain," Margaret said, leaning against her.

Maggie's hair tickled her face and Emelyn twitched, scratching her cheek. "Yes of course, you could never," she said, "though I daresay you took some pride in it."

Margaret released her, clearing her throat as she got to her feet. "Well I'm sorry if you think so," she said, extending her hand, "now will you come in?"

"Please go on."

Rescinding the offer Margaret turned to leave without another word, and Emelyn watched her go, half resolved to apologize . . . until the front doors closed, and she was alone.

The air was cold, but the waning moon was bright, and after a time she left the stairs to amble about the grounds, finding her way to the stable house where she stopped to stand by one of the saddles. Running her fingers over the leather seat she imagined Queen Bess, her own mare, standing ready at hand, and what it would be to throw the saddle over her back, and chase Mr. Arkwright into the unknown. The horses shifted, whickering softly in their stalls, and leaning her head against the kit Emelyn cried a few moments, before wiping her eyes with a sniff and continuing her walk.

Coming to stand at a granite railing between proud statue topped fountains, she looked down over the gardens descending away like mossy steps carved for giants. Meant to recall a natural falls, the fountains breathed cascading streams that poured down tier over tier, splashing to their rest in the wide glimmering pool at the bottom.

On she walked, the starlit solitude growing eerie and remote, and turning her weary thoughts to the vampiress she stopped with a shiver, thinking again of the dreamy calm she felt in her presence.

The natural sounds of night surrounded her, and standing in silence for some time Emelyn listened, feeling nothing at all. "Would madness be easier, I wonder," she muttered, resolving to return to the house . . . for what was darkness after all, but an endless want of light, devoid of all fascination, without Vaela to share it with.

Built just off the ill-kept main road, the township of Crawley and the sprawling George Hotel in particular, marked the halfway for many an ambitious traveller between the city of London and the harbours of Brighthelmstone. The sky was bleak and the hour late when Fitzwilliam Arkwright turned off High Street, trotting through the arch to enter a lantern lit courtyard under the gaze of the crescent moon. Like welcoming arms the wings of the inn encircled the bustling yard with candle warm windows, and though tonight the courtyard was louder than usual, with late coaches unpacking and respite minded travellers gabbling their way to the doors, Mr. Arkwright heard only her voice, and saw only her face . . . she whom he'd kissed upon the hill.

Sliding from his horse, he stood with the reins in his hand, oblivious to the lanky groom in overly large hat who approached. Garish music drifted over the roof of the inn from somewhere beyond, cutting strings and a jaunty flute.

Arkwright frowned, taking note of the lad. "What is that music?"

"They say if you can hear the music, you're enchanted already," the lad droned. "That is, it were the outdoor stage sir, penny for the gate if you like."

"Been restored to use has it," Arkwright said, handing over the reins as his horse snuffled at the ground. "He's earned some fruit if you've got. The toll road is a disgrace, we'll have a hard go of it to London tomorrow."

"We had lovely green pears, but all for kitchens now I'm afraid."

Mr. Arkwright tossed the lad a coin. "Well, whatever you can spare him."

Under oaken beams and lit by a swelling fire in a grand brick hearth, the taproom was alive with cheer, men and a few women eating, drinking and smoking in mud hemmed cloaks as tavern boys scuttled about to serve. Removing his hat Arkwright followed the scent of beer-basted roast to the counter, a walnut bar smoothly notched from decades of heavy elbows, behind which a familiar wide-faced fellow held court, his waistcoat stained with kitchen effusions.

The curly headed innkeep greeted him with a handshake. "Fitzwilliam Arkwright sir, back again are we!"

"Montag, back again," Arkwright replied, sinking onto an empty stool. "Hot supper, and a room . . . just tonight."

"Roast beef, potato, bread and boiled muscats for ninepence. Shilling for the bed."

Arkwright nodded, staring vacantly.

"You look right worn down sir, if you don't mind me sayin' it," Montag observed. "Something on your mind?"

Arkwright picked up his hat and dropped it again. "Naught to trouble an old friend. I'll have the porter."

The fare came dry but warm: a heel of bread with buttered potato, generous cut of roast, and a bowl of hot stewed pears beside. Making good use of the cold porter against the thirsty road, Arkwright quaffed his ale quickly, refilling once and again as the disorderly voices around him faded into the background. By the fourth mug he could no longer resist the relief of confession, and found himself reliving his abrupt embrace with a fire haired beauty whose name he would not speak, and how it had wounded him. "But can you know from a single kiss," he said quietly, "that you must never kiss again, unless it be she . . ."

Jostling into him a pair of laughing friends took their seats; the volume of the crowd increased, and Arkwright protected his drink, speaking what more he dared as the barkeep listened, until a young woman's voice whispered at his ear.

"I can smell your broken heart . . ."

Arkwright turned, but found only road worn men waiting for tables in the smoky haze of the taproom.

"I condole with you sir," Montag declared, wiping out a mug before hanging it over the bar, "but lady luck may find you yet. Take my sister by example, shovelled hay by the road for a month didn't she, waiting for a passing fletcher to work up his address."

Arkwright smirked. "Did she indeed."

"Oh aye she'd fork it out of the wagon, and back in again after he passed. They been married two years now. So if your lady feels any share in your regard, 'haps there may be hope still."

"Only hours ago I thought as much." Arkwright shook his head. "But after making so public an incident, and under the very nose of her friend . . . I'll know better than to sport with hope."

"T'were meant to be, would be." Montag leaned close. "But in the meanwhile I shall recommend to you an ample distraction. The Painted Players are in the midst of a riotous show on the stage round back, perform every month they do, drawing all sorts. Young lady that ends the show is a comely marvel and no mistake, gives as good as she gets. You'll be thinkin' of her sports for a week. Go and see for yourself; final act not started yet by the sound of it."

Arkwright opened his mouth and closed it, and taking up his hat he stuck it on his head. "Perhaps you're right, some distraction might be just the thing."

Outside the stars closed their eyes as heavy clouds drifted in. The hotel sign under the arch swung on its hinges, and upon crossing the courtyard Mr. Arkwright paid his fare to a small wooden toothed fellow before proceeding through the gate and down a little cobbled path that skulked around behind the inn.

Making the corner he found a few dozen gathered in hats and cloaks against the cooling night, mulling about before a wide wooden stage under an open frame with hanging drapes closed at the rear, the frame being strung with merry paper flags and lustrous oil lamps in coloured glass. The stage was bare but for three drably dressed musicians standing to one side, their faces hidden by long nosed plague masks. One tamped on a drum while the second piped his flute, the third swaying beside them as he bowed the strings of a fiddle. The crowd shuffled and murmured, and Arkwright was just imagining to turn back when a young man leapt onto the stage through the drapes. Very slender he was, tall and sharp in white tasselled coats, his face painted under a bright silver wig, as with an effeminate gesture he called out over the crowd.

"Ladies and gentlemen of discretion, we the Painted Players salute your patronage, with all such warmth as you properly deserve." The man bowed, folding with crossed ankles as he snapped his cuffs before rising with a broad smile. "Now as fair Demetria, clad only in moonlight, spake from her bower on the eve of her wedding, *come one, come all!*" There were chuckles among the crowd, and sweeping his hands as though to draw them closer he continued. "For our valedictory joy, I bid your speech cease flow, that ears might hear, and eyes might grow. You're not like to see her like again, Her Painted Ladyship, Afinda Faine!"

There was a blast of white smoke tinged with red, and in his place stood a very different creature, a petite young woman, immodestly clad in snug striped breeches, black hosen and heeled shoes, her pale bosom clenched in a low laced sleeveless bodice, with not even gloves to hide her arms. Her hair was ashen blonde, coiled up behind, her face painted white with round red dots on her cheeks and cherry dark lips. At once the crowd reacted, jeering heartily as she spun around, producing five green pears which she began to juggle, tossing them high as she tapped and kicked.

With remarkable grace the dancer flitted across the boards, drifting perilously close to the musicians and back again, tottering almost without balance, yet snapping her objects from the air with such precision they might have been tied to her fingers by string.

Arkwright gave an appreciative whistle, and the music played on as some of the louder members of the audience began to shout, clamouring for her attention.

A short plump faced gentleman came to a stop close by, sneering at the stage. "Ah, another person of quality for this gad forsaken entertainment," he said. "Tibworth Briggs my good sir, how do."

"Fitzwilliam Arkwright," Arkwright responded, mystified at the performance. "She's a fair acrobat; as graceful a hand as I've seen . . . and almost familiar."

"Lovely little coquette eh?" Mr. Briggs posed. "Yes thrice I've attended her show; but by sight and sound she's the spitting image of the painted witch in *La Femme Déchue,* that played in town years back, when I was an apprentice . . . The actress hanged herself over the crowd for a ripe trick; none too sure how she did it."

"It's theatre, Mr. Briggs," Arkwright said, watching as the dancer flipped backward feet over hands, tossing the pears high. "But I believe that's the ticket; *La Femme Déchue* at the Gramble I think it was. Must have been twenty years ago; the resemblance is striking."

"I've two hundred a year my dove!" one of the younger men blurted out, calling her attention.

"I'd drain you dry my love," the dancer quipped, blowing him a kiss between catches.

Mr. Briggs handed Arkwright a calling card from a silver case. "I'm in silver as it happens, wonderfully commercial of late."

"Is it indeed," Arkwright replied.

"I say if you've not invested, the hour is ripe," Briggs went on. "In fact I represent a group of forward thinking gentlemen aiming to reopen the old mines at Gravesend; I should be happy to chat it over . . ."

Arkwright gave no response, the music played a flourish, and the performing girl twirled with a jump, catching plummeting pears to whistles of approval before resuming her bawdy cavort, turning this way and that as the fruit danced in the air.

"Where is your mother lass?" a thick chinned fellow taunted, the crowd hooting in response.

"I'm eighteen you sorry sot, what she got I haven't got?" the girl called back.

"Eighteen and playing midnight at the George," Briggs chuckled. "But perhaps the actress we recall had a daughter, followed in her unhappy footsteps and fallen on hard times. T'would explain her advertisement of dress, such ripeness of form on display . . ."

Arkwright scowled, returning the card. "Thank you Mr. Briggs, but I've not the means for speculating on silver I'm afraid."

"Ah well, I suppose I mistook you for gentry," Briggs huffed, snapping the card back in its case.

"You're not the first, more credit to my tailor."

The girl capered about, eliciting a gasp as she caught one pear atop her foot, kicking it lightly back to her hand.

"I begin to fancy the daring doxy," Briggs said loudly. "What do you say sir, shall you wish me luck?"

"I've none to spare," Arkwright said, watching the stage.

The dancing girl's taunts carried on, as one after another she lashed out at her hecklers with humour and bite, until stopping abruptly she caught the pears in a stack, much to the awe of the crowd. "But here's a purse-proud raincloud," she declared. "Yon handsome lonely lark, why must ye pout in the dark?"

Finding her staring Mr. Arkwright cleared his throat. "Do your worst fair miss! I deserve nothing less."

"That's no way to start." The girl gave him a frown, leaning over as she flashed the fruit into the air to continue her juggling. "Shall he touch this cold jester's heart?"

Arkwright swallowed, feeling the eyes of the crowd upon him.

"Ten chips of the Golden Duke!" Mr. Briggs blurted, digging the coins from a monogrammed leather purse. "Ten guineas says you'll stop your fribbling and attend me."

The girl snickered, juggling short and quick. "But my tender touch comes for free sir, when you'd rather anyone but me sir . . ."

"I'll see his ten and make it fifteen!" another man put in.

"Two fish in a barrel circle the brine," she cackled, "one to the other *this barrel is mine!*"

The short Mr. Briggs spat on the ground. "Twenty guineas!" he shouted, and glancing at Arkwright, "I know these country wagtails; find her price she'll find her knees."

Arkwright twitched as the second man offered twenty-five.

"Thirty guineas!" Mr. Briggs countered, flush with impatience. "Come my cozy coquette, get thee down!"

"The shortest member still raises," the girl cheeked, twirling as she juggled. "Shall none better buy my praises?"

Arkwright raised his hand. "Fifty guineas!"

The dancer stopped her twirling. "*A hit, a very palpable hit!*" she laughed, snatching the fruit from the air.

"I beg your pardon sir," the silver merchant bristled. "What's your game?"

"She's little more than a girl; she should be home and safe at such an hour," Arkwright said, "not put to this."

"You plan to rescue her then? You know nothing of these creatures," and with a splutter of anger Mr. Briggs stuffed the coins back in his purse.

Amidst whistling applause the girl tossed a pear high enough to lose sight of it, looking to the sky with arms wide. There was a dramatic pause as she waited, parting her lips . . . and with a flash of green the pear slipped out of the dark, landing with a plop as she crouched, catching it in her teeth. The crowd cried out their approval and she lifted the fruit from her mouth, finding Arkwright's eyes.

"For your horse fair gent," she said, flicking it in his direction.

The pear streaked for his nose, stinging his palm as he caught it with a smack. "Thank you!"

From the sides of the stage erupted great blasts of smoke, and grabbing hold of her bosom the actress grinned into a bow, vanishing in a shower of red and white petals. The haze drifted over the onlookers who coughed with applause, and Arkwright swatted the air, finding the stage empty and quiet. "If you want for company sir, I'm sure there's others to answer," he said, but Mr. Briggs was gone.

Making his way round behind the curtain Arkwright found the minstrels removing their masks and wiping their faces. The tall actor in white smiled with pursed lips, looking him over. "Good even handsome sir, Her Painted Ladyship will return anon," and he snapped a gilded pocket handkerchief from his sleeve. "Souvenir perhaps? The monogram stitched by her own hand."

"Why not," Arkwright replied, watching as several hands set to dousing the lights. "Fine quality indeed, Mister . . ?"

The man swished his cuffs for a bow. "Christophe Lorne Blanchett," he said.

"Ah, Mr. Blanchett," Arkwright said, tucking away the pocket kerchief, "I should like to give what money I've pledged, for her welfare."

"Call me Lorne good sir, if you please," the actor answered. "But perhaps you'd care to keep your pledge in person; I might look for her in the stable if I were you . . ."

There was something in his smile that unsettled, but Arkwright nodded, turning to make his way back to the inn. The leaves in the trees began to twist, and holding his hat against the wind he crossed the muddy courtyard to the lantern lit dim of the stable building.

Finding no sign of anyone he searched the stalls for his thoroughbred, coming upon him in the back corner. The animal shivered, and clicking his tongue Arkwright presented the pear. "Whoa there Brendel," he chuckled, patting the beast on the nose. "A strange day we've had, haven't we . . . but is it the fattest pear you've ever seen?"

The horse snuffled after the treat, and employing a boot knife

Arkwright sheared himself a piece, handing over the rest. Brendel crunched happily as raindrops began to test the roof, their plinking notes joining a chorus of ale-addled patrons sloshing past outside. There came a jingling thump, and swallowing his bite Arkwright backed out of the stall, taking a lantern off its hook to look about him. The planks creaked overhead, and crouching to tuck away his knife he discovered on the floor the same monogrammed purse the silver merchant had drawn from his pocket, though spotted with blood.

"Mr. Briggs?" Arkwright stood quickly, raising the light, and looking overhead he caught a glint of white through the planks. Something shifted, and there was a sound, faint enough to mistake though it might have been a whimper . . .

The ladder was near, and he took hold of the rail to climb. "I say Mr. Briggs?" he called again, hearing a sudden sound, as of a violent twist, and then silence. Reaching the top he squinted in the flickering light, peering over tightly bundled packs of straw to find the face of the man he'd spoken to only moments before, his pale countenance slack with death. A shadow moved and he discerned a pair of eyes, brightly gleaming as they reflected the light, staring back at him.

"You," he breathed, his voice scarcely a whisper, and sliding to the floor he turned to bolt but stopped short as the stable doors slammed closed, the bar drawn.

"Would you fly away so quickly?" a young woman's voice spoke out of the gloom, "after buying my company for fifty guineas?"

Arkwright turned for a different path, but she was right there, her face painted still, red dots at her cheeks, and smiling with bloody teeth. "Hello lovely sir," she said, holding his gaze as she crossed her ankles for a curtsy.

Arkwright stood transfixed. "Afinda Faine," he heard himself say. "It was you . . ."

"Afaine," she said simply, "or so I'm known to those I love," and suddenly she was very close.

With a half step back he bumbled into the ladder, flinching as she sniffed him over.

"I smell your longing heart," she intoned, looking up at him.

"I saw you, upon the hill," he said, struggling to gather his thoughts against the pierce of her eyes. "Murderess . . ."

In a blink she leapt upon him, throwing her arms about his neck, and though stumbling for balance he was compelled to catch her under the thighs lest she fall.

Holding him tightly her silver eyes broke away, and again she sniffed at his neck. "My valiant gentleman," she cooed, her body warm though her breath was cold on his skin, "would you save me from this life by your generosity?"

Emelyn's face came back to him, and clenching his jaws he grabbed his attacker's waist, heaving to throw her off, but the girl only giggled, stuck fast, and losing his footing he staggered about, crashing to the ground atop her.

Puffing with humour at the impact she took hold of his face. "Hush, you'll wake the beasts, and the horses too . . ."

"Release . . . release me!" he managed, his head swimming.

The girl opened her mouth, and Fitzwilliam could only growl in protest as she pulled him tight against her. Her lips found his throat, sharp points dimpled his flesh, and she paused.

"You saw me upon the hill?" she puzzled. "What hill?"

"I saw your demon eyes . . . on the cemetery hill at Hastelbrook."

"Hastelbrook! Can you be the same Arkwright who pursues Emelyn Morley?"

"That is none of yours!" he gasped, straining to reach the knife tucked in his boots.

With an aggravated sound she shoved him off, and he rolled into the wall with a bang, sprawling face down to catch his breath.

"You know, it might have been me, set to watch over her," she said, a pout in her voice as she crouched over him, "but for my immoderate nature. So you it was not me you saw . . . that was another. And that you would confuse his eyes with mine, rather offends me."

Arkwright half turned to look up at her, raising a defensive hand. "Leave me fell spirit! On my honour . . . I will keep your secret."

"It's too late for that," she said, and grabbing his coat she rolled him to his back, straddling his waist to lean in with bared fangs.

The boot knife punctured her under the bosom and the girl shuddered with a noise, her eyes wide.

Cold blood wet his hand, and Arkwright pushed it to the hilt.

"Cut off even in the blossoms of my sin," she moaned, creasing her brows, and clutching the weapon she sagged off of him. "You've murdered me."

A horror of regret seized upon him, an appalling fear that he had mistaken her. "Miss . . . wait!" he pleaded, lowering her to the ground beside him.

But her little coughs turned to laughter, and sitting up she caught hold of his chin, close enough to kiss him. "I gave you a treat for your horse," she breathed, pulling out the knife to fling it away. "Is this your gratitude?"

She pushed him down, and flat on his back he opened his mouth to cry out, coughing as her bloodied fingers stopped his voice. The enchanted burn of her blood met his tongue, his mind reeled, and the blurry white of her face bloomed close. "Thank you for bidding on my liberty," she said quietly, kissing his nose. "I will drink you now . . . Goodnight, my lonely lark."

The dark pull of her gaze overbore his senses, and it were as though he sank through the ground into nothing . . .

Silver daylight expanded to fill his room, and Arkwright startled awake, tumbling from the bed with a curse. Finding himself clad only in breeches he shot to his feet, moaning at an ache of weariness in his back, though there was no trace of the liquor haze he might have expected. Sitting in the bedside chair he found he could not remember where the night had taken him, nor how it had ended.

At a loss to account for his shirt he was obliged to send down for another, which he bought from the laundress at thrice its worth before returning to the taproom for breakfast.

"Perhaps from your lady sir?" Montag said cheerfully, pausing over the dishes to hand him a letter.

Arkwright's heart pounded as he flipped the letter to open it, whereupon he found the regal seal of Lady Dhorings, and courage failed him. "I shall read it on the road," he said, tucking it into his coat. "Until next I'm called south! Farewell my friend."

The innkeep nodded. "Safe roads to you sir."

Finding Brendel ready and restless Mr. Arkwright loaded him up and set out, passing under the gates onto the deep rutted road north for London. Not an hour later he was obliged to hold to the shoulder, curious to pass what looked to be a covered hearse struggling its way south before a slow team of men on horseback, and tipping his hat he exchanged polite curses over the state of the road, leaving the pack behind to continue north.

The long hearse carried on, and dawn was high and bright when it trundled under the arch into the wide courtyard of the George Hotel. Ponderous wigged in heavy frock of mud darkened green, the weighty Magistrate Taffram Brule puffed for breath as he heaved from his horse, fetching out a kerchief to dab his forehead.

"Bloody ridiculous," he groused, addressing the driver. "Road to Hell if you ask me; if this wagon rattles to pieces on the way back you'll not see a shilling!"

"Your pardon sir," the sallow faced driver said, climbing down as a ruddy young lad dismounted from the other side. "The road is no good for wheels, made worse by the cargo, heavier than I'd like."

Magistrate Brule coughed into his arm, lifting thick black drapes to peer into the body of the hearse. There rested an ebony coffin, that which he'd been instructed to build, reinforced metal bands over wood, lined with silver within. "Then let us pray our errand succeeds," he said, and releasing the drape he turned to observe the remaining men, a dozen conscripted constables, as they corralled their horses to the stable and started out for the inn.

"Not a drop gentlemen!" Brule commanded. "Just now we'll be finding the cistern round back and setting the canopy, the well must be sheltered from every ray of the sun."

Resigned to grumbling obedience the men changed course, a few tipping their hats with broad smiles. "As it please Your Worship!"

Behind the inn the wooden stage rested empty, red and white petals scattered over the planks, extinguished lanterns strung overhead, glistening in the wet morning. Some fifty paces further back, through mud-bedded grass, there stood the well. Of old and weather battered rings of stone, it thrust from the ground but reluctantly, as though eager to return whence it came. The cistern stood waist high, with neither roof nor bucket, but only a plunging drop into rank shallow water some ten yards below.

"There milord, the old well just as your informer said!" one of the men spoke up.

"There is nothing unholy about an old well," the waxy faced magistrate responded. "We shall see."

The men set to work, and sneezing into his kerchief Brule presided, directing them to pound stout wooden poles into the earth, stretching across them a heavy tarpaulin of black canvas head-height over the well.

With their shade erected the men equipped the hearse driver's boy with a hooded oil lamp, tying a rope harness about his waist, and with a brave nod the lad tossed his hat to one of the others, disappearing as he climbed over the edge.

Mr. Brule shook, choking with wretched coughs as images of the monstrous man who'd set him on this course, whose vampire blood sickened his veins, swam before his eyes. "Hurry up lad!" he croaked. "Do you see anything?"

"I might espy a gap sir," the boy cried back, "just before the water line, if you'll give us a moment . . ."

A chair was brought, and Brule wheezed as he lowered himself to sit, pulling a silver flask from his coat to fuss off the lid for a drink.

Soon the boy yelled back, and the magistrate's heart leapt at the news: the gap was a hole, large enough for a body to crawl into, and there in the hole were lady's shoes, feet still in them and legs after; an entire woman it was, wrapped in a faded shroud.

"Or a corpse more like!" the boy added, accepting a rope to bind about her knees and ankles.

"Are you certain?" the magistrate called down.

"Cold as ice my lord! But fresh as you please; narry a niff o' death . . . all's I smell is wet stone and old water."

Dragged gingerly from the hole, the body was pulled up and over the top to be laid on the ground, the soggy lad following after, and huffing to his knees beside her the magistrate hissed for the others to keep their distance. Assuring himself the sun was blocked, Brule took hold of the edge of her garment, peeling the cloth from her face.

He was greeted by the sight of a comely young woman, painted forehead to chin in white makeup, smudged and cracked, red dots at her cheeks. With relaxed countenance and arms crossed at her chest she exuded a perfectly preserved serenity, as though she had died, if dead she was, that very minute.

"By damn!" Mr. Brule was fixed with wonder. The girl neither stirred nor breathed, and he chewed his lip, retrieving the flask from his pocket. "What you are about to witness my good fellows, is to be kept strict within this company, or Lord Dramen shall hear of it."

"Trespassers! Graverobbers!" a shrill voice shouted. "What have you done?!"

The men reacted aggressively, catching a frantic man to hold him at bay.

"Who shrieks? Let him through," Brule ordered.

Murmuring with curses the men parted, and a tall slender fellow robed as though for bed burst between them, his short hair tied in an ungainly knot, his eyes wide with horror.

"And who are you sir?" the magistrate grunted, squinting one eye.

"I sir am Christophe Lorne Blanchet, artist director and thespian! But this poor creature was lately of our troupe; it was only last night she was put to rest away from the inn, having died of a feverous plague!"

The men lurched back, several covering their mouths, but Brule only laughed. "Hold the fool where he stands! There is no plague here."

"Would you defile a poor girl's body!" the actor protested, the whole of him atremble as the men held him by the arms.

"Poor girl is it," the magistrate mused, holding up the silver flask.

"But she is dead sir, ain't she?" the boy asked, drawing nearer.

"Oh yes, dead as Queen Anne while the sun shines," Brule answered. "But half a moment . . ."

The actor shook with whimpers, Mr. Brule slowly lowered the flask, and with clenched lips he touched the silver to the base of the corpse's throat. At once a smell of burning fouled the air, and a light wisp of smoke drifted from beneath the metal.

A distressed sound escaped her lips, and Brule found eyes black as coal staring back at him. With a cry he lurched to his feet, watching her shiver as the flask seared her neck. Pale hands with nails like claws fumbled at the object, but her fingers recoiled with burns as audibly she choked, staring into the tarp above them.

Struggling like a madman the actor nearly broke free, but the men caught him fast, and under a hail of blows he surrendered, collapsing to the ground. Paying no attention the magistrate knelt to observe as the boy rushed forward, snatching the flask away from her throat. The girl heaved for breath, and the men stood transfixed as the flaking, fuming burn in her flesh began to collapse, drawing itself together until the skin was smooth once more.

"The burn is healin' my lord look see," the boy pointed, pocketing the flask.

Like a curious dog the heavy magistrate crawled closer, and the girl looked at him, the pain in her face relaxing.

"Can you speak?" he inquired, licking his lips.

A tear of oily black slipped from her eye, and she smiled. "*O Jenny go scrub ye the blood away,*" she sang in a small voice. "*T'were lucky was just me to have my way."*

"Have they a witch living in the well?" one of the men asked. "Can this be what we've come for?"

"Damned fools do you not see the miracle before you?" the magistrate shot back, and returning to the girl he grabbed her throat. "Confess your nature, vampire!"

The girl bared her teeth, turning her head, but there seemed no strength in her to resist. *"T'was I sir espied her upon the hay,"* she continued singing softly, closing her eyes.

"I know you hear me, spawn of Lilith," Brule whispered, buzzing with excitement as he spoke at her ear. "The coffin we've prepared for you is banded with steel and lined with silver, so I must suggest you keep very still for the journey . . . Lord Dramen will be delighted beyond measure to receive you."

"And what do we do with this one?" one of the men asked, yanking the sobbing actor to his feet.

"There will be others in their little troupe," Brule said. "We shall report this lot to the reformers. With a vampire in their midst and this one a molly no doubt . . . who's to say what depravities they're given to."

The actor was struck in the face and dropped, collapsing senseless in the grass.

"But is *she* not dangerous?" one man asked.

Brule sighed, and leaning down he kissed her forehead, releasing her throat. "Soft as a mewling kitten," he said, pulling the shroud over her face. "Bring the box!"

Bundled tightly in woollen blankets, their vampire prize was laid in the open coffin, her captor bidding the men pause as they moved to fit the lid.

"Your last chance to speak my dear, before we set out," Brule said, addressing her faceless wrapped form.

"She lay there, she stayed there 'til break of day," the girl sang softly.

"You hear that sir?" the coach driver snorted. "She mocks us."

Mr. Brule chuckled heartily, looking over his captive. "That she does my good man," he said, gripping the edge of the coffin to murmur close to her face. "Dear precious creature, by this adventure I must now account myself a true hunter of vampires," and wrinkling his nose he sniffed at her. "Evil incarnate, with no soul of your own . . . You shall be the guest of Charwell manor; the baron Lord Dramen is your master now."

The vampiress did not respond, but lay very still, and with a gesture he bid the men close the lid, locking sturdy chains across it. Three to a side they hoisted the box, plodding behind the others to make their way back to the hearse.

Montag the barkeep stood in the courtyard, squeezing out a wet rag as he looked on in bewilderment.

With a rumbling cough the portly magistrate approached him. "For your silence," he said, thumbing over a few gold guineas. "I'd not have the common sight of a funeral box bloom into gossip. And you do well to bar these *Painted Players* from your premises."

"Do I indeed sir?" the innkeep puzzled, accepting the coin.

"They are known for a troupe of ill repute," Brule said sharply. "Sin and depravity sir, every performance. I'll have the reformers see to them never you fear. Now fetch a mug of your stoutest for each of my men, and we'll be off."

Chapter 15
Invitations

Emelyn awoke from a dream she could not remember, finding herself in the deeply mauve northeast bedroom of Dhorings Park, a tender ache in her head from late games and drink. In a rush the impassioned kiss with Mr. Arkwright returned to mind, and with a mortified wail she stuffed her face in the pillows.

A noise made her start, and sitting up she discovered Breda was already in the room, standing by the foot of the bed selecting pins, a clean shift draped over her arm.

Emelyn blinked at her. "How long have you been in my room?"

"I've let you sleep longer than I should miss," Breda said, laying her petticoats on the bed. "It's nigh ten o' clock and we must be home with time to prepare for your gentleman."

"Lord Van Croft," Emelyn breathed, rubbing her forehead. "Oh any other day . . ."

Dressed in a simple gown of soft silver, having rinsed her face several minutes to soothe the ache, she came down with time for but half a scone by the windows, where she studied the stone grey sky, grateful at least there was no rain. Lady Dhorings joined her, and bobbing with a curtsy Emelyn heartily apologized for her strangeness the previous evening.

"Oh nothing to it," Lady Dhorings dismissed. "Now I have sent the note you requested by dawn post from New Haven; with any luck it shall reach Mr. Arkwright before he departs from Crawley, though I cannot promise the gentleman will respond."

"Thank you Your Ladyship," Emelyn said with a blush, a little surprised Margaret had done as she'd asked.

Outside she came upon her friend taking the view from the top tier of the stepped gardens on the rounded veranda growing outward from the hill, supported by Roman columns over the lower level. Watching Margaret as she stared over hunting fields and forest, Emelyn felt herself quite justified, should she opt to leave without a word . . . but the moment passed, and she approached to bid her good morning.

"Good Morning Emie."

They spoke briefly of unimportant things, and Margaret wished her luck with Lord Van Croft, which Emelyn accepted, hoping in turn to see her again soon.

"We are for Cornwall, a fortnight, then to London," Margaret said. "Perhaps I will see you there?"

"Oh I don't think so," Emelyn said quickly. "That is, we'll be here for the season, as you know. But I wish you a happy trip, of course."

"Of course."

The ladies embraced, their parting pleasant if cool beneath the surface, and moments later Emelyn sat in the coach, her eyes warm as she pondered why neither of them had apologized. The towers of Dhorings Park disappeared over the tree line, and Breda handed a kerchief across. "No thank you," Emelyn said. "It's always wistful, saying goodbye."

"But lucky it is miss, to live so close as we do."

Emelyn smiled. "Yes it is . . ."

<hr>

The infamous Baron Dramen's library was oppressive and gloomy as any room in the house, with deep shelves where windows might have been, and at one end a grand hearth of claw-footed iron, before which was placed a shield-back chair on the crimson Turkey rug. Upon the chair, her wrists tied to the arms, sagged the young vampiress Afaine, her narrow eyes black, her mouth open and fangs half-bared, with fresh blood spattered across the low neck of her bodice.

There were candles all around, pole candelabra having been brought in to fortify ceiling lanterns. The air was quiet and still, excepting the tick of a tower clock and the soft whistling mirth of Lord Dramen himself, who sat with his feet splayed, leaning casually back in a second chair facing the vampire. In reflective blue frock over pristine whites, Dramen wore his finest wig, of long and elegant grey curls.

The sagging magistrate Mr. Brule stood beside him, a pleased sort of befuddlement on his face.

Lord Dramen's accustomed air of displeasure was quite vanquished, and even as he tried to speak his glee got the better of him, obliging him to cover his mouth with a kerchief for another triumphant cackle.

"Shall I send for Miss Winter my lord?" Brule asked, his face greasy with sweat.

"Oh dear me no," Dramen said, shaking his head to compose himself. "Not yet. Pray sir what time is it?"

"Nigh one o'clock my lord."

With a bang on his armrest Lord Dramen stood quickly. "I've a mind to play a bit longer!" he declared, clapping the magistrate's shoulders. "Dammit man, how shall you not be giddy as I am? You've been paid well enough. I'd never have believed a word of it . . . and yet," the chuckles got the better of him again, and like a drunk he staggered back to her, stopping to lean on the chair.

"Yes my lord, I'm pleased as you are, she is under our power," Brule said, wiping his forehead.

"You are a changed man Brule!" Dramen pronounced, pointing at him with a grin. "Not so very long ago you only tolerated my instructions; you took the money quick enough, but you never believed, not in *vampires*. On the curb at the theatre I half wondered if you'd lost your mind . . ."

"No my lord . . . not yet."

"Then tell me, dear Brule," Dramen said. "Your description was enigmatical. Who is this informer? Some lucky lad exploring where he oughtn't have?"

"I know not his name," Brule replied, staring vacantly, "nor truly his plans . . . but he weren't like any man I've known sir, but a creature, giant and most foul."

Lord Dramen raised an eyebrow. "Were you smoking the poppy sir? But it doesn't matter . . . You must find him again, whatever he is. If he knows of any other such creatures hidden I'll have them, for any price," and his expression darkened as he grabbed his captive's chin, steering her to look at him. "What do you say to that, my handsome little hell spawn. Speak monster! Speak for me I charge you . . ."

Brule coughed. "Shall I remind you my lord, if she's not completely secured by dusk . . . she'll have us one and all. There's no fighting these creatures at night."

"Was it not I who taught you as much?" Dramen snapped,

squeezing her face to pucker her lips. "Not a year ago they laughed at me Mr. Brule, and how they laughed, to see the secret room I constructed below us, walled all in silver plate. But they'll not be laughing any longer, will they my dear," and bending low he pressed a kiss upon her mouth.

Afaine clenched her eyes, and slowly he released her.

"By the revelation of your sweet soulless self," he said, "we shall see the *Vampire Act* soar through Parliament, to be created law of the land . . . and I its chief prosecutor."

The vampiress murmured, her chin sagging to her chest.

"At last it speaks," he said, snapping at Brule for attention. "Repeat yourself if you please, good my gentlewoman, let us hear what you have to say."

Straining with the effort she lifted her head, speaking in hoarse whisper. "*By the stair his favourite fair, athirst in death espied him. Long-wig Jack did break his back, when down the steps she hied him . . .*"

"Wonderful," Dramen breathed, leering close. "Is there more?"

"*On his twig she danced a jig and left his guts beside him,*" she hissed, nipping at the air near his face.

Lord Dramen straightened up, and with an affectionate frown he placed his hand on her head. "What a strange specimen she is," he said. "Defiant even now, though her power is nothing, so long as the gaze of the Almighty burns in the sky."

"The sun my lord?" Brule licked his cracked lips, his eyes wide as the baron drew a mulling poker from the heat of the fire.

"Still," Dramen said, turning the red tipped implement in his hand, "defiance from such a creature, as from a dog, we dare not tolerate," and with force enough to kill he cracked her across the face.

Afaine crashed to the floor with a shriek, chair and all, an open gash across her skull. Looking on in awed silence the men watched as the wound closed and faded, leaving pure pale skin. The vampiress spit blood, and staring at Lord Dramen she fixed her smile, lying perfectly still.

Dramen stood over her, grunting with satisfaction. "Remarkable is she not?"

"That she don't breathe my lord, unnerving it is," Brule said.

"*She don't breathe* . . . elegantly stated sir." Dramen gave a contented sigh, crouching to examine her. "But her proof is only the beginning. Somewhere in the bountiful forests of Kent, lies the hidden city of the dead. *Saunmoor* and its immortal queen must be real as she is . . ."

The vampiress held her inscrutable grin, and Mr. Brule shivered.

"Yes sir, yes I suppose it must be."

"And as the sun doth shine, I will find it," Lord Dramen declaimed, getting to his feet. "I shall conquer, and pillage, and drag even their queen to the court of her judgment, for during the day she'll be no stronger than this poor vampire slattern."

"Yes my lord." Brule bowed his head. "And across the breadth of the empire, all His Majesty's subjects shall know your name."

Dramen tossed him the bloody fire iron. "See it properly scrubbed of her tainted blood, there's a good man," he said cheerfully. "Now, dinner I think! She'll be perfectly safe where she lies, until we secure her below. Send for Miss Winter."

■■

Arriving over hard roads a little after one o' clock, Emelyn and her companions found Hastelbrook in an uproar, with her father still abroad. Mrs. Leicester, the starkly dressed housekeeper, whom Emelyn rarely saw and had been terrified of as a girl, was sharply managing the maid staff to clean *as like for the Bishop of Rome* while footmen threaded between them moving chairs, tables and silver outside for a grand dinner. The affair was constructed under a white canopy in the lower gardens, Mrs. Morley complaining all the while that the captain had not been good enough to communicate *when* to expect him, which left little choice but to arm the house for dinner as quickly as possible.

Taking a brief respite in her room Emelyn helped Breda sort the clothes out of her trunks, discovering a folded note wrapped in a pair of gloves.

'Seek where the dolls heads were buried.'

Glancing at Breda to find her busy hanging gowns in the armoire, Emelyn tucked the note away, and unable to resist even a moment's curiosity over it she made her exit.

Coming to the low cemetery wall in the very place she'd shown Mr. Arkwright, she checked to assure herself no one was at the drawing room windows, and crouching to test the familiar earth found it to have been recently disturbed. A shallow dig unearthed a little parcel wrapped in linen, and unfolding the cloth she gasped to behold the grand ruby necklace.

Without the faintest idea how, or why, the jewel should have been returned to her, Emelyn had no sooner stepped back into the house than Comby informed her that her father had returned from Brighton.

Upstairs she dug up the bank notes, and after folding them for her pocket she came back down, turning from the stairs to pass through the long gallery. The black hooded statue loomed where she'd left it, and staring at the smoothly sculpted folds of volcanic stone she knocked on the office door.

"Enter!" Mr. Morley cried, jumping up from his cluttered desk as she did so. "Your mother tells me you were expected by eleven latest," he said. "We must we equip Breda with gunpowder, to wake you all the earlier."

Emelyn pulled the notes from her pocket. "The party went very late."

Her father scowled at his desk, rifling through papers as several dropped on the floor. "Ah well," he said. "I trust you enjoyed your trip?"

"Yes, brief as it was," she replied, unfolding the bank notes to count them.

"And how is our dear Miss Mettles?"

"We quarrelled," Emelyn said, surprising herself. "Never mind. And how fair our shipwrights?"

"I can't imagine what I hoped for," he said, slouching his shoulders to lean on the desk. "Perhaps some detail, something that might better qualify an Act of God for our defence."

"I would like to help."

"Emelyn my dear, would that you could," he said, removing his spectacles to rub his eyes. "But there is little point in pretending any longer. The trustee is intractable, and the estate may be called to answer . . . I must write to your uncle."

With such pitiable distress etched in the lines of his face, her father was a man she hardly recognized. "No Papa," she said sternly, "we shan't be losing the house, not today or ever."

Mr. Morley fixed his spectacles back on his nose with a scowl, taking from her the bills.

The clock ticked, and marking the wobbly gleam in his eyes Emelyn felt her own going wet. "Eleven thousand Papa, more than enough to meet their demand, for now, is it not?"

"I don't understand," he said, his expression a mix of wonder and trepidation. "My dear girl . . . what on earth have you laid down for such a sum? What have you promised?"

"Only the ruby necklace Papa, it is sold," she said, and wiping her eye she smiled with a little grunt, bewildered to recall the very item had found its way back to her pocket.

At his puzzled expression she cleared her throat.

"Ten thousand to the trustee, is it not correct? And one thousand besides. I know it to be only a fraction of our owe, but shall it not buy you time to negotiate?"

"Eleven thousand," he said, rising slowly to his feet.

"Chin up Papa," she said. "Let there be no more talk of debtor's prison."

Mr. Morley opened his arms for her embrace, and she came to meet him. "My dear Emie," he said, holding her tightly.

"I've paid Cavendish his fees," she said, her head against his shoulder, "and caught up your dues at the club."

"Have you?" he marvelled, releasing their embrace to look at her. "So, to my great fortune you have refused to heed my advice."

"There," she said, leaving him a kiss on the cheek. "Now I must go up."

"Half a moment," he said quickly, taking up an unsealed letter. "I nearly forgot . . . I've had a correspondence, from your Captain Van Croft."

Emelyn rubbed her head with a sigh, and drawing the chair she flounced into her seat. "And what does he write?" she asked. "Am I out of danger?"

Her father lowered himself to sit opposite, setting the money gingerly on the desk. "On the contrary my dear, he redoubles his pursuit. The captain has invited you to call with him upon his godparents, one Commodore and Mrs. Akehurst, at the house of Galecliff in Eastbourne. Perhaps a fortnight."

"To *call with him*? So then, he has invited all of us . . . Papa? He has invited all of us, surely."

"He has invited neither myself, nor your dear mother, nor sisters."

"What? Can he be so impertinent? Of course you have refused him."

Mr. Morley tapped the letter on his desk. "Nay my dear; the invitation is honourable."

"Is it?"

"He has invited Deacon as your chaperone."

"Deacon!"

"And you shall have Breda, of course. Naturally your mother is very keen that you should accept."

"Deacon," Emelyn repeated, stunned at the thought. "Lord Captain Van Croft has invited him, truly?"

"Indeed he has. He presents Commodore Akehurst as a fellow of great liberality, who having lost his hand at sea knows too well the plight of a man marred by accident. And there shall be a doctor in attendance, a man of no mean skill. But t'would be a good thing I think, for your brother to have some society outside these walls. Do you not agree?"

"I do, of course I do," Emelyn said, sitting up straighter. "But I don't believe it . . . Deacon."

"For a young lady so well furnished of speech you are quite repeating yourself," her father mused, removing his spectacles to dab his eye with a kerchief.

"But is he well enough to travel? Lady Dhorings is convinced there is ill report of his health."

"Deacon is in fine form, as well as can be expected. There now, any other news from the Dowager Countess?"

"She spoke of that smell-feast Charles Wellsea. She believes he is making plans for the estate."

Mr. Morley shook his head. "Your profligate cousin has been brought to heel. I've offered him an apprenticeship with the partners, which he has accepted."

"An apprenticeship? At his age?" Emelyn balked. "Papa we never hear from him, but he wants for money; you mustn't believe he has any desire to work."

"Gently my dear, you must put him from your mind," her father said. "I've no intention of losing my son; if Wellsea seeks the inheritance of Hastelbrook let him seek in vain." Mr. Morley stood, and coming to her side he took her hand. "Come now my Emie, you have provided us a gift I can never repay. Chin up."

"Yes Papa, of course," she said, rising to stand.

The day's preparations carried on under the critical eye of her mother, who being increasingly frantic over Van Croft's arrival saw to it Emelyn was wrapped in a snugly sumptuous gown of white with gold flourish, the pale skirts drawn back and pinned behind to display her golden petticoats underneath.

Her headache had blessedly run its course, though she found the tension in her chest was only increased by the costume, which left little to the imagination and no room for comfort. "It's too much," she said with a flush, heaving before the mirror as Breda tied back her hair in a twisted knot, pinning a cocked hat of beaver felt atop.

"A decorous blend of elegance and enticement," her mother said, fastening a jewelled lace band tightly about her daughter's throat. "This second meeting is paramount; it is on the effect of this encounter that he will settle his choice . . . Lest you forget our very future my dearest, is in the balance."

"Am I not anxious enough already?" Emelyn protested, stretching her shoulders as she strained for air. "But I can scarcely breathe enough to speak."

"Nonsense, it's only for the afternoon," her mother said, selecting her gloves. "You will strike him like lightning, and then we may all exhale."

There was yet no sign of the captain, and by half past two it was decided the meal could wait no longer. Dinner was spread on white draped tables by the lakes, and catching her breath between bites Emelyn ate her minced beef and asparagus with polite urgency, though she was scolded away from the bread. The family had just time to finish when there was at last a sighting of Van Croft's imposing coach-and-four on the road, and they bustled from their chairs back up the hill to the house.

Hurried moments later Emelyn sat straight as a spar in the drawing room, her sisters planted before her on opposite chairs, equipped with embroidery hoops to appear at their leisure, though by some miscommunication Isabelle was left without needle or thread. Deacon stood free of his crutches, supporting himself by the back of the sofa where Emelyn perched, her mother peeking through the windows, while Mr. Morley waited in the grand hall.

"Hush!" Mrs. Morley charged, wringing her hands as she flew to her seat. "He arrives!"

The sound of swift boot steps soon approached, and the footmen opened the doors, standing aside. Lord Captain Jonathan Van Croft was announced, and the women stood together as the gentleman strode into the room, speaking to Mr. Morley, who was on his heels.

"My apologies for the coach," Van Croft said, finishing his thought. "I shall have a newer in the week."

The captain was at least as handsome as Emelyn remembered, stern faced with his hair pulled back, ribbon tied over navy and gold-buttoned coat, high collar and powder white cuffs. With hat tucked under his arm he clacked his heels with a nod, marking her person with a sort of exhausted relief as he addressed the group. "Mrs. Morley, Miss Sarah, Miss Isabelle, Sir," he said, approaching to shake Deacon's outstretched hand as her brother struggled to keep his arm steady.

"An honour my lord," Deacon said.

"The honour is mine," Van Croft droned, releasing him to take Emelyn's fingers as she curtsied. "And of course, the incomparable Miss Morley," he said, planting a firm kiss on her knuckles.

"You grace us my lord," she said, her smile not quite reaching her eyes.

"Most agreeable it is, to find myself returned to Hastelbrook," Lord Van Croft declared, keeping Emelyn's hand as he addressed her mother. "I'd a frightful bother in Brighton, so it would seem I've skipped one dinner only to miss the second."

"Nonsense," Mrs. Morley said, "we shall send for it at once, whatever you like."

"Oh I'd not put you out," Van Croft said, releasing Emelyn's hand, "though if pressed I should relish a gently boiled venison stew. Veal stock, cream and onions, thick with rice."

Mrs. Morley blinked at him and snapped at the footman, who promptly vanished. "The kitchen shall see to it directly," she said.

"Excellent," the captain said, turning to Mr. Morley. "Now, if I might speak to your daughter alone sir, for but a few moments."

Mr. Morley nodded, meeting Emelyn's eyes, and he gestured to welcome the others back to the hall as Mrs. Morley hurried to usher them through. "With all haste my lord," she gushed, and Emelyn watched in dismay as her family filed out of the room, Deacon equipping his crutches to bring up the rear as quickly as he might.

Lord Van Croft checked his pocket watch as her brother stumped through the doors, followed by the footmen, and as the latch clicked the captain turned with a grin, arms spread wide as though presenting her on stage.

"My perfect beauty, how truly *torturous* these moments away from you have been."

Emelyn stared at him, feeling rather like a deer who'd elected to freeze rather than run. "Torturous?" she echoed, thinking of her dress. "You flatter me sir, but this being only our second meeting you cannot possibly imagine . . ."

"Fear not," he said, helping himself to a brandy. "I've not requested your solitary company to propose."

"But, there must be no other reason," Emelyn said, glancing at the doors. "Or have you committed a deception upon my family," and she started to walk for the exit, but Van Croft stepped quickly to stop her.

"A moment Miss Morley, please," he said. "First you must tell me who I'm to thank, for this ravishing presentation . . . your mother perhaps?"

"I am perfectly capable of selecting *ensemble* on my own," she said, "though in this case I'm happy to give her the full credit, for I can scarcely fill my lungs."

"Your sacrifice does not go unnoticed."

Emelyn blushed. "You study me with great care my lord. It makes one wish she had a fan . . . or perhaps a blanket."

Van Croft shook with a laugh. "Very good!" he said, holding her eyes as he coaxed her hand from her pocket. "Your clever silliness endears Miss Morley, but I've only excused your family that I might hear you accept my plan in your own willing words."

"Can you mean the invitation to Eastbourne?" Emelyn asked stiffly, employing her free hand to press her ribs, hoping to magic some room into her stays.

"Of course my dear lady," he said, rubbing her knuckles with his thumb.

"My father has presented it," she replied, "and I am perplexed with gratitude. I cannot help wondering at your including my brother."

"Can you think so unkindly of me?" He took a sip of his brandy. "But do you not love your own brother?"

Emelyn panted, waiting for her breath to catch up. "I do my lord, and I would protect him, as any sister must . . . while she has a heart."

"Then put yourself at ease; my motive is only to please you by his elevation," Van Croft said, finishing his drink.

"And can you make such a promise?" she asked, feeling painfully impatient. "Deacon is of uncertain constitution; I'll not endanger his health, nor will I permit he attend any such function only to be neglected."

"You needn't fear on that account," Van Croft said, setting his glass on the card table. "The Commodore is a congenial man, and Galecliff a long march from the clenched prejudice of London."

Emelyn knit her brows, feeling a tug of emotion to imagine her brother met with proper respect as a gentleman.

The captain smiled. "Stern in blushing beauty as the plucked rose. Will you accompany me to Eastbourne, to take my arm and acquaint my old friends?"

"If it pleases my brother to join us . . . then I accept."

The captain closed in. "Shall we seal it with a kiss?"

"No my lord, we shall not seal it with a kiss," she said, feeling inconvenient stirrings at his proximity. "You have stolen my company by deception, that must be reward enough."

"Save your smouldering for our enemies," he said, standing too close, "whom I shall see laid at your feet, to create you the goddess at my side . . ."

"You vaunt with the swagger of Caesar," she said, turning her head as he leaned closer.

"Then let me conquer."

"My lord we are alone; I require space, either you or the couch must move."

"So perhaps you should sit down, to make room."

"And demure in surrender," she said, meeting his eyes. "No my lord, I shan't be bullied . . . give me space."

Van Croft stood almost against her, and leaning away she overtaxed her balance, dropping to sit in the sofa.

"Excellent!" he laughed, retreating with a grand bow. "Ever the contentious kitten, and by the swell of her breath most deliciously vexed."

Emelyn's face grew hot. "My lord I begin to wonder if you're blind in one eye," she said, rising from the couch with deliberate dignity, "to so mismeasure the distance between us. I cannot stop you crowding me, but if you only mean to force my regard by your looming presence . . ."

"By gad madam!" he interrupted, returning to the crystal to pour a pair of brandies. "Your displeasure is more fetching than sincerest ecstasy on the face of a lesser woman."

"You mark well my face, but not my words," she breathed, her sides straining with ache.

"My dear lady I mark every *syllable* from those sweetest of lips," he said, offering her a glass. "There, I grant you all the space timid convention demands . . . Now let us toast, before I set off again."

Emelyn composed herself as she could, accepting the brandy. "Very well, quickly. To what do we toast?"

"We shall toast this silver Friday as the navy does," he said. "To willing foes and sea-room!" and he clinked her glass.

No sooner had she tasted her drink than the captain's stew was delivered, and drawing up a chair at the billiard table he tucked in. Emelyn watched with shallow breath, hands pressed to her sides, and feeling an abrupt temptation to faint she sat again on the sofa.

Lord Van Croft nodded with an affirmative noise, wiping his mouth on the napkin. "First-rate," he remarked, pushing back the chair. "I shall return to fetch you Friday next; we shall take the newer road to Eastbourne, skirting the cliffs for the view. I will take my place by the driver," he added, clattering his spoon into the bowl, "that your brother should have more room for his comfort."

"That is . . . most considerate." Emelyn winced, watching as he approached, and she gasped as he knelt before her, taking her hand. "No my lord! You mustn't think it, not yet . . ."

"Settle yourself!" he said, kissing her fingers. "I only mean to thank you for your patience, and bid you goodbye."

"Goodbye," Emelyn said, feeling a growing lightness of head.

The captain stood with a wink. "And good afternoon, my dear Miss Morley. Now see to those laces before you take your last breath," and turning on his heel he strode to the doors, pulling them open to the sound of surprised giggles.

Emelyn moaned, sagging into the sofa as the girls rushed to her side, Mrs. Morley close behind them.

"What a strange man!" Sarah exclaimed. "To finally arrive late for dinner and stay not an hour."

"But have you given him your answer?" Isabelle asked, fidgeting her hands.

"He's not proposed," Emelyn said. "Now I must escape the claws of this costume; help me up."

Mrs. Morley spluttered with confusion. "But you were alone with him my dearest, how has he not proposed?"

"By neglecting to propose!" Emelyn rasped, pulling as her sisters helped her to her feet.

"But you do mean to accept his invitation to Eastbourne?" Sarah asked.

"I do, Sarah, yes; I'll not deny Deacon the chance to attend a proper party away from home . . . if I do not die for lack of air."

The sun hung low in the sky, and free of her sharply boned bodice at last Emelyn leaned into the frame of her window, reduced to her cotton shift as Breda pushed into her back with balled fists, kneading against her soreness.

Emelyn heaved with the relief of it. "On my life you are never to lace me so tightly again, whatever my mother requires, do you understand?"

"I'm that sorry miss," Breda lamented. "I've never seen her so demanding; clear enough she's set her whole heart on the captain . . ."

"That she has," Emelyn said, grimacing as the maid's knuckles worked under her shoulder.

<hr>

Saturday June 18th

Just north of London, in the open Hertfordshire hills under a pale sky, the castle of Terra Lindsor presented a stark salt-white edifice against the manicured green of the land round about. Shielded by a wall of columnar trees, the encircling drive split into narrower roads, escaping the castle grounds by means of railed bridges, their bellies arching over a clear stream that surrounded the estate like a natural moat.

One of these bridges pointed westward down the hill to open miles of deer park, and there, leaning with laced cuffs on the rail stood the sour faced Baron Dramen. He was dressed befitting his reputation — skirted knee length coat of black over silken vest, with a long split wig of white under his hat and precious stones on the buckles of his heeled shoes. Standing tall and proud, a frown worn low on his face, Lord Dramen creased his brows as he looked into the burbling water below.

The endless afternoon sky swam overhead, tufted islands of grey scattered across powder blue, and with no mind for the scenery the baron turned to find his better in rank, the Duke of Lindsor just slowing his steed at the far foot of the bridge where Lord Dramen's coach waited. Clad in similar grandeur, a long coat of creamy silk and wig of cascading curls peaked higher than that of the baron, the young nobleman dismounted, taking the bridle to walk the horse as he made his approach.

"Your Grace," Lord Dramen greeted, sweeping his arm for a bow.

"My dear Dramen at last," the duke hailed. "Forswearing the house for the grounds I see; but it is a fetching day, well chosen."

"I find Your Grace two hours behind his time," Lord Dramen noted, surveying the rolling land about them. "Had I known I'd have given more pressing matters their due."

"My dear Gadoric you may fix blame on the Kent Roads Act," the duke puffed, "and what a singular bore it was; upon my word I'll never see the use erecting tolls through the downs. Most treacherous bit of road London to the sea . . .”

“Indeed Your Grace.” Lord Dramen snatched a silver topped cane from its lean on the rail as they began to walk. “That way is cursed.”

“By blood drinking ghouls and goblins,” the duke chortled. “But I hope you’ve not come to contend for your *Vampire Act* old fellow; nothing has changed.”

Lord Dramen smiled as they neared the end of the bridge, and he stopped to swish his cane, blocking his peer’s path. “On the contrary Your Grace, *everything* has changed.”

“Dramatic,” the duke sighed, brushing away the cane as he continued to lead his mount. “If you’ve devised some expedient to sway my position, by all means give it air.”

“Your Grace, I have in my possession a living vampire.”

“Have you? How diverting. And you’ve brought the creature to show me perhaps?”

“I speak in earnest,” Lord Dramen said, clacking the end of the rail as they passed. “My agents have seen it done; she was taken by the light of dawn, caught in her sleep of death.”

“A female, well-chosen again,” the duke said, chuckling as they strolled between pointed topiary trees planted like spears on either side.

“She is beautiful,” Lord Dramen added, “petite, and young, as it would appear.”

“And whatever shall you do with her, your lovely vampire, present her at the market fair perhaps?”

“Nay sir,” Dramen said, curing the duke of his smile. “I shall keep her close, for presentation of proof, to those I deem worthy of the invitation . . . to expand our coalition.”

“So you would make her a pet. A rather chancy prosecution I should think, or perhaps you’ve overstated the danger of these creatures.”

“Dawn till dusk the vampire is helpless, soft as a sick child,” Dramen said, looking ahead. “I have come here to invite you to try the pretty creature, for yourself.”

“To try her?”

Lord Dramen wet his lips. “That is to say, for even the most profane use of such a creature, a man could not be judged.”

“I’m not sure I take your meaning . . .”

“The unliving damned have no immortal soul Your Grace, they are but motes of dust, uncounted in the eyes of Heaven. Therefore my proposal is simple; for your generous support, her flesh your canvas."

"Well I can't imagine what you've heard of me," the Duke clucked. "But a fellow might find your overture too good to be true, only meant to expose him for blackmail."

"Not at all Your Grace," Lord Dramen said, dabbing the ground with his cane as they walked. "I mean to offer you a place of honour, as one of our founding subscribers with a stake in her ownership."

"Shall you sell shares?" the duke marvelled with a laugh, "create your little monster a commodity?"

"For but a select few," Lord Dramen said. "Understand, Your Grace, when vampires are proven the greatest enemy of Christendom, we the new Rosicrucians shall rise ascendent, empowered by king and country to hunt not only these feral drinkers of blood, but their slaves and sympathizers. The *Vampire Act* is only the beginning."

Cold drops of rain began to tick on the ground, and the smiling duke cleared his throat. "Oh my dear fellow," he said, biting his lip, "I see by the gravity in your face you'd spare no effort to convince me . . . but unless, and until I find the creature precisely as you describe, I might hazard you've only snatched some desperate drazzle and pressed her to the part."

"My dear Your Grace," Lord Dramen said, slowing his pace, "this is no deception. Rest assured her every corporeal aspect will be vetted. Of course, should she prove a fraud . . . well, then I shall leave her disposal to you; a private audience perhaps, shall we say this afternoon?"

The duke swallowed, coming to a stop. "A tempting bit of mischief to be sure. Alas, I've calls to make and leisure to take . . . Shall we say day after tomorrow?"

Lord Dramen fortified his smile. "The Duke of Lindsor must do as he pleases," he said, swirling his hand for a bow, "but I would caution Your Grace, that once the existence of vampires is proved to our credit, rank and peerage will count as nothing, for those outside the brotherhood . . ."

"Rousing trumpets Dramen," the duke said dryly, "and I would caution you in turn: should you design to make a fool of me, thinking to woo my investiture by deceit, I will introduce your *Vampire Act* to the House of Lords, but with every ridicule it deserves. You will be finished."

"Then perhaps we understand each other," Lord Dramen said, touching his hat as he started back across the bridge. "I shall expect you at Charwell at your earliest convenience, and when you have tested the creature yourself . . . I will accept your apology."

"Just a final query sir," the duke called. "Bethlem Hospital . . . can it be true you've bought your way to the chair? But it's a quagmire old fellow, good for nothing but bleeding parish coin. What possible use could you make of it?"

Lord Dramen stopped, turning on his heel to respond. "The hospital governors are among the first I've invited to view her. But what better place to study those living in death, than the incurable wards of Bedlam?"

"With not one but *two* wives in that hallowed place, you should know better than I," the duke mused.

Betraying a sneer Dramen bowed low. "And might I suggest wearing a mask to attend her, that she cannot name her tormenter, if ever it comes to it . . . Good evening Your Grace!" and tapping his cane he set off, crossing the bridge for the grand coach that waited on the other side.

Seated with hands folded, dressed in black to the throat, her dark hair pulled up tight, Miss Ariana Winter watched as Lord Dramen climbed in with a huff, muttering under his breath.

"Damned obstinate buzzard," he grumbled, finding his comfort, "he will learn better than to mock me."

The door closed and Miss Winter chuckled. "Shall I kill him my lord?"

"No," Lord Dramen said tersely, banging his cane to signal their departure. "The duke is an insufferable blatherskite, but a reliable hedonist. He will bear witness, and then he is ours."

Miss Winter crossed her legs with a smile. "Our immortal captive is a singular trophy to be sure, but I would caution against abandoning our designs upon Hastelbrook my lord. We know Philip Denlund's killer was a vampire; there could be no better confirmation something of great value lies beneath; evil is drawn to the place like flies."

"I've no intention of abandoning Hastelbrook," Dramen said, "but the man who hunts two hares catches neither. Patience, my dear Miss Winter; with a living vampire in our power, our season has come at last."

■■

Sunday June 19th

The cold rain came down hard, punishing the Hastelbrook gardens as Emelyn and her sisters watched through the high parlour windows.

"That's London off then," Sarah lamented.

"It's not fair!" Isabelle groused. "No Farinelli, no *Alcina*, no Vauxhall gardens; are we to go the entire season without culture?"

"The post was generous this morning," Emelyn said. "Perhaps you've a letter."

Isabelle dashed off, and Sarah sighed. "If you would still like a lesson at harpsichord, I shall be free all day."

"Yes I would like that," Emelyn said.

With her sister she adjourned to the music room, where hoping for distraction from anxious thoughts, she nevertheless found herself unable to focus on the instrument.

"I'm sorry," she said after a while.

"It's all right Emie," Sarah said, standing from the bench. "We'll try again when you're interested."

Left to sit at the keys by herself, Emelyn stared at the cascading windows. Margaret's doubt, compounded by the way they'd parted sat weighty upon her, and striving to return her attention to the music she set her fingers to try again.

That afternoon a light refection of tea and honey cake did little to buoy her spirits, and joining Sarah and Deacon Emelyn planted her flag in the small library downstairs, making it headquarters for another stab at research. Sitting in the bay windows surrounded by literature and papers she began with a thorough study of her journal, searching her written memory for anything she might have used to better convince Margaret of the truth . . . and wondering again what Mr. Arkwright must think of her, and how it all might have been different, had Maggie not interfered.

Pouring rain hammered the drive, making little rivers across the stones. Sarah rose to glower at the windows, closing her book with a snap. "I'm going upstairs."

The hours laboured on, and waking from a doze to find the grey daylight still thick with downpour, Emelyn rubbed her eyes, returning to Lord Cumberstone's book of poetry, which she'd taken to concealing in the open pages of larger works; in this case *Systema Naturae: Classes, Ordines, Genera, Species,* printed in Latin by Carl Linneaus.

A snort reminded her of Deacon's presence, though she could see only his outstretched legs as he slumped in a grand wing-back chair.

Clicking closed his snuffbox he stretched with a growl, leaning forward to peer back at her. "*Systema Naturae,*" he observed. "Holy Saxons Emie, where do you put it all?"

"Perhaps I find the new taxonomy diverting," Emelyn said, studying the page.

Deacon stared at her. "You're not reading it."

"I'm not."

"Go on then, what are you hiding?"

Emelyn sighed at him. "What do you think of Lord Cumberstone? Who is he?"

"There's no such peerage I can tell you, not in Great Britain," he said. "A pseudonym passed down; the first codex of songs published by that name was 1286 if I remember."

"1284," she corrected, adjusting her book. "But tell me what do you make of this: *Whence slipping Stour splits East in Tines, away a blue eyed startled Hind doth perish o'er jagged Cliffs by Fen, and crash to Foam alive again, brumed 'twixt lucent Windows flows, to purl blind 'neath iron Barrows, through Cavern Bones and stacking Stones, where long Dead sew deep Mere below, and raise her Rooms in ebon Blooms, until dark Towers pierce the Moon."*

"Goose plucking nonsense," Deacon pronounced, swivelling back to his book.

"But it's not *all* nonsense," Emelyn said. "The Stour river is real enough. I should say it sounds rather like directions to some hidden place. Saunmoor perhaps?"

"By Jove you're right," he said, turning his page. "Fetch my hat there's not a moment to lose."

"Oh come now. You've memorized every word the Socratics put to paper; the least you might do is tell me what you heard."

"Fine then," he said, still facing away from her. *"Blue eyed startled Hind?* Perhaps a quick stream off the main course, flowing over a falls to pass through fog by a village in the valley below, falling into the dark beneath some erected eminence or other, and the rest is piffle . . ."

"Perhaps, perhaps not," Emelyn said, fidgeting with the queen of Saunmoor's coin, which had by now found permanent residence in her pocket. "What of *deep mere below?* Is there an underground lake in Kent?"

"I don't know Emie, but if there were towers tall enough to pierce the moon, we shouldn't need directions to find them."

There was a bang at the doors, and dressed in floral white Isabelle burst in with a happy flush, shaking a letter in her hand. "Emie, Deacon," she said breathlessly, "it is confirmed, the most wonderful news!"

"Praise the nation your dolls' heads are found," Deacon said.

Isabelle puffed her lips. "No, of course not that; I've had a letter from John Lawford, Mama's just given it over; oh Emie he's written to me, and all is well!"

Emelyn set her books aside. "Really? And what does he say for himself?"

"First he apologizes in the most beautiful words," Isabelle said, snapping through the pages. "*I've been the most intolerable knave these past months . . . yes, and just here: hiding under such a burden of shame as your pure and darling self could be never be abased to comprehend. My dearest Bell, it is with the humblest most miserable contrition I can only beg . . .*"

"Why did he not write to you earlier?" Emelyn interrupted.

"If you will listen, I am telling you! *I can only beg your tendermost mercy, for cold deserved reproach from your lips would shatter my miserable heart forever, though verily I should expect it. Isabelle Marie, will you forgive a most desperate rogue . . .*"

"What else does he say?" Emelyn interjected, finding the syrupy confession ridiculous. "Does he explain buying his way out of the charge, that a *magistrate* of all people paid off Mr. Cavendish for the injury? How did he manage it?"

"It doesn't matter Emie!" Isabelle snapped, her colour rising. "The whole confrontation is put behind him, and the aggrieved party well satisfied."

"I cannot tell through the froth," Deacon puzzled, "has he found your dolls' heads or not?"

Emelyn coughed, stifling a laugh.

"I shall be certain to lament of the both of you in my response," Isabelle retorted, swatting her skirts. "Mr. Lawford is by all accounts reformed, and has even a patron now, a marquess in fact, that's better than your *Lord Captain* Emie."

"What marquess?" Emelyn asked, hesitant to believe it. "Does he name him?"

"Of course he does, here," Isabelle said, finding the passage. "*My illustrious patron, the Marquess of Crennock, who would deign to call upon you at some future time, and would speak in my defence whilst I am called to attend my father in Germany.*"

"Lord Crennock?" Deacon said, sitting up.

"Do you know him?" the women asked together.

"I know he made out like King Solomon in the South Seas crash fifteen years ago."

Leaving the bench, Emelyn came to stand by her sister's side.

"There, so you see I was not wrong to hope," Isabelle said. "He does not say when, but a *marquess* Emie just think, *Lord Crennock* here at Hastelbrook!”

“This is an intimate letter Bell,” Emelyn said, looking it over, “Lawford should never have written to you directly.”

“I think you’re jealous.” Isabelle batted her with the pages. “He addressed it to Mama of course. After holding it for the morning she gave it over.”

Emelyn frowned. “Did she indeed.”

Mrs. Morley was writing at her desk in the upstairs salon attached to her rooms. “If you’ve come to admonish me over Isabelle’s letter,” she said, finishing her own, “I should tread very carefully my dearest.”

Emelyn stood in the doorway. “John Lawford is a scoundrel Mama. Do you forget he pursued me before Isabelle? You cannot believe he’s sincere.”

“*I remain, your faithful and affectionate friend, Antonia Morley*,” her mother recited, signing her letter and blowing the ink to dry.

“Are you listening to me?”

“I read Lawford’s note before it ever touched her hands,” Mrs. Morley said, folding her pages.

“Yes I see . . . but I suppose the prospect of entertaining a marquess is of greater moment than Isabelle’s reputation.”

Her mother gave an exasperated sound, and softening a stick of wax in the candle she turned it in the flame before pressing it to the paper, which she stamped with her signet ring. “You’re not thinking my dearest; our Isabelle’s reputation could only be improved by acquaintance with Lord Crennock. Now, do you remember Miss Shelley Browning?”

“Of course,” Emelyn said. “She was at Dhorings Park for the shoot, though we hardly spoke.”

Mrs. Morley stood from the desk, her face stern with displeasure. “Well, I’ve just seen to the misfortunate obligation of penning a rebuttal to her mother, who maintains Miss Browning saw you in a heat of passion *kissing* Fitzwilliam Arkwright on the hill!”

Emelyn swallowed. “Shelley Browning is a tireless gossip.”

“I have assured her of her mistake, but from you I must have the truth . . . do you deny it?”

Avoiding her eyes Emelyn took a bracing breath. “I do not.”

“Emelyn Elizabeth . . . how on earth could you allow it? Did he attack you?”

"No Mama, nothing of the sort . . . but it was only a kiss, only a moment. We were hardly permitted sight of each other for the remainder of the evening."

Her mother heaved as though to temper her alarm. "Oh my dear deluded child; I am prepared to accept that he seduced you, but you must think nevermore of him! And we must be grateful it went no further."

"He never seduced me . . ."

"Then it could not have happened!" her mother exclaimed. "For he is in trade lest we forget, naught but the son of a cooper."

"Papa is in trade!" Emelyn protested. "We are not nobility Mama."

"We are well landed gentry; some of our wealth was *put* to trade, there is a difference."

"*Some* of it? Really? Is that why I'm to be married in all devilish haste, that we might keep the house?"

There was a pause, and her mother flushed. "Your poor father is doing everything he can."

Emelyn took a breath, feeling she'd rather over shot the mark. "I know Mama . . . but Fitzwilliam Arkwright must have a thousand a year by now, likely more; that is a respectable income."

Mrs. Morley laughed with performance. "And Van Croft shall have ten times as much. My dear girl we will not trade the gift of your beauty for a struggling interest in barrel making!"

"Mama," Emelyn crossed her arms tightly. "No one has proposed to me. I have done nothing wrong . . . beside one small misjudgement."

"Small misjudgement!"

"I have invited Mr. Arkwright to call," Emelyn said stiffly, controlling her tone, "so that I might properly explain. I should expect a letter from him soon."

"Incorrect my dear; you've nothing to explain to him, nor anyone else," Mrs. Morley said. "The matter is settled. The *Bloodhound of His Majesty's Navy* takes a keen interest in your future, and that is where we shall focus your powers."

Emelyn glared at her. "What can you mean *the matter is settled?* Has Mr. Arkwright answered already? Have you kept it from me?"

"We received his note from London only today. Quite presumptive of the gentleman, and you should never have involved Lady Dhorings. I have said as much on your behalf."

"You've said as much?" Brushing past her Emelyn rushed to her mother's desk, rifling through the papers. "Where is it? You've not sent your response already?”

“I held the post boy this morning; our answer is well on its way.”

Emelyn clenched her teeth, turning around. “So you have forbidden him?”

“My dear Emelyn Elizabeth,” Mrs. Morley said, taking her hands. “We are all the better for it, you will see.”

Emelyn pulled away. “Shall I have what he wrote to me, or have you burned it?” she demanded, feeling a sting of panic.

“Of course it is gone. The cooper is a passing fancy my dearest; you have accepted Lord Van Croft’s invitation, and he will expect your full attention. We shan’t disappoint him.”

“I will not have you refer to Mr. Arkwright as *the cooper*,” Emelyn charged, feeling tears of anger as she turned for the door. “My choices are not yours to make!”

“Very well my dearest, of course I meant no offence! I do not doubt you will do what’s right.”

“What’s right?” Emelyn stopped on the threshold, gripping the frame. “Mama, if you love me you will not stop my letters . . . and if you love Isabelle you will not receive John Lawford, nor his friends.”

“So you would champion your right to choose,” her mother said, sitting again at her desk, “while denying your sister the same.”

Finding no civil response Emelyn swished from the doorway and back down the hall.

The thunderous deluge continued, and retreating to the drawing room she joined her sisters for half-hearted games, sitting for a languorous match of backgammon with Isabelle, during which they took turns forgetting who was to move next. Emelyn’s darkness of mood was only aggravated by Isabelle’s air of contemplative joy, and she could not look at her. The competing spectres of Arkwright and Van Croft clamoured for attention, and silently Emelyn berated herself for parting with Margaret as she had, allowing her dearest friend’s protective nature to come between them. But when the grey masked sun finally set perhaps Vaela would be of some comfort, if only she would appear . . .

“I require you,” Emelyn grumbled softly, moving one of the black pieces.

“Who?” Isabelle asked, looking up from the board.

“Nothing . . . no one.”

By and by they drifted back to the wide front parlour windows to watch the rain, finding Deacon already seated by the warm glow of the hearth, smoking his briar. There was little conversation, and aside from sharing some amusement at the sight of the brave gardener chasing his hat across the tidal winds of the drive, the young ladies sat quietly in thought until the clocks chimed four.

"On my life we shall have nothing but water the whole week." Isabelle pouted, supporting her chin in her hand. "I wonder if Mr. Lawford is watching the rain . . . Do you suppose it's raining in Germany?"

Emelyn made fists in her pockets. "I'm going out," she declared.

"What?" her sisters exclaimed together.

"Lovely day for a walk," Deacon called after her, chewing his pipe, "if you're a duck."

Hastening to the grand hall Emelyn stopped before a startled Adam Comberland.

"Mistress?"

"Do not argue; help me out of my shoes," she ordered, pulling at her skirts to display her foot. "Yes, thank you, quickly."

Pleasantly surprised at his rapid compliance Emelyn kicked off the second short boot and pulled open the doors, dashing in her stocking feet down the stairs and into the rain. The wind howled about her, stinging drops flashing against her skin, and she laughed at the mortifying drench of it, splashing across the stones of the drive and between the boiling fountains to disappear into the hedge.

The cold grass squelched beneath her, and by the third turn in the path her sopping skirts dragged as though hemmed with stones. Panting with the effort she gathered her petticoats and pushed onward, stopping near the gazebo to pull at her neckline, wrestling her bodice until the fabric creaked and split. Arrows of water pierced her skin in their thousands, and untangling her hair to shake it out she opened her mouth to the effusive sky, basking in the invigoration of her escape.

Thunder broke across the clouds, and blinking in the pelting rain she imagined Vaela there at her side, or perhaps leaping atop the gazebo in a single bound, free from all earthly cares. *Come up and join me,* the vampiress would beckon. But the silver light of day yet gleamed through the clouds; wherever Vaela was she must be well hidden from the sun, sleeping until dusk.

Shivering in the soaking cold, Emelyn sheltered under the roof on the curving bench, hands between her knees as she smacked her feet on the flooded stones, her stomach twisting to think of the journey to Eastbourne and the high cliffs of Beachy Head, which she had never seen.

An aggressive fog rolled off the lakes, and again she thought of Mr. Arkwright, lamenting that she'd likely squandered the last of his company on so rushed and ridiculous a goodbye . . . But closing her eyes she could still feel the touch of his lips, and the urgency to have his response quickened within her. "I have committed no crime," she said aloud, watching the shallow water as it swirled, turning white stones to glass.

Comby burst out of the hedge with arms aloft, a heavy cloak over his head. "Miss Morley you must come inside! You shall catch a chill!"

"Comby we meet again!" she cried, raising her arms, and standing to accept his gift of shelter she huddled under the cloak, joining him to return to the house.

An hour later found her in dry shift and dressing gown, swaddled in woollen blankets before the grand drawing room fire as Breda brushed out her hair, Mrs. Morley pacing furiously before her.

"But it wounds me that you could indulge such recklessness! Is this your revenge for our disagreement? And what on earth was Comby thinking? Having you out of your shoes indeed . . . he must be turned off at once!"

"You will not dismiss him," Emelyn said sharply. "He did nothing but obey my command; I'd have pulled them off myself if he refused."

"Well, you are confined to the house tomorrow and I'll hear not one word of protest," Mrs. Morley puffed. "You will see Doctor Bayten my girl, and you will take to heart his every instruction."

Her skin prickled with memory of the rain, and Emelyn sighed as she watched the fire, warm and insulated from her mother's scolding. "Yes Mama, whatever you like . . ."

Chapter 16
The Black Citadel

In the small hours after midnight, under the rolling canopy of Kent Downs, a rushing stream split from the body of the Stour, running through secret ways of mire and bramble to a high rocky falls, where it plunged headlong into the hidden vale below. Emerging from the foam the little river reassembled its strength to thread a gentler course guarded by prodigious elms and oaks, their knuckled roots flush with flowering green, until the river slipped between planted fields to approach the centre of the valley, where a sprawling fog nestled village crowded its way to the banks, a thousand candles winking in a thousand windows.

From the heart of the village rose a vast craggy hill that straddled the water, permitting the river to wend its unsuspecting way through vaulted darkness beneath. Rising from the hill was a gargantuan eruption of iron and stone, its unbreakable walls surrounded by a choking wood of tangled trees, their bark dry and cracked as though chaste of all life. Thrust from the ground to a dizzying height, this the citadel of Umbremar was crowned with innumerable towers, their sharp edges cutting black against the sky, while at the outer edge of the valley basin, beyond village, fields, and forest, rose a massive wall of encircling stone, a sea of enchanted mist swimming just outside its guardian gates, the final boundary of Saunmoor, the dark queen's domain.

Tonight the dimly lit village streets were silent all but one, a steep lane making its way through the settlement down to the riverbank. Here there came a procession of nine children robed in white, led by an elderly woman shrouded and veiled as though in mourning, a cloudy lantern held high before her. The children were ordered from eldest to youngest, with Miles Grey, now eleven years of age, in the front, his heart thumping in his chest, while the littlest girl, aged but four, trailed behind, making furtive glances back.

Eerie lights played in the distance, keening voices wailed on the wind, and some of the children shook with audible fear, the older ones shushing them as the procession slowed to a stop at the open gate of a fenced dock, beyond which lay stairs to what looked to be a long jollyboat bumping softly in the current. There were no oars as far as young Miles could see, though in the curving body of the boat he espied rows of thwarts-straight spans for seating, carved with spidery patterns in the wood. A brass bell hung by the dock on a lantern pole, and the elderly woman turned like a statue to face it, reaching her withered hand to catch a length of rope tied to the clapper.

Too frightened to speak, the children waited, and the bell rang out sharp and strong, chastening the voices on the wind.

For a long moment silence reigned, broken only by the tearful hiccoughs of the smallest child at the end.

"Britt you must be quiet," the eldest girl, nine year old Amelia warned softly.

"Ammy," the little one protested. "Ammy I want to go back to the house."

Miles cleared his throat. "Are you to take us somewhere ma'am, on the boat?" he ventured, addressing their mysterious guide.

"I have not ferried the little ones to their fate, for many years," the decrepit woman lamented, her voice high and weary with breath, as though she had not enough air to speak.

Squinting in the haze Miles tracked the river, finding it plunged straight into the stony face of the mountain beneath the fortress, where it was lost to sight and sound save faint report of rushing water from somewhere below.

"My time is ended . . . the Painted Shadow will come," the woman said vaguely, and the children startled with fright as she faded to nothing before their eyes, lantern and all.

"Don't break out of line!" Miles ordered, the hair tingling on his neck.

"Do we run?" one boy asked, a quiver in his voice.

"We should back up the street, to the cottage where they put us," Amelia said, speaking over little Britt's increasing sounds of distress.

"Where they locked us in?" another protested.

"Yes and with food, and beds, and dry clothes," she replied, speaking to Britt.

"Shush!" Miles scolded, silencing the murmurs. "We dare not move," he said, taking in the impossible vast of the fortress over the river, a black mountain, sharp edged against the dead sky. "Stay together."

High above the children, at the end of a rocky path that wound its spiralling way up and around the mountainous hill, Vaela stood before the sealed doors of the citadel. Behind her a narrow bridge of stone pierced the creaking forest, fording a deep cleft like a natural moat, which plunged down and out of view, shot through with worming tree roots.

Ghostly lights swam in the dark about her, approaching shyly and dancing away. "My queen," Vaela spoke to the doors, bewildered to find no response. "Dire Lady Pazoa, I seek your audience; will you not open the way?"

The silent portal took no notice, and with a snarl she slapped her hand against the deadening metal, straining to hear the sound that would betray her welcome: a grinding from within as the ponderous doors split apart, swinging wide to reveal a crimson carpeted stair she had descended countless times.

But the doors did not open.

The chime of a bell tingled from the bottom of the hill, a lonely tone rippling over the water, and the vampiress smacked the doors again. "My queen will you hear me?"

Only the wailing wind gave answer, singing through grasping branches as the forest shifted around her. There came a second chime from the valley . . . but the bell never rang twice.

Turning sharply Vaela listened as the floating witch lights avoided her gaze, humming close behind her, and looking back to the entrance she lifted her eyes to the grand arched tympanum above the doors: an elaborate pictorial sculpture of legion skeletal figures swarming to the centre, where stood a tall imperious woman cast in tarnished copper, arms raised as though to gather her power, a high sharp tined crown on her brow. Craning her neck Vaela scanned the familiar walls, finding to either side of the intricate scene cobweb frosted statues, carved to hunch from their alcoves, as though glowering down at her through their marble shrouds. And higher still, dotted with distant lights beyond crenellated walks and bridges, rose the colossal cardinal towers, framing the great red eye of the cathedral.

The bell chimed again, and Vaela shot away, retreating across the bridge to retread the path, flashing down the hill.

At a humble dock by the water she found them: nine children in white, their strict order abandoned for a protective huddle. Gawping at the sight of her they drew back, and Vaela approached, lowering her hood.

"She's not a ghost . . . I see her face," a little girl whispered.

For some time children and vampiress stared at each other.

"My name is Miles Grey madam," the tallest boy piped up. "Beggin' your pardon, we know not why we was brought here, or what's to become of us."

"Where is your escort?" Vaela puzzled. "Where is Afaine?"

"Where is what?" one of the girls asked.

"Who rang the bell?" Vaela clarified.

The girl shook her head, eyes cast down.

"I did," Miles said. "We waited but no one came . . ."

"Afaine has not come," Vaela said, struggling to understand. "Then how is it I find you here?"

Collecting their courage the children began to speak, talking over each other to explain they'd been snatched from London some days past, that hers was the only unshrouded face they'd seen, and that a strange old woman had come to collect them, guiding them down to the water. Vaela picked through their turbulent voices, and by and by she gathered they'd been quartered in a cottage up the hill, locked inside until tonight.

Plucking up Miles Grey proceeded to introduce the other children. "But it's lovely diggins' they given us mistress, no complaints," he added. "We been warm and fed; new clothes an' pair o' shoes . . ."

"We followed the beldam," Amelia put in, "but then she was gone, disappeared like she never was. I don't know what she wanted . . ."

"All children are brought to the queen, on their thirteenth night," Vaela said.

"I don't want to go!" a tender voice squeaked, and the smallest girl burst from the group before Amelia could grab her, rushing forward to catch hold of Vaela's leg. "You're not a ghost," she pleaded, her eyes wet with fear. "Will you take us home? To the warm house?"

"Britt come back!" Amelia scolded.

But the little girl held fast, and at the sense of her tremulous heart Vaela sighed, crouching before her. "Britt? Listen . . . You are not afraid."

Transfixed in her gaze Britt settled, sniffing with a nod as the others crowded closer.

"Please mistress, will you help us?" one of the boys asked, a tremble in his voice.

Many hands pressed her, their innocent terror overwhelming her senses. "Do not crowd me!" Vaela chided, hissing to drive them back, though Britt clung to her hand.

"Will the queen eat us like Raw Head or Long Mary Wretch?" a horrified girl asked.

"Those are fictions, childish bugbears," Vaela said, allowing Amelia to fetch the little one back. "The queen beneath the mountain is real, and I must bring you to her."

"What is she wanting with children?" Miles asked.

Vaela looked at them one by one, gathering their eyes. "No more questions. Into the jolly boat, every one."

Obediently the children filed to the end of the dock, descending to clamber into the vessel as the vampiress held it steady, and bidding them to sit she posted herself at the stern, unwinding the mooring and taking up a long pole to push them off. Amelia and little Britt sat just before her, with Miles at the prow, the children facing front as Vaela guided them into the lazy drift of the river.

The impenetrable gloom of the tunnel drew near, and her young passengers shrank in their chairs. Softly the darkness parted, and they'd scarcely time to marvel at the vast open space before them when the watercourse charged downward. The children cried out, holding to each other as they braced for the drop, but the thrill of descent lasted scarcely a moment before the boat settled with a splash, carried forward on the current. High overhead the vaulted cavern ceiling curved like the ribs of a whale, while to either side steep mud banks gave way to artificial shores of pale carven stone. The high stacked walls were busy with columns and porches, hazy lights burning in empty windows, and the air was alive with the sounds of work: tinkering hammers, bangs and booms, sliding and cracking. Plodding figures moved up and down many a stair, dragging nets of broken stone, tools and timber as they disappeared into the deeper halls. The figures were gaunt, impossibly so, their tottering skeletal bodies moving with slow and deliberate pace, each in step with the others as they discharged their dreary tasks.

"They cannot be alive, they're rotting," Amelia said, and as the full measure of the unliving labourers became clear the boat was filled with whimpers of fright.

"Becalm yourselves," Vaela said. "These shades do not perceive you."

"Lord A'mighty they come from the water!" Miles bleated, pointing as a long figure of unnatural size, grey flesh stretched over its bones, ascended from submerged steps to the shore, dragging great split slabs by chains.

"They quarry stone under the river," Vaela said, using the pole against the swells. "Ever the citadel grows; the work does not sleep."

Here deep below the fortress, bisecting the subterranean hive of the dead, the running river bent slowly, losing sight of the entrance as they drew near the centre. The fortifications about them darkened: walls of stone turned to iron, square windows stretched tall, their open mouths toothed with bars, and from the narrowing water grew sentinel towers capped with sharpened points as heavy doors sealed entrances to the black shore on either side. Nothing stirred, though mournful voices echoed through the walls, joining a far off din like the rhythmic pounding of giant drums. Pale corpses, the witch light in their eyes, watched in stillness from an iron bridge as the children passed underneath, and the boat lurched to port, plunging through a yawning gate into the heavier murk of a descending hall.

"Hold on," Vaela instructed.

The way began to drop as the water rushed about them, causing the jollyboat to slip faster, and raising shouts of alarm the children clung to their chairs. Ponderous chains swam in the ceiling overhead, and speeding to a final splash the boat surged into the calm of a placid rounded passage, levelling out as its young passengers panted for breath.

Haunted sounds faded behind them, the vampiress employed her pole, and guiding them forward she made their way to a lowered gate under the sloping ceiling, draped in heavy drenched cloth. With a grinding churn the gate shivered and lifted, scraping up into the ceiling until the way was clear.

Their course continued slowly, and the passage ahead came to a solid end, where the shallow current rushed through balusters under an iron railing to plunge into immeasurable darkness below. This waterfall into the abyss was bridged by a broad stair ascending from the water side to an open corridor on the far wall; here the boat turned and came to rest, bumping softly against the railing, and Vaela bid them disembark.

Carefully the children obeyed, holding their breath as one by one they climbed from boat to the stairs, and step by step made their way up to enter the hall. The vampiress slipped by to lead them on, carrying a lantern from the vessel, with Miles Grey just behind her, Amelia next clutching Britt's hand tightly, and the others following as close as they might without tripping up.

The far end of the passage came into view, a yawning open space of denser shadow, and filtering into the room they found it dank and cold, with ancient tapestries hanging in vast loops, some drooping so low that the children were obliged to duck or brush them aside. The party's footsteps crunched wet and small on the grimy stone, the dull fabrics at last gave way, and Vaela held the lantern aloft. "Your tribute, my queen," she said.

There loomed before them a grand dais of coppery carven marble, faded green with age, atop which sat a wide backed throne, its design splayed outward like the petals of a great rose burned black. But the throne was empty.

Beneath Vaela and the children, flooded chambers and hollow depths of stone, in a grand council room that broke into columned arches at every side, the elder vampire Morion approached the end of a long dully draped table, his ebon hair breaking about his face as he walked, a single living rose pinched in his hand. Each setting at the table was marked by hanging banners from above, painted with symbols stained in blood, though the chairs were flung far aside, scattered and broken, all save one. At the head of the table in the tallest seat, carved of red veined obsidian glass, sat the faceless figure of a woman, bronzy umber of skin, shadowy silk adorning her slender form, her bare arms studded with jewels and resting on the table, onyx claws clicking against its surface.

A solitary candle burned blue before her, and as Morion drew near he found her, Pazoa Qiminossa, queen of Saunmoor, with her head pulled back against the chair by a yard of dark silk taut across her face, while a pair of hooded handmaids strained to hold it by the ends, pulling as though they meant to suffocate their immortal sovereign. The queen opened her mouth against the cloth, trembling as the women pulled it tight, and one of them raised a pitcher, pouring water over her forehead.

Morion dropped the rose, claws bared as the queen spluttered and coughed, the blessed water singeing her flesh, but she raised her hand, bidding him stay his approach, and seething in silence he watched as the water poured again, fuming and splashing over her upturned face. Cast in drenched relief against the binding, the contours of her ageless beauty stretched as she opened her jaws, choking beneath the water.

"Enough!" Morion roared, and like startled phantoms the handmaids vanished.

The queen slumped in her seat, the wrappings sagging about her head, and Morion tore them away, loosing sopping twists of voluminous raven hair to spill about her, obscuring her face.

"Have I come on a thirteenth night . . . to find you here, in such a state," he said, his eyes black.

The Dark Lady of Saunmoor smiled. "My precious Morion," she intoned, her voice a silken balm. "Be still, it is only a sensual diversion."

"It is holy water of baptism!" he charged, his lips curling. "I can taste it on the air."

"A few drops, stirred in the water to tickle my pain."

"Mother, will you not give me your eyes?" he said, leaning close. "Lord Simeon is returned from the continent, and with nothing to avail us, while Afaine stands in neglect of her duty . . . she is missing."

The table cracked under the splitting pressure of her claws. "Afaine is not missing," the queen replied, her tone hard with distemper. "She was taken in carelessness . . . taken by mortals from her rest."

"How is it possible? But I will show them their mistake."

"No!" Pazoa snapped, her voice rattling the table, and catching the edge of his coat she pulled him to her, embracing him about the waist as she sat. "Ever she spurns these walls . . . for shelters and burrows of her own making," she said, her face against him. "Afaine must free herself, or she is no more worthy to be my daughter."

"Would you abandon your own blood? The youngest among us, who loves you beyond death?"

The queen did not respond, but clenched his vest in her teeth.

"I am weary to the back of my heart for pleading with you," he said, holding her icy shoulders. "You languish in a prison of your own making; you must unmask your affliction, share with us of this pain!"

"I require the Bloodstone!" she said, her snarling lips framed by curtains of hair as she rose before him. "And you bring me . . . a shoemaker."

Morion dropped to kneel before her. "As I would bring every needful tradesman to our gates. As I would bring even the Chosen Child, to lay her at your feet."

"The girl is mine already," she said darkly.

"Then why do you hesitate? Bring her to the altar, test her blood; the stone will be found!"

Pazoa studied him, sliding cold fingers through his hair. "Do you suppose you have something to teach me?"

"Steps must be taken, whether you have the jewel or not," he entreated, looking up at her.

"And if the Old Man breaches the vault before I," the queen answered, rubbing his face with her thumbs, "I need only pluck the treasure from his grasp."

Morion closed his eyes, leaning his face in her hands. "Mother, it is innocent blood you require now. Vaela has ferried the children in Afaine's stead . . . you must drink them."

"Vaela . . . the little raven has defied me, taking counsel where it is forbidden. Send her away."

"You must take nourishment!"

"Poor creatures, my anguish frightens you," she said, bending to kiss his forehead. "Our prince and princess hunt the continent far away, Vorsadat is grown strange, Afaine is captured, Lord Simeon and Vaela turned insurgent . . ."

"Nay my queen, they are loyal to you, to the end."

"Even my precious Morion, Archduke of Saunmoor, hears me not."

"My life to preserve you," he said, his eyes wet with black.

Pazoa stroked his scalp with her claws. "You cannot reach me."

"What of the council, whose seats you have broken? My mother I beg you, if there is mercy in your breast will you not bestow it upon yourself? Summon their return, that we should with united force expel this influence upon you!"

The queen did not respond, but held his face to her belly with a weary sound.

"Please my queen; do you not see how we suffer by your concealment . . . What is this crucible? What is this pain upon you?"

"Son of my blood, this burden is mine alone," she said, holding him tightly. "That which haunts my spirit takes what shape must dismay me most . . . I am tested by illusions, cast up from the dark powers rooted beneath us."

"What shape must dismay you most?" he repeated, as like from the ashes of memory an ancient terror seemed to whisper out of the shadows around them . . . The candle flickered, and rising to stand he grabbed her, his claws biting into her arms. "You do not speak of your maker . . . brought to dust, before even the dream of Saunmoor. What could spirits of the black lake know of him?"

Runnels of blood seeped from her shoulders, and the queen lowered her head, growling softly.

"Command me," Morion implored, squeezing her tighter, "that I might deliver you from the source of this madness!"

With a twitch she broke his grasp, her palm striking his chest to send him hurtling away, and cracking off one of the columns he twisted like an animal to light on his feet, sliding backward as his crushed ribs reknit. Dust of stone shook from his hair, and wiping the blood from his mouth Morion looked up in dismay to find the candle on the table extinguished, the queen's chair dark and empty.

"Take heart my eldest," Pazoa's voice boomed from the walls. "I will accede to your admonition, for greatly I thirst . . . I will honour the thirteenth night, I will take the children at the charred throne and embrace them each. As for Vaela Audette, she reeks of the traitor Tredavius; even from here I smell his books and maps. I will not see her."

"But should we not discover *why* she sought him out?" Morion asked, looking about him. "Vaela has been our guest these hundred years; I see nothing for her to gain in defying you now."

"She will complete her duty to the Thirteenth Night," the queen rumbled. "And then, let her be dismissed with my warning: neither she nor her maker are to intercede on Afaine's behalf, lest they remain banished from our grace forever."

- -

Some hours later, in the haunted village at the feet of the queen's fortress, there gleamed a single candle in the loft window of a solitary cottage, wherein nine tired children clambered into their beds under quilted covers, set four to a side. The sound of quick feet patted across the floor, and little Britt climbed into Amelia's bed to be engulfed by the blanket as the children stretched back with yawns and sighs.

Sitting up in the bed nearest the stairs, a stout candle flickering on the table beside him, young Miles Grey slurped the last of his milk from a crockery mug as Vaela stood by.

"So the queen was not to devour us, after all," Miles said, setting the mug aside to scratch his shoulder, "but only taste our blood."

"The children of Saunmoor must nurse their mother," Vaela said.

"A mother does not harm her children."

"I scarce remember her bite," he said, "but I remember the scary trees, and them workers what was dead and still moving; how shall I be not afraid of 'em?"

"That is the queen's power," Vaela said, "you do not fear me, yet I am no more alive than those that walk beneath the fortress."

"But you ain't like them," he contended, fussing into the covers. "And how they come to be here? And who were they, when they was alive?"

Vaela sat on the bed beside him. "Their names are long forgotten," she said.

The lad watched her intently, eyes wide, and the vampiress continued. "Many, many hundreds of years ago, before the Danes, before the Saxons and Romans, before even the Druids, an ancient people dug great pits here below, into which they cast their dead . . . but something disturbed their rest, something that was here already; in the water, in the earth, perhaps in the *ugly trees*," she said, pulling the blanket up over his shoulder, "and the dead began to wake. Deeper and deeper the pits were dug, to keep them in the ground, until at last they delved so deep they had broken into a high cavernous space over an underground lake. That lake, far, far beneath us, is where the dead reside still, and where the first throne of Saunmoor may be found, rising from the water on an isle of bones."

"But why do the dead wake up?" Miles whispered.

"Even the queen cannot tell," Vaela said. "That is why she was drawn here, to understand the power that animates them."

"Please mistress, what is to become of us?" the girl in the next bed asked, blinking slowly.

"You shall grow up," Vaela said. "There shall be tutors and masters, and work befitting you each . . ."

"Might I be one of the Lurkmen," Miles inquired, "and see London town again, like Mr. Lorris?"

"Someday perhaps, if you're clever enough," Vaela said, adjusting his blanket. "But your hunch is right, Master Grey, only the Lurkmen among mortals are permitted to leave this place. Just like yourself, Mr. Lorris was only a boy when we found him, I daresay the very age you are now. He slept by the stench of the riverbank, at the foot of the Horseshoe Alley stairs . . ."

But Miles was asleep, his mouth agape.

Finding the girl beside him had drifted off as well Vaela stood from the bed, and her eyes flushed black as she detected shadows taking solid humanoid form behind her.

"You must not tarry," Morion said. "You must obey your queen."

"Is she really to carry on as though nothing has changed?" Vaela asked. "Will she disdain her own suffering until it breaks her?"

"She believes the power of the lake is testing her, antecedent to some revelation. Nothing will change until the key is found . . ."

The vampiress turned to face him, finding her elder long coated in black as was his wont. "And what of Afaine?" she asked. "*Where* is she?"

"Afaine was discovered in sleep, taken by mortals. She must look to her own deliverance; Pazoa forbids us to interfere."

Vaela bared her fangs as she stared at him. "Shall the queen's own daughter be thus cast away, forgotten?"

"Not forgotten, never," he said, stepping closer. "Our queen will find herself again, but until such time as you are summoned, you are not to return."

"My exile will profit her nothing. Vorsadat means to betray her; the very secrecy of Saunmoor is at stake."

"He only makes enemies of himself," Morion said. "Do not fear; I am forbidden to hinder him directly, but I will not permit his madness should threaten us," and he reached to take her hand.

Vaela drew back. "No. I don't want the guilty weight of your heart; You know the queen is wrong; she must accept the prophecy. She must accept it is Emelyn, and not herself, who will enter the vault."

Catching the neck of her cloak he pressed her suddenly to the wall, baring his fangs with a snarl as she hissed in protest, baring her own.

"Enough!" he growled. "You will depart in gratitude, for she is merciful."

The humming and heavy burden of his heart shuddered through her, and Vaela's eyes filled with black. "You are sick with fear for her," she breathed, grabbing his wrist. "I will not carry your demons!"

Morion's eyes were deep and dark as he beheld her. "An immortal with the heart of a child," he said quietly, letting her go. "Your presence vexes her; go and join your maker in the city . . . I will treat with the queen on your behalf."

Vaela swallowed. "Then you must give her this ring," she said, presenting him the obsidian band from Tredavius. "It was her final gift to the Old Man; she will know his sincerity by its return."

Morion looked it over. "She will not accept his token. Return it whence it came, or keep it. It matters not."

"But you spoke to him," Vaela contended. "He confessed as much."

Curling his lip Morion stepped away from her. "If he would earn her trust, let him return the Bloodstone. Now go, Vaela Audette, and do not return until you are summoned."

Vaela frowned, as for a moment more she held his eyes, and in a swirl of mist he was gone.

Stepping outside she paused to look upon the black bulk of the citadel, and the unblinking eye of the cathedral, which glowered red over village fields and forest, sheltering all the hidden city in its gaze. "You are blind my queen," she said, her voice thick with sorrow, and into the dark she vanished.

■■■

Rainy evening had made for a deep and misty night, and once again Emelyn could not sleep. Perched in a thin robe at her desk she brushed out her hair, just resolved to return to her journal when she gasped to see Vaela's face at the window.

Emelyn jumped to her feet, mastering her nerves as she set to unlocking and opening the panes. "Please," she rasped, clearing her throat to strengthen her voice. "Please come in."

At once the vampiress was inside, and taking Emelyn's hand she placed it against her heart, breathing with closed eyes as though to fortify herself. The sense of her presence charged the air, but Vaela's collar was cold, and studying her face Emelyn found a tinge of sadness about her.

"Vaela? Is something wrong?"

There was no answer, and feeling there was naught to do but draw closer, Emelyn embraced her.

With a soft hiss Vaela bared her fangs, and Emelyn craned her neck in anticipation, closing her eyes . . . but the teeth scarcely made contact before receding.

"No, you are yet recovering," Vaela said, withdrawing with a sigh.

Emelyn opened her eyes, her skin prickling with goosepimples. But to find the vampiress standing there, on the cream woollen carpet of her own room, it was wonderful, like a dream broken free to manifest among the real. "The necklace," she said, "it must have been you . . . who returned it, who left me the note."

"It must never again leave the grounds of Hastelbrook."

"So you stole it back for me. And have you murdered the jeweller?"

"Meritus Frusk is rotten, cheating those driven to sell their dearest treasures," Vaela said. "But I only glamoured him; he will not remember the jewel."

"That is good," Emelyn said, thinking again of the cryptic note. "But you knew . . . You knew where I buried the dolls' heads. Was it you who took them, when I was a child?"

"It was."

"Why?"

"I collect the pieces," Vaela said. "I make dolls when it pleases me, as I've done since the last of my days among the living. But here, I have a gift for you."

"A gift for me. Have you not given me enough?"

"I have not," Vaela replied, presenting a slender platinum chain with a small carven pendant of opal, bearing the profile of a woman's face.

Feeling somewhat in a daze Emelyn lifted her hair for the vampiress to clasp the necklace about her throat.

"There are earrings to match, and a nestled opal ring," Vaela said.

Emelyn touched the pendant as she turned to face her. "It is lovely . . . Did you steal these as well?"

"They are not stolen," Vaela said curtly. "I've a little hoard in London, in a forgotten place beneath Cheapside. This set was mine, given to me when I lived; when I was married."

"When you were married?"

"Yes. You and I share the same birthstone . . . October."

The fire crackled softly as they regarded each other, and Emelyn marvelled to think how little she knew of the woman Vaela must once have been, or how much of her remained even now. "Vaela, do you not ever wonder what your life might have been, had you not become . . . as you are."

"I do not think of it," Vaela said, though in the shining depths of her eyes Emelyn imagined she saw a distant kindle of life, as of a guarded heart that had been robbed of the world before its time.

"Of course you think of it," Emelyn said, taking her hand.

There came a knock at the door; abruptly their connection was broken, and the vampiress vanished.

"No! Wait please!" Emelyn exclaimed.

The knock repeated.

"Yes, who is it!"

"It's only me," Sarah's voice answered.

Emelyn yanked open the door to find her sister startling back, a candle in her hand.

"Emie, I was just . . . To whom were you speaking?"

"To myself Sarah, of course."

"To yourself? But it rather sounded like . . ."

"Were you listening at my door? How can I help you?"

"I'm sorry; it's only, I cannot rest for thinking of your terrible icy fever," Sarah said, her face stricken with concern. "And then, when you ran into the rain without your shoes . . . Are you sure you're quite well? Is there aught I can get you?"

"My dear Sarah you mustn't carry on. I am the picture of health; the bloodsick left not a trace."

"The *bloodsick*? Is that Bayten's diagnosis? What is it?"

Emelyn groaned at herself for the slip, blocking the doorway. "My apologies," she said, pretending a yawn, "but really I am very tired . . . I should rather speak tomorrow."

With some hesitation Sarah bid her goodnight, and Emelyn locked the door, putting her back to it. The energy of Vaela's presence lingered still, and she felt a nervous rush to realize the vampiress was still in the house.

Finding nothing at the window she took her candle into the dark dressing room, where at a creaking sound she looked to find the old wardrobe door ajar, drifting open by the press of a pale hand from within.

There she found Vaela sitting with her feet on the drawers, crowded by cheerful layered gowns.

"It smells very like my own once did," Vaela said.

"Does it," Emelyn said quietly. "Will you tell me of your mortal life, of your marriage?"

Vaela picked at one of the gowns. "My childhood was quiet," she said. "At sixteen I was given to a stranger; the Compte d'Orognac was not a cruel man, though he was often sick with drink . . . made the worse by three years of marriage in which I failed to bear him children. Ever longer he was away, until I scarcely saw him."

"He abandoned you?"

"He bestowed his love upon his sister, doting on her and her brood. When she died in childbirth, he drank himself to his end. The blame was put to me for my infertility, and for neglecting him."

"Good Lord how horrible," Emelyn murmured, feeling a swell of anger on her behalf. "However did you bear it?"

"I did not bear it," Vaela said. "I fled home, and for my sins I was locked in the turret. For some while hope endured . . . but when the last idea of deliverance died, I died with it."

Emelyn swallowed. "But you didn't . . . You came back."

Vaela stood before her, her eyes gleaming. "I did," she said with a smile, "though until I took on your guardianship, I was only adrift, without purpose . . ."

With quickening breath Emelyn tilted her head, baring her neck. "Let me give you something, in return . . . please."

The vampiress drifted closer, her fangs just visible between parted lips. "Perhaps just a sip."

Bracing for her immortal kiss Emelyn startled with a gasp as the bite pierced her throat, but the sting of dagger points melted into welcome warmth, and she cradled Vaela's head as she drank.

Their connection was brief, and after the little wound was mended Vaela shivered, stepping away to wipe her mouth. With a soft sound Emelyn touched her neck, following as Vaela returned to the bedroom, where stopping by the desk she produced a gold banded opal ring.

"Put it on."

Setting down her candle Emelyn sat at the desk, doing as she was bade. "It's beautiful, like the profile on the pendant," she said, touching her neck as she studied the little cameo carven stone. "Is it meant to be you?"

"It is."

"You said he was often ill," Emelyn said, fidgeting with the ring. "You know it might have been your husband, and not yourself, who was infertile."

Vaela's face was inscrutable, but she stood stock still, her eyes wide and black.

"Medical science has come some way since your time," Emelyn suggested.

Vaela appeared to collect herself. "It doesn't matter," she said, placing a pair of opal-backed earrings on the desk.

"I know it doesn't matter now, but if ever you blamed yourself . . . you mustn't."

Vaela's eyes softened to their natural brown. "Your counsel is welcome," she said, "but those memories are cold, they're only stories now. Here, you must try them on."

Guided to the mirror Emelyn faced herself, testing the fit of the earrings, whereupon she noted Vaela's reflection which, though clearly visible, was dimmer than her own. "Your image . . . it is almost ghostly, do you see? But have I not read that vampires should cast no reflection?"

"It is lost to us gradually, over time," Vaela said. "There are those older than I who have none at all."

Emelyn stared at her, bracing for the question. "The man with the burning eyes? And I suppose your queen . . ."

"Yes. Were she here you would find no trace of her in the glass; mirrors are forbidden in the citadel."

"No trace of her in the glass," Emelyn repeated, imagining with horror what it would be to stand before a mirror and see only the empty room. "But for every reflecting surface to bespeak one's nonexistence . . . How does she endure it?"

Vaela stood close behind her. "Every waking dusk the queen is encircled by portraitists, and painted for a ceremony of dress, that she may remember her beauty, and witness her attirement."

"And the Lurkmen? I've meant to ask . . . the children they abduct, are they taken for the queen to consume?"

"They are not consumed, only taxed as vessels for their blood. Those taken by the Lurkmen find more life in the haunted city than they were ever spared in the world outside. The queen becomes their mother."

Emelyn felt a kiss on her shoulder, but before she could respond Vaela vanished, reappearing outside the window, clinging to the edge of the frame, her bright eyes gleaming in the dark.

"Wait!" Emelyn almost shouted, rushing to the open panes. "What of the Order? Have you learned nothing of they who covet whatever treasure is to be found beneath us?"

"They shall covet in vain. Goodnight little one."

"Wait please!" Emelyn protested, but she addressed only the rain misted air, for the vampiress was gone. The curtains fluttered in the window, the feeling of Vaela's presence slipped away like a dream, and the practical world returned.

With a sigh Emelyn dropped to sit at her desk, her eyes wide and unfocused. "And how shall I sleep now," she muttered, rubbing the opal pendant at her throat.

Monday June 20th

Just north of London, along the Shoreditch road, an easterly gale drove the early evening rain against the windows of Charwell manor, where in a dimly lit room the young Duke of Lindsor perched on a claw-footed chair, a crimson clouded bowl resting on the tea table at his elbow. His eyes were masked, his gaze fixed on the sputtering candles of the chandelier above. With no wig to cover the crushed blonde of his hair, he wore a blood specked chemise without his coat, as with nervous hands he clenched a sweat soiled rag.

Footsteps sounded in the hall, and blinking from his trance he struggled to untie the mask, tearing it away.

The door to the little study opened, setting the delicate lights aquiver, and a familiar woman entered the room, gowned in sombre black. Dark of hair and gloves, her mouth and nose obscured by a silken mask, the lady smiled with her eyes before turning to latch the door behind her.

The Duke of Lindsor leapt to his feet, and lowering her mask Miss Winter came to face him, a small wrapped implement in her hand.

"A souvenir Your Grace, to celebrate the cure of your unbelief on this new moon," she said, unwrapping the item to present an elaborate glass handled knife, polished to a brilliant gleam. "You will display it proudly in your home, as agreed, while its twin remains here."

"Miss Winter," the duke breathed, dabbing sweat from his face, "I assure you . . . I took no pleasure in it, whatever you may have seen . . ."

Miss Winter smiled. "Oh Your Grace," she said, taking his hand to close his fingers about the knife. "You needn't pretend with me."

"I only meant to adduce *proof* of her vampirism!" he declaimed, lowering himself to sit. "I was certain Dramen was having me on."

"But we expected nothing less," Miss Winter replied, moving to pour him a brandy at the table. "And now that by this faithful dagger you have carved the truth from her, shall we discuss your induction into the Order?"

"The Order . . ."

"The world festers with unholy secrets Your Grace, and we mean to uncover them, foremost those of the vampire, as you have witnessed."

"The vampire," the duke repeated, staring into nothing. "But it were as though time marched in reverse, her every wound mended before my eyes . . . and yet, with each stroke I was certain she should wake to her powers and tear out my heart!"

"You were very brave Your Grace," Miss Winter fawned, passing the brandy to his trembling hands.

"She'd no strength to resist me," he said, his eyes wide, "like a delicate dream . . . Does gentle daylight truly master them so?"

"It does," Miss Winter said, touching his chin for attention. "Of course your ministrations would have killed a mortal woman many times over, but you dare not regret . . . These creatures less deserve our mercy than the biting flies. Now, shall I suppose we have earned your support?"

Drinking the brandy quickly down he coughed into the glass. "You have it!" he rasped, wiping his mouth. "Whatever you need; ten thousand, twenty!"

"Generous," Miss Winter allowed, folding her hands. "But I know you for a competitive man . . . I confess an investment of fifty thousand were enough to match the interest of my patron."

"Fifty . . . Has Lord Crennock put down fifty thousand?"

"Indeed he has," Miss Winter said. "And for such an amount, well I can't imagine but Lord Dramen would make you an equal partner. Then of course you might see her . . . whenever you like."

The duke nodded numbly. "Yes . . . partners; fifty thousand, you shall have it."

"Very good," she said, and leaning close she took his hand, pressing a kiss upon his ring. "Now you must wash your hands once more; the blood of vampires is neutralized by water of baptism, but it must be scrubbed away with great care."

"I can hear her still," he said, his expression fixed with wonder as he fingered the blade, "that sweet and desperate voice . . . But I've not ended her, you're certain?"

"Perish the thought, Your Grace," Miss Winter tutted. "We'd never allow you should cause our prize lasting harm; but a few drops of mortal blood, and the little succubus was quite herself again."

"Good, that is good," he said, tucking the knife in his belt. "Then I shall make the arrangements. Will Lord Dramen attend me?"

"Lord Dramen is indisposed," she said, turning for the door, "but in two nights he means to call a special meeting at the Inn. Ten o'clock sharp. I would strongly urge your attendance. Now, I suggest you collect yourself, have another drink . . . Good day Your Grace."

The waning light of day spread golden over the rooftops as Arkwright Cooperage closed for business, working men with oil stained hands and patchy trousers making their way down the lane to Castle Street. In dark breeches and rolled shirt sleeves under his vest, Fitzwilliam Arkwright remained on the dusty shop floor, hammering a metal driving wedge on the side of an unfinished barrel, tightening the wooden hoop around the staves. Pausing to drag an arm across his forehead he took a mighty breath, turning to the only other person in the warehouse: a small faced gentleman with ashen hair and matching coat who stood by the wall, squinting over the single page of an unfolded letter.

"Go on Mercer." Arkwright gestured with a smirk, pointing the hammer, "read it aloud."

"Egads man." Mr. John Mercer winced, looking at the paper. "Whatever possessed you to write to Miss Morley herself? You might rather have evaded her mother's wrath by a cordial response to Lady Dhorings."

"There were things that needed saying, and only to *her* . . . I knew the risk. Anyway it's not as bad as that, wait and see. Read it aloud."

"Very well then let's have it," Mercer said, and clearing his throat he began to read:

> *'Dear Sir,*
>
> *It appears incumbent upon me to reflect to you my great displeasure, and ensuing relief, to have intercepted the grave misjudgement of your correspondence to my eldest daughter, who is only lately recovered from a crisis of body and spirit. The libidinous details of your note I will not support by repetition, except to denounce the passionate attack you so affectedly describe. In truth I find your boasting impropriety to be little more than salacious fantasy over a young woman known throughout the county to be above reproach, and as much in earnest as any mother might be in defence of her child, I exhort you to see there can be no further efficacy in your address, except to distract our precious Emelyn from a most preferable and worthy courtship well in the undertaking.*
>
> *Lady Dhorings my kinswoman I do not condemn, except*

to say she will doubtless come to deplore her part in cosseting the thoughtless request of a vulnerable girl. The dowager countess should never have written to you on Emelyn's behalf, and naturally I must release you from any expectation to accept her ill-advised invitation to Hastelbrook. Thus it is with solemn exigency that I rely upon your good sense as a gentleman, in the immediate cessation of all commerce between yourself and my daughter, real or imagined.

In this request I remain,
Your humble advisor, Antonia Morley'

John Mercer grimaced, folding the page. "Well now old fellow, I should say you've plucked quite the wrong string; she'd as soon have you kill her daughter as court her."

Arkwright turned over the barrel, using a small implement to finish an inner bevel for the disc at the head. "First, you understand Lady Dhorings is a nation unto herself," he said, flipping the container again to tap the disc in place. "If not for her reassurance I'd not have written at all . . . though I must regret seeing her dragged into it. Even so, if you take stock of what Mrs. Morley *does not* say . . ."

"Well . . . I see she makes no attempt to speak for her daughter's inclination."

"Precisely; by *intercepted* I take it to mean she withheld my letter against Miss Morley's will, and if that be so, all hope is not lost."

"But perhaps it should be," Mercer said thoughtfully. "It does appear the young lady is spoken for; sleeping dogs old fellow . . ."

Arkwright sighed, setting the barrel upright to sit atop it. "Certainly I've not title nor fortune enough to tempt her mother, but my character at least is answerable to the good opinion of Lady Dhorings, or she'd never have sent the message. Heaven knows how protective she is of the Morley girls."

"But would you defy Mrs. Morley, and invade Hastelbrook on the advice of her better? The gentleman I know would not think of it. But is her daughter suffering from some illness, or crisis of spirit as friend and mother attest?"

"That I'll not believe," Arkwright said, turning the hammer in his hand. "Emelyn Morley is of rude health and the most sure-footed young lady I've ever met . . . If you could but see her Mercer, her emerald eyes smiling upon you; a man might drown in those eyes. She is free as fire; I tell you artifice is unknown to her! If that is illness I should be grateful to suffer the same.”

“Careful there.” Mercer chuckled, picking up a wooden stave to play with, “you may be afflicted already. Was it not the very next morning you lost all account of yourself . . .”

Arkwright groaned at the reminder, reaching into his pocket to withdraw a little pouch belonging to the silver merchant, Mr. Briggs, which he tossed to his friend.

“Is this the very purse?” Mercer marvelled, turning it over. “Have you remembered anything?”

“I remember the man it belonged to; I spoke to him before the stage,” Arkwright said, “and then he was gone, and I’m left only a gnawing certainty . . . that he is no longer to be counted among the living. I have no proof of it, but I could swear there was someone else that night, or some horrible danger, though it’s only shadows in my mind. I cannot account for how the bloodstained purse came to be on my person, nor for the pocket handkerchief,” he added, producing the little white monogrammed kerchief the actor had given him, with the initials A.F. clearly monogrammed in elegant stitching.

“Yes I see that,” Mercer said.

“And my boot knife,” Arkwright added, scratching his face, “it too stained with blood.”

“My dear Fitz have you murdered a man in your sleep, over a woman named A.F. perhaps?”

Arkwright dropped his head with a good humoured sigh. “If the initials were E.M. I might account myself in danger, but *this* I can make no sense of. I thought picking up the tools would do me good, but there’s nothing for it . . .”

“Then how do you intend to solve for the purse, or the pocket handkerchief?”

“I do not know.”

Mercer gave him a half smile. “Then perhaps Crawley warrants another look, which as luck would have it is halfway along the road to your heart.”

Chapter 17
Paths of No Return

Wednesday June 22nd

Guarded with all the zealotry of a private club, the sprawling Fleet Street tavern known as the Devil's Inn was generally avoided by those with any sort of reputation to protect, though tonight by descent of a dingy back stair a group of particular noblemen, with no business to conduct in the open, ducked through the weathered basement gate to disappear within. Here in the building's cramped understory, packed to the walls with untapped casks of wine and spirits, the long darkly lit room terminated at the doors to a private chamber, well hidden from stairs to the common room above. Before the doors Mr. Thomas Attridge stood guard, carving a little hooded figure of wood, meant to resemble the unearthly woman who had delivered his daughter safely home, and he from his illness. Opposite his post, snoring by the foot of the stairs in a chair just stout enough for his bulk sat a great burly man, a red sash across chest, unwashed hair spilling from beneath his cornered hat, tipped low to cover his eyes.

Inside the secret room, under the frosted glow of an elegant chandelier lay a grand oaken table. Six well wigged gentlemen of quality shuffled in to take their seats, with the weighty magistrate Taffram Brule already sweating into his collars, seated at the end nearest the door. One by one the men noted with some surprise the presence of Miss Winter, who stood near the head of the table like a statue gowned in black, a silver crucifix at her chest, her face veiled and indistinct. Before her stood her patron and chair of the meeting, the tall and gaudily dressed Marquess of Crennock. A squint eyed rail of a man with lace at his cuffs long enough to conceal his hands, his frothy jabot cravat spilling from neck to waist over sky blue coats, he was periwigged far grander than the others, with ostentatious full-bottomed silver curls, his aging face powdered with makeup.

Lord Crennock snapped his cuffs with a frown. "My lordly brothers of the Order," he began, his deep voice belying the bright colours of his presentation, "it is no embroidery of words to say we are come to a crossroads of history. The seeds of Lord Dramen's new order are planted, and every man shall be counted either among its champions . . . or among the damned."

"Ominous words," a stern faced man in cropped wig and coats of white spoke up. "But I've a point of order, a grievance on behalf of Robert Edward, my son and heir."

"My dear Lord Abbott," Miss Winter said, speaking beneath her veil, "Lord Dramen shall address your grievance in due time."

Abbott flushed with ire. "Shall he? And precisely where, pray tell, is our illustrious leader?"

Miss Winter started to answer but the rotund Lord Bellantross spoke over her, drumming his fingers on the table. "What's this? A *woman* in attendance for the brotherhood minutes?"

"Miss Winter is of invaluable experience in these matters," Crennock answered, taking his seat. "Any disrespect shown her is the same shown to me. As for Lord Dramen, I am empowered to speak on his behalf. It is upon the effect of this meeting gentlemen, that we shall anticipate your full support . . . for the *Vampire Act.*"

"Shall you indeed? But here we are eight for ten," the young and sharp-eyed Lord Staunton said. "Pray where is our newest popinjay Duke Lindsor? Don't tell me tales of vampires have put him off?"

A silver knife struck the table before him, stuck fast, and there was a collective hush. "I'll not be discounted sir; we are nine for eleven," Miss Winter corrected, stepping forward to claim her blade. "Duke Lindsor is free to take his leisure, for he has proven his commitment, by a pledge of fifty thousand pounds."

"Fifty thousand!" the elderly Lord Hurlington exclaimed. "And how by the grace of Providence did you convince him to invest such a sum?"

"Dramen's got some card up his sleeve," Lord Staunton said. "The way I heard it he's summoned the governors of Bedlam hospital for a private audience, to bear witness to something . . . extraordinary. Perhaps Duke Lindsor has seen it?"

"Is that to do with Hastelbrook?" Lord Hurlington pressed. "Has Dramen come upon some legal means by which we might excavate at last?"

There were rumblings of agreement, and Lord Crennock gestured to Miss Winter. "Gentlemen, Hastelbrook is a difficult question, but I think you'll find the larger goal is now closer than ever. I have here a box . . ."

Taking from a side table a small parcel draped in black, Miss Winter brought it to the presiding marquess, setting it before him.

Lord Crennock tapped the box with a smirk. "My brothers of the *Argentum Serpentis*," he said, "under the steady hand of Lord Dramen we have for longsuffering years hunted the forbidden occult. For our efforts we have won the mystical crucifix of Saint Adamo, which Miss Winter, being the most veteran hunter among us, now wears about her neck. But here, that which rests inside this little shrouded case represents a far greater victory," and with a flourish he pulled away the cloth, revealing the box to be of glass over a crushed velvet base. On the inside centre were mounted two pairs of sharpened fangs, upper and lower, pure white root to tip. Arranged in a circle about them lay ten pointed claws, black as night.

"Behold!" Crennock pronounced, spreading his arms. "*Immortalis quae sanguine vivit*, the immortal who dines upon blood, is scientifically proven."

For a moment silence reigned; the men leaned in, eyeing the objects with suspicion.

Lord Bellantross spluttered in amazement. "It cannot be! Are we to find these for teeth and claws taken of the undead?"

"My worthy Lords," Crennock said, gesturing to the wheezing magistrate at the other end of the table, "by the wiles of our own Mr. Brule, we have now a living vampire in our power. She is held at Charwell manor in Lord Dramen's keeping, in a room especially designed to contain her. She is to be presented at Kensington Palace, pending the secure construction, under Miss Winter's direction, of a box fortified to transport such a creature."

"And what of the box she came in?" the hunching, pockmarked Lord Mulgate asked. "Or however did you drag her to Charwell?"

Magistrate Brule cleared his throat, a sickly retching sound. "The road Crawley to London is a broken slog," he said. "The coffin was cracked in the jostle; we shall need another, and all the stronger, to present a living vampire at court."

The men stared transfixed, their faces set with wonder, and fear.

"Quail not gentlemen," Lord Crennock continued. "Every

precaution has been taken; the little bird is harmless in her cage, and before she is moved we invite each of you to pay her a visit, to test her immortality for yourselves."

"Good God man!" Lord Bellantross blurted, his face pale. "If the creature is real . . . can this be how Dramen means to conquer the House of Lords, to employ his captive monster for the purpose of scaring us out of our wits?"

"Come now Bellantross," Lord Staunton said, "what have we to fear from a vampire stripped of fang and claw?"

"Correction, the creature is whole as she ever was," Miss Winter said. "The extraction of teeth and claws, however brutally done, is but a few moments of agony to the vampire, for unless she is utterly starved of blood, both will regenerate to their full extremity in a matter of seconds . . ."

"A matter of seconds?" the small and bespectacled Lord Crabtree interjected. "You speak of nothing less than biblical regeneration!"

Lord Abbott slapped the table, commanding their attention. "This is a distraction. I will have justice for my son!"

"Robert the Blade is a notorious rouser," Lord Crennock said impatiently. "What justice do you imagine you're owed?"

Abbott pushed back his chair to stand. "My eldest was brutally attacked in St. Giles, sir, and by servants of Miss Emelyn Morley, the *Succubus of Sussex* herself!"

"Really sir. And how should we be certain your son has ever even met Miss Morley?" Crennock asked.

"We've proof enough of that," Abbott retorted. "Do not we know her for an unnatural beauty, witch-red of hair? But if this does not satisfy, in the very hour of my son's grief she paid a call on our own Mr. Gapplethorpe, and stole from him a precious coin."

"Very well, and why should she command an attack upon your son?" Crennock asked. "Was it in defence of her honour perhaps?"

"I do not concern with wherefore!" Abbott bellowed. "My son and heir might have lost his life, and by God's wounds the house of Morley will pay for it!"

"Lord Abbott, with respect," Miss Winter said, "as far as I'm aware the Morleys do not employ Moorish giants. Now, it is about town that your son and his friends were basted to pulp by a man who fits that description, but perhaps he was only coming to the girl's aid."

There were low chuckles about the table, and Lord Abbott hissed with anger. "*Basted to pulp*? Do you mock me madam?"

"Come now sir," Lord Crennock interjected. "Hastelbrook will be ours in due time, but good sense must have the mastery of spleen."

"Good sense," Abbott growled, looking at the others. "Gentlemen, invest in Dramen's vampire conspiracy if you must, lies and tricks to shore up investment I'll be bound, but I mean to settle a debt of blood," and with a short bow he made for the door.

"Your anger is understood," Lord Crennock said loudly, "but having made a dog's breakfast of this meeting, I should advise you allow yourself the benefit of reflection, before you act."

Lord Abbott turned with an angry chuckle. "Yes my lord, I shall bring my *benefit of reflection* to Morley's doorstep. Perhaps his beauteous daughter only wants for the strap."

"Hastelbrook is not to be touched, not until Lord Dramen wills it," Crennock answered.

At the sound of Miss Winter chuckling Lord Abbott spat on the table, his face all the redder. "Does Dramen not seek to breach the vault? Then I shall assist him by turning up every stone. I shall descend upon Hastelbrook with fifty men. Let the father of the witch stand in my way if he dares. I will have her, and her darkish servant too; I'll see him swing."

"Will you *invade* the house sir?" Crennock shouted. "Stand fast, and see reason!"

Lord Abbott made a dismissive noise. "If the Morley girl had *reason* in her pretty head she'd not have trifled with the house of Abbott. Goodnight gentlemen!"

Crennock was on his feet, but Miss Winter grabbed his wrist, and the startled assembly watched as Lord Abbott stormed out of the room, banging open the door with a curse and shouting for Thomas Attridge to clear a path.

"Patience my lord," Miss Winter said softly. "If Abbott is wrathful as his word we shall disavow him, and the sooner gain Morley's trust. Remember it is only the vault that concerns us, we care not a whit for the girl."

"I've never seen the man so incensed," a flushed Lord Staunton said. "His son must truly be at death's door."

Lord Crennock groaned in frustration, lowering himself to sit. "Very well my lords, if you will oblige me to forget this little outburst, we shall proceed with our . . . demonstration," and he gestured for Thomas Attridge to shut the door.

Outside the room Mr. Attridge strained to hear as he worked to carve the tiny figure. Voices within grew softer, and looking back into the wine cellar he checked to find the massive guard by the stairs still rooted to his chair, mouth open and snorting with sleep. Satisfied the brute would not wake, Attridge continued his whittling, leaning close to hear.

There were noises, as like the hiss of steam. *"My lords, do look closely,"* Miss Winter instructed, *"both fang and claw scorch at the slightest touch of silver, for it is a deadly poison to all vampires, while they live."*

"I don't say it's a trick, but I've no mind to see a living vampire!" Lord Bellantross exclaimed, his voice cracking with fear. *"Collecting antiquities, forgotten treasures of material worth, but that's all I ever signed on for . . ."*

"Nevertheless, we will require you all at Charwell in the coming week," Lord Crennock said sharply. *"There the last of your doubts should be put to rest. Now gentlemen, we are adjourned. I bid you good evening."*

The men scraped back their chairs, and striving to hear audible speech over the noise Mr. Attridge nicked his thumb. The door opened, knocking against him, and the carving dropped from his hand as he lurched back, standing at attention.

"Heavens I've startled you," Miss Winter said, staring at him as the men made their way out.

For a moment Mr. Attridge stood transfixed by the lady in black before him. "Forgive me madam," he bumbled, dropping to paw after the wooden figure, "I thought for a moment you was someone else . . ."

"Is it the veil?" Miss Winter posed, crouching to help him search. "Have you never seen a widow in the weeds?"

"Yes ma'am," he said. "I am sorry for your loss."

"Oh I've never been married," she clucked, snatching up the figurine as the men shuffled past. "But I find people easier to watch when they think you lost in your bereavement," and with a smile she returned it in two pieces. "For your daughter Penny I presume? But dear me, it's broken."

"Yes, yes madam . . . but it were only a toy, no harm done."

"Well, I'm grateful for your watch at the door," she said, "keeping us undisturbed while that laze-about sleeps off his drink . . ."

"Just as you please madam."

"Here you are," she said, handing him a guinea coin. "I must stay and speak with Lord Crennock and the magistrate, but you've earned yourself a rest. Go home, Mr. Attridge."

"Oh . . . yes madam. Thank you kindly then," and giving her a bow he took up his satchel to make his way out.

Watching until the door at the top of the stairs had closed behind him, Miss Winter addressed the massive sleeping man in his chair. "Mr. Grouthe!" she said, and marking no response she slapped him.

The hulking fellow was on his feet in a flash, snarling like a tiger.

Miss Winter shushed him. "Does Lord Dramen pay you to sleep?"

"Your pardon mistress," the greasy haired fellow said, straightening his coat with a wry smile.

"How long was that man listening close at the door?"

"I dunno, he were just stood by his post as usual, from where I sat. So it's all buttoned up then?"

"No you great golem, it is not buttoned up," she replied. "My business here continues. You must return to Charwell at once. Deliver to Lord Dramen that he is to reduce the creature's ration; pig's blood only, no more mixing with human. By Lord Abbott's quick temper we may yet find Hastelbrook the nearer target, but if we're ever to present our vampire to Kensington Palace, she must be absolutely docile . . ."

■■

Outside, upon reaching the thoroughfare of Fleet Street, a vengeful Lord Abbott thought he espied Mr. Attridge, the porter from the basement, speaking to a shadow in the alley across, but when he looked closer he saw the man was alone, examining a little carven figure in his hand.

Muttering to himself, he made his way along the muddy stones to the waiting coach, a luxurious rented carriage emblazoned with the Hack & Humble company crest.

Lord Abbott found his driver nodding. "Mr. Parmish are you asleep sir?" he called up.

Startling awake, the day worn coachmen grabbed his hat to climb swiftly down.

The carriage door opened from within, and red-faced in drunkenness, his shirt untucked, Robert the Blade leaned out, revealing a snoring young lady in the seat beside him, her modesty all but slipped from her bodice. "Welcome thee Father, I trust your meeting was an all enjoyable affair!" and receding back inside he shut the door with a laugh.

Lord Abbott was incensed. "What is this?" he demanded, addressing the open-mouthed driver. "Well? Shall you stand there catching flies man?"

"Apologies my lord!" the coachman spluttered. "My Lord Robert insisted we abscond to the Rose sir, we've only just returned."

With a growl Abbott yanked open the door to climb aboard. "Your injuries are yet mending," he said, sitting opposite his son, who slumped happily into his companion as she murmured in a stupor. "Could you not soberly have waited for me, as I asked? There's word here to the river of your embarrassment."

"My apologies, Lord Abbot," Robert grunted, navigating a bottle to his lips.

"Damn your apology. Did it ever occur to you to let the girl alone? Your *weakness* reflects upon me!"

"Aye, rib roasted her good I suppose," Robert muttered, admiring the drink. "Might rather have kissed her, and worse if that great Moorish ogre hadn't come 'round."

"Too long have I tolerated your moral infirmities," Lord Abbott growled. "It shall require great show of strength, to repair what you've done."

"For whom?" Robert wheezed with a sleepy chuckle, tipping back for another swig. "Shall I remind you, your illustrious Lord Dramen is only a baron, and yourself an earl."

"Dramen alone among us is connected to the Invisible College of Rome."

"Those naturalists turned *vampire hunters*? They must have more time on their hands than I do."

"Robert Edward, I'll not be made a fool of in the Order!" Abbott snapped. "Do you understand?"

"All for Miss Emelyn Morley," Robert mused, rubbing his face. "But I wish I'd never set eyes on the little jilt; I'd no idea to lose a tooth over it."

His father groaned in exasperation. "My son, I can remember the careless streets at your age . . . *hunting a beauty* we used to call it. Nevertheless, it was thoughtless, to violate a woman of name in the bright afternoon. But her man should never have touched you, as we shall teach them both."

"And how is that? We're not like to find her waiting by the alley again . . ."

There was a knock, and the door opened. "Your pardon my lord, shall we be off home?" the coachman asked.

"Nay sir," Lord Abbott answered, looking over the woman. "We'll be returning this buxom baggage to the Rose, and there find our first recruits."

"Recruits?" Robert asked, scratching his bruised mouth.

"Yes my profligate eldest," his father answered. "I mean to move on Hastelbrook, and you shall lead the charge."

Robert blanched as the bottle lolled out of his hand. "Myself to lead the charge? Nay Father, you'll find me otherwise engaged," and snatching the young woman's arm he shook her awake.

"You will obey!" Abbott warned, "or I shall stop what monies you employ yourself to waste in my name."

"Will you," Robert said, pulling his companion close as he pushed open the door. "And how shall you stop me using your credit? Shall you disavow me before every brothel keeper in London?"

Lord Abbott crossed his arms with a bemused frown, watching as his son hauled the irritated woman outside.

"Ouch! Leave it!" she cried.

The drunken couple argued to the curb, moving briskly away from the carriage.

"Shall we wait for him my lord, or be off?" the coachman asked.

"In drink and skirts he's out of harm's way," Lord Abbott said. "Let him go. But we're not above pressing his sycophants and comrades into service. And I shall swell their number with thief-takers, the very worst. To the Rose, Parmish! And quick about it."

The coach set out, and so consumed was he in contriving his plan that it was only upon turning down a sparse and unfamiliar road that Lord Abbott sat up to glower through the window, finding he'd no idea where he was. "What the deuce," he grumbled, and rapping on the roof he signalled the driver to stop.

"Are you mad sir?" he shouted through the open door as the coach bumped along, veering off the road to make between trees on level ground, leading to an open field. "I'll have your job and your hide! What are you playing at?"

He marked no response, but as they cleared the narrow woodlands for the field there came a splitting crack, the sound of startled horses and scampering, and the vehicle rolled to a stop. For a moment Lord Abbott sat listening, and hearing no other sound he slid a box out from beneath the seat, which he opened to retrieve a pair of ivory handled flintlock pistols, before clambering out and slamming the door with a bang, breaking several panes. Drawing the weapons he turned, seeking a challenger, but all was still. Above him the driver sat, head bowed beneath his hat, and as

Abbott approached the front he found the crossbar broken and leather traces on the ground; the horses were nowhere to be seen. The coachman was much changed, no longer layered in the shoulder cloaks of his station, he appeared slighter of frame, robed in shadowy silk.

"What is the meaning of this?" Abbott demanded, tucking one of the flintlocks in his belt. "You're not Parmish. Get thee down at once!"

The driver sat very still, and Abbott waggled the pistol with a huff, unhooking a lantern from coach. "I suppose Crennock has put you up to this? Am I to thus *pause and reflect*, before avenging my son?"

Surveying the damage in the dim light he adjusted his position, moving to face the driver square on, but when he looked up the bench was empty.

"Lord Ephram Scott Abbott," a woman said, speaking from behind him.

With a start he turned, aiming the pistol to find the very person he'd mistook for his driver: a pale woman, ageless and comely, shrouded in black. The coachman's hat was on her head, and plucking it off she tossed it away, revealing raven hair wild and loose, her eyes dark as pits of shadow.

"You!" Sweat tingled on his upper lip. "Can you be Dramen's monster . . . broken free of your cage?"

"I am not that unfortunate creature," Vaela said, "but I am the last face . . . you will ever see."

The pistol fired, her image flickered, and it were as though the ball passed straight through her.

"You are a spirit," Abbott charged, dropping his gun to snatch out the second.

"I am flesh and blood," she said, raising her hands as though in surrender, "but not so slow as you'd like."

Snarling, Lord Abbott retreated a step, aimed and fired. Again she flickered, and the shot missed.

"Have you a third?" she asked.

The nobleman blurted a curse, hurling his lantern at her feet. The glass broke, sending up a great fume of smoke, and the woman was gone. Seized with animal fear he bolted across the field, running as fast as his heeled shoes could manage, until one was lost to him, and in half stocking feet he stumbled on, dashing through the cold grass. Holding a course for friendly lights by the distant road he wheezed as he ran, though there came over him a chilling sense that those lights were as far out of reach as the fingernail moon. Icy alarm tingled through his back, his pursuer overtook him, and bodily he was snatched, a shriek escaping his lips as the woman crashed him into the side of the coach, pinning him to the door.

Like a rabbit caught its last, Lord Abbott shrieked in a madness of terror, until pressed so hard into the cracking wood he could scarcely breathe. "No! I fear no darkness," he managed, staring into the sky.

The vampiress made a seductive sort of noise, holding him close. "This is the part I most cherish . . . when I feel the rot in a man's heart, and permit myself to drink, just before I taste the blood."

Lord Abbott clenched his lips in a dignified frown. "You dare not! You dare not threaten a man of Christian charity!"

"Christian charity?" Vaela repeated, sniffing at his neck. "You would attack Hastelbrook, and hold it hostage, to revenge yourself upon the eldest Miss Morley, and the man you believe she employs . . . all to impress your rank in the Order."

"Hence from me hell spawn!" The nobleman spat, making feeble attempts to break her grip.

"Your son is rotten as you are," Vaela tutted.

"Deceiver! You will not touch him!"

"Robert's debt is paid, for now," Vaela said. "And your missing driver is safe, though I know you care not. Mr. Parmish will wake to find himself at the coffee house, with a sovereign in his pocket."

"Spare me!" Lord Abbott puffed. "Spare me and I shall lay a thousand guineas before you . . . ten thousand!"

"You might have escaped my notice," Vaela said, ignoring the plea as she bared her fangs, "but for your threats upon Emelyn Morley . . ."

"I will not beg, I regret nothing," he said coldly, trembling in her grasp. "Take my blood . . . and I shall go to my reward; those my stalwart allies will not rest until you are dust!"

"You overestimate your importance," Vaela spoke in his ear. "Your disappearance will never be solved."

Lord Abbott opened his mouth to speak but could only splutter as she fastened to his throat, bearing him to the ground . . . and there was nothing in his power but to gurgle and choke, pawing at her back as she drank him.

A low wind rustled the grass, his limbs grew heavy, and as the pain subsided the dead sky washed away.

The vampiress leaned back on his lap with a breathy sound, licking her teeth. "I suppose your wife will miss you, in her way," she said. "Your servants will celebrate the end of your cruelty, your wayward son will have the title, and when he inherits, I've no doubt he shall waste all you've left him."

"And so fades the house of Abbott," a man said.

Slowly Vaela stood, recognizing the voice of her maker. "Afaine is captured," she said, staring into the dark, "and we are not to lift a finger."

"The queen will see reason; she will not abandon her own," Lord Simeon replied, drawing near.

"Can you be certain?" Vaela snarled, turning to find him by the coach, his silver hair tied back, his spectacles gleaming in the dim light as he examined the door.

"To kill a peer of the realm is discouraged," he said.

"I understand," she replied. "Alas, I would not suffer Lord Abbott to live."

"But must my carriage suffer?" Simeon asked, opening and shutting the door to test it.

"Hack & Humble shall have hundreds by now. The night coaches have flourished, in your years away."

Lord Simeon was running his hand carefully over the wood.

"It was he who broke the window," Vaela said. "I only pinned him against it . . . Yes, I see the door has been split; I apologize."

"You might have glamoured him."

"He did not deserve it."

Lord Simeon sighed. "It is yours to watch Miss Morley; we are agreed she must be protected, but you needn't fear for Hastelbrook itself. Lord Abbott's invaders would have been dealt with."

"By the Lurkmen? The queen would never risk exposing them so," Vaela contended. "Abbott threatened to bring fifty men. Or can you mean she would employ Vorsadat? T'would be using a cannon to remove a stain, and he cannot be trusted . . ."

"Is this the counsel of Tredavius?"

"I felt his heart; the Old Man is sincere. He would buy his way back to her grace, but Pazoa would not see me, nor receive his message."

"Mortals expect change, they embrace it," Lord Simeon said, removing his spectacles to study them. "We do not, our queen especially."

Vaela appeared before him, her eyes flushed black. "I am not afraid of change."

"No." Lord Simeon smiled, replacing his spectacles. "Miss Morley has taught you the useful virtue of impatience. But now my dear, is precisely where patience is most required of us. We have no precedent, for what is coming."

. . . .

Friday June 24th

The week passed in rainy gloom, with every morning Emelyn obliged to endure Doctor Bayten's examination: standing in her dressing gown before the mirror, rolling back her eyes, presenting her tongue, and receiving with performative gratitude a fresh dose of his elixir, which she poured from her window as he made his notations.

Confident his treatments had now twice preserved her, first in curing her freezing fever twelve days prior, and second in preventing a chill after her flight into the rain, the doctor spared not a breath instructing her anew.

"Barefoot foray in an icy downpour," he chastened, accepting the spent vial. "It might have cost you dearly Miss Morley; we can by no means rule out a recurrence of the original condition."

"There is no *original condition* doctor, but I understand it was foolish to run out in the rain," she conceded, seeking the shortest path to his exit.

"And have you anything unusual to report?" he asked, listening to her back. "Unaccountable weakness, lightness of head, excessive wind?"

"No doctor, nothing of the kind."

"Well I find no jaundice, no irregularities of breath or pulse," he said. "Doubtless my regimen is having an effect. We shall continue the draught of tar water, shaken with oil of sulphur and liquorice, to be taken thrice daily with your tea while you are away."

"I shan't rest until every vial is emptied."

Afternoon came on dismally grey, and after a tasteless dinner Emelyn sat in the small library, propped in the window with her journal. The injury she had incurred in London, being healed without a trace, had taken with it the terror of the attack, but the prospect of departing Hastelbrook for the stormy cliffs of Eastbourne, and with her mother's emphatic expectation that engagement was to come of it, brought on flights of nerves, which she endeavoured to transcribe:

‘I have given Papa the money, which I trust shall delay the proceedings of our creditors. And now the whole county will talk, as it must, for in accepting Lord Van Croft’s escort to Galecliff, am I not supporting gossip of the intimacy such an errand must imply? Shall I imagine him the man to win me from Hastelbrook forever? I feel in my heart I must not be taken from home, not yet, and I know so little of him, though I confess some small exhilaration, for the daring of it.’

Compounding such doubts was the indelible sense memory of her impassioned kiss with Mr. Arkwright. Here she imagined to find secret comfort in Vaela’s counsel, but there was only dismay, for the vampiress had not reappeared, and her recent visitation, now four days past, had taken on the same unreal quality as those before it, less a remembrance than a dream.

‘though it is in precisely these anxious moments I long for the enchanted stillness of her company. Indeed since London, and Vaela condescending to tell me of her past, I find myself restless and frustrated. Is it that my quest in the city was largely bamboozled, as Mr. Townsend might be apt to say? If there is truly an ancient vault beneath us, what could be its purpose? And what does the Order want with it?
My skin feels cold, my appetite is vanquished. In moments I dread the bloodsick might return. But even 11,000 pounds cannot preserve us for long. Therefore am I only nervous for the state of our finances, or the expectation that I must wed at once to repair the books? Can Lord Van Croft truly believe he’s already won me?
But perhaps I’m only sick of this nettlesome doctor, or yet angry at being denied Mr. Arkwright’s letter, which I cannot stop guessing at. Mama had no right to destroy it. She’s never done so before, and she does not hear when I argue the point. Nor does she see the folly in allowing Isabelle to correspond with so low and ridiculous a person as John Lawford. No good will come of it.’

With an audible groan Emelyn set her feet on the bench, staring through the rain warped glass into the garden labyrinth. “Nothing but dull and damp . . .”

“You’ve been groaning all week,” Deacon observed, rattling the paper in his favourite chair.

“Where is Mama?” she asked.

“Fancy another go at her? She’s upstairs.”

It was after three o'clock when Emelyn found Mrs. Morley perched on a sofa in the music room for Sarah's practice.

"My dearest, I have decided you shall have the last word," her mother said, sitting very straight as she watched the harpsichord. "I should like to be quiet while I attend the music."

"I've not come to argue." Emelyn took a seat at her side. "But I do worry for how quickly Isabelle bestows her heart."

"*Advice to the Unwary*," Sarah announced, setting her fingers, "by Lady Buckham of Bristol."

"I think you're only afraid the same might happen to you,' Mrs. Morley said. "Of course the Bell of Brighton's impossible standards are to be expected, but you cannot demand the same of your sisters."

"Have I impossible standards? I don't think I have; Fitzwilliam Arkwright was a most unexpected . . ."

"Not another word of the cooper!" her mother hissed, touching her forehead, "I've not life enough left in me."

Emelyn swallowed her words, making fists in her pockets as she followed her sister's hands on the keys. The melody was intricately pleasant, if sharply technical, as was Sarah's habit.

"I cannot imagine but the captain's new carriage will be very fine," Mrs. Morley suggested.

"Yes I'm sure of it."

Sarah had begun to sing, her voice high and thin. *"The wounded deer flies swift away . . ."*

"The sky is darkening," Emelyn said, glancing at the window. "Unfavourable is it not, for a journey along the cliffs I mean."

"the bearded arrow in her side, still vainly hoping that she may . . ."

"Nonsense," Mrs. Morley said. "The thunder is afar off, and it's rained not a drop. No, you need only think of our brave captain falling hopelessly, desperately in love with you; I daresay he's half there already."

"among the herd be yet unspied . . ."

"Our brave captain? You do understand I hardly know him," Emelyn said. "But should we not wonder, if it is wise after all for me to go?"

"Perhaps just the keys for now dear," Mrs. Morley said loudly, waving for attention.

Sarah closed her mouth, hunching closer to the instrument as she played.

"Lord Van Croft is our superior by every measure," Mrs. Morley continued, tapping her fingers to the music. "He is not the sort of man to be refused, not if you're to have any chance at such a future."

"But I hardly know him," Emelyn repeated, her hands sweating. "If we prove unfit for each other, would not this errand be a grave distraction from other . . . from whatever else may be pressing."

"My sweet darling," Mrs. Morley said, turning to face her, "you do not know him now, but you *will*, that is precisely the objective. You need only consent to his attention, and let nature see to the rest. I'm quite sure he will find you indispensable."

Emelyn swallowed, her mouth dry. "And if there is more to me than he is prepared to find?"

"Emelyn Elizabeth you are not so complicated as you imagine," her mother said. "You need to be challenged, and I daresay Lord Van Croft is up to the task."

Wiping her hands on her skirts Emelyn stood. "Well, I suppose you know me better than I know myself . . ."

"Don't be smart," Mrs. Morley said. "Now, your trunks are downstairs, but you must change before his arrival, and find your smile my dearest. You'll not be sharing the road six hours to Eastbourne with a gloomy demeanour."

"Yes Mama," Emelyn said curtly, and thinking of Vaela's opal jewellery, she determined to bring no other but the ring, necklace and earrings the vampiress had given her.

The family was gathered outside, and ere long Emelyn was waiting at the top of the steps, gowned in summer white with rich lime inlay, an elegant cardinal cloak about her shoulders, her hair tied up under a cocked hat. Vaela's opals sparkled at her ears and throat, and she embraced her sisters, kissing them each, as drawn by sleek stallions Van Croft's carriage was sighted rolling its way up the road.

"A new Berline with steel springs, just think," Mrs. Morley enthused. "You shall swoon away from the comfort!"

"One can only hope," Emelyn said, watching its approach as she wondered how Vaela would discover where she'd gone, though it was comforting to remember the vampiress might find her even in dreams.

"Emelyn what's wrong?" her mother asked. "What are you staring at?"

"Nothing Mama, I was just thinking . . . surely there must be more to my fate, than to stand behind a husband, and bear him children."

"Oh tosh," her mother said impatiently. "You are too radiant to stand *behind* anyone. Now, I will remind you to keep close to your brother . . . Galecliff shall have fewer staff than we, but you must treat them with dignity."

"Yes of course," Emelyn said. "But if, that is, should Mr. Arkwright write to me again . . ."

"There's no chance of that," Mrs. Morley said sharply. "Now Deacon, if the servants expect vails you must not pay; your walking cash is for medicines and whatever necessities come about."

"Yes Mother," Deacon said, leaning on his crutches.

Mrs. Morley cleared her throat, adjusting Emelyn's cloak as though reluctant to let her go. "So if the footmen line up for gratuity it must be the captain who provides it them," she said. "And you will treat the lady of the house with deference and patience; who's to say what she's heard of Hastelbrook, but she is Lord Van Croft's godmother and like to be protective of him."

The list of cares and cautions went on, and by the time Lord Van Croft's imposing coach had reached the drive Emelyn's nervous tension had redoubled. The carriage rolled to a stop, mother and daughter shared a brief embrace, and Mrs. Morley released her to her father.

"Well my dear, I suppose it is adieu for now," he said, taking Emelyn's arm to escort her down the stairs, "You must be sure to enjoy the cliffs, but not too closely!"

"Yes Papa," Emelyn said vaguely, waiting as he kissed her forehead, "thank you."

Van Croft's arrival was hurried, and after greeting her with a light pinch of his teeth on her knuckles, he bowed to the assembled family and helped her brother into the coach, tossing his crutches to the footman at the back. Breda climbed aboard next, equipped with a basket of fruit stuffed castagnole pastries, to present the lady of Galecliff upon their arrival.

Escorted to the far side of the vehicle, Emelyn found the captain's hold on her fingers endured even after she'd taken her seat, and she was obliged to lean, stretching her arm for several kisses more. "My perfect rose," he said.

Her heart pounded, and meeting Breda's scandalized expression Emelyn retrieved her hand at last, losing her glove. With a laugh Van Croft tossed it inside and closed the door, before scaling the front to take his seat by the driver. The reins lashed, and with a thunderous rattle they were off.

The glove had landed on Deacon, who passed it across. "Another glove sacrificed in the arts of courtship. That's five this season, I believe."

Emelyn plucked it from his hand. "Four," she corrected.

"But why wear them at all, if they're only to slip off at the first sign of a gentlemen."

"You might have caught it on its way down my wrist," Emelyn said, grabbing her hat against the jostle as the coach made its turn. "You are my chaperone, are you not."

Deacon smirked. "But it's nice to find you still in humour, after so gloomy a week."

Emelyn did not respond, and as she looked through the window at the fading eminence of Hastelbrook there came a twinge of panic, making her sit up. A wild fantasy came over her, and she wanted to burst outside, to dash back up the hill for the safety of the house, to ensconce in the small library, upon her favourite window bench for study. Perhaps she'd find something she'd missed, perhaps the very secret to unlocking the vault, and so unearth a treasure to solve her father's debts forever . . . but the moment passed, and she tilted back her head, staring into the rocking lantern that hung from the ceiling.

The bumps began to smooth as the wheels gained in speed, and with a dramatic sigh Deacon lay down flat, struggling to come to terms with a pillow for his head.

"Turn it upright," Emelyn suggested, holding tightly the coin in her pocket.

But it was little use. New and vexing thoughts took shape, coming first in the form of Lord Van Croft, handsome as he was arrogant, who would doubtless be laughing with the driver just now, at how easily he'd stolen her away from home.

Light rain stencilled the windows, and she toyed once more with her memory of the kiss, burning with unquenched curiosity for what Mr. Arkwright might have written to her . . . And then there was London. Dank and drear, rolling in smoke and squalor, it had never seemed so foul to her, so awfully far from the world she knew. But if Margaret could not believe in vampires, what would she say to the Mohocks and their ringleaders, bent on stealing the secrets of Hastelbrook, or the Lurkmen, their captain in particular, whom Emelyn was certain had saved not only herself, but Adam Comberland's life as well.

These phantoms swirled together, seasoned by rehearsal of arguments with her mother over the rogue John Lawford, whom she could not bear to find near Isabelle again.

Anxiety clenched in her chest, and Emelyn took Breda's hand, imagining it was Vaela's . . . but her maid's fingers had not the grace of the vampiress, and she was disconcertingly warm.

"All right miss?" Breda asked.

Emelyn breathed hard against her stays, realizing with some horror that during the light of day Vaela would *never* exist to her, except as a muted shadow in the back of her mind, longed for and unreachable.

"Emelyn?" Deacon asked.

She did not respond, but pressing her hand to the window softly hissed, unable to stop herself picturing her father locked in the Fleet prison for his debts. Dutifully she would bring him books and food, making what cheerful conversation she could bear, as his wife and children prepared for their imminent eviction from the estate . . .

"What's wrong miss?" Breda troubled.

"I need air," Emelyn gasped, feeling faint as she reached reflexively for the door.

Emelyn Morley . . .

It was as though a voice had whispered in her head, and with perfect clarity the image of the hooded statue in the long gallery came upon her, interrupting her spiralling thoughts. Closing her eyes she could almost feel the cold smoothness of the stone under her fingers, the grounding sense of it. Calmer, more rational notions returned, and she took a long breath. In some hours the sun would set as always, to welcome returning nightfall, to welcome the woman in black who watched over her . . .

"*. . . yours is the surest, the strongest heart I have ever felt.*"

The carriage jostled along, putting comfort to ill use. But the memory of Vaela's words was as a shaft of light, breaking through brittle darkness.

"I'm an imbecile," Emelyn said, untying her hat.

"Agreed," Deacon grunted, squinting at his book. "But why should it bother you now?"

"I'll not fear marriage, nor destitution, nor some secret brotherhood designing upon Hastelbrook, nor any of it."

Deacon raised his brows, turning the page. "What are we on about?"

"And if Lord Van Croft thinks my company to Eastbourne is tantamount to accepting his proposal, he shall be disappointed. The one does not precipitate the other."

"So that's that then," Deacon said thoughtfully. "I suppose we'll be turning around."

"I'm not in jest," Emelyn said, pinching the opal charm on her necklace. "I will not be married simply for wealth or title, nor any other reason . . . not until such time as my heart approves."

Deacon sat up to bully his pillow. "Emelyn, do you imagine any of us really thought otherwise, even Mother? For my part I say it's brave of you, to have accepted the captain's challenge. And I am transported with joy to be included. I shall find new corners to glower from, I've no doubt."

"You won't." Emelyn kicked his foot, feeling suddenly vested in his part. "You shall be welcomed for every festivity, if Van Croft expects any sight of me."

"Fine, but I've little desire to stand jig by jowl in a crowd of navy men . . ."

Breda made a sudden noise. "Oh miss I cannot bear it! I've brought something I shouldn't have."

"What on earth do you mean?" Emelyn asked. "What have you brought?"

"My lady bid me dispose of it, but it weren't right, being the first time she ever asked such a thing," Breda said, fishing into her pocket to produce a folded letter. "I came to the kitchens to see it burned, but I could not."

Emelyn's heart leapt at the sight of it. "That's not from Mr. Arkwright?"

"Yes miss, if you'll forgive me, I dared not reveal it in the house; sworn on pain of dismissal as I was."

"While I live you shall by no means be dismissed," Emelyn said, accepting the letter.

"Is it scandal already? We're scarcely out of the drive," Deacon marvelled.

"You're not to breathe a word of this," Emelyn warned him, unfolding the paper to find it a single, densely written page:

'Dear Madam,

I cannot overstate my surprise regarding the receipt of your generous invitation to Hastelbrook, which I heartily accept, though finding it addressed by your worthy advocate Lady Dhorings, I had expected little more than a record of banishment for my rash and disgraceful behaviour on the hill, made all the worse by a miserable heart's unwillingness to regret it.

I am by no means unconscious of the dishonour such amorous advance, even so heavenly a kiss, is keen to inflict, further qualified by the alarming intelligence I had of your loyal friend Miss Mettles, though her report of your impairment by some illness of mind or spirit is one I cannot accept. Indeed, I treasure with abiding conviction that you of all ladies shall never want for spirit, nor sense, nor beauty, and our shared risibilities were to me a grateful tonic.'

Emelyn heaved with an emotional breath, blocking her face with the page as she leaned into the corner.

'Therefore, finding neither any defence for my wretched hope, nor the means to extinguish it, I can only say that even allowing for the ghostly lights we spotted beyond the cemetery, I have never breathed a more natural air than I found walking at your side.

Thus, my dear Miss Morley, until such a time as I may again share in the blessing of your company, I shall remain,

Your most affected and humble servant, Fitzwilliam Arkwright'

Moved with tenderness at his words Emelyn made an involuntary sound, carefully folding the letter. But *ghostly lights* gave her pause, and she shivered to think of the monstrous man with the hellish light in his eyes. *"Do not fear him; he will not harm you,"* Vaela had promised.

She unfolded the paper to read it again, and Mr. Arkwright's heartfelt hope, so well expressed, struck her all the more.

"Oh dear," Deacon said. "Good for tears is it?"

Emelyn shook her head, refolding the letter for her pocket. "He writes beautifully."

"*He writes beautifully,*" Deacon repeated. "Is that all? He writes to you in person, while you lecture Isabelle over the same from Mr. Lawford."

"They cannot be compared," Emelyn said. "Lawford *attacked* our solicitor; he's very lucky Cavendish was made right by his betters . . . Of course if the knave had tried that with Mr. Arkwright, he'd have been beaten to hot mash, except Arkwright would never, because *he* is every part the gentleman."

"Beaten to hot mash," Deacon chuckled, glancing at Breda. "So it's the captain or the cooper . . . and if history instructs my sister shall reject them both."

Outside great streaks of coloured cloud followed after the sinking sun as the heavens faded behind them, and invigorated by the deepening dusk Emelyn smiled at him. "You cannot predict such a thing. But this excursion is not only for me. I'm determined you will enjoy yourself; you may even meet a lady."

Deacon returned to his book. "Some of us fall in love Emie, and some of us watch; that is the way of the world. Anyway, you're not my chaperone, I'm yours."

"Well I'll not see you withdraw yourself as you do at home. And surely everyone is deserving of love."

"Have you read that?" he said, finding his page. "Who needs love Emie; I'd settle for dancing."

Breda cleared her throat. "Galecliff looks over Beachy Head miss; I hear the chalk cliffs are the highest in the country; five hundred feet!"

"I hear the same," Emelyn sighed, and watching Deacon attempt to read in the low light she felt a surge of hope, that perhaps the doctor friend of Van Croft would be of material help to him, her elder brother whom just now she liked to imagine standing unassisted, a lovely young lady on his arm.

"I see you smiling," Deacon said. "No more whinging, no more ill-humour for the journey?"

Emelyn folded her hands in her lap. "On the contrary, I am quite at ease," she said, and feeling yet the warmth of Arkwright's letter, she resolved to put aside all trepidation over the future, whether of marriage, or Hastelbrook, or even her place in Vaela's mysterious *prophecy*, which as surely as night followed day she would come to learn more of.

With a long sigh she relaxed, and gazing out into the welcome darkness she wondered what it would be like to dance with the swaggering captain, and whether there could be more to Lord Van Croft than bravado, after all.

COMING SOON: **Saunmoor Book 2**

Emelyn Morley and the House of Galecliff

Having reluctantly secured the favour of a man known as the Bloodhound of His Majesty's Navy, Emelyn has agreed to travel with Lord Captain Van Croft to the secluded house of his godparents, high upon the chalk cliffs of Beachy Head. Chaperoned by her brother, she soon discovers the ancient prophecy of Saunmoor has followed her here, and Vaela is not the only one watching.

A dark force descends upon the House of Galecliff, even as Emelyn confronts her feelings for Van Croft, whom she finds both impossible and intriguing. Meanwhile the haunted Mr. Arkwright, unable to forget her, is drawn closer to Emelyn's orbit by a most unexpected and courageous act.

In the city of London a proud order of vampire hunters, under the direction of the ruthless and visionary Lord Dramen, sets its sights upon Hastelbrook. Black storms loom from the west, and Emelyn learns there is more to the legendary vault hidden beneath her home, and more to her power in its story, than she ever imagined.

Acknowledgements

This book would not have been possible without the love and relentless support of my parents Joan and Grover, the pointed artistic inspiration of my sister Laurie Carswell, and the unwavering enthusiasm, faith and dedication of my editor Dr. Susan Manring.

I'd also like to acknowledge close friends, teachers and guides, who have provided crucial feedback, acting as lights along the road for this journey: Jan and Bee, Stephanie, Michael, Nate and Ryan, and my various beta readers, who through six years of writing, rewriting, research and editing have helped me refine Emelyn's world, namely Colleen, Terry Anne, Georgia, Alice, Jacqueline and Jill, my brother-in-law Matt, my uncle Johnny, Anna, Kristen, Janie, Maika, Trisha, Kija, Jodie, Sabine, Jordan, Lisa and Bruce, Mary and Paul, and my old school buddies Teddy, Sandy, Byron, Jay, Tei, Matt, Arie and Jon.

www.ingramcontent.com/pod-product-compliance
Lightning Source LLC
Chambersburg PA
CBHW032013310726
48972CB00002B/387